Praise for *Almost Heaven*

Tim Norbeck's opus is a sweeping testimonial to small town West Virginia, high school football, family values, racial equality, and the Greatest Generation. This is a nostalgic, panoramic view of a post-World War II America buttressed by strong character and moral backbone. It is through this undercurrent of decency that the *Almost Heaven* community learns to deal with disappointment and cope with tragedy.

As one who spent many summers visiting relatives in the Mountain State, I am so impressed with the way Norbeck captured the spirit of the hearty souls fortunate to call West Virginia home.

Clark Bell | Veteran journalist, educator, and foundation executive

Almost Heaven is a real page turner! A great heartwarming story with many twists and turns. The novel contained everything from true and interesting historical events to several engaging love stories— peppered with memorable relationships and some frontier justice mixed in. Couldn't put it down!

Ed Smoragiewicz | Attorney, Connecticut and Florida

Almost
Heaven

Published by Why Not Books

Paperback ISBN: 978-1-7367266-5-5
E-book ISBN: 978-1-7367266-6-2

Cover and interior design by Tessa Avila
Author photo by Megan DePiero Photography

Almost Heaven is a work of fiction. All incidents and dialogue, and all characters with the exception of some well-known historical figures, are products of the author's imagination and are not to be construed as real. Where real-life historical figures appear, many of the situations, incidents, and dialogues concerning those persons are actual true events. In all other respects, any resemblance to actual persons, living or dead, events, or locales is entirely coincidental.

Also by Tim Norbeck

Two Minutes
No Time for Mercy

To my Uncle Hank Comstock

and a special thanks for their service
to the countless veterans
who returned home from WWII
to restart their lives

CHAPTER 1

The war was all but formally over, but the pain for most returning veterans was just beginning. This is the story of one of those heroes. He fought, he survived, and then he came home to a life full of uncertainty and trepidation. He had no job or prospects, no home of his own, no car, no wife, and no money. Throw in an unwanted divorce and a son he had never seen, and the bleak and seemingly hopeless circle was complete. While hardly a consolation, he understood that his plight was shared by too many of his fellow returning vets from World War ll. The calendar was creeping towards September of 1945, and it was now crunch time for new civilian Jack Morgan.

Stepping off the plane into his hometown of Buffalo, New York, Jack took a deep breath and walked toward the arrival gate. There they were. He saw them seconds before they spotted him—his sister, Nellie, and his parents, John and Mary, craning their necks, hoping to see him first. Several other servicemen and civilians stood in line ahead of him, all probably more desirous than he to interact with the sea of greeters milling around. He loved his family very much, but his head was somewhere else. For the first time in his life, twenty-seven-year-old Jack Morgan felt he was a burden to them, and he worried about his future.

"There he is!" Nellie shouted, racing toward him so fast she almost knocked down two people.

"Give him a chance, Nellie!" Mary admonished, moving to smother her son with kisses.

John Morgan dutifully waited before stepping forward with an extended hand, followed by a heartfelt hug. Many men of his vintage limited any show of affection for fear of being seen as unmanly, but the elder Morgan had no such inhibitions.

Jack, like many of his comrades, disdained any talk about his experiences as a Marine. Many experiences were too gruesome to mention, and few who survived wanted the remembrance of things past, as the French novelist Marcel Proust once noted. His mother didn't need to hear about the savagery and barbarity of so many conflicts or the number of enemy soldiers he killed. It would all come out someday, perhaps, but that day had yet to come.

On the way back to the Morgan home, Nellie Kent broke the awkward silence. "Jack, you know I'm a widow now." Tears welled in her green eyes.

Sadly, he nodded.

"Jim had just shot down a Japanese Zero when two ambushed him from behind," she said bitterly.

Jack reached from the front seat to stroke her hand.

"It was June 5, 1942, the Battle of Midway," she continued.

John and Mary shifted uneasily in the back seat, having heard the unhappy tale several times before.

Tears rolled down Nellie's cheeks as she relived the pain of that day. "They never recovered Jim's body. That was the toughest part."

That was only part of the tragedy. Nellie was three months pregnant at the time. Five months later, she felt an unusually sharp pain in her abdomen. She knew in her heart she'd lost the baby, but unfortunately, even that didn't signal the end of her woes.

As the result of her miscarriage, the doctor told her she'd never carry a baby again. Fortunately, her parents and friends helped her through most of the anguish, but such support went only so far. Nellie, brave woman that she was, had to gather herself and go on, and she did.

Possibly to change the painful subject, Jack recounted the tale of his own marriage and how it ended on such a sour note. His family knew some of the details, but he hadn't shared the entire story with them yet.

All three Morgans remembered his marriage to Cathy Mumford in Philadelphia in June 1941. They recalled how arrogant and pompous the bride's father was and how they felt cautious when meeting him. Lewis Mumford of Philadelphia was a wealthy, controlling man who wore both traits on his sleeve. If someone didn't notice when first meeting him, he soon demonstrated it. A little man with a pencil mustache, Mumford was a cunning, conniving misanthrope who happened to be very financially successful. It was obvious the nasty old man didn't like Jack and thought him beneath the standards he set for his daughter's husband. Cathy even confided to John Morgan her father's antipathy for his future son-in-law but love prevailed. Eventually, the bully father appeared as soon as opportunity presented itself. It did on December 7, 1941.

Cathy was almost six months pregnant with the son they would name David, and Jack just completed his first semester teaching English and history at a Philadelphia area high school. On Monday, December 8, like so many other young men in the

United States, Jack responded to the outrageous sneak attack the previous day against the American Pacific Fleet in Pearl Harbor by enlisting in the Marines. He was assigned to Parris Island, South Carolina, for basic training.

He never imagined when Cathy saw him off at the Philadelphia airport on December 10 that he would never see her again. Initially, her letters were warm and loving, but the tone changed abruptly after David was born in late March 1942. The letter informing him of his son's birth read like a form letter. He continued to write Cathy when he could, telling her about his training, and, more importantly, how he missed and loved her and their new son, how he was looking forward to being home with them again. Trusting soul that he was, he attributed her rather cool letter to a tired young mother raising a child alone. Far from it. Lewis Mumford sensed a rare opportunity to do what he did best.

The letters from Cathy ceased, and his letters were returned. Then came a short, terse divorce notice. Finally, furloughed in late June, he flew to Philadelphia to restore his relationship with his wife and see his new son.

He was shocked to find their old apartment vacant, and their few meager pieces of furniture gone. There was no forwarding address. He soon discovered that Mr. Mumford was as devious as his parents suspected. The scoundrel absconded without a forwarding address, and no one at his company would tell the frantic young father anything.

He spent his entire furlough, wasting time and effort. It appeared that the Mumfords—daughter and father—had vanished. Totally crushed and in despair, the disconsolate Marine returned to his unit at Parris Island for additional training before shipping out to the action zone in the Pacific.

CHAPTER 2

The remainder of the ride home with his family was quiet and somber, even though Jack's return was a happy event. The four passengers were lost in thought, and Jack's mind raced, as he relived some of his war experiences.

The sad Philadelphia experience toughened him for the battles ahead, which wasn't a bad thing. He had absolutely no idea what lay ahead, despite the very vivid, formidable pictures his drill instructors and others painted for him. No training in the world could adequately prepare Jack and his comrades for the horror and carnage they would soon experience. As he drilled and trained, the crestfallen Marine was sobered that he would soon be using his bayonet to pitchfork an enemy, not a bale of straw.

The Marines turned him, fully willing, into a killing machine.

In early August 1942, Jack Morgan was part of the U.S. First Marine Division that landed on the humid jungle island of Guadalcanal. Unfortunately, little was known about the mosquito-infested, disease-plagued island, nor did any of the Marines have any knowledge of the difficult terrain, tides, or weather. Their first objective was to establish a two-thousand-yard beachhead and take control of the Japanese-built airfield. Helping them was an American submarine S-38, which sank an enemy transport dispatching troops to repel the Americans.

When three hundred and forty-two men quickly perished, the Japanese diverted the remaining ships away from Guadalcanal. They soon returned, however, and the Marines were ordered to hold Henderson Field, the newly captured airstrip. It wasn't easy. Their enemy controlled the sea, making it difficult to provide supplies to those defending the island.

Jack lost forty of his comrades in the first battle for Henderson Field but only a few in the second, decisive battle. The Japanese incurred heavy losses in those savage engagements that left the Americans permanently in control of the coveted, strategic airfield. Bayonets were drawn, and even rifle butts were used in the brutal hand-to-hand combat.

He wasn't proud of killing three combatants in five minutes, but it was that or be killed himself. It took the Army, Navy, Marines, and Air Corps six months to defeat the Japanese in what some called a battle of attrition.

There was little time during that horrid six months to think of anything other than survival. During the final week, Jack was sent to the field hospital with fever and chills. Fortunately, malaria was ruled out, and he missed only one day of fighting. When the battle ended, he and many of his Marine comrades flew back to the States and settled for some rest and recreation at Camp Pendleton, California.

Back home now, with time to ruminate and rest his weary bones, Jack found his mind drifting back to his miserable former father-in-law, Lewis Mumford. It was no wonder he insisted the newlyweds settle in Philadelphia. Jack assumed that was part of Mumford's grand plan, making it easier for the old man to exercise control and influence over his daughter and to arrange the quick divorce and disappearance. Mumford was a miserable son of a bitch, worse than Jack suspected. Jack hadn't liked the crusty bastard to begin with and tolerated him only for Cathy's sake. How could Cathy have allowed her father to turn her against Jack? Was it part of the plan or did she merely succumb to that overbearing, officious wretch? Would Jack ever know? Would he see his son?

He almost regretted that he had time to think of such things, instead of dodging bullets.

At six feet two inches tall and a solid one hundred and eighty-five pounds, Jack very much looked the part of a man no one took lightly. Square-shouldered and jut-jawed, he was a Marine's Marine. Large blue and expressive eyes above a prominent narrow nose gave him the appearance of a patrician. He was nice looking but not what most women considered handsome, although he walked tall and with a confident bearing that made him more attractive. His face was chiseled with a few scars from football along with an additional mark on his right cheek, the result of a strafing incident on Guadalcanal. The experience there, replete with the omnipresent bloodbath, hardened him into a true warrior, and he felt he was a fully-fledged, battle-hardened Marine.

CHAPTER 3

After their long rest at Camp Pendleton and a few minor assignments, Jack and almost twenty thousand other Marines were sent to a hellhole called Tarawa in the Gilbert Islands. They arrived on November 20, 1943, and the next seventy-six hours were among the bloodiest of the entire war.

Tarawa was strategically important due to its location as the gateway of the overall U.S. effort in the central Pacific aimed at the Philippines. It was imperative that the Marines capture the airstrip. They were familiar with the scenario by then.

Almost five thousand Japanese defended it, aided by a labyrinth of what seemed like endless pillboxes and bunkers, all connected by tunnels protected by wire and mines. The setup was just a prelude to what followed.

Jack was in the second assault boat, which unfortunately landed at low tide, forcing the Marines to disembark far from shore. The first wave of troops to run in encountered disaster. Many soldiers were sitting ducks for the enemy, who fired from fortified positions. Jack reached the beach safely in the second wave, but he heard bullets zipping past. Many soldiers died before they hit the ground.

The Japanese position at Tarawa seemed so impervious to attack that its commander said, "A million men couldn't take this stronghold in one hundred years."

Almost Heaven

It took the Devil Dogs from the 2nd Marine Division just seventy-six hours to accomplish the deed. The Japanese fought almost to the last man, with only seventeen survivors. The stench of the dead was overwhelming. One thousand Marines died in the frightful carnage, and another two thousand were wounded, but it was over by November 23.

During those days of fierce fighting on Tarawa, Jack noticed a Marine holding a movie camera and darting between trees and foxholes to film the action. Seeing the man almost get hit twice, Jack couldn't believe his heroism. A buddy told Jack the man was Staff Sergeant Norman Hatch, sent there by the Marine Photographic Services Branch to document the heroism and horror of World War II. The Boston-born Hatch couldn't have chosen a more dangerous spot to begin his film career. Jack never had a chance to meet his twenty-two-year-old Marine colleague during those three days of ferocious action, although the day came fifteen months later at a place called Iwo Jima.

Battle weary but relatively healthy after the brutal combat, Jack and most of his fellow Marines got some much-needed rest before they embarked on their next assignment. After a few mop-up jobs, they headed to the island of Saipan, one of the Mariana Islands.

The Marines were there with the Army's 27th Infantry Division almost a month, from the middle of June to July 9, 1944, before they prevailed over the 43rd Infantry Division of the Imperial Japanese Army. After additional R & R, they had to capture another important airstrip on a small coral island called Peleliu, which was occupied by almost eleven thousand elite Japanese troops and fortified by the usual elaborate series of bunkers and caverns. The Battle of Peleliu began badly for the Marines.

The landing beaches were filled with obstacles, such as mines and artillery shells buried with exposed fuses that would detonate when run over. The Americans landed on September 15. The battle raged for seventy-three days before the island was declared secure. Thirty-five Japanese soldiers held out in the caves of Peleliu until April 22, 1947, finally surrendering after a Japanese admiral convinced them the war had long been over.

In early February of 1945, the United States began an air and naval bombardment of an eight-square-mile island called Iwo Jima to soften opposition for an invasion planned to commence on February 19. Only five hundred and seventy-five miles from the Japanese coast, the volcanic island provided an air base for their fighter pilots to intercept American B-29 bombers and doubled as a safe haven for Japanese naval units under attack.

Joining Marines from the 3rd, 4th, and 5th divisions, Jack Morgan prepared for another bloody conflict to advance the Allied efforts to end the war. The first landings at Iwo Jima began just before nine o'clock in the morning. The forty thousand troops braced for enemy artillery as they hit the black, sandy beaches, but the bombardment never came. The Higgins boats did their jobs, landing ashore and releasing troops, and still there was no sign of enemy fire. Once the Marines reached the beaches, however, they took fire from twenty-seven thousand Japanese operating from a vast underground network of tunnels and caves. The Marines were forced to crawl, inch by inch, across the fiery terrain. There was little place to hide on the black volcanic soil.

Once on the beach and somewhat safe from enemy fire in his foxhole, Jack was joined by the Hatch fellow he first saw in Tarawa.

"Hope you don't mind my joining you," the photographer said, landing beside Jack with a huge thud, carrying his heavy, thirty-five-millimeter camera.

Jack made an instant friend by offering Hatch a cigarette from Jack's rations; Jack wouldn't have missed it because he rarely smoked.

"Thanks, friend."

Norman Hatch's response was a prelude to a warm discussion between the two men under harrowing conditions. Norman began his photographic career by sneaking a camera into a downtown Boston burlesque theater and secretly photographing the salacious dancing.

"I joined the Marines in 1939, basically because I was eighteen and needed a job," he explained.

Jack was taken aback by the man's answer to his next question. "Why do you risk your life so many times while filming the combat?"

"Because I consider it a sacred duty. You and others on the front line have told me countless times that I didn't need to be here with you. I felt I did, because the public, the American people, need to know what the Marines are doing."

By nightfall, the brave photographer moved to another position, and he and Jack never saw each other again.

Twenty-two Marines and five Hospital Corpsmen received the nation's highest award, the Congressional Medal of Honor, for acts of heroism on the island of Iwo Jima. Jack rode in the Higgins boat with one of them, a young Marine named Jacklyn Harrell Lucas.

His was one of the most interesting stories of the war and a fascinating profile of courage in a conflict that held an abundance of them. Any young boy unfortunate enough to be named Jacklyn at birth had to learn to fight at an early age. From Plymouth, North Carolina, the thirteen-year-old took the Japanese sneak attack on Pearl Harbor personally. He left military school, hitched a ride to Virginia, and bribed a notary public to say he was seventeen.

Huge for his age at five feet eight inches tall and weighing one hundred and eighty pounds, he marched through the door of the Marine Corps Recruiting Station like he owned the place and forged his mother's name on his enlistment papers. At the tender age of thirteen, Jacklyn Lucas shipped out to Parris Island for U.S. Marine Corps boot camp. He became a full-fledged Marine at fourteen but wasn't pleased with the menial jobs he was assigned, so he left the base. In the flurry of wartime preparations, he was able to finagle transportation all the way to Pearl Harbor via hitched rides and hiding on an airplane or two.

Much to his chagrin, the corps made him a truck driver at the base and denied his numerous requests to fight on the front lines. He stayed around Honolulu for several nondescript years, passing the time by drinking and engaging in bar fights.

He finally got his chance to enter combat on February 19, 1945, five days after his seventeenth birthday, when he and Jack Morgan, along with forty thousand other Marines, hit the beaches at Iwo Jima. The next day, Lucas and his buddies came upon a dangerous Japanese machine gun nest. Suddenly, the position fell silent, and to their horror, they found eleven enemy soldiers behind them.

Turning quickly, the Marines gunned down most of them, but a live grenade appeared in their midst, directly at Jacklyn's feet. According to his comrades, he didn't hesitate to fall on the grenade and shield them from the explosion, shouting at them to take cover.

When a second grenade landed within reach, he pulled that under himself, too. The first one detonated. The second failed. Inspired by the seventeen-year-old's heroism, the other Marines stormed another Japanese position and put it out of commission. When they sadly trudged back to collect Jacklyn's dog tags, they were incredulous to find him still alive. He was taken to a hospital ship, where he needed twenty-one surgeries over several months to remove over two hundred and fifty pieces of shrapnel from every major organ in his body.

The youngest recipient of the Congressional Medal of Honor in the entire 20th century walked unassisted up to President Harry S. Truman to receive his award in person.

The epilogue to his military life was almost as captivating. After the war, when he was still only seventeen, he returned home to North Carolina and fulfilled his promise to his mother to finish high school and go to college. He married three times and survived his second wife's attempt to murder him with the help of a hit man. At the age of forty, he enlisted in the 82nd Airborne as a paratrooper, his main objective to conquer his fear of heights. In typical Jacklyn Lucas fashion, he plummeted thirty-five hundred feet through the air on his maiden jump without an operable parachute, but his life was saved through some good luck and a commando roll. Miraculously uninjured, he soon was back in a plane for his second jump. He had become America's version of the indestructible Rasputin. Strangely, Hollywood never called him. A movie of his life would have been compelling.

CHAPTER 4

As Nellie maneuvered the family's 1939 Buick up the driveway, Jack's mind was a blur as he contemplated his less-than-promising future. He successfully excised some of the Lewis Mumford nightmare from his system, and, at the moment, he didn't want to discuss his war activities. Much of his reticence was due to his not wanting to acknowledge the savagery of the battles to his family and also to protect himself. He often woke suddenly drenched in sweat, and, while in that sleepy state, thrashed about the bed in a frantic effort to escape perceived danger. Such was the life of a returning military veteran who saw the worst war could offer.

Although filled with trepidation over his unknown future, Jack was still somewhat excited to begin his new life. He understood that job opportunities were limited, and it was possible he wouldn't find anything in Buffalo.

After getting his first night's sleep in a long time, in his own bed and the comfort of his own room, he spent his first full day home calling his high school buddies, many of whom never left the city and still worked in Buffalo. Jobs were scarce. It soon became painfully obvious to Jack and the over four hundred thousand military personnel returning home that the America they left in 1941 and 1942 was far different from the America they found when they returned.

The homecoming for the troops was just one of the ways in which America changed. While returning home was something to celebrate, it was also a very difficult transition for many servicemen and women. For some, it was almost impossible. A return to "normalcy," a word coined by President Warren Harding to describe the calm political and social order he promised the United States after the rather chaotic Woodrow Wilson years, was something the troops sought, but it was anything but for many. Post-traumatic stress afflicted Jack and other returning troops, manifested in difficulty sleeping, recurring nightmares, flashbacks, moodiness, and, in some cases, withdrawal from socialization. Even those who weren't in direct combat witnessed the deaths and gruesome injuries sustained by their comrades. Although welcomed back as popular heroes, many were forgotten. It was another blight on America at those times. Despite government attempts to ease the burden of transition, unemployment for returnees soared.

General Omar Bradley reported to the American Legion National Employment Committee in 1946 that unemployment among veterans in the nation's workforce was triple that of civilians. As writers David Chrisinger and Samuel Greengard noted, pre-war experience, not to mention one's wartime experience, wasn't perceived as having much value to civilian employers. Compounding that realization was that many veterans feared another depression like the one that crippled the U.S. economy and brought unprecedented numbers of women into the workforce, which, in turn, lowered unemployment from 9.9 percent in 1941 to only 1.2 percent in 1944. There were many fears over assimilating the more than twelve million veterans into the tight workforce.

By 1944, well over one million women with husbands in the U.S. military were employed. The independence forced upon those women during the war, followed by challenges brought on by the return of surviving soldiers, had an impact on gender relationships and became one of the seeds of the women's rights movements that followed in later years. Even the traditional role of fathers was compromised due to military-absent dads. Some children were undisciplined because of the lack of male influence, which was further exacerbated by time constraints on working mothers. Many feared their fathers would leave them again or remained angry at them for leaving in the first place.

The times were changing.

On top of the challenges caused by the new order of things was a further trial—homelessness. Despite the passage of the GI Bill, many returning veterans had great difficulty finding suitable lodging. The fortunate ones had families who could house them until they died. Receiving four thousand dollars toward the purchase of a new house wasn't very helpful if there were no homes available to buy. A shortage of building materials contributed to the problem.

Very few houses were built during the Depression, and even fewer during World War II, so the implied promise of affordable housing for veterans in the GI Bill fell far short of the well-intentioned pledges. The result was many veterans living wherever they could—in barns, on tractors, in streetcars, and in cars and garages. A 1947 study by the Veterans Administration shockingly reported that sixty-four percent of all married veterans and eighty percent of those who were unmarried still lived with friends or families two years after the war ended.

The GI Bill, also known as the Servicemen's Readjustment Act of 1944, was intended to prevent many of those heartaches. It was signed into law on June 22, 1944, by President Franklin Delano Roosevelt. Returning servicemen and women were to receive low-interest mortgages, low-interest loans to start businesses, cash payments for tuition and living expenses to attend high school or college, and fifty-four weeks of unemployment compensation. Debates involving such benefits for returning veterans of World War I in the 1920s and '30s were lengthy and acrimonious. Politicians in 1944 wanted to avoid the same bitter experience. FDR also wanted financial assistance on an as-needed basis for the poor, but Congress rejected its inclusion. Only veterans would receive that help.

Jack faced all those issues, as he attempted to transition back into civilian life. He mulled over his options, and his first realization was he didn't have any. He had no job prospects and no home of his own. His friends couldn't even help him secure an interview. The situation was that tight. He thought about coaching football and teaching, but there were no positions open in the Buffalo area. His old high-school football coach wasn't able to find anything for him, either.

Nellie continued working in Buffalo as a nurse, but the outlook for Jack wasn't as good. He felt totally stymied by what he perceived as rejection. He was a freshman during Vince Lombardi's senior year at Fordham when he was part of the "Seven Blocks of Granite." He called his old college football coach, the legendary Jim Crowley, who left Fordham shortly after Jack. Unfortunately, Crowley didn't have any advice, either, nor was he aware of any work available in the immediate New York area.

An optimist at heart, Jack found it difficult to remain positive about anything. At night, when he didn't dream of the hell on Tarawa, Iwo Jima invaded his thoughts. More than a few times, he woke up suddenly in a fright, perspiring profusely, thinking he was dying. The nightmares persisted, but he calmed himself with the sad but somewhat consoling realization that his returning buddies suffered the same fate.

That recognition calmed him a little, but he felt guilty whenever it entered his mind. How could he feel bad about himself when many others died? The famous, pertinent observation of the blind poet John Milton remained in Jack's thoughts.

"The mind is its own place," the prolific literary craftsman said, "and can make a hell of heaven or a heaven of hell."

That's probably the best description ever of why people feel the way they do, Jack thought. *It's why millionaires who appear to have everything commit suicide, while a beggar who has nothing is upbeat about his life.*

Jack also noted that Milton had never fought at Tarawa or Iwo Jima.

The situation remained the same for several weeks. He felt like he was leeching off his parents and began to wonder if he would ever be able to move on and find a new life for himself. Thinking of his son only made the situation worse. Surviving the war saved him from real personal tragedy, but never seeing his son almost negated any feeling of reprieve.

Then he received a phone call.

CHAPTER 5

66 Jack!" Jim Crowley bellowed. "I have some good news for you, if you're still looking for a job."

Quickly leaning forward so hard he almost bashed his teeth on the black desk phone, Jack tried to keep his composure and said calmly, "I sure am, Coach."

"Well, it's probably not what you're looking for, but it's a possible job."

Not discouraged, Jack asked, "Where is it, Coach?"

"In Bentley, West Virginia. The high school history teacher took a job in another state, and he was also the assistant football coach. My old college roommate is the principal of the high school. Your pay as teacher would probably be around two thousand a year. You could earn another five hundred by coaching the football team. Everything is technically negotiable, but I doubt they'll budge on the salary."

"When do they want me to start?"

"They want you right now. There's little time to decide."

The thought of living off his parents added to his anxiety, and his answer was easy. "I'll take it. How can I ever thank you?"

"Glad to help one of my boys, anytime. I'll call the principal right now. I suggest you call him yourself within the half hour."

"Will do, Coach. I can't thank you enough." Jack quickly wrote down the name "Patrick Mahon" and a phone number.

"I'll call right after you," Jack said exuberantly. "Thanks a million!"

Hearing the excitement in Jack's voice, Nellie and her parents gathered around when he hung up.

"I think I have a job," he explained. "It's in West Virginia."

Their joyful expressions turned to grimaces.

"When would you be leaving?" his mother asked with a hint of trepidation.

"I don't know yet, Mom, but I'll find out soon. The job isn't finalized until I talk to the school principal on the phone."

For Nellie, the news was bittersweet. She knew how badly Jack wanted a job, and she was happy for him, but they were close, and the past few weeks were a wonderful reunion and rediscovery for both of them. Nell, Jack's name for her since they were little, was a remarkable woman. At a diminutive five-feet-two-inches and only ninety-five pounds, with a quick wit, she was a little fireball who wasn't easily intimidated. She held herself erect and didn't slouch like many others. Her teeth were white and nearly perfect. Her natural light-brown reddish hair highlighted her persona along with her prominent cheekbones. With voluptuous red lips and a small nose that accented her flashing green eyes, she was "beautiful in form and feature, lovely as the day," as Longfellow wrote in his *The Masque of Pandora*. If pressed to describe her in one word, Jack thought "radiant" was probably the best. Even after losing her husband and unborn child, her self-confidence and independent spirit made Nell an attractive package.

As promised, thirty minutes after his call with Crowley, Jack called West Virginia.

"Good morning, Mr. Mahon," he began. "This is Jack Morgan following up a call you had with Jim Crowley."

"Oh, yes," he said with obvious pleasure. "I've been expecting your call."

"Sir, I'd love to have that job if it's still available."

"It is, and you come highly recommended. Our history teacher, Bill Roberts, had to move to Pennsylvania at the last minute. We could pay you two thousand a year for the teaching job and another five hundred if you're interested in assisting Don Adams, our football coach." He spoke with finality, clearly not willing to negotiate.

"I'll take both positions, Mr. Mahon. When do you want me there to start?"

"Terrific. School begins on September fourth, the day after Labor Day, so you might want to get here the Friday before to get acclimated. Jim said you're in Buffalo, so it's probably a five-hundred-mile drive and could take as much as twelve hours by car. If you arrive here on Friday the thirty-first, please come have dinner with my wife, Kathryn, and me at our home, so we can get acquainted. Jim didn't say if you're married. Is there a Mrs. Morgan?"

"No, Sir. I'll come alone."

"I'm glad you want the job. Call me if you have any questions."

Jack, hanging up, felt a rush of ambivalence. He'd never been to West Virginia; much less did he know anything about the state. The only thing he knew was that the battleship *USS West Virginia* was sunk during the sneak attack on Pearl Harbor on December 7, 1941.

Jack joined his parents for lunch after speaking with Patrick Mahon. Nellie had already left for work. John and Mary leaned forward in their seats, as Jack told them the news. They were happy for him but also crestfallen.

Mary couldn't suppress her tears, and John tried in vain to console her.

"When?" was the only word she could manage.

"How many more days do you have here?" John asked.

"Dad, I need to be there on the thirty-first. It'll take at least two days to get there. I probably have to leave next Wednesday."

Mary, sobbing uncontrollably, sputtered how sorry she was for her unabashed display of emotion. Jack fidgeted in his seat, trying to reassure them while explaining the rationale for his decision.

"I can't continue to live off you and keep my self-respect," he said. "I appreciate all you've done for me. If I could find work here, that would be different, but I can't find work here or anywhere. I really don't want to go to West Virginia," he said, becoming more emotional, "but I don't have any other choices."

"I know, son," his father said. "We just got used to having you around the house again, and we loved it. Of course, we want you to be happy and fulfilled. It's a shame there aren't enough jobs for the men and women who gave so much of their lives for the rest of us."

Mary reached out, through her tears, and squeezed Jack's hand. "How will we tell Nellie? She'll be devastated."

During his emotional explanation with his parents, Jack hadn't considered Nell. They had a special bond, far stronger than any other sibling relationship he knew. The thought of telling her terrified him but also deeply saddened him.

He had a week to explain to her and buy a car for the long trip to his adopted state of West Virginia. That afternoon, he allowed himself to feel euphoric for having landed a real job at a difficult time, as well as a fresh start. That feeling was tempered by the sense of trauma he would feel when he said goodbye to his sister.

After a hearty dinner that night, John and Mary put on some records and gave Jack a knowing glance. It was time to tell Nellie. She went upstairs after dinner, so Jack went to her room and knocked gently on the door.

When he walked in and closed the door behind him, she knew something was amiss. "What's the matter?"

He sat on the bed, where she was stretched out, reading. "I got the job," he said matter-of-factly.

"The one in West Virginia?" she asked calmly.

"Yeah, that one. It's a teaching and coaching job, but I wish it wasn't so far away."

She dissolved into tears. Her next words came as a shock. "Take me with you. Let's go together."

He never considered that, even for a moment. "But you have a job here. What would Mom and Dad say?"

"They'll manage. After all, they got along fine before we were born." Her tears stopped, and her green eyes flashed. Nellie was fully engaged and wasn't going to let him refuse.

"Why not?" she asked. "It makes all the sense in the world. I love Buffalo, but I need a fresh start, too. Mom and Dad are wonderful, but they're a constant reminder of the baby Jim and I lost."

He shook his head. "It would kill Mom and Dad to lose us both. What about your nursing job?"

Never easily intimidated, she pursued her argument without acknowledging his question. Undaunted, she said, "I'll give you three good reasons why you need to take me with you. First, you don't have a car, so we can use mine. Second, with Jim's life insurance, we can buy a fairly nice house."

Jack began to smile. "And number three?"

"I can get a nursing job in West Virginia, and I can keep up the house. You're a terrible housekeeper."

"That's four." He chuckled. "Let me think about it."

"Well, don't take too long. I have to give notice." She was clearly excited, while he felt only mildly interested.

He saved about two thousand dollars—more than enough to buy cars priced around eleven to twelve hundred dollars—but she was right about the house. He could rent a place, but it would be much nicer to own a house.

He hugged Nellie good night and sauntered to his room to mull things over. She was right about most things, plus she'd be a good companion, but how would they tell their parents? If his mother was so emotional about his moving, she would be almost apoplectic about losing her daughter, too. He decided

Nell was right. Their parents would just have to accept it. They could always come visit, and Jack and Nell could visit in return.

After thinking it over for an hour, he marched back to Nell's room and knocked on the door. When he walked in, he said, "OK. You're in."

She jumped up and threw her arms around him. "It'll be wonderful, and so much fun, too!"

"On one condition."

Suddenly, her enormous smile changed to a scowl. Standing back with arms akimbo, she asked, "Like what?"

"You tell Mom, and I'll tell Dad. Mom almost went ballistic when I told her I accepted the job. God only knows how she'll react to your leaving, too."

"OK. I'll do it. I'll tell her tonight if she's still up."

After listening to Glenn Miller records most of the night, John Morgan was ready to turn out the living room lights when Nellie approached her mother on the stairs, and Jack asked his father to remain downstairs with him for a few minutes.

During their conversation, they heard wailing from an upstairs bedroom. It was clear Mary wasn't taking the news as well as her husband.

"It'll be hard on us," John said, "but you must do what you and Nellie think is best for you. I always told you that there comes a time when you have to do whatever is necessary."

He hugged his father and thought how much he respected the older man. While not college-educated, he was a carpenter by trade, and he was an intelligent, caring, kind, and understanding man.

He and Jack climbed the stairs together and found mother and daughter in tears, hugging tightly while sitting on Nellie's bed.

"Mother," John said, using the term many men of his generation did when addressing his wife, "enough of this palaver. We have to accept this. It's their lives. We must respect their wishes."

Jack embraced his mother, while Nellie went to hug her father. "Thank you, Mom and Dad. We won't let you down."

"Mother," John added, "it's not like we won't see them again. It's only a few hundred miles to get down there. We can visit them over Christmas."

It was settled. Nellie and Jack had a week to finalize their plans to drive to West Virginia and begin their new lives.

Later the following afternoon, Nellie took her 1942 black Studebaker coupe in for servicing in anticipation of the nearly five-hundred-mile trip.

Jack called Principal Mahon to ask if there were any houses available in the Bentley area.

"You know, I might be able to help you out," he replied, "but the house will probably be too big for you. Remember Bill, the history teacher you'll be replacing, is moving to Pennsylvania with his wife, Joan."

"Yes, of course."

"He and his wife have four children and live in a large old farmhouse near the school. It's a sprawling old structure, and I think it's got five or six bedrooms. I was there for a party once, and it's pretty big. Maybe it'll be too big for you, inasmuch you'll be living alone."

"That has changed, Sir. My sister, Nell, wants to come with me. She's a nurse who lost her flier husband in the war. She wants a fresh start."

"That's great, Jack. It's not great she lost her husband, but it'll be nice for you to have a companion. I suspect Bentley Hospital will find a place for her, too. Please bring her with you when you have dinner at my place on the thirty-first."

"Mr. Mahon, do you happen to have the Roberts' phone number? I'd like to talk to them about that house."

Nellie called Joan Roberts that day, and they had a long talk. When she met with Jack later, she said, "They're asking four thousand dollars. It's a big farmhouse with six bedrooms, and it was built in 1861. There are three bathrooms, and it sounds like it has a nice porch, too. Believe it or not, it's fully furnished. If we want the house as is with all the furniture, it would cost forty-five hundred. We could buy it outright."

"Sounds pretty neat. I promise to pay you back."

"I know, but don't worry about it. Let's go down a day or two early and look at the house and see some others, too."

"I'm in," he said in approval. "Great work, but I *will* pay you back."

Nellie scheduled a meeting with the Roberts family at their farmhouse on Thursday, August 30. That meant she and Jack had to leave Buffalo on Tuesday, the 28th. They had only a few days to prepare for their trip.

Buffalo General Hospital was sorry to lose one of its best nurses, but Nellie's supervisor promised to call Bentley Hospital and give Nellie a strong recommendation. That conversation led to an interview scheduled for Friday morning, the day after their intended arrival.

They left Buffalo at six o'clock in the morning in Nellie's Studebaker coupe, hoping to make at least three hundred miles that day. Their parents, fighting tears and holding each other in the driveway, hugged and kissed them both. Mary handed them a sack of goodies for the road before holding onto John for support. John made them promise to call once they safely reached West Virginia.

Jack and Nellie had tears in their eyes, too. It was a very difficult day for the elder Morgans. They promised they would keep in close contact with their parents, who were so supportive and did so much for them during difficult, trying times.

Their journey occurred well before President Dwight Eisenhower signed into law the Federal Aid Highway Act of 1956. Signed on June 29, it created the interstate highway system to ease the burden of motorists driving across the country.

The seeds for Eisenhower's vision were sown during the time he participated in the U.S. Army's motor caravan from the nation's capital to San Francisco. The endless weather problem that turned dirt roads into mud and ice added to the difficulty of navigating through rickety wooden bridges and the like.

The usual mechanical difficulties encountered by vehicles at that time lengthened the trip further. It took sixty-two days, convincing the general and future president there had to be a better way. Germany discovered the solution when it created the autobahn network, and Ike never forgot it.

Traveling across the United States in 1945, as Nellie and Jack did, presented challenges. They planned to drive south and slightly west from Buffalo to Pittsburgh, about two hundred and thirty miles and at least five hours away. After a stop for lunch, they would travel southwest for another sixty miles and hopefully arrive in Wheeling, West Virginia. Figuring the journey would enable them to arrive by three o'clock if all went well, they could then decide to stay overnight or forge ahead for two more hours to Clarksburg. That town was only one hundred and thirty miles from Bentley, and they'd be able to arrive by dinnertime.

Since they were both determined, they decided to drive all the way through to Clarksburg, barring any unforeseen problems. If they made the same trip twenty years later, the nearly ten-hour journey could have been shortened considerably.

Fortunately, they arrived without incident in Clarksburg, West Virginia, at five forty-five in the afternoon. Auto camps and motor courts, the forerunner to motels, sprang up in the 1930s and '40s. They came in response to what *The New York Times* characterized in 1946 as an "eagerness to take to the open road, which swept in like a wave over the nation." Soon, rural entrepreneurs built small cabins and even somewhat fancy bungalows to accommodate the new demand.

It was simple for Nellie and Jack to find suitable lodgings at a roadside motor court. Fortunately, they had a small room available with twin beds. Both felt excited about the trip and the start of their new lives, and they discussed it over chicken dinner at a small diner.

Having spent almost twelve hours on the road, they knew sleep would come easily for both of them, but not before Nellie got Jack to open up to her about his Marine and war experiences. She knew he didn't like discussing them, especially in front of his mother, but this was different, just brother and sister. She nagged him all the way from Buffalo until he reluctantly agreed to talk.

Once he started, it was like someone turned on a spigot full blast. Stories, gore and all, poured out. Even though both were exhausted, the recitation of his experiences took several hours.

Finally spent, Jack fell into a deep, memory-free slumber for the first time in ages. Nellie gazed at him from across the room, knowing her husband had probably experienced many of the same things. She thanked God for bringing Jack back home safely, then blew a kiss to her late husband before going to sleep.

The next morning was hot and humid in Clarksburg. After eating a quick breakfast and adding gas to the car, they drove south toward Bentley. Jack assumed it would take about three hours to cover the one hundred and fifty miles. Both felt enervated by the long trip to West Virginia but were refreshed by the shared camaraderie. A good night's sleep and the excitement of the unknown were all the tonic they needed.

A flat tire in the small town of Summersville slowed them a bit, but Jack fixed it easily, and they forged on toward their destination.

CHAPTER 6

"Welcome to Bentley, West Virginia," read the sign. Nellie noted the time was one fifteen in the afternoon. Neither she nor Jack could resist the temptation to call Joan Roberts, and they quickly found a pay phone.

"Come on over," Joan said. "You can have some soup I just made. Bill already went to Pittsburgh for his new job, but he'll be back Friday afternoon."

It wasn't Buffalo, but they enjoyed the countryside as they drove to 7 Mountain View Road. Finally, they saw a sprawling white farmhouse that needed paint and a little TLC, but otherwise, it seemed in good shape.

Joan greeted them in the dirt driveway, where a few puddles had accumulated from the early morning rain. After exchanging the usual pleasantries, the three went inside. Jack noticed the screen door was a bit loose and was missing a small section of screen near the handle.

"Joan," Nellie began, as Jack collapsed onto the upholstered sofa, "we're so sorry to bother you now. I know we agreed to meet tomorrow."

"Oh, goodness, it's no problem. Please don't mind the mess. Bill and I hope to leave permanently on Labor Day, which is only five days from now. I told Bill I wasn't sure I'd make it by then."

Joan Roberts was a stout woman, probably twenty pounds overweight on a frame that was barely five feet tall. A turned-up nose accented her perpetually friendly, expressive smile. Twinkling blue eyes and a rather prominent jaw gave her a notable look, especially with a hint of gray in her stylishly shaped short hair. She was probably in her mid-fifties and spoke plainly, from the heart. If she was indicative of their soon-to-be West Virginian friends and neighbors, Nellie and Jack knew they were in good hands.

Joan served lemonade and homemade chocolate chip cookies after learning Nellie and Jack had already had lunch. Jack looked around the expansive room from his nestled position on the couch. He loved the fireplace at the end of the huge main room, and there was a feeling of warmth in the home. After lemonade, cookies, and small talk, they toured the rambling homestead.

There were two large bedrooms on the first floor with an adjoining full bath. Four more bedrooms were on the second floor, which they viewed after climbing a rickety staircase. A chipped newel post supported the handrail at the top and bottom of the stairs. The four bedrooms, while on the small side, were certainly serviceable. Besides, they didn't need them unless they entertained guests from back home.

The two upstairs bathrooms were old, but the fixtures seemed in good working order. Scattered rugs lay throughout the house on the beautiful wooden floors. Nellie wasn't thrilled about the kitchen, thinking it was a tad small, but it looked out onto the huge main room.

The backyard was considerably larger than the front. Along with the side yard, it provided a beautiful scenic view of the mountains ten miles away, but they found an even greater attraction. After walking fifty yards from the house, they came upon a large garden somewhat obscured by a small tool shed. A pile of cordwood was stacked in a neat pile nearby. There it was—the most-beautiful vegetable garden Nellie had ever seen. Joan proudly showed them a more-than-ample supply of tomato, pepper, and lettuce plants, and she pointed to some bountiful, thorny blackberry and blueberry bushes. Another fifty yards away stood cornstalks and potato plants near an apple tree.

"We have so much," Joan said. "We always give some to the neighbors."

Suddenly, Jack and Nellie felt a greater affinity for the house.

Farther away, they saw similar farmhouses of equal size, with a few hundred yards on each side between them.

The three sat down over hot tea to talk.

"The neighbors are very nice and friendly," Joan added, trying hard not to oversell the place.

Jack looked at Nellie and concluded that she, too, felt enamored with the place. He realized it would take a lot of work to finish up, and he wasn't very talented in that regard, but the house had plenty of potential.

Nellie sensed Jack's interest, too. "Joan, you said the asking price was forty-five hundred furnished. Does that include the pots and pans and other kitchenware?"

"I'll be glad to throw them in if you want. We could also leave the lawnmower."

It was almost five o'clock when Nellie and Jack stood to leave.

"Jack and I will discuss this over dinner and will get back to you in the morning," Nellie said.

They had nothing else to compare it to, but that didn't stifle their interest in the property.

"If you don't have a place to stay tonight," Joan said, "why not stay here? I'd offer dinner," she added regretfully, "but I was just going to have leftovers."

Nellie looked to her brother for some approbation. "We don't want to put you out too much, but we'd love to stay here tonight. Jack and I can go out for dinner and return in a few hours. Would you like to join us?" she added without much enthusiasm.

"Oh, no. You two have too much to talk about without me."

Nellie nodded and walked toward the front door.

As soon as they were out of the house, Nellie asked, "What do you think of the house?"

"I really like it, but it's a tad too big for us. Still, it has warmth and character. I hope the fireplace works." He tried to mask his enthusiasm. "How about you? Can we swing it?"

"I really like it. The kitchen's a little too small, but it's manageable. We wouldn't have to buy beds, furniture, and all the other stuff. A beautiful garden isn't the sole reason for buying a house, but I loved it. Are we moving too fast? Should we look at other prospects?"

They decided to tackle those questions over dinner.

Pulling up to the diner on the main street of town, Nellie and Jack went inside and were seated in a booth by the window. Their friendly and attentive waitress seemed to know instinctively they had things to discuss, so she didn't bother them. They ordered a hearty chicken dinner with mashed potatoes and green beans, then relaxed over cups of coffee.

"Nell, do you think that place is too big for us?" Jack asked.

"At first I did, but it's such a charming place. It needs some work, but nothing major. Perhaps we could take in a boarder or two. That would help supplement our income."

"Not a bad idea, Nell. It does have a certain character. I have a great feeling about the place. I just hope the fireplace is functioning. It's a bit cooler out now. I hope Joan has the fire going when we get back."

They returned and saw smoke emanating from the chimney, which pleased Jack.

"Let's do it, Jack!" Nellie blurted. "Let's buy it tonight!"

Not as impulsive as his sister, he paused. "Are you sure?"

"You like it, don't you?"

"Yes, quite a lot, but we could look at other places, too."

"We could, but do you want to risk losing this one? We aren't desperate, but we don't have much time to look before you start your new job."

"I agree. This is a good place for us. I'll pay you back."

She pretended not to hear his last words.

Joan, greeting them by the front door, led them inside. Logs crackled in the fireplace, and the heat was a welcome respite after the cool night air. They sat down and marveled at how cozy and enchanting the house was with glowing heat from the embers to enhance the magical setting.

"Joan," Jack said, "Nell and I love the house and property. Let's do it."

She smiled. "I'm so glad, not just to sell the house but to sell it to you two."

Those were the uncomplicated, halcyon days when one could agree on something, even purchasing a house, with a handshake. There was no house inspection, no attorneys, and no threat of litigation. The consent of both parties was enough.

They had to sign a few forms to ensure the title and ownership of the house were properly transferred, but that was all.

Before retiring, they had hot tea after Joan called Bill with the good news.

Jack stood from his comfortable place near the fire. "I'm roasting from the tea and the wonderful fire, on top of wearing a sweater. I want to cool off with a walk."

Left to themselves, Nellie Kent and Joan Roberts got to know each other better. The soon-to-be new owner explained how she was three months pregnant when her husband, Jim, died. Months later, she lost the baby to a miscarriage. Joan, the mother of four children, dabbed at her eyes with a handkerchief.

Sensing Nellie's deep grief, Joan attempted to change the subject. "One of our friend's sons fought in the Battle of the Bulge. He didn't come back, either."

CHAPTER 7

J ack returned to the farmhouse's cozy living room, feeling thoroughly refreshed from his walk in the brisk nighttime weather. The two women were still enjoying the conversation, and the crackling fire's heat continued to permeate the room. They cradled a second cup of coffee in their laps along with a corn muffin.

"Would you like another corn muffin?" Joan asked.

"That would really hit the spot," Jack replied.

Jack and Nellie slept in bedrooms upstairs with an adjoining bathroom. Although excited by the purchase of their new house, both drifted off to sleep easily.

Two hours later, Jack felt the need to visit the bathroom and maneuvered as quietly as he could toward it. He heard boards creak underfoot and hoped Nell wouldn't awaken.

After flushing the toilet, he started back to his room, chuckling slightly, because the simple act of flushing a toilet wasn't taken for granted in 1945. Just five years earlier, only fifty-four percent of American households enjoyed complete plumbing—running water, a private bath, and a flushing toilet. Certainly, that number was higher by the time Jack and Nellie purchased their farmhouse, but it wasn't by much. They were lucky the farmhouse had such facilities.

Upon reaching his bed, he nestled his head on the soft pillow and heard wind whistling against the exterior of the house.

I should expect that in an old house, he thought, feeling content and eager to meet Principal Mahon the following day and learn more about his new job.

Joan had eggs, bacon, muffins, and orange juice ready for them by the time Jack and Nellie rose and navigated the stairs.

"Coffee or tea?" she asked.

Both wanted coffee, and they thanked her profusely for the wonderful breakfast.

Nellie had an interview at Bentley Hospital scheduled for eleven o'clock that morning, so she excused herself after breakfast and left Jack on his own.

"Please make yourself at home, Jack," Joan assured him, cleaning the kitchen. "I hope you'll forgive me for going upstairs to pack some things."

"Of course. Do you need any help?"

"No, thanks. It won't be too difficult, because the kids are all scattered about and already have the things that matter to them."

Jack's meeting with Principal Mahon wasn't until the following day, so he sat back to read an issue of *Collier's Magazine* he found on a coffee table. On the month-old August 4 cover appeared a seemingly carefree American sailor and equally happy-looking servicewoman.

Little did they know, Jack thought, *that two days later, the atom bomb would be dropped on Hiroshima, followed by the bomb on Nagasaki three days after that.*

He noticed a basket on the floor with other magazines, including a February 1945 *Reader's Digest,* Jack's favorite. An article titled "An Ex-Marine Returns to High School" caught his eye, and he turned to page thirty-two. A seventeen-year-old Marine named Kenneth Merrill served at Guadalcanal and was later sent home due to combat fatigue. He went back to finish high school.

"What a great story," Jack muttered, thinking of his seventeen-year-old friend Jacklyn Lucas, who earned the Congressional Medal of Honor for his courage and valor at Iwo Jima on that fierce, combative February day.

Jack was snoozing on the couch, with Joan working upstairs, when Nellie arrived in her Studebaker. She walked through the front door and called, "I'm home! Jack, I think I have a job! They loved my experience as a trauma nurse, and the director promised to call me tomorrow morning."

She looked up and saw Joan leaning over the banister and called, "I may have a job, but I won't know until tomorrow morning. I hope you don't mind that I gave her your number."

"Of course not."

The phone rang promptly at nine o'clock the following morning. Joan reached it first and handed it to Nellie, when Nursing Director Sylvia Thomas asked for her prospective employee.

After a moment, Jack and Joan heard Nellie declare, "That's wonderful! When do you want me to report? Yes, Tuesday would be great. Thanks so much, Ms. Thomas."

Things were looking up for the new West Virginia residents.

Before visiting the Mahons for dinner that evening, Jack and Nellie scouted the Bentley area, including the high school. Main Street was a long avenue with several stores and office buildings. They saw a pharmacy and a Woolworth's adjacent to it.

Jack and Nellie parked the Studebaker and walked into a small bookshop beside Woolworth's. They introduced themselves to the shopkeeper as new residents from Buffalo, New York. He was the owner and was a lifelong resident of Bentley, having been born there in 1875. Now seventy, his passion was books, and he enjoyed puttering around the shop. His name was Stephen McCarthy, and he loved to travel around the state, looking for interesting old books. Tall, frail, and lame, he walked with a cane and wore thick glasses.

They exchanged pleasantries and soon the couple went out to explore the town further. As they walked down the sidewalk, everyone greeted them with a smile and warm hello. The pharmacy and more introductions came next, followed by an early lunch of lime Cokes and grilled cheese sandwiches at Woolworth's soda fountain and lunch counter. The waitress greeted them with a big smile and welcomed them to Bentley.

"I can't wait to make your lunch experience a great one," she said.

After the waitress walked away, Nellie said, "I like Bentley and its people, Jack. Don't you?"

"Absolutely." He was equally impressed. "I have a good feeling about this move."

After more pleasantries, they motored back to their new home on Mountain View Road, passing a bakery, hardware store, dry cleaners, barbershop, beauty salon, a flower and gift shop, and the local post office.

Joan continued packing while the couple was away and greeted them when they returned.

"I love the people here," Nellie gushed.

"It's a close-knit community," Joan agreed. "Bill and I have loved living here. If you ever need help, you can count on it in a minute. While Bill and I aren't West Virginians by birth, we have come to love this state and its people. They're warm and friendly, and there's a strong sense of community spirit. You definitely picked the right place. Bill and I will miss it."

Her enthusiasm made the Buffalonians even happier about their decision. After an afternoon nap, they drove to the Mahon home at the other end of town. The neighborhoods and homes they passed, while sparsely populated, appeared less affluent than their new abode.

CHAPTER 8

66 Good afternoon," was the enthusiastic greeting they received at the Mahon homestead. Kathryn ushered them in with a warm smile, and Patrick, Jack's new boss, soon joined them from his study. They were a handsome couple—tall, stately, and in their mid to late forties. Patrick was Jim Crowley's roommate at Notre Dame, even though Patrick didn't play football himself. Kathryn attended Indiana University, and the two met at a college dance.

Soon, Robbie, their twelve-year-old son, appeared. He was tall for his age and a bit gangly, as well as a bit shy. After politely meeting Jack and Nellie, he disappeared quickly back to his father's study to listen to the radio.

Over a salad, grilled steaks, and baked potatoes, the four sat down for coffee in the living room.

"Love your house," Jack said. "It's spacious."

"And I adore your kitchen," Nellie told Kathryn.

"Thank you. Patrick and I moved here five years ago from Morgantown. "

"There aren't a lot of opportunities in today's education world," Patrick said, "but we're very happy here. Kathryn works at the library, and I hope someday to get into college administration. Working at the high school is a challenge but a delightful one."

While the ladies cleaned up the dishes and talked about Bentley's offerings, the two men went into Patrick's study.

Patrick lit a cigarette and offered one to Jack.

"No, thanks," Jack said. "I never took up the habit."

"Lucky you. I wish I never started. I grew up in a small town in Indiana, and all my friends smoked, even at the age of thirteen. Kathryn is after me about it all the time, but it's tough to stop."

"I know what you mean. My mother and father have been trying to give it up for at least ten years, and I know I'd have the same problem if I ever started. I did smoke a little when I was in the Marines, but my comrades were thrilled when I refused my ration of cigarettes and gave them away."

Jack didn't mention the time he spent in foxholes at Tarawa and Iwo Jima, when cigarettes helped calm his nerves and pass the time while anxiously awaiting the next enemy attack. As a war hero, he didn't want to mention the experience and appear immodest.

The conversation soon shifted to Bentley High School.

"Like a number of others," Patrick said, "we're a fairly poor state. The people are wonderful, and they come from all walks of life. Many are disadvantaged, and you'll see it immediately. They're the salt of the earth."

Jack nodded.

"One of the things I love so much about Bentley is that we're a melting pot, but no one sleeps with the doors locked. Here's a packet of information and some paperwork for you to complete. You can hand it in to the main office secretary on Tuesday morning. Do you have any questions?"

Feeling comfortable with his new principal, Jack said, "Not really, but I'm sure I'll have a few once school begins. I look forward to learning more about the schools, students, and meeting other teachers and the football coach."

"I'm sure you'll have questions, Jack," Patrick replied with a broad smile.

Jack felt Patrick was a nice guy who wasn't full of himself.

On the way home, Nellie said how much she liked Kathryn. Despite their age difference, she envisioned a warm friendship with her. Jack replied similarly, saying Patrick was potentially a good friend and boss.

They spent Saturday grocery shopping and helping Joan. On Sunday morning, they attended the local Presbyterian Church accompanied by Joan and Bill Roberts.

Bill was a large, robust man who stood six feet three inches tall and weighed two hundred and fifty pounds. When Jack met the jovial man, he couldn't avoid an amusing thought of Bill in bed with his stout, five-foot wife. Dismissing that thought quickly, he went along with the business of knowing his host. Bill was affable enough, but it was difficult to overlook his bulbous, almost-purple nose while addressing him.

The large proboscis reminded Jack of a possibly apocryphal story of J. P. Morgan, the American financier and banker, who had a similar affliction. Allegedly, Morgan once offered one hundred thousand dollars to anyone who could explain why his face was red and his nose a blue/purple. The answer was that he had rosacea, but no doctor at the time could diagnose and cure it.

Supposedly, a young waitress was serving Mr. Morgan breakfast one morning and couldn't get over the sight of his bloated, colorful nose. The more she tried not to think of it, the more she focused on it. Finally, it was time to serve coffee to the old man.

"Do you want a lump of sugar on your nose?" she asked nervously and was instantly mortified, and Morgan was miffed.

Just as the waitress couldn't get over Morgan's nose, Jack had trouble getting over it, too. Fortunately, unlike that young woman, Jack didn't have to serve Bill coffee.

Early on Labor Day morning, Jack and Nellie said goodbye to the Roberts for what was likely to be the first and only time. Hugs from the women and handshakes from the men would be their last acts together.

As they turned back to their new house from the driveway, Nellie threw up her arms in excitement.

"This is fun! I have a good feeling about being here."

All Jack could think of was the handyman work he faced. The house needed painting, a few boards on the porch and stairs needed repair, and the newel post and front door screen needed replacing. That was just what he could see after only a few days, without seriously looking.

I'm sure there will be some unpleasant surprises ahead, he thought. *At least West Virginia looks pretty good. The people are nice and seem to share our values.*

They had trouble sleeping that night. Their permanent bedrooms would be the two downstairs, with an adjoining bath, but the excitement of starting their new jobs kept them up well past midnight.

CHAPTER 9

After breakfast on Tuesday, Jack dropped Nellie off in front of the hospital. He drove to Bentley High School two miles away. He wore dark-gray trousers, a white shirt, and black sweater, and, after dropping off his paperwork in the main office, was ready to meet his new students.

It was eight-thirty as kids filed in for their history class. Some looked quizzically at him, while others passed by without noticing.

When it seemed all forty students were seated, he stepped forward from the desk in front of the chalkboard and introduced himself.

"As you probably noticed," he began with a twinkle in his eye, "I'm not Mr. Roberts."

Those who listened giggled or laughed, but a few students weren't paying attention.

"My name's Jack Morgan," he said over the merriment.

A rather disheveled young man shot through the door and past Jack to a seat in the back of the room.

"That's just Jimmy Warren," a girl in the front row said. "He's always late."

More giggles ensued.

"Sorry, Teach," Jimmy blurted.

"It's nice to see you, too, Jimmy, though I expect you to be on time tomorrow."

More laughter followed.

"Mr. Roberts moved to Pennsylvania. He took another job in Pittsburgh. He wanted me to say goodbye to you for him." He grinned. "He told me what great students you are and how you're never late."

They chuckled. At Jack's request, each student stood at his or her desk and gave a name. Jack wanted to start his teaching experience as pleasantly and positively as possible, and he wasn't concerned about any particular assignment that day.

A few kids elicited laughter from their classmates when they gave their names, especially Jimmy, but the process went smoothly.

"Do you have any questions for me?" Jack asked when they finished.

Several hands went up. He called on Sally, a pretty, though somewhat emaciated, young woman.

"I'm Sally Hawkins," she said with a nervous smile, her hands fidgeting with the inkwell on her desk.

"Yes, Sally?"

"Well, Mr. Martin," she began.

A cacophony of voices erupted.

"That's Morgan," he corrected.

Clearly the students were enjoying themselves, but that was OK. They laughed.

"Sorry, Mr. Morgan. Do you give much homework?"

All the students, including Jimmy, leaned forward, eager for his answer.

"It depends on how much we accomplish in class," he replied. "If we aren't late and don't laugh too much," he quipped with a grin, "there probably won't be a lot of homework."

Some applauded softly.

"Yes?" Jack asked, acknowledging someone six rows back.

"My name is Kevin," a big, strong-looking youth said. "Will you be staying here, or are you just subbing for Mr. Roberts for a while until they find a replacement?"

Again, all students pitched forward to hear his answer.

"I'm here for the long run. I'm also coaching the football team."

"See you on the field, Coach," Kevin said.

Other questions came.

"Are you married?"

"No."

"Were you in the Army?"

"No, the Marines."

"Do you live here?"

"Yes. I just bought the Roberts' house."

"Where are you from?"

"Buffalo, New York."

"Do you like West Virginia?"

"Yes, very much. So far, so good. I look forward to exploring the area more."

Soon, class was over. Before dismissal, Jack reminded the students to continue reading about the Revolutionary War, which Mr. Roberts assigned them before the Labor Day holiday.

"We'll discuss the Boston Tea Party tomorrow," he said. "I look forward to getting to know each of you."

"Thank you, Mr. Morgan," the students chorused.

As each one paraded past his desk to leave, he studied them. Many were skinny. Some, like Sally Hawkins, looked especially thin. A few wore new clothes, but most, like Jimmy Warren, looked a little disheveled and wore well-used, somewhat tattered garments.

His first class over, he went to the faculty room to meet some of the other teachers. He sat down with Mrs. Helen Marsh, a pleasant-looking lady in her early sixties. She taught math, and it was obvious she cared deeply about the kids at the high school. She had piercing, deep-set eyes behind old granny glasses, a tiny nose, no makeup, and teeth that needed work. She wore her hair in a bun, which didn't help make her look any younger. She was very nice, and, after talking with her for a bit, Jack felt comfortable with her and shared his concerns about the students he met.

"Is it my imagination or are some of these kids underfed?" he asked.

"Jack, some definitely are. That cute little girl, Sally Hawkins, is one of them. You probably don't know her yet, but she's one of many."

Her sympathy was clear. Like many high schools of the day, Bentley didn't have a formal cafeteria or lunchroom, so students brought bag lunches and ate at their desks. Mrs. Marsh noticed over the years that many kids quickly devoured their sandwiches and probably wanted more. She strongly suspected some had a small breakfast or none at all. It wasn't that all the families were poor, or the parents didn't care, but the war and its aftermath created hard times in West Virginia and many other states.

The Mountaineer State of West Virginia did more than its part to aid in the U.S. war effort. Based on population, it reported the fifth-highest percentage of servicemen in World

War II—218,665. Almost six thousand were killed, and eleven Medals of Honor went to the residents. Among them was the first person to break the sound barrier, Charles "Chuck" Yeager, who became an ace in a single day by shooting down five German planes, thirteen in all.

Some two thousand West Virginian women were in military service during the war, too. In every way, West Virginia distinguished itself in the war effort. More than six hundred million tons of coal came from the state, along with steel used for battleships and tanks. The Kanawha Valley housed the largest synthetic rubber plant in the world and became America's premier supplier of synthetic rubber.

Like all the other states, West Virginia rationed gasoline, butter, sugar, and many grew their own food. Children helped in the effort, like children throughout the country, collecting paper, scrap metal, and old tires. Everyone pitched in. The steel industry, well represented in West Virginia by Weirton Steel and Wheeling Iron & Steel companies, converted their production lines to respond to specific needs, such as howitzer shells, bombs, and steel drums.

While prospering during the war years and for another fifteen years afterward, West Virginia's industry finally started showing a decline. Coal was king in West Virginia, but, after its phenomenal contribution to the war effort, the coal industry felt the pinch of competition from other fuels.

The move from coal to alternative fuels such as oil, natural gas, and even nuclear power forced the coal companies to reduce costs to survive in a much tighter market. One county nearby to Bentley, lost more than half of its hundred thousand residents. Mines closed, leaving thousands jobless. Major increases in poverty were the unfortunate result, and people were forced to move away to find work.

Jack met with Don Adams, the head football coach. Jack sized up Don almost immediately as a rather gruff, intense, control freak. Six feet tall with a pronounced gut, which Buffalonians called a "Milwaukee tumor," the head coach had unruly black hair, a ruddy complexion, dark deep-set eyes, and a nose that obviously had been broken a few times. His mouth was unusually wide and contained a set of unattractive yellow teeth. He was probably in his mid-fifties, and Jack felt he was the quintessential drill instructor in the service.

As they talked, it was evident Don had no sense of humor and very little personality.

"You have to establish order, especially with the poor kids. They have no sense of discipline. You have to come down on them hard."

He wasn't entirely unlikable, although he pushed the limits. Jack recalled a general he met during basic training. When the general addressed the men, he said, "No man is a total failure, because he can always serve as a bad example." The general must have been thinking of Don Adams.

"I heard you were a running back and linebacker at Fordham," Adams said. "I'd like you to run the offense and take responsibility for managing the game clock. Last year, we had a chance to beat Middletown with fourteen seconds left, but the damn clock ran out before we could run another play. I don't want that to happen again."

"What should I call you?" Jack asked.

"Coach will do."

This won't be fun, Jack thought.

Before practice that day, while the boys donned pads and uniforms, Don sat down again with Jack and told him some of the challenges. "'We won only one game last year and just one the previous year. Our nearest rival, Central, over in Oakville, has our number. We've never beaten them. We don't get as many good players as they and the other schools in the mountain conference do. Their schools are bigger, too."

Once on the field, Coach Adams ran the kids through very rigorous wind sprints. There were few laughs or any other signs that anyone was having fun. If a boy missed a block, the punishment was ten pushups and a lap around the track. Out of the corner of his eye, Jack saw a thin Negro man observing the practice from behind a fence.

After a while, Jack ambled over to the DI, Jack's pet nickname for Adams, and asked about the visitor.

"Oh, he's just the janitor," the coach said, "trying to pass the time. I don't even know his name."

Nellie got home before Jack that day. He gave her a hug and peck on the cheek, and asked, "How was your day?"

"It was fun, Jack," she said, beaming. "I think I'll like it very much. How about you?"

"The school's a good fit for me, but the head football coach is a jerk."

Nellie made pork chops that evening, and they discussed their experiences and the people they met in more detail over dinner.

They next day at practice, the same Negro man stood at the fence to watch.

"Maybe he knows his football and can help us," Jack suggested.

"How the hell could that Black son of a bitch help us?" Adams spat in a contemptuous voice. "I should probably just chase him off."

After practice, Jack approached the tall observer as he was leaving the premises. "Hi," he said, his hand outstretched. "I'm Jack Morgan. I just moved here from Buffalo, and I'm teaching history and trying to assist the Drill Instructor."

The old man's dark eyes twinkled, and he laughed. His smile indicated he shared Jack's disdain for Coach Adams.

The man was Henry Parker, the school janitor for twelve years, and he'd played a little football in Connecticut back in 1902. Tall, well-spoken, and sixty-years old, he had coal-black eyes above high, prominent cheekbones. His ebony skin accented his white teeth, which were somewhat stained yellow, probably from tobacco.

"I love football," Henry told Jack. "But I must admit I was a scrub at Connecticut. Not many Negroes played back then."

His voice held no resentment or complaint. Strangely enough, Henry's face was almost free of wrinkles, and he wore his gray-white hair short, with a slight mustache under a thick nose.

"Can I give you a lift home?" Jack offered.

"Oh, no, Mr. Morgan. I live just a few blocks away."

"It's Jack, Henry, and I insist."

They drove several blocks north and one west, then the old gentleman signaled that was where he got off.

"Thanks again, and see you tomorrow," Henry said, trudging toward a nearby apartment building.

CHAPTER 10

J ack's students in both of his classes were well-behaved in general, which was a victory for a new teacher, but several of the boys and Sally Hawkins appeared distracted by something.

Don Adams wasn't any friendlier at football practice, and Jack wrote him off as a dork. Henry returned to watch.

"How about a ride home?" Jack offered.

The old man declined. However, they shared some friendly banter, and Jack eventually dropped Henry off at the corner before driving home.

Over dinner that night with Nellie, Jack spoke of his concern about some of the students in his classes.

"I don't think some of these kids have breakfast," he said. "I know it affects their attentiveness and ability in class."

"Do you have any ideas?"

"As a matter of fact, I do." He leaned forward and set aside his fork. "I need your input. I was thinking about taking a few things with me each morning, like Grape-Nuts cereal or something similar, along with bananas and apples. What do you think?"

"Well, it sounds like a terrific idea, something that's typically thoughtful and generous of you. It will cost us a bit, but the apples can come from our trees." Nellie felt enthusiastic. "Maybe we can get Mr. Rider at the grocery store to help provide some of it. I'm sure he'll think it's a good idea. Why Grape-Nuts?"

"It's about as filling a cereal as you can get, especially cold." He remembered somewhat ruefully that Grape-Nuts were part of the lightweight jungle rations he and his fellow Marines ate on the beaches of Tarawa, Guadalcanal, and Iwo Jima. "Their motto is, 'It fills you up, not out,' and it worked for us."

Grape-Nuts, developed in 1897 by C. W. Post, was made with wheat and barley. Despite the name, it didn't contain any grapes or nuts. Nellie offered to buy some extra milk, Grape-Nuts, and bananas the following day after work.

After football practice the next day, Henry didn't bother protesting the ride home. He willingly took his place without argument in the front seat. At the corner, he hopped out of the car, waved a hand over his shoulder in a goodbye-thank-you gesture, and ambled up the sidewalk to his apartment.

Jack waved goodbye and pretended to drive home, but he stopped just out of sight at the corner to watch. When the older man thought Jack was gone, he walked in the same direction he'd come from. Jack remained far behind and watched Henry return to the school.

That Friday night, Jack and Nellie went to visit Rider's Grocery. Mr. Rider, enthusiastic about the idea of providing children with healthy breakfast food, wanted to contribute a gallon of milk, a box of Grape-Nuts, and a few browning but still-edible bananas for Monday's class.

"Let me know how it goes," he told them. "This could be the start of something good."

Jack was in class early Monday. Without saying a word, he placed the goodies, which included the items from Rider's Grocery, along with bread, peanut butter, and jelly, on the back table with a few bowls and plates. Some of the kids asked why it was there.

As other students filed in, Jack said matter-of-factly, "I just thought some of you would like a snack."

One-third of the students helped themselves, and the success made the class begin fifteen minutes late, at eight forty-five, but no one cared. Jack saw Sally had cereal with bread and peanut butter. The scene pleased him immensely, but he had to be careful that his gesture wasn't interpreted as charity. He didn't want to threaten their dignity and sense of pride.

Football practice went well that afternoon, better than Jack expected for kids who just had a weekend off. Henry watched from his usual vantage point and met Jack after practice.

The two drove to their usual drop-off point. As the tall gentleman walked away from the Studebaker, Jack rolled down his window.

"Come back a moment, Henry."

"What is it?"

"You don't have any place to go, do you?"

"No." Henry lowered his head and looked embarrassed.

"Why the charade of coming out here?"

"I didn't want you to feel sorry for me."

"Henry, we need to talk."

They drove back to the school.

That night at 7 Mountain View Road, Jack and Nellie had a lot to discuss.

"How did your breakfast experiment go?" Nellie asked.

"Great! There was hardly anything left over."

"That's wonderful!"

"What about you? Did you have a nice day?"

"I did, and I didn't. There's one nurse, Ellie Fleming, who I'm afraid is a bit jealous of me."

"Well, I'm not surprised. You're a very attractive, personable, smart young woman. I'll bet she was the pretty one until you arrived."

"Oh, Jack, you're just saying that, because you're my brother."

"Look in the mirror, Nellie. Ellie was probably top dog with all the doctors. Now she's not."

"Well, that's possible, I guess, but she's far prettier than me."

"I doubt that, but if she's that pretty, maybe you should introduce us."

"Maybe that's not such a bad idea, Brother Dear."

He looked at her seriously. "Nell, there's something else we need to talk about. I met a wonderful older gentleman at the school, and he's a terrific guy. He's the janitor and used to play football at Connecticut. I just found out he doesn't have a place to live. He's homeless. I found out accidentally. I think he's sleeping in the school."

Jack explained how he and Henry met, and their conversations on the way to Henry's phantom apartment. "He's a very proud, honest man."

"And you want to bring him here to live with us?"

"Well, kind of."

"How do you know he's honest?"

"I just know he is, and he has character."

Much to his surprise, she simply said, "I suppose we could try it."

"Oh, Nell, you're the best! There's one other thing."

"Here it comes. What's the catch?"

"He's a Negro."

She paused, then asked, "So what?"

"I hoped that would be your response. It's just one of the many things that make you special."

The Morgan siblings were raised to respect everyone regardless of race, color, or religious creed. Their father, a carpenter, told them something they always remembered: "Everyone you meet is your superior in at least something. Don't ever think you're better than anyone else."

Jack thought it was a shame that Don Adams didn't share that attitude.

Tuesday was a repeat of Monday with the food. Almost half the students arrived fifteen minutes early. The self-made peanut butter sandwiches were a particular hit, and the bread vanished quickly. Some made sandwiches to save for lunch.

Word got around fast, and soon other kids availed themselves of the treats. On Tuesday morning, Jack saw five kids he'd never seen before who helped themselves to the food before going to their classrooms. He also noticed his students were more attentive to the day's lesson, participated more in discussions, and asked questions. He was clearly onto something.

Jack could hardly wait until football practice. After laps around the field, for which he always joined his charges, he sauntered up to Henry and asked, "How's it going?"

"Hi, Jack. Same old, same old."

"How would you like to move in with my sister and me?" he blurted.

Henry was incredulous. "Are you kidding me?" A small tear trickled down his right cheek.

"Nope. I'm absolutely serious."

"But...but why would you do such a thing for me?" he asked earnestly.

"Let's just say, Henry, that we could use a helping hand. Besides, Nellie and I could use the company. Let's go get your things."

Henry's possessions consisted of a large paper bag filled with old T-shirts, a gray sweatshirt, some socks, a few pairs of underwear, and a pair of blue jeans.

In the car, Henry was the first to speak. "You know, I'm a good handyman. I can paint your place and do some repairs. I was there once before when Miss Joan had me out to cut some wood and repair the woodshed."

That answered the question Jack was about to ask. "That's great. The old farmhouse could use some love."

As they pulled up the dirt driveway, Henry wasn't through. "One last thing, Jack. Does Nellie know I'm a Negro?"

"That doesn't matter, but yes, she does."

Nellie greeted their visitor with a big hug before Jack could even introduce them. "Hi. I'm Nellie. Welcome to our home."

Tears rolled down both Henry's cheeks, as he returned the embrace. "Miss Nellie, I want you to know how much I appreciate what you and Jack are doing for me. I promise to earn my keep. I'm a really good handyman and can help you fix up this beautiful place."

Over dinner that night, Henry told them about his life.

"I was born in New Haven, Connecticut, in 1885. My dad was a chef at Yale, and I had pretty good grades and played football at Hillhouse High School. I ended up with a football scholarship to the University of Connecticut in 1902. I wanted to play at Yale, but no Negro ever played for them back then or now.

"After Connecticut, I drifted from one job to another, mostly handyman work. That was when I learned you can't beat demon rum. I was all messed up but was fortunate to meet a wonderful woman I loved dearly. She already had a kid when I moved in with her.

"One day when I was gone," he said slowly, taking a deep breath before continuing, "her old boyfriend returned and beat both of them to death. For a while, the law blamed me, but they finally caught up with him. Eventually, I moved south to Virginia and then here, where I began working as the high school's janitor twelve years ago."

CHAPTER 11

For the next few days, the traffic around the back table in Jack's homeroom at the school increased. Soon, he was bringing in two loaves of bread daily and extra peanut butter and jelly. His students seemed to thrive in their class work.

One Thursday afternoon, Jack had a very unpleasant encounter with the irascible football coach. The stodgy, insulting, unsavory coach came up to him after practice with a smirk on his face and said, "I understand that Black lowlife is living with you."

Nearly purple with rage, Jack put his face right up to Don's and backed him to the gym wall. "I don't like that word, and I really don't like when someone uses it. Henry's a fine man. He played college football and can help us right now with our kids."

He stared Adams in the eye, clearly not backing down an inch. If there was to be a fight, Jack was more than willing.

Coach Adams saw the look in Jack's eye, as well as a vein popping on Jack's neck. "I'm sorry," he said sheepishly. "I shouldn't have used that expression."

Jack was shocked, assuming either they would have a fistfight, or Jack would be fired. *There are certain things a man must stand up for*, he thought. *This is one of them.*

Fortunately, Henry wasn't there to witness the near brawl.

Friday passed without incident until Jack, sitting in the faculty room, saw Patti, Principal Mahon's secretary, making a beeline toward him clutching a piece of paper.

"Mr. Morgan, the principal wishes to see you as soon as possible." She handed him the paper and left.

He looked at the note and knew the summons wasn't entirely unexpected. He wondered if he had a future at Bentley High. *I'm here barely two weeks, and now I'm gone,* he thought.

There were twenty minutes left before lunch, and he wandered toward the principal's office, contemplating what he would say when he was fired. Principal Mahon peered out the office door and saw Jack approaching.

"Come in," the principal said.

Jack strolled into the room and stood before the desk.

"Sit down." Mahon gave him a stern look.

Jack sat down immediately and assumed his job was over.

"We've got a problem." The principal paused while Jack sank back into his chair and exhaled softly.

I can't believe I'm going to lose my job because of that scumbag foot-ball coach. What will I tell Nellie?

"Jack, you have to stop it." Seeing Jack's quizzical look, Mahon said, "The food, Jack. It has to stop. Several faculty members have complained it makes them and the school look bad."

Relieved but angry, Jack collected his thoughts before replying. "Pat, the kids are hungry. Obviously, some don't get breakfast, and it affects their schoolwork and attention span. I've been here only two weeks, and the problem sticks out like a sore thumb. If the other teachers are whining about it, then they can do what I do. Better yet, why doesn't the school provide the food? I would pay more than my share to contribute."

Principal Mahon sat back in his swivel chair and nodded. "You know, Jack, that makes sense. Let me think about it over the weekend. In the meantime, please don't bring any goodies on Monday."

"But they'll still be hungry on Monday," Jack insisted.

"I know. Give me a few days to figure it out."

At football practice, Don Adams went about his business as if nothing happened, and Jack wondered what that meant. They had one more week to prepare for their first game, and it seemed they needed it.

Monday morning came, and, as requested, Jack didn't bring any food to his classroom. Some of the kids arrived early, as usual, and their expressions showed their disappointment when they realized there were no snacks for them that day.

Jack thought a few even looked distraught, but he knew he couldn't do anything without going against the wishes of the man who gave him the job.

Right after Jack's history class, Patti found him in the teacher's lounge. "My boss wants to see you."

Jack set down his coffee cup and followed the perky secretary to the principal's office.

"Jack, please sit down. I've thought a lot over the weekend about what you said about this problem, so here's what we'll do. From seven forty-five until eight fifteen, we'll have several loaves of bread, peanut butter and jelly, bananas, and dough-nuts available for the kids. I saw Tom Rider at the grocery store on Saturday, and he's willing to contribute most of the food with some help from the school.

"Heidi Miller from Heidi's bakery promised us any dough-nuts she can't sell for two days, and they'll still be plenty good for the kids."

He watched, as Jack fought to contain the smile that blan-keted his face. He stood and offered Jack his hand. "Thanks for this idea, Jack, and for caring so much about the students' welfare."

"Pat, you're a good man and a fine principal. I'm glad I work for you. When does this go into effect?"

"Tomorrow. We'll tell all students and faculty."

"Tremendous!"

Football practice went especially well that afternoon, with almost no extra push-ups or laps needed. Coach Adams seemed pleased by the players' progress, and the quarterback and leader of the team was throwing the ball with confidence. Most teams built their play around the running game, and Adams added a few new wrinkles to their passing game that might catch some opponents by surprise. He was in a rare good mood, and the players responded positively to it.

After a shower and a drive home with Henry, Jack thought about another engagement. That night he would go to the hospital for a social gathering, courtesy of an invite from Nellie.

Bentley Hospital was hosting an hors d'oeuvres and cocktail mixer after work, so Nellie asked Jack to join her.

"Besides, perhaps you can give me some suggestions on how to handle Ellie Fleming."

His eyebrows rose in confusion.

"You know, the girl who doesn't seem to like me."

"Oh, that one. I remember."

Jack freshened up and dressed in khaki pants and an open-collared white shirt topped by a blue sport coat. He bid Henry good night, and, as he passed the mirror on his way out the front door, he smiled and mused that maybe he wasn't so bad looking after all. Driving to the hospital, he thought it might be fun to meet a few nurses.

After he arrived, he gazed around the room, seeing if he could find Ellie. She was supposedly good-looking, perhaps the best of them all—until Nellie arrived. The theory made sense, because the belle of the ball never liked competition.

He saw a striking brunette, but her nametag read "Molly."

At that point, Nellie rushed up from the corner and gave him a fierce hug, placing a name tag on him. "You look really nice."

"Why, thank you, ma'am. And so do you." He grinned.

Soon a short but attractive female came up to them and said, "So, this is your brother." She offered Jack her hand.

"Hi," Jack said, shaking her hand. "It's nice to meet you."

"Likewise, I'm sure," she purred.

He stood awkwardly, not knowing what to say.

"Want a glass of punch?" she asked.

"That sounds great."

With that formality behind them, the woman took his arm and ushered him to the punch. "By the way, I'm Ellie Fleming, and I work with your sister."

They found two bowls of punch on the table.

"Do you want just punch, or do you want punch with something in it?"

"Since I'm driving, I'll take the undoctored stuff."

She laughed and chose the same punch for herself. He guessed she was barely five feet three inches tall, with a small body to match. She had blue eyes, autumn-brown hair with bangs, and perfect teeth. Her nose was small, and her lips were full and red. The thing he noticed most about her, however, was her skin, which was very pale white and appeared as if she spent little time outdoors. She seemed nice but a bit too sure of herself.

Jack soon learned she grew up in Morgantown, north of Bentley, and graduated from West Virginia University. They found an empty table and two chairs, where they could continue their discussion. Ellie went to nursing school at the university and was engaged to a young doctor, but it didn't pan out. She wanted to work in rural West Virginia anyway, so she took the job in Bentley two years earlier.

"That's enough about me," Ellie said. "What about you?"

Nellie walked up to see how Jack was doing. He gave a subtle "thumbs up," so she continued to another table. "Well, my story is kind of boring." He told her a little about his life. Concerning the war, all he said was he was a Marine.

Soon, the mixer ended, and Ellie gave Jack her phone number. The evening went well, and he envisioned seeing her again.

"So, what did you think of Ellie?" Nellie asked, after getting into the car.

"She's nice, very nice."

"Would you want to go out with her?"

"Maybe."

They drove home and found Henry hunched over the kitchen table, eating a peanut butter and jelly sandwich.

"I would have made something for you, Henry," Nellie said in disappointment, although she actually felt relieved. The hors d'oeuvres were plentiful, and she didn't feel like making dinner.

Nellie went to bed early, but Jack and Henry had a cup of coffee and sat on the couch to talk. Henry had become not only a good friend but a confidant. They ate apples and discussed baseball.

Henry had been an ardent fan for years, although understandably focused on the Negro leagues. He was convinced that players like Josh Gibson, the power-hitter for the Homestead Greys, would have been a star in the Whites-only major leagues. Gibson hit .369 in 1944 and had eighty-four home runs in one season. Born in Buena Vista, Georgia, the six-foot-one-inch two-hundred-and-thirty-pound slugger was one of the best and most prodigious home run hitters in baseball history.

"Jack, do you think Josh would make the Hall of Fame if he played in the Major Leagues?" Henry asked.

"Are you kidding me?" he replied, his eyes wide. "Does a bear shit in the woods? Of course he would make it. He's the Negro Babe Ruth."

The two knew they would have many future discussions about baseball.

Nellie was a bundle of energy when Jack picked her up from work the following day. "Well, Jack, you'll never guess who's now trying to become my best friend."

He suspected she meant Ellie.

"She came up to me the morning after the mixer and brought me coffee. She likes you. Do you like her?"

"Yeah. As I told you last night, she was nice and kind of cute."

When they got home, they saw Henry had finished painting the inner door a light tan color, and the screen was repaired.

"Fantastic job!" they told a beaming Henry.

"Well," he said, obviously happy with their approbation, "I still have a lot of work to do."

After a dinner of grilled steak, vegetables, and fruit salad, they moved into the living room for conversation and hot tea. Nellie retired early. Henry wanted to share some of his observations about the football team with Jack, so they lingered.

The next day, after practice, Don suggested he and Jack have a beer at Keeley's, a bar over the town line in Oakville. They could review prospects for the coming season and discuss any necessary changes.

Jack was a few minutes late when he opened the door and saw the head coach up near the barstools, being tossed around like a rag doll by three unsavory-looking characters. Two wore beards, and the third had a nasty-looking scar extending down his right cheek.

"What the hell's going on?" Jack asked, moving toward them.

"Well, looky here," one said. "It's the war hero. Come on over." He beckoned with both hands. "We'll kick your ass, too."

Just like in an old Western, the patrons got up from their tables and retreated to a safer place by the door.

Somewhat baffled, Jack asked, "What's the matter? We don't have a quarrel with you."

"Well, let's just say," the scar-faced man said, "we don't like anyone from chickenshit Bentley High."

Don, blood dripping from his nose, slipped from their grip. "Let's get out of here," he told Jack.

The guy with the scar was clearly the ringleader. He stepped between the two coaches. "Not until I get a piece of this chickenshit."

Close enough to smell the thug's foul breath, the sturdy Marine unleashed a thunderous right fist squarely on his jaw. The punch couldn't have traveled more than eighteen inches, but the burly man crashed to the floor so hard that empty glasses from a nearby table toppled and shattered on the floor.

"Anyone else feeling tough?" Jack asked the two remaining thugs through clenched teeth, his face was purple with rage.

The man with the scar was completely unconscious. His comrades backed away, raising their hands in the air.

"OK, gentlemen, and I use the term loosely, if I ever see you again, you'd better move in the opposite direction." He took Don's arm and pulled him toward the door.

"Thanks, Jack," Don said, as they walked to their cars. "I didn't know you were a brawler."

"I'm not, but he got what he deserved. A Marine boxer friend told me once that it's always best to get in the first punch if a fight is inevitable. Just make sure it's a good one. Also, if you swing, aim at the guy's Adam's apple. That way, if he ducks, he'll catch it squarely on the nose. Either way, he's disabled."

CHAPTER 12

Jack's history classes went well the following day, and the kids seemed more attentive. He couldn't help feeling a sense of pride that his idea for a food program helped with overall conduct as well as students' grades.

Football practice went well, too, and he noticed a distinct change in Don's behavior toward him. He showed Jack more respect than usual and was even deferential to him when addressing the kids. Don had a black eye from the skirmish, but no one dared ask why.

Once again, Don thanked his assistant coach for bailing him out of trouble, although he did it privately. They talked about the upcoming game against Hartnett, a school from a similarly small town fifteen miles away.

"They have most of their boys coming back from last year," Don said. "That includes a fast-running back named Bill Darby. We lost 13-6 to them last year at their place, but I think we have a chance to beat them this time."

It wasn't to be. In Friday night's home game, they lost soundly 25-6. Jack spoke briefly to Don and the boys after the game, then headed home with Henry.

It was after nine-thirty by the time they reached the house and sat down with bottles of Coke.

"Would you like my observations on the game tonight," Henry asked, "or would you rather not?"

"Fire away, Henry. I definitely want to hear your opinion. It wasn't pretty out there, and Don really thought we had a chance to win. It was rather obvious by the end of the first quarter that we were overmatched."

"I noticed two main things. You'd best shore them up quickly, or it'll be a long season."

Jack took a long swig from his Coke and leaned forward.

"The defensive ends don't seem to understand their job. They have to force the runner into the middle of the field and not allow the wide, outside sweeps that killed you all today. Those two consistently tried to rush the quarterback, leaving the outside exposed." Jack nodded, listening intently.

"The other thing is that the defensive backs need to watch the quarterback's eyes to know where the pass is going. At this level, probably only a few high-school quarterbacks in the country are smart and talented enough to look one way and throw the other. Those elite players aren't in this league."

Quite perceptive of him, Jack thought, agreeing with both points Henry raised. Bill Darby had a field day on his sweeps around the ends, and Bentley's defensive backs were late all day in contesting Hartnett's passes. Henry's criticism was on the mark, which gave Jack an idea.

After practice the following Monday, Jack asked to meet with a rather subdued, disconsolate head coach.

"I was surprised," Don said. "I really thought we had a great chance to beat them, but seems like if we played ten games against them," he added sadly, "they'd beat us every time. Maybe I'm a bad coach."

Jack pondered that and offered a suggestion. "Don, I spoke with Henry after the game. You'd be surprised at how much he knows about football. You know he played at Connecticut." Without waiting for a reply, he continued, "His critique of the game is right on."

Jack described Henry's observations in detail. "Don, you're a very good coach, and I think I'm an adequate one, but we need more help. Did you notice that Hartnett seemed to have three or four coaches? There's only the two of us plus Danny, who played for you two years ago. Let me see if Henry will step in and coach the ends and maybe the defensive backfield."

Don mulled that over. Much to Jack's surprise, he said, "Sure. See if he'll do it."

Upon hearing such unexpected news, Jack acted as nonchalant as possible, promising to take care of it.

He couldn't wait to meet Henry at the car that afternoon.

"How'd you like to be the ends' coach and also work with the defensive backs?" he asked, getting into the car.

Henry's eyes lit up. "Me? Do you really mean it?"

"Absolutely. Coach Adams wants you to do it."

"I didn't think he liked me or even knew who I was."

"He told me," Jack said, fibbing a little, "that he respected your knowledge of the game. Your appraisal of the ends and defensive backs opened his eyes."

Henry's face broke into a wide smile. "I can't believe it," he muttered. "Me, Henry Parker, a high-school football coach."

"Well, get used to it. Coach."

They drove up the driveway to the front of the farmhouse.

Nellie was delighted to hear the news, and they hugged. "This calls for a celebration."

She fetched a bottle of Jack Daniels the former occupants left in the cupboard.

"This is the perfect occasion to break that open," Jack agreed.

They sat back and enjoyed a few sips of straight whiskey and talked about Henry's new venture.

The new assistant coach had an immediate, positive effect on the play of the defensive ends and the backs. The Bentley Bears prevailed in their second game against Derby, 13-12. Coach Adams was pleased and acknowledged Henry's contributions in the locker room following the contest.

They never won again, though. To make matters worse, Central crushed them in the final game of the season, 54-6. In fairness, Bentley was the smallest school in the conference, and there were fewer boys to choose from to make up the team. Jack and Henry tried hard to console Don after the season, to no avail. The numbers were hard to explain away. His four-year coaching record was 5 and 27.

For Henry, though, the season was an unqualified success. Most players didn't know any Negroes, so having him as assistant coach was a new experience. With each practice, it became more and more obvious to Jack that Henry won them over, both as a friend and coach. Their parents soon felt the same

CHAPTER 13

By late fall, at Thanksgiving time, Henry completed the major repairs on the farmhouse and looked for additional minor ones. Jack went out with Ellie Fleming several times and enjoyed the time he spent with her, but there was no real fire. Perhaps he was looking for too much. Maybe he was still gun-shy from his experience with Cathy Mumford. Whatever it was, he didn't know, but he was reasonably certain Ellie wasn't the one.

Meanwhile, Nellie met Ted Lewis, a young physician at the hospital, and they basked in each other's company. Jack was happy for her, and he liked Ted. He secretly hoped they would progress beyond being an item.

Henry reminded Nellie one night that he was an assistant chef earlier in his life, considering his dad had been a chef and taught Henry his way around the kitchen. Henry offered to assist Nellie in the kitchen, if she didn't mind. She didn't, and they agreed, much to her delight, that he would take over preparing the meals on weekends. The older gentleman proved himself a valuable, integral part of the Morgan family, and they loved having him around. He was amusing, smart, kind, and genuinely thoughtful.

Over the course of several months, Jack and Nellie remained in touch with their parents in Buffalo by telephone and through newsy letters. They broached the subject of visiting over the holidays, and John and Mary were thrilled.

"We've missed you both so much," Mary gushed.

"It will be wonderful to see you," John said. "We want to hear all about Bentley and what you two have been up to."

Jack would be on school break during the holidays, and Nellie planned to take a few days off. They would fly into Buffalo and stay for four days with John and Mary. Their trip was thankfully uneventful, and they were fortunate not to experience the typical winter Buffalo snow that might impede travelers.

The Morgans shared a wonderful holiday visit, with home-cooked meals around the family table, catching up on everyone's activities over coffee and eggnog in front of the living room fireplace, enjoying a midnight service and caroling in the neighborhood.

All too quickly, their time was up, and Nellie and Jack had to return to their jobs in West Virginia. They promised to keep in touch and hoped their parents might be able to visit them sometime in the coming year.

Christmas came and went. Jack once again sent the son he'd never seen a present and card, only to have both items returned as usual.

The big news over the holidays, other than their visit to Buffalo, was that Nellie bought a black Ford pickup truck for her brother for only three hundred and fifty dollars. It ran well and would free Jack and Henry from having to pick her up every day at the hospital.

CHAPTER 14

The second half of the school year began.

One afternoon, Jack decided to visit the local bookstore. While puttering around in the aisles, he ran into a young woman who stepped from behind a bookshelf.

"Whoa!" he said, as they collided.

His hands flew up to protect himself and managed to strafe her breasts.

"I'm so sorry!" he blurted in embarrassment.

While she seemed familiar, he couldn't remember why. Fortunately, she didn't show any signs of anger or annoyance and flashed a pleasant smile instead.

Her right hand extended, she said, "Hi. My name is Molly Rivers. I work as a nurse at the hospital. Somehow," the vivacious brunette continued, "I think I've seen you somewhere before."

As she spoke, he remembered seeing a very attractive woman across the room at the hospital mixer that fall, just before he met Ellie. It had to be the same woman.

He apologized again, taking her hand and shaking it. "I think we were both at the hospital mixer in September. My name's Jack Morgan. My sister, Nellie, is one of your colleagues."

"Of course. I remember seeing you there, but we never talked. I wish we had. Nellie's a good friend."

Not one to feel comfortable or confident around women, Jack summoned all his courage and asked, "Unless you're in a hurry, Molly, would you like to go next door and grab a cup of coffee?"

He was pleasantly surprised when she said, "Sounds great, Jack. Lead the way."

They talked for an hour at the coffee shop, describing how both had first love affairs end badly. She, too, was previously married, but the situation soured when her husband cheated on her with her best friend. They divorced three years earlier in Charleston, and she moved to Bentley to avoid the further pain of seeing one another at the medical clinic where they both worked.

Jack listened carefully, fully able to empathize. When he explained his own sad tale about the unwanted divorce, that he'd never seen his son, she reached across the table and took his hand. Her gesture of empathy and affection touched him, and he squeezed back.

Clearly, something was developing between them, and he didn't want to release her hand right away. Looking into her beautiful soft blue eyes, he couldn't help noticing that she had full, rounded lips, and he fought back the urge to kiss her right then. She was the most beautiful woman he'd ever met. Her skin was flawless, without a single blemish, and her nose was small and straight. She had long, black hair and prominent, well-kept eyebrows, and she seemed every bit as nice as she was modest. He felt an upwelling of emotion and was sexually aroused for the first time in years. He wanted to dive across the table and devour her, although he carefully warded off such thoughts.

"Are you seeing anyone regularly?" he asked. *I can't believe I just asked that,* he thought. *What an idiot!*

"No, I'm not."

"Would you like to have dinner with me sometime?"

"I think that would be fun."

Four nights later, perhaps a bit eagerly, Jack arrived at Molly's apartment five minutes early, at six twenty-five.

When he opened the passenger door for her, he said, "I hope you don't mind riding in a pickup truck."

He had spent the afternoon cleaning the windows and vacuuming the floor mats, wiping down the seats and arm rests, cleaning out paper clutter, and even washing the exterior. He felt confident the vehicle would make a good impression.

"Not at all," she said with a wide smile.

Their dinner at DeMarco's, a nice, casual, local Italian restaurant, went very well, and they became deeply engaged in conversation. They talked about their upbringing and where they grew up, their favorite pastimes and interests, and how they liked the atmosphere in Bentley. He was pleasantly surprised at how easy Molly was to talk to and hoped she felt the same.

It was nine o'clock when he pulled up to her apartment. As he got out of the truck to hold the door for her, he wondered if she'd ask him inside for a cup of coffee or an after-dinner drink. She didn't.

At the apartment building door, he stood near her, pondering his next move. *Should I?* he wondered, trying to summon some courage.

Not feeling very brave that night, he let the opportunity pass and thanked her for a very pleasant evening. He was so bewildered, he forgot to ask if she might like to go out again. She stood at the door, ripe for the plucking, and he didn't even have the nerve for a good-night kiss.

She must really think I'm a wimp, he thought. *She expected me to kiss her, and I stood there like a wuss.*

He wasn't happy with himself, though he was very pleased with Molly Rivers. She was a complete package—gorgeous but didn't act like she knew it, had a great sense of humor, was fun to be with, was smart, had a good job, and was just plain nice.

Nellie greeted him on his return home and couldn't wait to ask Jack how his dinner date went. He explained they had a great time over a delicious dinner. Each had one glass of wine, and they talked about many things.

"I may have messed up not kissing her good night," he added. "Maybe she didn't enjoy the evening. She didn't ask me in for coffee or anything. If she had, I certainly would have kissed her."

Like many self-doubters, he added, "Perhaps she doesn't like me, my truck, the way I dressed, or something else, so her non-invitation was what I deserved."

Nellie was a great help. "The only reason she didn't ask you in was she didn't want to appear too forward. It was only your first date, you know. You might've thought she was easy, and that would have ruined everything."

By the end of their conversation, Jack almost believed his first date with Molly ended on the right note. Nell always looked at things positively. Her judgment and advice mattered to him, and she had an uncanny ability to turn a seemingly negative thing into something positive.

The year 1946 was a notable one in the lives of Jack, Nellie, and Henry, and not all for the good. The relationship between Jack and Molly, despite a slow start, thrived, and the two seemed in lock step together.

Don Adams voluntarily left his position as head football coach after another dismal losing season. The Bears won only one game and were decimated by Central in the finale match-up 34-6. Jack accepted the job and the thousand-dollar raise that came with it. His expectations rose, too, and he felt more pressure as the head coach. It was his team now.

Nellie became recognized as one of the top nurses at Bentley Hospital and became a nursing supervisor. Her relationship with Dr. Ted Lewis didn't pan out and left her disappointed. Happily, she met a wonderful physician named Carl Norton, and their relationship grew stronger each month. It was clear they were serious about each other, and Nellie hinted to Jack there might be future plans.

Henry officially became the assistant head football coach for the Bentley Bears, and Jack made sure Henry was paid five hundred dollars for his new role. Henry was in a happier place than he had ever known, feeling accepted by the players on the football team, their parents, and the community.

CHAPTER 15

I n January 1947, Jack and Henry engaged in a lively baseball conversation one lazy Saturday afternoon. Henry would turn sixty-two that July and read an article about the Brooklyn Dodgers and their general manager, Branch Rickey. Rickey planned to bring up Jackie Robinson from the Dodgers' minor league farm team, the Montreal Royals. What made it so noteworthy and exciting was that Jackie was Negro, and the Majors had heretofore been a White-only league.

Robinson, no average player, led the entire International League with a .349 batting average in 1946. Jack knew that his Buffalo Bisons also played in the International League with Montreal, and that the Buffalo fans must have had an opportunity to see Robinson play.

"Tell me more about Robinson," Jack asked Henry.

"It says here that Jack Roosevelt Robinson was born in Cairo, Georgia, but grew up in Pasadena, California. He was a phenomenal athlete at UCLA, recognized as a top college football, basketball, and baseball player."

He explained that Jackie was a track star who won the NCAA broad jump. In basketball, he led the Southern Division of the Pacific Coast Conference in scoring twice. Playing before over ninety-eight thousand fans at Soldier's Field in Chicago in 1940, he scored a touchdown for the College All-Stars against the Chicago Bears in a 37-13 loss. Those same Bears destroyed the Washington Redskins 73-0 in the NFL title game.

"On April 15 this year," Henry said proudly, "the Dodgers will open the season against the Boston Braves. On that day, Jackie will break baseball's color barrier. What a shame that Josh Gibson didn't live to see it or play himself."

Jack, agreeing wholeheartedly, felt a pang of guilt for being a White man in what was only a White man's game until that time. "I sure hope he does well. Can you possibly imagine the pressure on him? What if he isn't good enough to stay with the team and gets demoted back to the minor leagues?"

Henry considered that for a moment. "You're right, Jack. If he fails, we probably won't see Negroes again in the major leagues for a long time."

"Sad, but probably true." Then Jack remembered that Henry's sixty-second birthday would be on July 26, and he had an idea.

CHAPTER 16

It was a cold, snowy, wintry night in late February in Bentley. Carl Norton, pediatrician, made a house call to nearby Portledge to check an eight-year-old patient named Jimmy Abbott. The boy had a severe fever that manifested after dinner. His temperature was over one hundred, which frightened Dorothy and Harold, his parents. After a thorough examination, Dr. Norton told them not to worry, gave Jimmy an aspirin, and urged them to apply cold compresses. If the fever still raged, the doctor said, the boy should be immersed in a cold bath.

Thanking him profusely, Dorothy gave Carl some cookies she'd baked. He got into his car for the return trip home and traveled over a narrow wooden bridge that had become icy. He lost control and plummeted off the bridge and down a rocky embankment into an eight-foot-deep pond. The impact knocked him unconscious and threw him out of the car, but he landed face down at the pond's edge. He drowned in only a few inches of water.

There were no witnesses, and the police found him only because Nellie called and said Carl hadn't arrived to pick her up for a dinner date, nor had he called about a delay. In a larger town, the police would wait for more information before checking the situation, but it was Bentley, where everyone was a neighbor.

When the police knocked on the farmhouse door, an anxious Jack answered. Before any words were spoken, Nellie knew it was bad news and fainted in Jack's arms. All he could think was, *not again.* She and Carl were so close by that time, openly talking about marriage.

The funeral service was the saddest event Jack ever attended. Nellie, though visibly shaken, performed admirably. She delivered the eulogy along with Carl's brother. Although she paused often to collect herself, she labored on like the special person she was. Dr. Norton was only thirty-eight when he died.

No stranger to tragedy, Nellie returned to work the next day and found solace from her patients and nurse colleagues.

If anyone can handle this horrible event and move on from it, Jack thought, *it's my resilient, resourceful sister.*

Still, he knew the situation was unbelievably difficult for her. He occasionally saw her at the kitchen table with tears running down her cheeks, picking herself up to carry on after a short time. He guessed it would be a very long time before she would test the romantic waters again.

CHAPTER 17

On April 12, 1947, Jackie Robinson's Major League Baseball debut was only a few days off. The newspapers focused on Jackie, his accomplishments, his overall responsibility, and the impact his play would have on the game.

"Look at this," Henry said on Saturday morning over coffee while reading the newspaper. "Apparently, Jackie isn't the only star athlete in the family. It says here his big brother Mack was a phenomenal track star."

Mack was a great athlete, indeed. Also born in Cairo, Georgia, four and a half years before Jackie, Matthew MacKenzie "Mack" Robinson won a silver medal in the 1936 Berlin Olympics in the two-hundred-meter dash. He broke the world record with a time of 21.1 seconds without a coach, using the same old track shoes he wore in college. The problem for Mack was that Jesse Owens bettered his time by four-tenths of a second. Instead of offering him a hero's welcome, his hometown of Pasadena, California, where he and his family moved years earlier, hardly noticed. Upon his return, despite a record-breaking four gold medals, there were no job offers for Owens or Mack. Instead, Mack was reduced to wielding a broom, cleaning the streets of downtown Pasadena. While that proud, accomplished man toiled, he wore his Olympic sweatshirt with his silver medal hanging from his neck.

His younger brother, Jackie, always remembered that slight, and it rankled him the rest of his life, although the city later honored them both with the Jackie and Mack Robinson Memorial statues, across from the Pasadena City Hall. There may have been something about those track shoes. Adolf "Adi" Dassler, the founder of the German sportswear company, Adidas, followed Owens' success at the Olympic trials in the United States and was eager to have the sprinter wear his shoes at the actual games. After trying on several pairs, Owens chose the last one, and the rest became history. No one would ever know if Mack could have made up the difference of 0.4 seconds if he had better shoes. Nothing ever diminished the Olympic accomplishments of Jesse Owens.

There was another interesting and obscure storyline about the 1-2 finish of Owens and Robinson in the two-hundred-meter event. It involved the bronze winner, Martinus "Tinus" Osendarp, a Dutch runner who also captured the bronze in the one-hundred-meter event. Unlike the experience of the two Negroes who beat him in the two-hundred-meter run, upon his return to the Netherlands, Osendarp was hailed as a hero and the best White sprinter at the Games. An airplane was sent to fly him home from Berlin, where he was honored wherever he traveled across the nation.

For Owens and Robinson, their greater accomplishments were ignored. When Germany occupied the Netherlands in World War II, Osendarp was a Dutch policeman. He became a volunteer member of the German SS and helped in the deportation of Dutch Jews. He later spent twelve years in prison for those acts.

"That's a lot of interesting history to come from running one race," Jack said, "albeit the Olympic Games. I wonder if Mack would have won with better spikes."

"We'll never know," Henry replied. "It's an interesting thought."

Three days later, on April 15, 1947, the day Jackie Robinson would change baseball forever, Henry and Jack eagerly listened to the radio when they got home from work. It was a Tuesday afternoon game at Ebbets Field against the Boston Braves, and Brooklyn won 5-3. Playing first base, Jackie unfortunately didn't get a hit on that momentous day, going 0 for 3, but he scored the winning run. In his first-ever MLB at bat against Boston's Johnny Sain, Jackie hit a grounder to third baseman Bob Elliott, who made the easy throw to first baseman Earl Torgeson.

They didn't play the following day due to rain, but Robinson registered his first hit in his second big league game, a bunt single to third in the bottom of the fifth inning and went 1 for 3. He must have been under intense pressure.

Henry kept up with Robinson's early-season games, fearful he might not play to expectations and be demoted to the minor leagues. Robinson promptly put an end to that concern by going 2 for 4 and hitting a home run the next day against the Giants at the Polo Grounds.

Henry breathed easier. Robinson was hitting .300 and had two RBIs and one home run in three games.

CHAPTER 18

Spring came late and wet to West Virginia. Jack was worried about Nellie. She was no longer her fun-loving, ebullient self after Carl Norton died so tragically. He tried to get her to double-date with Molly and him, but she always had an excuse. She'd clearly lost some of her zest for life, and Jack felt frustrated with his inability to help her.

On Friday, July 25, Jack sprung his surprise on Henry. Over dinner, he told his friend he had to drive to Pittsburgh the next day to visit an old friend, and he really wanted Henry to come along. A little hurt that Jack seemed to have forgotten his birthday the next day, Henry nonetheless nodded in acceptance of the invitation.

They left at six in the morning on Henry's birthday, and Jack still gave no indication he remembered the occasion.

They arrived at twelve-thirty in a parking lot, where a stained old billboard stated, "Welcome to Forbes Field. Today's game at 1PM vs. Brooklyn Dodgers."

Upon reading the marquee and seeing the smile on Jack's face, Henry was dumbfounded. "Oh, my goodness. I can't believe you did this for me, Jack. This is the happiest day of my life!"

Built in 1909, the ballpark was named for General John Forbes, a British general who captured Fort Duquesne in 1758 during the French and Indian War and renamed it Fort Pitt. Not a large facility, its capacity was only thirty-five thousand, which made it seem cozy.

On July 17, 1914, the park was the scene of a twenty-one-inning game against the Giants, in which both pitchers went the entire distance. The New York Giants, behind Rube Marquard, beat Babe Adams 3-1. It became the answer to a very difficult baseball trivia question: Forbes Field hosted the last triple header ever played in the major leagues on October 20, 1920, against the Cincinnati Reds, with the visitors winning two games.

Upon entering the park, both men realized they were famished and bought two hot dogs. They looked for a vendor who sold beer but to no avail, so they settled for soda. Jack had tickets right behind the Dodgers' dugout on the third base side, and they happily found their seats.

"Look out there." Henry pointed at a player wearing the number 42 taking infield practice at first base. "It's Jackie Robinson!"

He was batting a solid .299 at that point in the season and would end the year with a .297 average. At Montreal the previous year, Robinson wore number 10 on his uniform, but Brooklyn catcher Bruce Edwards received that number in 1946 when he broke in with the Dodgers.

They watched the game begin, and Jack noticed a man nearby drinking beer.

"Where'd you get your beer?" Jack asked.

"I brought it with me. They don't sell it here, but you can bring it in." He generously offered them each a bottle from his six-pack.

The Dodgers were leading 1-0 in the third inning, when Jackie stepped up to bat with a man on base. A loud crack reverberated throughout the ballpark. Jumping to his feet with all the other Dodger fans, Henry watched the white sphere head for left field and disappear over the fence. He was beside himself. Jackie delivered a home run on his birthday! He had one more hit that day, which helped top off a 6-4 Dodger victory.

On the way home, Henry repeated many times how much fun, he'd had. "I will always remember this day. I can't believe anyone would do this for me."

"Well, you're a special friend," Jack replied, "and I'm glad you enjoyed your surprise. Besides, I'm also a big fan of Jackie Robinson."

It was a long trip back to Bentley, but traffic wasn't bad, and the two weary travelers enjoyed the time of their lives. That Robinson hit a homer while they were in the stands was special. He would hit a total of twelve home runs that rookie year, and to think they witnessed one! Henry always pointed to that day as the best of his life, but he would have a few more just as good.

Nellie was fast asleep when the two men arrived at the farmhouse. It was almost eleven o'clock; they'd stopped for gas and food on the way home. Once in the door, Henry held out his hand and clasped Jack's shoulder.

"Thanks so much again," Henry said.

"You're family to us, Henry. I'm glad to have spent your birthday with you. Sleep well."

CHAPTER 19

Molly and Jack's relationship was thriving and had reached the tipping point of many similar relationships: Either it was time to move toward a commitment, or they should back off to reassess and perhaps go in opposite directions.

Jack considered escalating the level of intimacy but was at loggerheads with his own psyche. Part of him was ready, but he feared being rejected and embarrassed. The only real relationship he had prior to Molly was with Cathy. He was a shy, diffident youth in Buffalo, with few opportunities to become comfortable with women. While he attended some parties with members of the opposite sex, he never really felt comfortable around them. Most of his free time was spent playing football, hockey, and other sports, and he dated only casually, with the word "date" being an exaggeration. Was it really a date to hang out with another couple for cherry Cokes at the soda fountain? What about attending a Sunday-afternoon matinee movie followed by a burger and a milkshake, always in the safety of another couple?

He couldn't understand the mentality of several of his friends who were ladies' men. Friends like Bobby Batten and Dave Lauter seemed so at ease with women. He envied them, but confidence wasn't something like a water spigot one turned on or off. Fear of rejection could be a powerful motivator, either to act or hold off. For Jack, when it came to women, it was always the latter.

One Saturday afternoon, Molly and Jack saw a movie called "The Best Years of Our Lives," a powerful real-life drama about three World War II servicemen who returned home to small-town America only to discover that assimilation back into society was more difficult than expected.

Molly saw Jack dab at his eyes several times during the movie. She didn't say anything for fear of embarrassing him, but she knew that Jack, a tough Marine, was a gentle, empathetic soul.

While driving back to Molly's apartment for dinner, Jack mentioned how much she resembled Teresa Wright, his favorite actress. He first saw Teresa in "Pride of the Yankees," a movie he saw while in the service in 1943 about Yankee great Lou Gehrig. It was actually a 1942 movie, but it took time to get overseas. Gary Cooper played Lou Gehrig, but the female lead caught Jack's attention. A five-foot-three-inch little dark-haired beauty, Muriel Teresa Wright was born in New York City on October 27, 1918, and was the only actor or actress ever to be nominated for an Academy Award for her first three films.

"I swear, you and Teresa Wright could be twins," Jack said.

Molly blushed. "Don't I wish."

"You could." He compared their features, including her soft, light-blue eyes, narrow straight nose, and radiant smile. They even wore their hair the same way, shoulder-length and wavy.

After a light dinner and glass of wine, they sat on the couch while nursing cups of hot tea, listening to Vaughn Monroe's orchestra on CBS radio. Both set down their cups simultaneously and fell into each other's arms.

Suddenly, without a word, she took his hand and led him into her bedroom. Taken aback by her boldness, Jack stood and gawked at her. She smiled, as she removed her light-blue sweater and tossed it onto a chair with a flair. Her tight bra revealed her ample bosom. Molly looked directly into his eyes with a naughty smile and unfastened the clasp, letting the bra fall to her feet. He felt a rise in his pants while staring at her beautiful, voluptuous, milky white breasts.

She walked up to him and placed his hands on her breasts. Jack kneaded the nipples with his thumbs, making her moan softly. Tearing off his own T-shirt, he moved so she could feel his bare chest. It was his turn to sigh. He felt her hands unfasten his belt and tug down his pants and boxer shorts. He moved each foot, freeing himself from the garments. He was fully aroused.

"My, oh, my," she said, feeling his excitement. She helped him pull down her navy-blue slacks and pink panties.

They were naked and alone. Molly led him to the bed, where they gently lay on the bedspread.

When they finished, and he held her in his arms, he said softly, "I think I love you."

She cooed softly and replied, "I think I love you, too, Jack."

The timorous Marine had finally taken their relationship to the next level. From then on, it felt like a given that they would be together a long time.

For the first time, Jack spent the night with Molly.

CHAPTER 20

Jack and Henry were eager to begin coaching football that season for the first time as head coach and assistant coach. The team won only one game during Don's final year at Bentley, and Central beat them badly in the last game. Nevertheless, both coaches took away a few positives from the debacle.

For one thing, experience would be on their side. Seven of their starting players would return, including the all-important position of quarterback. Furthermore, a new sophomore moved to Bentley from Mexico, when his mother took a job at the hospital. His name was Felix Cantara, and, while he hadn't played much football in a country that embraced soccer as its main sport, he was fast and could run a hundred-yard dash in ten seconds. He was also a nice, respectful, coachable lad.

The boys, reporting to their first practice after Labor Day, seemed in good shape. Jack and Henry decided to design a few trick plays around their quarterback and all-around athlete, Jake Hammer. He was an excellent deceptive ball handler who caught the football as well as he threw it. While they practiced plays several times a week at school, they waited for just the right time in a game to execute them, assuming the game was tight.

The one game they won during the previous year in 1946 was by a single point, 13-12. They lost six games by an average of sixteen points, and they were demolished by Central by a 34-6 score.

Both coaches felt they could shore up the defense enough to make most games close. Henry once accurately said, "It's a lot easier to coach kids to play good defense than it is to instill offensive skills."

That was a truism for most sports. Offensive skill in most cases was a God-given talent, but almost anyone could learn to play good defense. While Jack and Henry spent their time play-calling and focused on offensive play, they also concentrated their efforts on the principles of blocking and tackling. It sounded simple, and it was. It was difficult to teach someone to run faster or instinctively find the right hole to get through. One could show a player how to position his body for an effective block or tackle. They could also teach hustling and finishing a play, and they could make sure their players were in top shape with enough stamina for a long haul. That was good coaching, and those things were relatively easy to achieve.

Jack and Henry focused their practices accordingly, spending the bulk of their time on teaching what the players could easily grasp. With good coaching and encouragement, the players were psyched and ready to change their school's record.

Their theories were put to the test in mid-September in their first game, an away encounter against Hanford. The Hawks weren't a powerhouse team, but they beat the Bentley Bears easily the previous year, 26-6. That time, it was a close, 6-6 contest at half-time. The smothering Bears defense showed what good coaching could accomplish.

Bentley had the ball on the Hanford 14-yard line, down 18-13, with less than two minutes to play. It was time for their now-you-have-it-now-you-don't special play, a precursor of the "flea-flicker."

Jack didn't want to try it on the fourth down in case it failed, so they attempted their trickery on the third down. Taking the snap from center, Jake Hammer handed it off to one of the running backs, Harry Carson, who ran forward toward the line, while the quarterback drifted back.

Suddenly, Harry turned and tossed the ball back to Jake. The quarterback threw a perfect twenty-yard strike to the open receiver, Josh Malloy, who easily reached the end zone. He was open, because the Hanford defensive backs came toward the line, thinking Carson had the ball.

The game ended with a good, extra-point kick with Bentley winning 20-18.

There was pandemonium in the visitors' locker room. Malloy and Hammer hugged each other, while players milled around in various states of euphoria. They loved the feeling of winning a game and took great joy in the surprise manner it was done. The two coaches, shaking hands, wore broad smiles.

On the bus trip home, the players went up and down the aisle, high-fiving each other. It was a great start to the season, but it wasn't all good. They had three more wins to follow, interspersed with three losses.

On Friday afternoon before their final game with Central, Jack answered a knock on the front door and saw a hawkish-faced young man about his own age.

"I'm running for the West Virginia House of Delegates," the visitor declared, stepping inside.

He had a pointed nose, high brow, dark hair, substantial ears, and a big smile. He also carried a fiddle.

"I sure would appreciate your vote. I promise to do what I can to protect our water supply and keep taxes down."

With that, he began playing the fiddle. As he readied himself to leave, the candidate thrust his hand toward Jack and said, "My thirtieth birthday is in three weeks, and I sure would appreciate your vote in the meantime."

Jack promised his vote and wished him luck, but he already forgot the man's name. *Oh, well. I'll probably never hear it again.*

There was no Central blowout, but the Bears lost that night by 26-6. There were many good things to take away from the season. The kids played hard, tackled well, were in good condition, and stuck together. Five of eleven starters returned, including quarterback Jack Hammer. The ascent of running backs Harry Carson and Felix Cantara was something to see. They suddenly took their places among the better running backs of the league.

After what everyone considered a successful maiden season for Jack and Henry, despite the 4-4 overall record, they went out for dinner to celebrate the team's success with Molly and Nellie. Reaching for milk to add to her coffee, Molly felt a slight tug in her back and winced.

Nellie noticed and asked, "Are you OK?"

"It's gone already," she said.

Jack and Henry, deeply engaged in football banter, were oblivious to the incident.

After dinner, they dropped Molly off at her apartment and went home.

"How about that, sports fans?" Jack shouted, throwing his hands into the air, as he entered the structure. It was definitely a good season for the two coaches.

It hadn't taken Henry long to show his mettle and prove his worth to the Bentley football players. A man of great patience, blessed with an innate ability to express himself, he was an immediate hit with the whole team. He knew his football and took aside players who'd made a mistake, reassuring them with his natural friendliness and an arm dangling over each boy's shoulder. The avuncular Henry Parker was well-received by most of the boys, though some hadn't met a Negro before. It took time for them to realize what a kind, special man he was.

Henry knew how to get the most out of his players, recognizing that some needed prodding, while others thrived on praise. Never having been in a coaching position before, he rose to the occasion.

The parents responded, too. Their sons often came home from practice with a "Henryism."

"Mr. Parker said there are no shortcuts to any destination worth going to, whether it's in the classroom or on the field. I know, because I've tried them all."

That was probably their favorite quote, although there were many more.

"I want you to improve, not be perfect."

"Leave it all on the field or in the classroom."

That one resonated with student-athletes and their parents. Henry wanted them to give their all every time. If they did, he explained, they would always be winners regardless of the score.

Initially, like some of the boys, it took a few parents time to warm up to Henry. It wasn't bias or prejudice that caused their caution but the fact they'd never had contact with Negroes before. Time and getting to know Henry better took care of that. Circumspection soon gave way to embracing the man and his innate integrity. The effect Henry and Jack had on the kids was noticeable and all positive. Henry, a born teacher, never had a chance to prove it. Recognizing his talents was one of the smartest things Jack ever did. The old man had a strong impact on the team and helped the kids develop their character.

Jack and Henry knew the influence they had on the players. Those responsibilities carried over into the classroom for the head coach, too. Both men spoke of how important it was for them to always present themselves as good role models. Developing character was foremost in their thoughts, and they knew, just like the parents, that their noble goal was to help those young people become good citizens. One of Jack's favorite sayings came from his father, although it wasn't a John Morgan original: "Character is what you do and how you act when no one else is around."

As Jack's relationship with Molly intensified, both encouraged Nellie to join them in some double dates. She certainly had ample opportunities, but the memory of the two tragedies in her life with men she loved had gotten the better of her. She wasn't a recluse, but she was close. More than a few eligible bachelors in town were eager to pursue her, including some doctors on the hospital staff, but she would have none of it.

Jack felt increasingly guilty about being so happy with Molly, while his sister was stuck with her nursing duties and reading. Several times over the following months, he prevailed on her to go out with Jim Warner, a teacher friend of his, but their double dates didn't lead to anything more than friendship.

"Jim looked too much like my husband," Nellie rationalized to Jack.

Another time, she explained that her lack of interest in a nice Bentley physician came from the fact that he had once worked with Carl.

"Will she always be this way?" Jack asked Molly one night.

"We can't rush her," she replied. "Nellie needs to set her own pace. Eventually, the timing will be right for her."

CHAPTER 21

Halfway through the next week, Nellie received a phone call one night.

"Hi, Nellie. It's Molly. I wanted to ask you about sharp pains I have in my back and pelvis. They've persisted for several days, but I don't know if it's anything. Please don't tell Jack. It's probably nothing. I've been really tired lately, too, but I don't know if that means anything."

"I'm sure it's nothing, but it's always best to be careful. Can you come by the hospital tomorrow, or would you rather see your own doctor?"

"Dr. Logan has always been good to me. I'll call him tomorrow."

"OK. Call me after you've seen him."

While cleaning her desk in preparation for leaving the hospital, Nellie's phone rang.

"Nellie," Molly said in a shaky voice, "Dr. Logan wants to give me a pelvic exam."

"That's good Molly. He wants to be thorough."

The following day, Molly had a pelvic exam and a biopsy. While she waited for the results, she visited Nellie at the hospital. When Nellie saw her coming through the door, she walked over as casually as possible to greet her. Her experience as a nurse painted a picture of ovarian cancer, but she wouldn't reveal her suspicions to her friend.

She took Molly's hand and embraced her. Tears formed in Molly's eyes, and Nellie spoke quickly.

"It might be nothing," Nellie said.

"I must admit that I'm scared," Molly said.

Two days later, Molly had good news. "It's only a benign cyst!" she gushed over the phone to Nellie. "It's really nothing." Relief filled her voice.

"I just knew everything would be OK," Nellie said, though in her heart, she feared the worst. Two terrible tragedies in her life tended to lead her toward unhappy or negative conclusions. That time, though, the news couldn't have been better.

While the cyst had to be removed, it was a simple procedure, and recovery was expected to be easy and quick. Molly finally told Jack about it. The four of them, including Henry, went out to dinner to celebrate.

CHAPTER 22

The 1948 football season saw the Bentley Bears win four and tie one. A 4-3-1 was a winning season, something that never happened before in the previous twenty-five seasons the school fielded a team. The town was proud of such an accomplishment.

Jack and Henry downplayed the importance.

"It's all about building character and team spirit," they agreed.

The winning season was a terrific success, but the wins and losses were secondary to the sportsmanship exhibited by the boys and their bonding as a team to do their best. Most parents agreed and were grateful to the coaches for emphasizing those principles. A few parents cared more about the number of wins and how much time their sons played, but the majority rallied behind Jack and Henry. Almost all parents recognized and accepted that the talent pool at Bentley was smaller than at other schools.

Nellie and Jack kept in touch with their parents in Buffalo, calling every week to give them their news and check up on them. Both parents were doing well and in good health, according to Mary. Nellie urged them to visit the place she and Jack called home.

"We have plenty of room for you both," she said, "and we'd love to show you around Bentley and the area. Take a few days to drive down. Thanksgiving would be a great time."

One other event during that time was unforgettable. It was September 30, and Jack, Molly, Nellie, and Henry huddled around the fireplace, soaking up heat to combat an early winter's wind and cold.

Molly looked up from reading her newspaper. "President Truman is coming to speak tomorrow night in Montgomery. It says he's coming in on his Freedom Train. After speaking in Charleston at eight-thirty, he should be in Montgomery by ten-thirty."

"Let's go up there," Henry said. "It's Friday night, so we can sleep in on Saturday. Thank goodness there's no game tomorrow. What a break for us."

"How far is it?" Nellie asked.

"About fifty miles," Jack said. "At that time of night, it'll probably take no more than ninety minutes."

All were filled with enthusiasm over the idea. They planned to see the president of the United States the next evening.

It was a crisp night with little wind when the four piled into Nellie's car for the trip to Montgomery. Nellie bought gas that morning and packed snacks and beverages for the journey. They went down the driveway at eight fifteen, leaving early to get a good spot for viewing the president as he spoke to the throng from the rear platform of the train. None had ever seen a president before, and the thought made them very excited. Halfway there, a drizzle began.

"Looks like we'll get wet tonight," Henry commented, "but it'll be worth it."

They brought hats and light jackets in case the weather acted up, and they were glad of it.

They arrived shortly before ten o'clock, in plenty of time for the president's visit. Others were arriving, too. Leaving their car in a small parking area, they walked through the station house and outside to the platform to take places under the "Montgomery" sign.

The rain abruptly stopped at ten-thirty.

Henry went to the track and bent over to place his ear against the rail. "I don't hear anything yet," he said.

The four of them pressed closer to be nearer to the action. The crowd had grown from twenty people to at least eighty by ten thirty-five.

Suddenly, someone shouted, "Here he comes!"

They saw the Truman Freedom Train come into view from the darkness and chug into Montgomery station. The president stood on the rear platform in a dark suit and gray fedora with his wife, Bess, at his side. He smiled and waved enthusiastically. Nellie, Molly, Jack, and Henry were only ten feet away, standing precariously on the gravel between the tracks.

The president moved forward and leaned slightly over the platform rail as he spoke to the throng. "I never expected to see a crowd like this at this time of night. I'll tell you what I want. I want one of you expert photographers to come up here and take a picture of this crowd, because this picture should go in all the newspapers in the country!"

One old gentleman pushed through the crowd of onlookers and snapped a picture. The crowd laughed and cheered.

President Truman concluded his brief fifteen-minute campaign speech by assuring them, "I'm not going to worry about this country, but I want each and every one of you to vote. That's the one thing I want you to do. West Virginians will provide the necessary majority. Be sure that you elect Okey Patterson as governor."

While saying goodbye, the president seemed to reach down. Henry impulsively stepped forward and reached up to clasp his hand as the Freedom Train moved away from the station.

Henry stood there in astonishment. He had shaken hands with the president. It was all he could talk about on the drive home.

Election day was Tuesday, November 2. The incumbent president won twenty-eight of the forty-eight states, three hundred and three electoral votes, and the popular vote by more than two million. Closer to home, Truman won West Virginia by more than a hundred and twelve thousand votes, taking the state with fifty-seven percent of the votes. Okey Patterson was elected governor, and the young man who came to the farmhouse and played fiddle was elected to the West Virginia House of Delegates. Jack noted the man won only because the newspaper had his photo in it. Something in Jack recognized that the fiddler had a nice, friendly manner and special quality. Jack guessed he would go far in politics, although Jack understood he knew little about the subject.

The Truman victory over Dewey was a huge upset. Almost every pollster called the results "wrong," and almost everyone saw the embarrassing November 3 issue of the Chicago Tribune, which trumpeted "Dewey Defeats Truman" on the front page. Considered the world's most-famous newspaper error, it illustrated just how big an upset it was for Truman to win.

Probably no political photograph was more famous than W. Eugene Smith's shot for *Time and Life Pictures*, showing a victorious and ebullient president holding aloft the newspaper with the erroneous headline. His sheer elation and joy were obvious.

On Truman's way back to Washington, D.C., from his Independence, Missouri, home, two full days after the election, the train stopped in St. Louis. Once off the train for a brief respite, the president was handed a two-day-old, now-famous copy of the *Tribune*. No one knew if he had already seen the newspaper's humiliating blunder, but that wasn't important. It was that moment when Smith snapped his famous picture.

Jack also appreciated that the president popularized the phrase, "The buck stops here." Truman took ownership of it and kept a sign on his desk with those words. He was stating unequivocally that, as president, he was the ultimate responsible person.

The difficult decision to drop the atom bombs on Japan was a perfect example of his taking responsibility. He made the choice and never wavered in his belief that it was the right thing to do.

One week after the election and thirty-eight days after the wondrous night at the Montgomery train station, Henry was in the kitchen, washing his hands.

"I'll bet," Jack kidded, "you haven't washed your right hand since that night."

Henry almost doubled over in laughter. "You've got that right!"

The Christmas holiday was approaching, and Nellie, Jack, Molly, and Henry walked through the downtown streets as they had the previous year. Wreaths with red ribbons were in abundance, especially on the front doors of all the stores. Reverberating through the area, piped in from city hall, was the sound of Bing Crosby singing Irving Berlin's "White Christmas," Jack's favorite holiday song since he first heard it while overseas. Crosby performed it on a Christmas Day broadcast in 1941, eighteen days after Pearl Harbor. The following year, the crooner sang it in the popular movie "Holiday Inn," and it won the Academy Award for best song.

Many American GIs, including Jack, adopted the tune as their "anthem of longing and homesickness," as one author put it. "White Christmas" eventually became the best-selling single record of all time.

Although 1949 was a nondescript year, it was a good one for the Morgans and Henry. Life continued as before. The relationship between Molly and Jack grew and became more intense. Nellie went to visit her parents in Buffalo for a few days to check on them and make sure they still were doing well. They told her they wouldn't be trekking down to West Virginia for Thanksgiving. They felt the trip was too much.

The Bentley Bears regressed to a 3-5 record that season. Although that was disappointing, Jack and Henry consoled themselves with the knowledge that it was a very young team.

CHAPTER 23

On a cold, snowy night in early March 1950, Jack had a surprise for Molly. Although they saw each other almost every day, they made it a point to go out for a special dinner every other week. Their relationship had lasted over three years, and even Nellie suggested to Jack that he "shit or get off the pot." That made him think. The day before their dinner, he stopped at the jewelry store.

They dined on a wonderful meal. Jack had ribeye steak, potatoes, and broccoli, while Molly had broiled fish, rice pilaf, and roasted vegetables. Jack ordered a bottle of wine. The candlelight and small vase of flowers on their table at Morey's Restaurant provided a perfect romantic setting.

"Molly Rivers," he began, "we've been seeing each other for over three years, and I think you're the most wonderful woman I have ever known, and I love you." Before giving her a chance to speak, he continued, "I want to spend the rest of my life with you." He fumbled in his pocket, finally producing a little black box.

"Molly Rivers," he asked, "will you marry me?" He opened the box and offered a beautiful, glittering diamond ring. His eyes misted.

Across the table, Molly dabbed at her eyes, too. "Oh, Jack, yes! Yes, I will."

His hands trembling, he gently placed the diamond ring on her finger.

"It's so beautiful," she said. "I'm so happy!" She jumped up from her chair and gave him a big kiss.

Morey's owner was so happy that such a blessed event happened in his establishment, he told them their dinner was on the house and wished them much happiness.

Thanking Morey profusely, they promised to return on their anniversary. They left the restaurant arm in arm, feeling a warm glow as they drove to the farmhouse to share their news with Nellie and Henry.

They decided to make it a short engagement and planned their wedding day for Saturday, June 24.

Thirty miles away, while Molly and Jack were dining, George and Edna Kelly were heading home from Charleston, where they went to purchase supplies for their hardware store in Bentley. Kelly's Hardware was in the family for seventy years, a popular place in town where shoppers could even get a free cup of coffee while browsing. George and Edna were well-loved in the community, as were their children—fourteen-year-old Philip and sixteen-year-old Paula. Both teens worked in the store regularly.

Life was good for the Kellys. All four were West Virginians by birth and were hardy people with a strong sense of character and matching personalities. George, always upbeat, felt his Irish blood mandated his self-appointed role as joke teller, and he was good, too. Edna, of Welsh descent, was the serious one in the family. Philip and Paula were excellent students and sensible, likable kids.

It was snowing hard by the time they reached the outskirts of Bentley, and the road signs were barely visible. The windshield wipers could barely keep up with the falling snow. The couple was eager to get home as soon as possible because they'd left the kids home alone.

Both children were resourceful and capable of fending for themselves, something they'd had to do several times before. Nonetheless, George and Edna didn't want to leave them in that state any longer than necessary, especially in winter.

In the darkness, without warning, a big truck barreling too fast in the opposite direction skidded on some ice at a bend in the road, heading right for the Kellys.

George didn't even see the vehicle until it was too late. The truck slammed into the front of their car, killing both of them instantly. When the truck finally stopped, the driver, very shaken, jumped out and raced to the car that sat on the side of the road. By the time he was able to pry open the passenger door, it was clear both passengers were dead.

The crash left two teenagers without a family and no relatives to help or comfort them. Bentley was overwhelmed by the tragedy, and at the funeral service, the church was filled to capacity, a rarity. The West Virginians rallied around the two stricken teens. The big question was: Where would they live?

After the service, Nellie, Jack, Molly, and Henry sat around the fireplace, discussing the situation.

"Guys," Nellie said, "I think we should offer our home to them. Unlike many in this community, we have room for them."

"That's a wonderful gesture, Nellie," Jack said, "but can you imagine how that would disrupt our lives?"

She looked at the other man in the room. "Henry, what do you think?"

"I don't have a vote here," he replied.

"Oh, yes, you do," she corrected. "You're family."

Henry looked at Jack, who nodded. "You both have been so good to me," Henry said, tears filling his eyes. "You know where I stand. Without your kindnesses, I wouldn't have a place to live or a job. You gave me hope where I saw none."

"I'm all for helping them," Jack said, "but we need to understand what it means for us. I know them at school. They're great kids, smart and motivated. George and Edna did a wonderful job raising them, but we're talking about a major change in our lives, with less privacy and free time, as well as taking on the responsibility of looking after them. None of us has ever raised a teenager. Molly will be part of this family, too, and she has some say in this decision."

"But, Jack," Nellie said, where else can those kids go? They're grief-stricken, lost, and don't have any relatives."

Molly was quiet during the exchange. "One of the things I love about Jack and this family is how kind, caring, and supportive you are. That includes you, Henry. I can't wait to be an official part of it." Shifting closer to Jack, she placed a hand on his knee. "These two children have been through a traumatic experience, and it will take a lot to get them past it. I can't think of a better place or more loving, caring people to help them. If I can have an early vote, I think you know what I'd say." She snuggled against Jack, looking at him hopefully.

Jack's heart took over, and he agreed, as long as everyone else was all right with the idea.

"All those for it," Nellie said, "raise your hand."

All four hands went up.

"OK. Let's tell Reverend Miller that we've volunteered to take them in."

Nellie placed the call, and Reverend Miller was greatly relieved that Philip and Paula could find such a place to call home. He was a good friend of Jack and Nellie's family, and they enjoyed his Sunday services and sermons.

The question was whether the two teens would accept the invitation. Reverend Miller enlisted the support of Beth Rooney, a parishioner, who was probably the closest person in Bentley to the Kelly family. She lived alone in a small apartment and couldn't possibly take the children herself.

She thought it was a wonderful idea and volunteered to broach the subject with the teens. They both knew Jack from taking his classes at the high school and liked him a lot. They also knew Henry, although to a lesser extent, and they were fond of him, too. Nellie came into the hardware store occasionally, and they remembered her. Molly was the nurse the one time Philip was sick and went to the hospital.

Through their tears, they assured Miss Rooney that living in the sprawling farmhouse would be OK with them. She hosted a dinner the next night for the two grieving teens and the four from Jack's house.

The evening could not have gone better, and the matter was decided. Over the weekend, the transition would begin, and the farmhouse instantly became a livelier place.

The responsibilities of parenthood arrived prematurely and unexpectedly for the four adults, but they stepped forward and accepted them. There was little other recourse for the kids.

The community responded to their gesture with praise. Any time one of the four adults met someone in the community, he or she was told, "There will be chairs in heaven waiting for you."

They knew they had to earn those chairs by facing many challenges. None of them had any parenting experience. Nellie and Molly visited the library to find books that might help them through their new perilous journey. The new residents in their house were children, not objects, and the awesome responsibility of preparing them for adulthood was at stake.

Fortunately, the Kellys laid out plans regarding the hardware store, house, and other assets through their attorney and accountant in the event something happened to them. Those matters were handled through the appropriate legal and probate channels, so at least the Morgans didn't have to deal with those difficult matters too.

Over the weekend, Philip and Paula moved into the farmhouse with help from Jack and Henry. Nellie made sure they felt welcome, and each chose a room. Molly joined them for dinner that night. It was a quiet scene, with some nervous but general chatter. Clearly, the kids were still in mourning, and only time would heal that. Efforts to open up about school were almost ignored, and it was difficult to elicit more than a "yes" or "no" answer.

One week passed without a change in the kids' demeanor. Jack and Henry felt more pessimistic each day, but Nellie and

Molly urged them to remain calm and patient.

"They need to have the room to move at their own pace," Nellie said. "It will come."

Occasionally, Nellie heard soft sobs coming from Paula's room. Philip wasn't very demonstrative and stayed silent most of the time. When another week passed without any change, Nellie got an idea.

It was April when Nellie told Molly, Jack, and Henry about the idea. They agreed to the strategy. On a Friday afternoon when Nellie had the day off, she went shopping and ran some errands, then embarked on a special mission and returned to the farmhouse before school let out.

When Jack pulled up with the kids in his Ford—he traded in his truck for a used sedan—they saw sitting in the front yard an amber-colored, eight-week-old female Golden Retriever pup.

Paula jumped out of her seat and raced over to it, picking it up and smothering it with kisses. Philip, enthralled too, eagerly petted her whenever he could get a hand in.

"Come on, Paula, let me hold her, too," he complained.

Nellie gave Jack and Henry a knowing smile, and they nodded and joined in the fun.

"Does she have a name?" Paula asked.

"Not yet," Nellie replied with a bewitching smile. "I hoped you and Philip would find a suitable one."

"How about Daisy?" she asked, glancing at her brother.

"Shoot," he said, "you always get your way."

"Well, what do you suggest, Mr. Know-It-All?"

"How about…" He couldn't think of any suitable idea. "OK. Daisy it is."

Daisy's presence made a huge difference in the teens' demeanor. Paula was clearly the most changed, and she cherished every moment with Daisy and heaped as much love on her as she could. Paula had a lot of love saved up after the loss of her parents. Soon, Daisy was sleeping with Paula at night, and Philip seemed the odd man out.

"There's only one thing we can do," Nellie told Jack, Molly, and Henry one night. "We have to see if Daisy's brother is still available."

Fortunately, the other pup had yet to be claimed, and his surprise presence at the farmhouse the following Wednesday afternoon completely transformed the stoic boy. The two puppies, happy to be reunited, raced all over the yard, frolicking endlessly. Philip named his dog Quincy, after the sixth president of the United States. He'd been studying the presidents in school and had written a paper about President John Quincy Adams.

Someone who wasn't familiar with or didn't like dogs wouldn't understand the complete metamorphosis that happened at 7 Mountain View Road. Both teens, who'd been suppressing their love after losing their parents, had beautiful puppies to shower it on. It would never make up for their loss, but it helped them get beyond it and continue their lives.

Nellie, Jack, Henry, and Molly added two dogs to their overall duties. They made it perfectly clear to the teens that for the good of all, they had to assume most of the work caring for Daisy and Quincy. Unlike some teens, the two embraced their new chores without complaint and followed through.

There would be many challenges ahead for the Kelly children and their new foster family, but the happy teens were finally making the difficult adjustments necessary for their lives without parents. Daisy and Quincy were the catalysts for that adaptation.

CHAPTER 24

Once everyone was settled with Philip and Paula moving into the farmhouse and adjusting to the constant motion of Daisy and Quincy underfoot, Molly and Jack could devote some of their time to their upcoming wedding. They decided to make it a small gathering of their closest friends and family. Nellie would be maid of honor and Henry, best man. Molly's parents were West Virginians who resided in nearby Charleston, so there was no question they would attend the ceremony and festivities. There were, however, questions about John and Mary Morgan making the journey from Buffalo. Neither was in good health, with John having the most trouble. His back spasms came without warning. Arthritis was another issue, particularly in his knees and shoulders. He was an old sixty-eight.

Mary was luckier. Her only malady was a sore elbow that flared up only in cold weather. She'd played a fair amount of tennis very successfully as a girl and into early adulthood. Her affliction seemed to be some type of tennis elbow. She was a young sixty-six. It was questionable whether they could make a long trip.

Flying was out—both shared an inordinate fear of planes. There weren't any direct train routes from Buffalo to Bentley. When it appeared doubtful they could come to the wedding, Henry volunteered to drive to Buffalo to bring them back.

"This is a special occasion, Jack," Henry implored. "Your parents want to share in your happiness and definitely want to meet Molly. I'd like to meet the people who raised two such wonderful adults. They'll be even more proud when they see what you and Nellie have done."

Henry would take Jack's car to Buffalo and return with the elder Morgans for the special event. Nellie called them that night and told them about the plans. Both were excited at the possibility.

"Thank you so much, Nellie, for making it possible for us to come," her mother said. "We wouldn't want to miss this for anything, and we look forward to meeting Henry, too. We've heard so much about him. Your father and I have already started packing."

It was a two-day trip each way, and Henry looked forward to seeing some of the countryside and meeting Nellie and Jack's parents.

Molly wanted to include Paula and Philip in the ceremonies, and Nellie suggested that Philip could be a groomsman, while Paula could be a bride's maid. Paula was more enthusiastic and comfortable with her role than her brother.

The teens continued getting good grades at school, Paula as a junior and Philip as a freshman. Their teachers noticed a temporary decrease in their grades and attention span during March, but that was attributed to the loss of their parents. In April, with help from Daisy and Quincy, the teens bounced back academically and returned to their normal high marks. They did very well in their finals and maintained straight-A averages. There would undoubtedly be problems for both of them in the future, but all seemed to be going well.

CHAPTER 25

June 24, 1950, was a bright, sunny day in Bentley, and Reverend Miller married Jack and Molly in the early afternoon in a small ceremony conducted in the backyard at 7 Mountain View Road. It was a simple affair, but there were beautiful floral arrangements everywhere, and a festive feeling filled the air.

The bride looked radiant and beautiful in her simple, elegant dress, and Jack felt tears come to his eyes when he saw her. Molly's parents were there, courtesy of Henry, and they were thrilled. Nellie was stunning in a cornflower-blue dress and beamed in her role as maid of honor for her best friend. Paula and Philip fulfilled their roles with aplomb and relished the joy of it all. It had been some time since they felt so happy, and they loved being part of the Morgan family.

After the nuptials, Henry raised his glass of champagne and gave a moving toast to the newly wedded couple. He looked quite dapper in his rented black tuxedo, his gray-white hair glittering in the early afternoon sun.

"This will be longer than your usual customary toast to the bride and groom," Henry began. "I hope you'll forgive me. I'm so happy for Molly and Jack because I know few, if any, people who are more deserving of happiness. You're both so lucky and fortunate to have found each other. I wouldn't be here today— or be alive today—if not for the kindness of this man and his sister, Nellie. They took me in when I had no home and gave me the chance to be a football coach. All of you know of their big hearts and how much they've done for this community."

He gazed at Nellie, Philip, and Paula. "God has blessed me to know and live with Jack and Nellie, as well as with Molly, Paula, and Philip. The Lord also blessed me by giving me the opportunity to watch Philip and Paula grow into wonderful, caring, responsible teenagers. I have no doubt whatsoever that when they take their places in society, they will give back to the same degree as their benefactors. What a rich example of loving, unselfish behavior we've seen in this family."

Tears streamed down his face, as he began his final words. "I only wish I could be half the man that Jack Morgan is each day of his life. Now, he'll have a beautiful, loving wife to walk with him on their journey together."

Henry offered his hand to the groom, but that wasn't enough. He leaned in and gave Jack a big hug, pointed at him, and applauded. He reached for Molly and warmly kissed her cheek.

Everyone at the intimate gathering stood and joined in the public display of affection, raising their glasses to toast the newlyweds and Nellie. Henry was one month short of his sixty-fifth birthday and was physically fit, happier than he had ever been in his life. He looked ready to live forever.

John and Mary Morgan were elated to see their children again and share in the festivities. John rose shakily from his chair, cleared his throat, and began his toast.

"Your mother and I feel blessed to have you as our son, and, of course, we feel the same for our wonderful daughter, Nellie. You've become exceptionally fine people who make us proud.

Now Jack has the great fortune of having a beautiful, smart, funny, loving woman to be at his side. Molly, welcome to this ever-growing family! We wish you both a lifetime of happiness together."

With tears in their eyes, Jack and Molly rose to embrace the elder Morgans. Everyone saw the love they shared.

John and Mary spent three days at the farmhouse with the family, learning about Bentley. They visited the high school and hospital, meeting Jack's, Nellie's, and Molly's friends and coworkers. They were especially happy to spend time with their new "grandchildren," Paula and Philip. Family meals were festive and entertaining. When it was time for the elder Morgans to return to Buffalo, Henry offered to drive them home.

"Thanks, Henry," Jack said, "but Molly and I will drive them and spend a few days as a sort of honeymoon. Besides, I don't know when Mom and Dad will come back down here again, if ever. We want to spend a little more time with them."

"That's great, Jack," Henry said, chuckling. "A honeymoon trip with your parents? I'll hold down the fort while you're away."

Their goodbyes were emotional, happy, and bittersweet. Hugs were given all around, and the Ford sedan finally drove down the Mountain View driveway for the trek to Buffalo. Nellie sighed, dabbed her eyes, and returned to the comfort of the farmhouse.

Molly and Jack decided to live in the farmhouse instead of in Molly's apartment for several reasons. Jack felt an obligation—although he didn't express it in those terms—to help with Philip, Paula, and the four-legged members of the family. He also wanted to be close to Nellie and Henry.

"Are you sure?" Jack asked Molly. "Please be honest with me. It'll take some adjusting on everyone's part, but we should have plenty of room. I think it would work out."

"Jack, I love you and know we can make it work. I've known Nellie longer than you, and we're like sisters. I love Henry to pieces. If I can have any influence with the kids, I'd be happy to do it.

"Besides, we'll save money because I won't be paying rent anymore. Don't worry. It'll work out. But," she added with a grin, "I won't agree to take the dogs out at six in the morning."

She pounced on her new husband, smothering him with kisses, thinking, *I love this man. We'll have a wonderful life together.*

Molly and Jack agreed to join the entourage at the Mountain View farmhouse. Molly's belongings and some furniture were packed up, and Jack, Henry, and Philip brought them to her new home.

One Saturday morning in mid-July, it was quiet in the house. Jack and Philip were outside cutting the grass and cleaning up the yard; Molly was out running errands. Henry was away visiting a friend.

Nellie sat down with Paula to discuss her future. Paula would be a senior in the fall, and it wasn't too early to discuss college.

Most of her classmates didn't plan to further their education, but Paula was determined.

"I want to be a doctor," Paula said, "but not just any doctor. I want to be a neurosurgeon."

Nellie was floored. "I don't think there's a single woman neurosurgeon in the country." She quickly realized the possible impact of her words and added, "That doesn't mean you can't be the first." She winked.

Nellie knew firsthand how difficult such a track would be. She'd wanted to be a physician, too, but the medical field was so strongly dominated by men, she gave up and chose nursing instead.

"I don't know for sure," Nellie said slowly, "but I would guess that only a small percentage of women, maybe as low as five percent, go to medical school. We'd better plan now. You need to attend the kind of college that will help you get into medical school."

"I've thought about it, Aunt Nellie. I want to go to Smith College in Massachusetts, then to Yale Medical School in Connecticut."

"Wow. That's ambitious. You'll need excellent grades. We need to find someone who's been to those schools to learn more. Why Smith?"

"My favorite book is "Gone with the Wind" by Margaret Mitchell. She went to Smith. I'd like to go there, too."

They talked for over an hour. Nellie knew it would be a stretch for Paula to achieve her goal but didn't want to discourage her.

Unfortunately for Paula, in the 1950s, there was an overt inequality in the workplace in the United States—not only for minorities but also for women. Women earned half what men did, working in the same jobs. Women could be fired for no more reason than becoming pregnant. In some places, women weren't allowed to serve on juries.

It would be very difficult for Paula to penetrate the male-only medical field. Women probably constituted only three to five percent of medical school graduates, and Smith College required very high grades.

Nellie made tea, and the two women continued their discussion. "Why neurosurgery? It's probably the most difficult medical specialty of all, especially for a woman. I don't want to discourage you. I think it's terrific that you have such ambition."

Paula swallowed hard. "I wrote a paper last year in science class about Harvey Cushing. He was a pioneer of brain surgery and seems to be the father of neurosurgery."

Harvey Cushing was an interesting, accomplished physician. The youngest of ten children, he was born in Cleveland, Ohio, in 1869 and died in 1939. Cushing went to Yale, which piqued Paula's interest in the institution, and he continued into Harvard Medical School. A recipient of the Distinguished Service Medal by the U.S. Army for his services during World War I, Cushing also authored a Pulitzer Prize winning biography, *The Life of Sir William Osler.*

Paula knew from writing her paper that Cushing used X-rays to diagnose brain tumors and was known as the world's leading teacher of neurosurgeons in the early decades of the 1900s. His most famous discovery was Cushing's disease, a disorder of the pituitary gland which, if left untreated, could result in extreme symptoms such as fatigue, skin, muscle, and bone changes, and could sometimes be fatal.

One of the most fascinating stories about Cushing was his connection to the thirty-second president, Franklin Delano Roosevelt. His daughter, Betsey, married James, the president's eldest son, and she was allegedly FDR's favorite daughter-in-law. Her relationship with Eleanor Roosevelt was strained.

Cushing and Roosevelt developed a strong bond and frequently exchanged letters. The president seriously considered a national comprehensive health insurance plan during the Great Depression when he first took office in 1933. It was alleged that the neurosurgeon was responsible for FDR backpedaling on the proposal.

The day before he publicly announced he wouldn't push for the federal health insurance plan as part of the Social Security Act, the president and Dr. Cushing discussed the issue over lunch. Those who knew the doctor understood that he didn't favor a federalized health insurance plan for the country. No one knew for certain if his thoughts influenced FDR's decision.

"I was enthralled reading about Dr. Cushing's medical career," Paula said, "and I wanted to be like him. I fell in love with the man the more I read about him."

Knowing how important it was to Paula, Nellie launched a mission the next day. She checked all the bios of the physicians who had Bentley Hospital privileges and found one who fit the criteria. Dr. Frank Clark came from Massachusetts, attended Boston College, and graduated from Yale Medical School in 1939. After his residency up north, he moved to West Virginia and opened an orthopedic practice in Parkersburg before finally settling in Bentley.

Nellie and Molly knew him and planned to approach him for any ideas he might have to further Paula's ambitions. His connection to Yale was only through the medical school. When they met, he agreed that at the appropriate time, he would be happy to write the admissions department at the college.

"I want to sit down with her first and get to know her," Dr. Clark said.

"Of course," the women replied.

One week later, Jack had a similar conversation with Philip. He was just a sophomore in September, but it was never too early to start preparing. Philip said he wasn't sure he wanted to go to college, but, like his sister, he felt motivated by a school paper he wrote as a freshman.

He researched the life of General Douglas MacArthur. That project, combined with a few discussions he'd had with Uncle Jack, meant he was leaning toward a military career. Jack was surprised and initially a bit disappointed, although he hid it well. If such a fine lad was interested in the military, who was Jack to try to deny him his wish? He hadn't explained much about his own experiences with his foster son, but they were too painful to live through again.

Philip's history paper pointed out that MacArthur graduated first in his class at West Point in 1903. That fact impressed him, and he wondered what it would be like to graduate first at such a prestigious school.

After graduation, MacArthur fought in World War I and later became commander of the Allied Forces in the Pacific during World War II.

"Did you ever see or meet him?" Philip asked hopefully.

"No. We were in different places," Jack replied. "He spent much of his time in the Philippines and eventually liberated that country from the Japanese."

Philip wanted to go to West Point and follow in MacArthur's footsteps. The Kelly kids clearly had strong ambition. Paula and Philip knew what they wanted.

CHAPTER 26

Despite that the fighting ended in 1945, it was still a volatile world in 1950.

At dinner one early September evening, Philip and Paula received a pep talk. The school year would start the following day, and it would be an important one for him and a vital one for her.

"Paula," Nellie began, "you'll probably have to be class valedictorian if you hope to get into Smith."

She was third in her class in her junior year but duplicating that might not be enough.

"I know that puts a lot of pressure on you," she continued, "but it will be very important. If that's too much of a burden, we can reexamine your goals and modify them."

"Aunt Nellie," Paula vowed through clenched teeth, "I *will* be valedictorian."

"Philip," Jack said, "your grades will be important, too, even if you're only a sophomore. Getting into West Point is a challenge even with top grades. They look for students who are not only intelligent but who possess great character and are physically fit. It will help a lot if a member of Congress nominates you. I don't know any," he said with regret, "but we can work on that."

He didn't realize it, but he would soon know a congressman. The fiddler politician would be elected to Congress in two years.

Henry and Molly joined the discussion.

"Extracurricular activities will boost your efforts to attain your formidable goals," Henry said.

"It can't hurt," Molly added, "that you both did volunteer work at the hospital the last two summers."

Henry nodded. "It's the total package."

Fortunately, money wasn't a concern for funding the two college educations. Life insurance and the proceeds from the sale of the Kelly house and the hardware store business were more than sufficient to cover both tuitions and living expenses. If Philip made it to West Point, there would definitely be funds left for both of them, as there was no tuition cost to attend the military academy.

While the Morgan clan had their conversation, a nasty fight broke out in apartment five at 1268 Clover Lane in Bentley. A middle-aged couple shouted angry words at each other and became violent. As the man assaulted his wife, the neighbors in numbers four and six heard the screams. They peeked out their doors. It wasn't the first time they'd heard such sounds.

Soon, policemen knocked heavily on the door and demanded it be opened. When it was, they saw a man in his fifties, disheveled, his face filled with rage. His wife cowered in a corner of the eating area, hands over her face. When the policemen saw her injuries—black eye, bloody nose, loose teeth, and scratched arms—they cuffed the man.

Ray Tompkins needed only a few drinks to become violent. The police were familiar with his address, having been called more than once to intervene during the last eighteen months. Tina Tompkins, in her late thirties, shy and demure with a slight build and only five feet one inch tall, was no match for the physically powerful brute who towered over her and was at least twice her weight.

Tina was taken to the hospital, and Ray rode in the cruiser to the station for the third time and was booked. It was the same old story—man attacked wife or girlfriend, but no charges were to be pressed.

Nellie saw the woman in her hospital room the following morning. Her face was battered, and she had purple welts over her back. Tina didn't want to press charges.

Nellie tried to change Tina's mind. It was a common story. The man was nice enough without alcohol, and he always apologized after the carnage.

"I have nowhere else to go, no money or anything," Tina said through her tears and swollen mouth.

"How often has this happened?"

"We've been married ten years, so probably eight or nine times. He lost his job recently and has been under a lot of pressure."

"Does that give him license to abuse you?"

"No, of course not, but it's a difficult time for him."

"And for you," Nellie said harshly.

Tina was in the hospital for several days, and Nellie continually encouraged Tina to press charges against Ray, but he was released from police custody and came to the hospital to pick up his wife. Without charges against him, there was no way to keep Ray under a restraining order and away from her.

Nellie couldn't conceal her contempt for him. The spirited, courageous woman walked up to him and began berating him. "What kind of man beats his wife?"

Without waiting for a response, she said, "You're such a coward, beating up a woman half your size."

Several doctors and nurses assembled outside the room.

"Watch your tongue, you bitch!" he shouted, purple veins almost popping from his forehead.

Nellie refused to back down. "I'm not afraid of bullies like you." Her face was only an inch from his.

He gave her a vicious shove that sent her up and over the bed, where she crumpled to the floor. Realizing he'd gone too far, he quickly hurried over in a weak attempt to apologize.

It was too late. Two physicians grabbed him and were quickly joined by a burly policeman. The cuffs went on while Nellie tried to collect herself. She remained on the floor and decided to milk the moment as long as she could.

Her arm and shoulder hurt, she told the others. Tina felt terrible but had a new perspective on her violent husband. She decided to press charges after all.

When the rest of the Morgan clan were told about the incident with Ray Tompkins, Nellie didn't admit that she deliberately baited the man. Her arm and shoulder were sore but all right.

After dinner and a discussion about the violent episode, Nellie had a question for the others.

Jack had something to say first, though. "Nell, you know how much I admire your guts and spunk, but you went too far this time. You could've been badly hurt or worse."

"I knew what I was doing. Besides, I saw help outside the door if I needed it."

"Yes, but let's agree that you won't do anything like it again."

The others nodded, and Nellie finally consented. All of them were eager to put the unpleasant Ray Tompkins incident behind them.

"What's the question you have for us?" Jack asked, breaking the mood.

"As you know, Tina Tompkins has nowhere to live. I wonder if she could stay with us until she's able to get a place of her own."

"When might that be?"

"I'm not sure, but this family helps people, and she desperately needs help."

After a brief discussion, they agreed to open their door and hearts to a woman they barely knew. Molly and Nellie said they'd look for jobs for Tina at the hospital to help her get started on her own. Jack also offered to ask if there were any openings at the school.

Tina Perry Tompkins was born in Macon, Georgia, to a couple who divorced when she was only twelve. She and her younger brother, Ben, were split up, each staying with a grandparent. Young Tina lived with her maternal grandmother in nearby

Milledgeville, while Ben stayed with his father's parents in Atlanta. Both retained their last name of Perry.

Tina graduated from high school and showed an affinity for playing the piano. After holding several jobs, she decided to pursue her music and became a waitress at Lorenzo's Café, where she also played for the patrons. Unfortunately, one patron was Ray Tompkins, who took an immediate interest in the pretty, diminutive twenty-five-year-old. They dated for three years before he proposed. Her grandmother didn't like or trust the man, who was nearly a decade older than Tina and a bit of a rogue. She strongly advised her granddaughter against the marriage, but impetuous youth won out, and the two married in a small ceremony at the Kiwanis Club.

The Tompkins' marriage was a disaster from the first day. Ray drank often and became a nasty, hostile drunk. At first, he didn't hit Tina but was verbally abusive. Standing six feet three inches tall and weighing two hundred and forty pounds, he towered over his ninety-five-pound wife. He never smiled and only snarled. His bottom lip protruded over his upper, making him look like a belligerent bulldog. Bushy black eyebrows were his most-prominent feature, along with a large nose that had been rearranged several times. Coal-black eyes were the perfect complement to his thuggish and intimidating appearance.

After one year of marriage, Tina realized she'd made a horrible mistake. As Ray's behavior degenerated and became more egregious, it eventually transitioned from verbal to physical abuse. She tried to leave him. Her grandmother was dead, and Tina had no place to go to escape. She feared for her life but was powerless to do anything about it.

Eventually, the couple moved first to Charleston and then Bentley, where Ray got construction work. When his supervisor caught him drinking on the job, Ray was fired. That quickly led to the ugly scene at the hospital with Nellie, but only after he'd mistreated Tina badly.

Somehow, through a mistake of the court magistrate, police error, the skill of an attorney, or a combination of all and some luck, Ray Tompkins escaped punishment and left the area. His excessive bad behavior should have resulted in jail time, but he was long gone.

Jack was furious, particularly because the man had manhandled his sister, and Jack suspected foul play on the part of someone in authority, but he never uncovered the culprit.

Tina, the frail, nice woman, came to 7 Mountain View Road to live with the Morgans. All six bedrooms in the sprawling farmhouse were occupied.

When Jack first met Tina, he was taken by how attractive she was, despite the bruises and black eye. She had deep-green eyes, beautiful white teeth, and a radiant smile in spite of her swollen lips. Although her nose was bloodied, it was still cute and straight. She was humble and very likable, and Nellie's judgment again appeared sound.

A little convalescence was in order, then Tina could look for a job. One of the gifts Tina brought to the household was the ability to play piano. The instrument in the house was there when Jack and Nellie bought the place from the Roberts, but no one had played since the brother and sister moved in. Nellie didn't want the instrument at first because it took up a lot of space. The Roberts didn't have room to transport it, nor did they wish to pay someone who could, so it stayed untouched in the house since September 1945.

The first night in her new home, Tina sat down to play a few songs. The piano was out of tune but nevertheless provided entertainment for the whole family.

It was a Saturday night in mid-September. Forty miles south of Bentley, in a dimly lit little room in a sleazy, seedy rooming house, a surly man hell-bent on vengeance sat on his bed and ate a sandwich, washing it down with beer. Cigarette butts filled the tin ashtray on the bedside table, and he could barely fit the ashes from his latest Lucky Strike into it. The small room reeked of stale cigarette smoke and beer, permeating the space and its meager furnishings.

A miscreant by any definition, Ray Tompkins was a big kid, and he enjoyed bullying and intimidating other kids in the schoolyard. Orphaned at ten, he took out his bitterness on small animals. He was expelled from his Richmond, Virginia, high school in his junior year and moved on to petty crimes and other misdemeanors before a failed attempt at bank robbery. That botched effort left a teller dead and his assailant on the run. It didn't matter to Ray that the man he killed had a wife and small child. He was never apprehended for the crime and began to feel he led a charmed life.

It was time for payback. He needed to settle his score with Tina and that nervy, upstart nurse to gain some overdue revenge.

It was six-thirty in the evening, and he had to reach his destination by seven-thirty. A quick knock on the door, and it would be over in five minutes. Once inside, he would order everyone on their knees with their backs to him, hands behind their heads. If anyone refused or became a problem, he would threaten to kill the women. First, he would assure them he didn't plan to kill anyone, just rob them. His ski mask would hide his identity. By the time anyone knew who he was, it would be too late.

Making sure he had everything he needed, Ray walked to the door. It would take less than an hour to get there. He would make Tina kneel first, then the nurse bitch who should have minded her own business. The others would have to die, too, to get rid of witnesses. He'd killed before without getting caught.

If he executed them quickly, he wouldn't even leave a trail, especially after he doused the bodies and floor with gasoline and dropped a match on it. Everything would go up in flames, and his vengeance would be complete.

He acknowledged the cops might suspect him, but he would lay low; they'd never find him. In the unlikely event they did, he would no longer have the weapon and gas can—after dropping them in a nice, deep lake. There would be no evidence of the deed anyone could connect to him.

He turned the key in his car's ignition, and the old engine started. The grim slaughter he planned was only forty-five minutes away.

During dessert in the farmhouse, Paula asked Jack, "I keep reading about GIs, and I don't know what that stands for. I asked Mr. Collins in math class, and he didn't know."

"That's a great question," Jack said. "I didn't know what it was, either, when I entered the service. GI Joe was the popular expression during the war, and most didn't understand it. People described all our soldiers in the Army, Navy, Marines, and Air Corps as GIs, because it included general-issue equipment. Officially, GI stood for Galvanized Iron, like in metal cans."

"Boy," she said with a giggle, "I thought there was more to it than that."

Henry wasn't feeling well, so he excused himself to go upstairs and lie down.

"If you need anything," Nellie called, as he ascended the stairs, "just holler."

Molly, Tina, and Nellie cleared the table and tidied up the kitchen, then they went to the main room for conversation.

Ray approached the driveway and pulled onto the shoulder to avoid being seen. It was seven twenty-seven. To allow for the possibility there were dogs in the home, he brought two large steaks. Daisy and Quincy heard the car and approached with a bark. He tossed the steaks at them, and they ignored him.

The element of surprise was important. He had to put his victims at ease as much as he could while holding a single-action .38 special revolver. He carried a one-gallon can of gas in his left hand, annoyed at the sloshing sound it made.

Stepping carefully onto the porch, he peeked in and saw everyone sitting in the living room, talking. He wasn't pleased to find two teenagers there, but that wasn't enough to deter him.

Carefully setting down the gas can without a sound, he gulped, took a deep breath, and pulled on the ski mask. He knocked. Nellie answered, and he shoved her aside, stepping in with his weapon out for all to see.

"This is a hold-up! Here's what you're going to do," he said flatly, his grim voice devoid of emotion. "All of you kneel with your backs to me and place your hands over your heads!"

Molly, Paula, Nellie, and Tina shrieked. Jack moved toward the masked man, who immediately aimed at his chest.

"One more step, mister, and I'll shoot the women. I only want to rob you, not kill you."

The mask indicated otherwise, but the six trembling hostages dutifully obeyed. Tina was nearest to the stairs, and he stepped directly behind her to begin his ghastly work.

Jack was the only one to speak. "Look, we'll give you our money and whatever else you want, but let us get up, and let us go."

"Shut up." He wasn't sure if anyone, even Tina, knew his identity, and he was sorely tempted to tell them, but he didn't. He couldn't wait to start shooting.

Suddenly, two shots rang out, and the masked gunman pitched forward onto his knees, then lurched backward, slumping to the floor and bleeding profusely from two holes in his chest and neck.

Everyone's head snapped to the left, where they saw Henry crouched on the stairs with a smoking Smith and Wesson .38 in his hands. Henry displayed remarkable *sangfroid* in the middle of the confusion and terror.

"Thank God you were there, Henry," Jack said.

Nellie went to check the gunman, who lay prostrate on the floor, blood oozing from his wounds the gun still in his hands. "He has no pulse, Jack."

"Henry," Jack said, composing himself. "Do you have a permit for that gun?"

Henry, clearly emotionally shattered by his dramatic intervention, merely shook his head.

Nellie reached for the phone receiver to call the police.

"Hang that up," Jack said sternly. "Here's what we'll do. Listen carefully. This is important. When the police come, I'm the one who shot this guy, not Henry."

Seeing his friend ready to protest, he shook his head. "You have to follow my plan."

Molly, Tina, Paula, and Philip stood there, shaking, unable to believe what just happened.

"Molly, please take the kids upstairs and settle them down. We'll leave Quincy and Daisy outside in the backyard. I wonder why they didn't bark.

"Everybody, listen. When the police arrive, we must have the same story. I was upstairs and heard the commotion. I was the one who shot this masked intruder, not Henry. Do you understand? This is important."

Again, Henry tried to object, but Jack silenced him with a gesture. "Henry, you must do this my way." He looked at all of them. "Do you understand?" he repeated.

They slowly nodded.

"Now, quickly," he told Molly, "take the kids upstairs." He grabbed her arm and whispered softly, "You'll hear another shot, but don't worry. It'll just be me firing the gun, so I'll have residue on my hand."

"Oh, Jack," she sobbed, "this is so horrible. Be careful. I'll tell the kids it's OK. I love you."

"I love you, too. Now hurry."

Jack took the gun from Henry, who still held it with all his strength. "Go wash your hands and forearms thoroughly with soap to remove any gun residue."

He quickly wiped fingerprints off the gun and grabbed it himself, then he told Tina, Henry, and Nellie not to watch what he had to do next.

"Before you call the police, Nell, please take Tina and go onto the porch with Henry," Jack said. "It will only take a moment."

As soon as they were out of the room, Jack assumed the same position on the stairs Henry took when he fired at the masked man. He shot another round into the lifeless body, making sure he didn't wipe his hands afterward. The body jerked with the impact. Upstairs, he heard Molly assuring the kids all was fine.

"Nellie, you can call the police now," Jack said.

The entire episode, from the time of the knock on the door to Nellie calling the police, took less than ten minutes, but to all of them it felt like an hour of slow motion. Jack's curiosity got the better of him, and he went to the dead man to remove his mask. His suspicions were confirmed when he saw Ray Tompkins.

Tina and Henry came in and said they found a gas can near the door.

"Don't touch it," Jack cautioned. "The dirty bastard planned to kill all of us and incinerate the evidence. I'm glad I killed the son of a bitch."

Tina had a hard time with the gruesome aftermath. "I put all of you in danger," she sobbed, "and you were so good and kind to me."

She dissolved into Nellie's arms, and both of them shared a good cry.

"Remember the story," Jack said. "I killed the intruder after he had all of you lined up on your knees."

The police arrived in ten minutes, with Sergeant Brown in charge. Nellie knew him from the hospital and considered him to be tough but fair. He had a grim expression and asked for an explanation.

Jack told him what transpired and that he came partway down the stairs to shoot the masked gunman.

"Looks like he wanted to burn all the evidence, too," Brown observed, seeing the gas can. "Unless that's one of yours?"

"It isn't," Nellie said.

Seeing the mask beside the bloody body, Sergeant Brown asked, "Did one of you remove it?"

"I did," Jack admitted. "I thought it might be him."

"You knew the intruder?"

Tina came forward, sobbing and leaning on Nellie, and told Sergeant Brown about her husband's prior assaults on her and on Nellie.

"I remember this guy," Sergeant Brown said. "It sounds like you performed a public service, but you shouldn't have touched the mask, sir."

"It was the only thing anyone touched, officer. I apologize."

"Do you have a permit for that gun?"

"No, sir, I don't. I keep it only for protection. I brought it back from Iwo Jima."

"You fought in Iwo Jima?" Sergeant Brown sounded impressed. "I understand, Mr. Morgan, and I don't think that will be a problem. Eventually, scumbags like this meet their end in some violent way. From what you told me, it didn't happen too soon."

After he left, medics removed the body from the farmhouse. Philip let the dogs inside and fed them dinner, which they ate despite their snack. They spent a long time sniffing the area where Ray Tompkins' body had been, but the women had already scrubbed the area clean with bleach and covered it with a scatter rug.

The seven finally had a chance to sit down. All were shaken. Molly sat closer to Jack and kept her arm entwined with his. Occasionally, she laid her head on his shoulder. The kids had cups of hot cocoa, but the adults decided something stronger was needed for their shattered nerves.

All sat in silence for a few minutes. Tina, though still shaking a bit, had calmed considerably. The dogs lay quietly on the floor, sensing something disturbing happened. Philip sat on the floor with them and stroked their necks. That helped calm all three of them.

"I think everything went well," Jack said. "I doubt we'll have any trouble with the police."

"Why did you say you were the one who shot that man?" Paula asked.

"I was the head of the household, and it would be more plausible if I were the shooter."

Nellie, Molly, Henry, and Tina seemed to understand what he implied, but the two teens didn't. Nellie looked at Jack and sent a silent message that it was a teaching moment that should be addressed, and he nodded.

"Paula, and you, too, Philip, there's another reason why I took responsibility for the shooting," Jack said. "Unfortunately, at this time in our history, there are some people who can't look beyond the color of a person's skin." He glanced at Henry, who nodded for him to continue.

"Henry's a Negro. We love him as a member of this family. Everyone in the community loves him, too, but if Henry, a Negro, shot a White man, even though he was a bad person, Henry could possibly be arrested and sent to jail."

Jack sighed. "It's not fair. We all have to work on changing the way people think about it, but unfortunately, that's how it is right now. I didn't want to put Henry through such a horrible, unfair, humiliating experience. That's the real reason I took credit."

Jack and Henry shared a knowing look.

The two teens nodded their understanding. Paula stood and went over to Henry to give him a warm, understanding hug.

They all went to bed late that night, hugging each other earnestly and not wanting to leave in the wake of their recent experience.

Sergeant Brown visited again the following morning, accompanied by a serious-looking man with thick glasses, who was introduced as Inspector Ryan. They wanted Jack's fingerprints to test against those on the gun. They went around the house, looking for anything of interest. They'd already confiscated the guns and gasoline can. The matches in Tompkins' trousers completed the picture. He obviously came to the farmhouse intending to murder everyone and burn the place down.

"There's no doubt," Sergeant Brown said. "He didn't plan to leave any evidence. His car was parked just down the road. We'll have it taken away."

Jack worried he might be in some trouble. The police might want to reprimand him for not having a permit or license for the gun, but nothing ever came of it. It was a stroke of genius for Jack to mention he brought the gun back from Iwo Jima. There was no one else who might have any questions about the incident. The evil Ray Tompkins was dead, and the case was closed.

Paula and Philip needed help after such a horrific, terrifying experience, and several sessions with a counselor got them through it.

It took Tina weeks before she could rid her mind of the near disaster. Her benefactors could have died because of her. Eventually, with the help of the newly tuned piano, she was able to move on.

Among popular songs that summer were "The Tennessee Waltz" by Patti Page and Nat King Cole's "Mona Lisa." Tina played them many times. "You Ain't Nothin' but a Hound Dog" by Elvis Presley was another favorite, although it was difficult to play on the piano. The rest of the family enjoyed listening and dancing to her music after dinner.

All at 7 Mountain View Road liked Tina and felt sorry for the trauma she endured. They also felt very fortunate, indeed, that Henry heard the commotion and acted so swiftly. The consequences had he not done so were obvious.

Week by week, Tina grew stronger, physically and emotionally, and soon, she was ready to seek employment. Nellie got her some work in the hospital cleaning rooms, taking out bedpans, and performing other caretaker duties. At least it was a job, and Tina was glad to have it. It was a start.

CHAPTER 27

The 1950 football season for the Bentley Bears was marked by ups and downs. On the positive side of the ledger was a victory over the Ridgemont Raiders, a team they hadn't beaten in ten years. The low point came against their vaunted rival, Central, to whom they lost 45-14. A victory would have given them a winning season. Nevertheless, a 3-3 season with two ties wasn't bad.

Easily the highlight of the year came in the triumph over Ridgemont. Trailing 24-23 late in the game, the Bears faced a fourth and twelve from the Raiders' twenty-yard line with less than two minutes to play. That was when Jack invoked the new trick play involving Don Bailey, the quarterback.

Bailey took the center snap, drifted back, and threw a lateral pass down the field to fullback Henry Wharton. The quarterback drifted right and sped toward the end zone. No one chased him.

The ball arrived in time, thanks to Wharton, and the Bears scored the winning touchdown. That was another trick play that worked.

The elections in West Virginia in November 1950, were noteworthy to the extent that the fiddler politician, the same man who stopped at the farmhouse several years earlier while running for the House of Delegates, was elected to the West Virginia Senate.

The great Appalachian Storm of November 1950 moved rapidly through the Eastern United States, causing significant wind, rain, and heavy blizzard conditions. It cut a swath through West Virginia, extending as far as the Carolinas and Northern Florida. Pickens, West Virginia, reported fifty-seven inches of snow. November 1950 would be remembered as the snowiest month on record.

As the spring of 1951 approached, everyone was proud of how hard Paula worked in her attempt to become class valedictorian. It would be a struggle, because Laura Patton was generally considered the top student in Paula's class. Laura didn't have the same incentive and motivation that made Paula excel. It would be a close battle. Philip worked diligently, too, but there was little chance of him even reaching the top three of his class.

Dr. Frank Clark, Nellie's friend who graduated from Yale Medical School in 1939, wrote a nice letter for Paula to the Admissions Office at Smith, urging her acceptance. Paula's science teacher did the same, as did a Yale graduate who was a lawyer in Bentley. Being valedictorian wouldn't assure Paula's admission, but it would give her efforts a boost.

The news came soon. Paula was named valedictorian, nosing out Laura Patton by one-tenth of a point. Waiting for the result before he wrote to Smith, Bentley High Principal Pat Mahon swung into action and sent a very positive letter to Smith admissions, urging her acceptance.

Philip ended up seventh in his sophomore class, which was a very good showing for him.

Nellie began dating, much to Jack and Molly's delight. It seemed a romance was clearly blossoming. George Fox, an ambitious lawyer, moved to Bentley the previous year from Charleston. They met at the hospital, where he was being treated for appendicitis, and they saw each other for four months. Nellie told Jack she could envision marrying George sometime if the circumstances were right. He was smart and funny, and he treated her with respect and kindness.

Jack and Molly, who were very happy together, wanted the same for Nellie.

On another front, joined by other ladies in town, Nellie, Molly, and Tina petitioned the Bentley Town Council to fund a Battered Women's House, one of the first in the country. A house was donated to the cause, and Tina would be its first director, at a salary of one thousand dollars a year.

George asked Nellie out for dinner, and she told Molly and Tina, "I have a funny feeling he's going to propose."

She dressed with special care that night and waited eagerly for his familiar knock on the door. Molly and Tina, equally excited, pretended to be involved in mundane housework, although they kept glancing at the door.

George arrived on time, looking as spiffy as ever in a white shirt and red-striped tie under his jacket, which looked particularly good on his tall, well-proportioned frame. He was a handsome man with a full head of wavy, dark-brown hair and piercing blue eyes. A square jaw housed an almost perfect set of teeth and led to a straight but too generous nose and bushy eyebrows.

The women greeted him nonchalantly, but it wasn't easy to curb their enthusiasm. They sent the couple off with best wishes for a nice evening and wonderful dinner.

At a rather upscale restaurant, Nellie and George each had a drink. She chose white wine, while George had Jack Daniels on the rocks. They talked easily for a while about their jobs and other matters, then George shifted uneasily in his chair and adjusted his tie. As he inched closer to her across the table, her instincts told her the moment had come.

"Nellie, I've received an offer from a law firm in San Francisco, and I was hoping you'd come with me."

That didn't sound like the marriage proposal she anticipated. His words hit her like a punch in the stomach, and suddenly, she felt ill.

They ordered dinner, but Nellie only picked at her salad and chicken. During dinner conversation, George mentioned he'd be leaving in four weeks.

Sensing her obvious discomfort, he asked gently, "Would you consider going there with me?"

She still hadn't recovered from the first blow. He hadn't said a word about engagement or marriage, but simply that he was leaving and wanted her to accompany him. Trying hard to mask her considerable disappointment, she took a sip of her wine before replying.

"George," she said, her voice shaking, "I don't think I can do that. I have many responsibilities here that I can't just leave."

Translated, that might mean an offer of marriage could alter her thinking, but he either didn't understand or chose to ignore it. "You're very special to me. I'd hate to lose you."

Nellie felt herself becoming agitated but remained calm. "I'm fond of you, too, George, but there's too much at stake here in Bentley."

He awkwardly took her hand and continued trying to convince her. She wouldn't have it and wished she could leave.

"Would you please think about it?" he asked.

"I will, George, but under the circumstances, I don't think I can do it."

Either he was too dumb to pick up on her hidden meaning concerning a marriage proposal, or he was too savvy and didn't want to make one.

Their goodnight kiss wasn't as passionate as those that had preceded it, and she sensed she might never see him again.

Two anxious women waited for her at the front door, and they immediately knew something was wrong.

"I'm through with men," Nellie said emphatically, before dissolving into tears and collapsing into her friends' warm, compassionate arms.

They shuffled her into the kitchen, where cups of hot tea helped soothe Nellie's nerves. Between tears and sobs, Nellie told them what transpired over dinner.

"Maybe he would have proposed if you had said you'd go," Tina offered.

"Maybe, but maybe not. He should have asked me to marry him first, then asked if I would go to San Francisco. I might have said yes, but he'll never know."

Among those disappointed over the breakup, Jack was the most distraught. He desperately wanted Nellie to know the same love and joy he shared with Molly.

CHAPTER 28

Once school was over, Paula was the first one to check the mailbox each day. Her goal to become a neurosurgeon hadn't dissipated a bit, and she knew Smith and Yale would furnish her with the best path toward the goal.

Henry and Jack prepared for the upcoming football season. Henry, still remarkably fit at sixty-six, hadn't lost any of his enthusiasm for life or football. Both men understood Bentley was short in the talent pool, and most of the promising athletes went to Central or other nearby schools. They had no feeder system to bring in new talent, which vexed them.

Central and other high schools got kids who played sandlot or other kinds of organized football. Bentley freshmen reported for the football team without any prior experience. It was a formidable challenge for both men to produce a competitive team, but they met it squarely, and the Bears were no longer a team to take for granted. The two men knew that good coaching was the only way to be competitive in the Mountain Conference.

Nellie was in the kitchen one late June afternoon when she heard a scream and ran onto the porch.

Paula stood there, a torn envelope in her hand. "I made it! I made it! I got into Smith!"

"That's wonderful!" Nellie said, hugging her and dancing around the porch together. "All that hard work was worth it, wasn't it?"

That night, the family celebrated over dinner. Paula's first step toward becoming a neurosurgeon was complete. Her destiny appeared to be in her hands.

She seemed to float on a cloud for days afterward, and her happiness was contagious. She spent a lot of time with Philip; she knew how difficult it would be for him to be separated from his sister for the first time. Paula assured Philip he could visit her at Smith, and she would be home for the major holidays.

During the remainder of her summer vacation, Paula spent time reading about Smith and the Northampton, Massachusetts, area. Molly, Nellie, and Tina took her on several shopping trips to buy things she needed for her dorm room—linens, bedding, and personal items. That included several new outfits and shoes, too.

Eventually, it was time for Paula to depart for Massachusetts. On the weekend before the Smith school year started, they shared an early farewell dinner, with laughter, hugs, and tears. Paula's belongings were packed into the family car after dinner, because the trip would take almost twelve hours. They didn't want to waste any time packing in the early morning.

Jack and Henry would drive her there and help her move in. Nellie packed lunches for all of them for the trip.

Before dawn the following morning, they all gathered on the front porch.

"I think we have everything now," Jack said. "Are you ready to start your new adventure, Paula?"

She grinned, nodded, and assured them she would call and write. After one more brief hug, they got in the car and drove off, with Daisy, Quincy, and Philip trotting alongside for a bit.

When they reached the end of the driveway, barks and good-byes were exchanged, and the college student was on her way, waving excitedly out the window.

They arrived in Northampton at five-thirty that evening. The journey was uneventful but long. They kept occupied with conversation and the beautiful scenery along the way. Jack and Henry wanted to start back to West Virginia while it was still light out, so they helped Paula move into her new room and bade her farewell.

She hugged them fiercely. With tears in her eyes, she said, "Thank you, Uncle Jack, and you, too, Henry. I'll make you and the whole family proud. I'll work hard. You'll see."

As the two men walked toward the car, Jack turned and saw another young woman greeting Paula and welcoming her to campus. Paula already looked a bit homesick when they departed, but the pep talk both gave her would help her make the transition.

Henry was thrilled to see Connecticut again after so many years, even for a short time, and he regaled Jack with anecdotes about his past on the way out of town. They decided the trip home was too long to cover in one night, especially after their long drive to Northampton.

They agreed to drive for a few hours, have dinner, and find a motel to spend the night.

When they stopped three hours later, Jack called Molly and told her of their decision.

"That's smart, Jack," she said. "You've had a long drive, and it's better to be safe than sorry. I'll miss you. We haven't been apart since we married. Sleep tight. I love you."

"You, too. We'll see you tomorrow."

CHAPTER 29

There were several reasons why the 1950s were good for West Virginians. The state contributed the fifth-highest percentage of servicemen in World War II, with over two hundred and eighteen thousand participants, and a majority of them returned to a welcome reception by a grateful state, although 5,830 West Virginians died during the conflict. More than half of the eleven thousand Negroes representing the state were students at West Virginia State College. Two thousand women from the Mountain State also entered military service during the war.

Ruby Bradley, an Army Nurse Corps administrator, received two Bronze Stars for her heroic acts in the Philippines and assisted in more than two hundred and thirty major operations and the delivery of American babies—all while being held captive by the Japanese in Manila.

Another West Virginian who distinguished himself was pilot Chuck Yeager, who became an ace in one day by downing five German planes. Another West Virginia native, born in Fairmont in 1923, was twenty-one-year-old Marine Hershel Woodrow Williams, who was one of eleven in his state to receive the Medal of Honor. He fought with Jack's friend, Jacklyn Harrell Lucas, the seventeen-year-old who fell on two grenades that day in Iwo Jima to save his comrades. Corporal Williams won his Medal of Honor three days later when he risked his life, attacking the Japanese for four hours with a flamethrower to minimize the casualties in his Marine unit. West Virginians more than paid their dues to keep America safe and free.

Still another West Virginian contribution to the war effort was the use of Seneca Rocks, an unusual formation of jagged peaks that jutted out nine hundred feet high, three times taller than London's Big Ben. The site, located in Pendleton County in the northeast region of the Mountain State, was used as a wilderness assault camp in 1943 to help U.S. troops prepare for scaling cliffs during the Normandy invasion on June 6, 1944.

The up-and-down economy of the fifties didn't match the initial post-war euphoria. Even before the war, the state experienced a steady decline in agricultural employment. Mining also fell off due to a reduction in the demand for coal, compounded by automation being promoted in the mining companies. That left the state looking for new industries and other potential employment opportunities.

The state had an abundance of important minerals. Bituminous coal was West Virginia's most valuable asset, and the state had the country's second-largest coal reserves, surpassed only by Wyoming, as well as natural gas, crude petroleum, limestone, building stone, rock, brine salt, sandstone, glass, sand, clay, and gravel. There were copious supplies of water and hardwood timber, which indicated a successful place to live for returning veterans.

A steely man with bushy eyebrows who was born in Iowa and never lived in the Mountain State, John Lewis' influence ranged far beyond the state borders. By the 1950s, his power was diminished, but in his twenties, thirties, and forties, he held considerable sway over king coal. In 1920, he became the president of the United Mine Workers of America, known as the UMWA. His election coincided with the turmoil in West Virginia between coal operators and miners.

The situation grew violent and out of hand as far back as 1912. Among the first coal strikes in the United States occurred in the Mountain State near Cabin Creek. The coal miners unionized and demanded safer working conditions, higher pay, the right to trade where they pleased, and recognition of the United Mine Workers.

The mining companies predictably refused to meet the demands, and the war was on. They hired men with high-powered rifles to guard the mines, and the situation grew worse. The union responded by supplying the miners with rifles, ammunition, and even machine guns.

Over six thousand unionized miners crossed the Kanawha River on the morning of September 1, 1912, on their way to kill the guards, but Governor William E. Glasscock declared martial law and prevented the carnage.

Five years earlier, the worst coal-mine disaster in the country occurred. Tucked away in Marion County in north central West Virginia was the town of Monogah, which included a network of mines operated by the Fairmont Coal Company. A huge explosion erupted at ten twenty-eight in the morning on December 6, 1907, rocking the town and leaving three hundred and sixty coal miners dead, two hundred and fifty widows behind, and more than one thousand children without fathers.

The year 1907 was a terrible one for U.S. mining, with accidents killing 3,242 miners. That year also served as a catalyst for the enactment of regulations and safety reforms that helped reduce miner death rates in West Virginia and other mining locales.

Although it was commonly believed that the first Father's Day was celebrated on June 19, 1910, in the state of Washington, its genesis was really the Monogah mining disasters. The first recognized Father's Day occurred in a church in Fairmont, five miles east of Monogah. It was held seven months after a mining catastrophe on July 5, 1908, to honor the men who died.

After nine years of mine wars, United Mine Workers membership plummeted in West Virginia, dropping to fewer than one thousand paying members by 1930. John L. Lewis, who became president of UMWA ten years earlier, concentrated his membership efforts there. With the help of President Franklin Delano Roosevelt's New Deal, union membership soared in the Mountain State and throughout the country, but all was not good for the miners. The quid pro quo for New Deal help was mechanized union mines, a change that ultimately cost tens of thousands of miners their jobs.

CHAPTER 30

The Bentley Bears' first game in 1951 was at Bentley Field against the Millersville Marauders. That team beat Bentley four times in a row but failed on the fifth attempt, losing 18-12. Junior quarterback Gus Rogers ran for two touchdowns and threw for one. The momentum didn't last long, though, and the Bears lost the following week to Smithville, 25-7.

Henry began feeling his age, despite his overall fitness. At sixty-seven, arthritis plagued him, and he couldn't participate in the physical drills with the players anymore. It discouraged him, but Jack reminded him how lucky he was to have gone head-to-head with the boys for so many years.

"Most sixty-seven-year-olds I know are sitting on the porch somewhere in a rocking chair," Jack said.

The sexagenarian remained the assistant coach, but Jack also hired Cliff Hogan, who played at Bentley and just graduated from West Virginia University, to run the defense with an emphasis on the defensive backs. Cliff played at the university as a starting safety. Coupled with his new degree in physical education, he had the bona fides to step right in. His steady presence freed Henry from defensive chores, enabling him to spend more time developing game plans.

The three men worked well together but couldn't produce a regular winner. Central was still a powerhouse, and Derby lost only one game that year. The Bears, despite good coaching, came out with three wins, four losses, and one tie. Jack and Henry desperately wanted to duplicate their first winning season in 1948, but it didn't happen.

One night after the season, between Thanksgiving and Christmas, Henry talked with Tina in the kitchen, as Nellie walked in.

"Hi, guys," Nellie said. "What's going on?"

"Nothing," Henry said sheepishly.

"We were just wondering when it might rain," Tina said quickly. "Daisy and Quincy seem rather agitated."

The same thing happened to Jack when he walked into the house and caught Molly and Tina in conversation.

"Can I join in?" he asked.

"Just girl talk," Molly quipped.

It seemed to go that way most of the week for Jack and Nellie. They encountered various combinations of the other occupants of the house in conversation, who were evasive when one of them asked to join the conversations. It seemed that Henry, Molly, and Tina were in cahoots.

One Tuesday night, they planned to go out to dinner together at Riley's, where they had a reservation for six, but Molly led them to the town hall instead.

"I just have to pick up something," she explained. "Then we can go to the restaurant."

They never reached Riley's.

Once inside the front door of Town Hall, Jack and Nellie were shocked when over two hundred people cheered. Brother and sister, totally bewildered, stared at the crowd, then at each other. High above them was a sign that read, "Thank You, Jack and Nellie."

Totally nonplussed, they threw up their hands in surprise. Jack was frozen with a broad grin on his face, while Nellie burst into tears.

Mayor Bill Dixon took the microphone. "I'd like to inform you two that you have received Citizens of the Year awards."

No such award had ever been given in Bentley before, but, as the mayor added, "We've never been graced by such generosity before!"

On a small platform sat a raised head table covered with a tablecloth decorated with a bouquet of flowers where the guests of honor would sit. There was also a small podium and microphone. Another twenty tables of ten filled the large room. It wasn't a fancy affair, but the townspeople came together in spectacular fashion. Wine, which was donated by two local package stores, along with iced tea and other beverages, was served in plastic glasses before dinner.

People brought appetizers, salads, and enough main dishes to feed an army. After enjoying the libations and appetizers, the throng went to their seats.

Mayor Dixon and his wife sat at the head table, along with Bentley High School Principal Patrick Mahon and his wife, Kathryn, with the guests of honor—Jack, with Molly at his side, and Nellie. Henry, Philip, and Tina took seats at the first table near the rest of their family.

There were no glasses to clink, so Mayor Dixon tapped the microphone to get people's attention. "Thank you all for coming, and for bringing all this food and drink. This isn't fancy because we aren't fancy people. We're family."

They cheered.

"Six years ago, we were blessed by the arrival of two very special people from Buffalo, New York. There was no fanfare to signal their coming, and they took their places silently and modestly in our wonderful town.

"What an effect they have had on this community! In just six short years, they have touched all our lives." The mayor saw many people set down their knives and forks to listen respectfully, but he urged them to continue eating.

"There are four people who wish to say a few words before I present these awards. Henry?"

The tall, aging, distinguished-looking Black man with a crop of white hair walked up to the platform. "Ladies and Gentlemen, Jack Morgan is my best friend and has been since the day we met. I wouldn't be here tonight, maybe not even be alive," he said passionately, his eyes filling with tears, "if not for this man's kindness. Jack Morgan gave me a sense of purpose and a reason for living."

Several ladies in the audience dabbed their eyes with handkerchiefs.

"He took a chance on me. He didn't know me and didn't owe me anything. Not only did he make me assistant coach, but he and Nellie gave me a place to live. I love them both and will until the day I die."

Even Jack and Nellie were tearful, but that was nothing compared to the tears streaming down Henry's face. As the older man, overcome with emotion, moved to embrace them, the audience stood and applauded vigorously.

The next speaker was Tina Tompkins. "I had no real life," she said hesitantly, "until I met Nellie Morgan Kent. I was a battered wife with nowhere to go when she stepped in between me and my husband one day at the hospital to stop him from hitting me again. Without even knowing me," she said, wiping her eyes, "she and Jack and his wife, Molly, took me in. I now have a job, thanks to Nellie and some of you, and a purpose to help others who weren't as fortunate as I was. I, too, can't thank Jack and Nellie enough and will be forever grateful to them."

The audience stood and applauded.

Mayor Dixon then introduced fifteen-year-old Philip Kelly. His hands shook, as he took a piece of paper from his pocket and walked to the microphone. Speaking in front of everyone would be very difficult for him, but he insisted on doing it.

The audience felt his anguish and pain and knew what he and his sister went through with the sudden death of their dear parents. He cleared his throat and accepted a glass of water from the mayor's wife.

"I...uh...am very grateful to the Morgans for giving my sister, Paula, and me such a wonderful home. They even got us the most beautiful dogs, Daisy and Quincy. During those first hard months for us, they helped us with our homework and were always there for us. Paula and I don't know what we would have done without them. We became part of another family, along with Henry, Molly, and, now, Tina. Paula's away at Smith," he said sadly, with tears in his eyes, "so she can't be here tonight, but she and I love the Morgans and our new extended family, and I'll always remember their kindness."

As he began crying, Mayor Dixon rushed to his side. Henry came up and walked Philip back to his seat. For a third time, the audience stood and applauded the brave young man and the people who helped him.

By then, most of the people were crying, even the stoic men. Seated between his beloved sister and adoring wife, Jack rested his hands on their arms during the emotional tributes.

Principal Patrick Mahon shuffled to the podium after patting Jack's back. "Six years ago, Bentley welcomed a brother and sister from Buffalo, New York. We had no idea how great an impact they would have on all of us. Nellie is a wonderful nurse in our community hospital, and Jack has taught in our high school and coached our football team.

"When he first arrived, Jack saw many of our kids didn't have adequate breakfasts. He brought in his own food until we decided it was an appropriate responsibility for the school to take on. Then he saw our janitor, Henry Parker, and realized what a fine builder of men and coach he could be, so Jack hired him. Henry and Jack have done a wonderful job as coaches of our football team and have emphasized how important good character and sportsmanship are to the game and our boys. In teaching history, Jack made his classes fun and created the perfect learning environment for our young people. We're so much better for knowing you two." He stepped down.

The mayor walked up and sipped from a glass of water. "Forgive me if I repeat anything that has just been said. We have been very lucky that Jack and Nellie chose our community as a place to settle. Had we known anything about you," he added, looking directly at them, "we certainly would have chosen you."

Applause and cheers erupted from the audience. Once the clapping subsided, he continued.

"As you know, they not only opened their hearts to strangers. They opened doors for them, too. Henry, Tina, Paula, and Philip know the generosity of these wonderful people, and we owe them a debt of gratitude. Nellie was instrumental in securing approval from the Town Council for a refuge for battered women. They worked with the council to reinstate a soup kitchen for our disadvantaged citizens. They helped staff it on Saturday mornings, and it's no coincidence that Henry, Tina, and Molly chip in, too. Nellie has upgraded the fine work done at Bentley Hospital."

Looking at the brother and sister, he said, "Jack and Nellie Morgan, I don't know how two talented and selfless people could possibly contribute more to enrich our society."

People jumped to their feet and cheered loudly. The mayor walked to the table and presented Jack and Nellie with medals from the town.

"Would either of you like to say a few words?" he asked.

Nellie nudged Jack, indicating her preference that it be him. Modest as he was, he was reluctant to take the microphone, but he did it to spare his sister.

Molly gave him a hug as he left his seat. He drank from his wine glass and walked up to shake hands with Mayor Dixon.

"Friends," Jack began, "I obviously don't have any prepared comments because this is a total surprise. Nellie and I feel blessed to be here with you and warmed by your wonderful comments. Our father would have enjoyed them," he said with a smile, "but our mother would actually have believed them."

People laughed.

"Seriously, thank you for your friendship and support, which mean a great deal to us. We remember how kind you were when we first arrived in Bentley. Nellie and I feel fortunate to have come to such an incredible community, and we'll always remember your kindness. We feel fortunate to be able to adopt, if you will, such wonderful people into our extended family. Henry, Tina, Philip, and Paula have been amazing additions in our lives. We wouldn't trade any of them for anything in the world. We only did what any good neighbor would do. They have greatly enriched our lives with their friendship.

"Molly, you're amazing to have taken on this Morgan project. That's one of the many reasons why I married you, and we all love you. We love our adopted state of West Virginia. Wherever and whenever we have traveled in this state, people have been incredibly kind and friendly. West Virginians are a hearty, honest, noble folk. You've made us feel like real family. Thank you to everyone."

People stood and walked to the dais to shake Nellie and Jack's hands and hug them.

Jack didn't mention it in his comments, but his idea for a soup kitchen came from a strange source. Like so many cities and towns throughout America during the Great Depression, Bentley established a soup kitchen to aid its impoverished citizens. During 1929-1939, men worked to support their families, while women remained home to care for the children. If a man lost his job, the family lost its means to support itself. Out of work, he would often nobly stay away from home during mealtimes, so the children could eat.

Joining countless others, he waited patiently in a breadline to get some form of sustenance, like bread, coffee, or soup. Brothers and sisters took turns eating each day. Unemployment grew rapidly, from 3.2 percent in 1929 to 25 percent in 1933. The courage and stoicism in those times were remarkable. Some keeled over from exhaustion and starvation while standing in a bread line. Others, subsisting on as little as a cracker a day, barely stayed alive or died from tuberculosis or dysentery from malnutrition. Local governments and the Red Cross tried to supplement aid efforts from the federal government, but those usually fell short.

Grisly stories were plentiful. There were reports of a Pennsylvania man in 1930 who, out of shame, hanged himself in his basement because he was caught stealing a loaf of bread for his four hungry children.

Older children joined their fathers in staying away from their homes during mealtime out of fear that the temptation to snatch food from younger children or babies would be too great.

As many as forty or fifty men fought over a few morsels of food left when garbage trucks unloaded their contents. Others lined up behind restaurants searching for anything to eat. Some of the most desperate stories came from rural areas like the hills of Kentucky and West Virginia, where milk was considered a life saver. A cow that gave milk was invaluable.

As the situation in the country worsened in 1933 and unemployment numbers rose, the nation faced a paradox. While too many were forced to eat what meager amounts of food they could find, American farmers produced a surplus of crops and livestock. The situation wasn't that good for farmers, either.

Prices for farm goods dropped dramatically, due to the American consumers' inability to pay for them. The surpluses continued, but there weren't enough resources to get those necessary foodstuffs to those in need.

Under President Franklin Roosevelt, the federal government responded to those problems with many programs, among them relief projects and the first Food Stamp Program on May 16, 1939.

Eggs were an extremely important food for depression families, providing needed protein. Sometimes it was too hot to grow crops, but chickens survived. They kept producing eggs and found themselves not only on farms but in family backyards.

Coffee was another important American staple during the Great Depression. By the late 1920s and thirties, South American overproduction of coffee beans made the prices drop dramatically, from twenty-two cents per pound to eight. Still, many couldn't afford it at any price.

A saving grace for many families was a garden and a few chickens. Beginning in 1926 and capitalizing on the popular name Uncle Sam, the U.S. Department of Agriculture ran a daily fifteen-minute home-economics radio program featuring Aunt Sammy. Using a sweet, soothing, friendly female voice,

Almost Heaven

Aunt Sammy instructed women how to stretch their dollars in cooking and other household chores. Her useful, money-saving tips proved so helpful and popular that a resulting cookbook sold over one million copies.

Jack thought one day about the need to establish a Bentley soup kitchen, which operated successfully throughout the Great Depression. He saw several people wandering the streets at night, obviously hungry.

One night he read a magazine when an article caught his eye about the Chicago gangster, Al Capone. Alphonse Gabriel "Al" Capone was born in Brooklyn on January 17, 1899. His parents were Italian immigrants, both born in the Province of Salerno. The Capones had nine children, one of whom was named Vincenzo; he later changed his name to Richard Hart, so he could become a Prohibition agent in Homer, Nebraska.

Most of the people in the United States knew his reputation as a ruthless mob boss and for his nickname, "Scarface," which he loathed. Apparently while working the door at a Brooklyn nightclub one night, he insulted a woman and was slashed on the left side of his face by her vengeful brother.

Al liked Lena Gallucio's looks and wasn't hesitant about telling her. She finally asked her brother, Frank, to stop the man from staring at her.

Allegedly, Capone said, "Honey, you have a nice ass, and I mean that as a compliment, believe me."

Frank was enraged. Capone charged him, but Frank pulled out a pocketknife and slashed Capone three times. He aimed for the neck, but he got the left side of Capone's face, leaving him with a gash that required thirty stitches, received at Coney Island Hospital.

Ironically, after apologizing to his assailant, Capone hired him as a bodyguard. Sensitive about being photographed after that, Capone hid the left side of his face and claimed his wounds were war injuries.

After that incident in 1917, few photos, if any, showed him from that angle. He became renowned for his role in the 1929 Saint Valentine's Day Massacre, an assassination attempt to wipe out his rival, Bugsy Moran.

The part of one article that most drew Jack's attention described another side of the mobster's life. It said that many attributed the creation of the first soup kitchen to Al Capone. He established it at the onset of the Great Depression because he wanted to repair his very negative reputation. Apparently, his motives weren't entirely altruistic.

His Chicago soup kitchen served three square meals a day, ensuring that those who had lost their jobs could get a free meal. The act certainly helped the public see him as a Robin Hood. *The Chicago Tribune* helped foster that public perception with a headline in 1931 proclaiming that one hundred and twenty thousand meals were served by Capone's free soup kitchen.

An army of ragtag, starving men assembled three times a day to eat a hearty meal in a storefront at 935 S. State Street, thanks to the gangster's generosity. Soon, they told newspapers that their friend was doing more for the poor than the federal government. They toasted him over hot coffee and sang his praises. Allegedly, some of them were even offered jobs. Seizing the opportunity, Capone visited the storefront to shake the men's hands and offer encouragement.

During the cold months of November and December, the kitchen served three meals a day. On Thanksgiving Day in 1930, Capone's public relations reached a zenith. On that day, five thousand hungry men, women, and children were served a hearty beef stew, something many hadn't tasted in over a year.

Reading that article prompted Jack to bring the idea to Molly, Nellie, Tina, and Henry. The subsequent approval from the Bentley Town Council meant the Bentley Soup Kitchen could become reality.

The year 1952 came in with a bang, with a cold, snowy winter for West Virginians. The timing for a soup kitchen was perfect.

CHAPTER 31

Paula thrived with her new Smith curriculum, and Philip was in his junior year at Bentley High. The 1952 elections loomed.

Jack realized the only way for Philip to gain acceptance into West Point was to secure a government nomination from a member of Congress. By law, each member could nominate only ten candidates a year to each of three of the four military service academies, whether that was the U.S. Military Academy, which was Philip's choice, the U.S. Naval Academy, or the U.S. Marine Merchant Academy.

The U.S. Coast Guard Academy didn't require a congressional nomination. After doing some research, Jack found out that since the candidate could apply only during his junior year in high school, it was important for Philip to begin the process. One could also apply after high school, but college credits would not be transferable. Further research told Jack that upon receiving a nomination and appointment, the candidate had to be tested and placed at the appropriate academic level upon entrance to the academy. Each successful candidate had to be a U.S. citizen between the ages of seventeen and twenty-two. Jack told Philip that the academies all required strong math and science skills to help prepare for a rigorous academy curriculum.

"Philip, your class rank, grades, extracurricular activities, SAT test scores, and leadership achievements also weigh heavily on your acceptance. The ball's in your court, young man. You really need to apply yourself."

"Yes, sir. I know. I'll do my absolute best and plan to succeed. You'll see, Uncle Jack. I'll make you all proud."

Since Philip was in his junior year, a letter from his congressman was in order. There was one problem—their congressman, Erland Harold Hedrick, better known as E. H. Hedrick, thought he might run for governor. An up-and-coming star in the Democratic Party was the same fiddler who appeared at Jack's door in the fall of 1947, and he was running for Hedrick's congressional seat. Philip's letter had to go to Congressman Hedrick, but if the fiddler won, he would hold the key to Philip's nomination to West Point.

As the election heated up in the fall of 1952, Paula and Philip completed very successful years. As a junior, Philip was third in his class and played on both the soccer and basketball teams. Paula was fourth in her freshman class at Smith and participated on the debate team.

Henry's arthritis continued to plague him, but he wasn't bedridden or immobilized. The Home for Battered Women and the Bentley Soup Kitchen were thriving, which was a good thing, though it was a shame that more than a few women needed the help.

Jack and Henry endured their worst season as coaches. The Bears fell to three wins, five losses, mainly due to a number of injuries, particularly at the skilled positions of quarterback and fullback. The only positive note in the frustrating season was a surprisingly close loss to Central at 20-12.

Nellie and Molly still enjoyed working at Bentley Hospital, and Tina thrived as the director of the home. Even Quincy and

Daisy seemed content and kept each other company while the rest of the family was at work or school.

Halfway through the football season, on a sunny Saturday morning in early October, the fiddler politician knocked on the front door when only Jack and Henry were home. Jack did some research on the election and was ready to court the man's favor. The fiddler was a favorite to win the election, especially since the incumbent was leaving his seat to run for governor. The congressman, also a physician, lost in the Democratic primary and Hendrick died two years later.

Jack invited the fiddler for a glass of lemonade, knowing how much he needed the man's help to get Philip into West Point.

That wasn't the topic of conversation that day, however. The coaches pledged their support to the man and offered to put up yard signs and encourage their friends and neighbors to vote for him. He eagerly accepted their offer and promised he wouldn't forget it.

They shook hands vigorously, and the happy fiddler left. Jack knew that quid pro quo would come soon after the election.

The election went as expected, and Jack and Philip drove to Charleston one rainy February morning to the office of the newly elected congressman from the Sixth District.

"Congratulations, congressman," they said almost in unison.

In the corner of the cramped office sat a fiddle. Newly elected Congressman Robert Byrd beamed, greeted them warmly, and motioned for them to sit down.

"I sure appreciated your help," he began. "What can I do for you, or is this just a social visit?"

Jack was there for one thing, though. "Thanks for seeing us. This is my foster son, Philip, who wants very much to attend West Point next year."

"And you'd like a nomination letter from me?" interrupted the jolly congressman with a sharply featured face.

"Yes, sir, if you would. He's a fine boy and has a chance to be valedictorian of his senior class."

"That's wonderful. I was valedictorian of my class. Of course, that was a few years ago in 1934." He looked at the young man. "Philip, is this something you really want to do? It's a rigorous program and will require a great deal of dedication and hard work on your part."

"Absolutely, sir. It's been a goal and dream of mine since I was eight years old. I'm committed to working very hard to make this happen. I can't thank the Morgans enough for giving me the opportunity and support. I want to serve our country like Mr. Morgan did. I couldn't thank you enough if you would nominate me."

The congressman's face broke into a broad smile. He was a very likable fellow. Standing behind his desk to signal the discussion was over, he asked Jack and Philip to send him the necessary information. "I'll be glad to communicate his attributes to West Point."

With their mission accomplished, they walked to the door.

"Thank you again for your help during my campaign," the congressman said.

Byrd was actually born Cornelius Sale, Jr., on November 20, 1917, in North Wilkesboro, North Carolina, and as a politician he knew how the game was played. His story was an extraordinarily interesting one.

The beginning of his life was difficult. While not even a year old, he watched his mother die in the influenza epidemic. His father sent him to live with his aunt and uncle, according to his mother's wishes. They adopted him, and his name was changed to Robert Carlyle Byrd. Sadly, despite living relatively near his son, his biological father never made a *bona fide* effort to see him. Byrd didn't even learn his birth name until 1933, when he was sixteen.

They moved to a farm in the rural part of West Virginia, where coal was king. He went to Sunday School at the local Baptist Church and learned how to play the fiddle. The instrument became such an integral part of him that he carried it everywhere, even years later when he ran for political office. An excellent student, he finished at the top of his Mark Twain High School class. Sadly, as was common in those days, he couldn't afford college. It wasn't until years later, when grants, loans, and scholarships abounded, that other poor high school students could further their learning experience.

He married his high-school sweetheart right after graduation and spent World War II as a shipyard welder for cargo ships in Baltimore, returned to West Virginia, and opened a grocery store in Sophia. When a radio station in nearby Bentley began broadcasting his fundamentalist lessons while teaching an adult bible class, he became a local celebrity. That wasn't enough for Robert Byrd, who wanted much more.

Candidate Byrd was fortunate to be elected to any office. During that 1952 primary for Congress, the Democratic opponent revealed to the voters that Byrd was once a member of the Ku Klux Klan in the early forties. Referring to it as "the greatest mistake of my life," Byrd continued his campaign.

After he won the Democratic primary, but before the general election, his Republican opponent charged that he wrote to the Imperial Wizard of the KKK three years after Byrd's claim that he was no longer a member. The letter contained a sentence that read, "The Klan is needed today as never before, and I'm anxious to see its rebirth here in West Virginia and in every state in the union."

This incriminating sentence would have ended the chances of almost any other candidate, and the furor it provoked was deafening. Even the governor demanded that Byrd withdraw from the Democratic ticket. Everyone was certain Byrd was finished as a politician. Even most of West Virginia's newspapers questioned his right to remain in the race, and it appeared his candidacy was over.

His friends and neighbors donated what little they could to keep Byrd's campaign going, and, miraculously, he won with 57.4 percent of the votes. Undoubtedly, had Nellie, Jack, Molly, Henry, and Tina known anything about the Klan controversy, Byrd would have had five fewer votes.

The new congressman owed part of his desire for leadership to the KKK. The first two parts of the name, Ku Klux, were derived from the Greek word *Kyklos*, which meant circle. Klan was attributed to the English word *clan*, which meant family. He joined the group in Sophia, where he owned a grocery store and was chosen as its local leader.

The Grand Dragon of the region suggested Byrd use his talents for leadership by going into politics.

As Byrd later acknowledged, "Suddenly, lights flashed in my mind, because someone important recognized my abilities."

As his political career evolved, he always claimed that his *klavern*, as local Klans were called, wasn't engaged in racial violence, and he joined because he shared its anti-communist creed. That enabled him to associate with the leading people in his part of West Virginia. The hawkish figure with the pointed nose, steely eyes, and florid words was clearly on his political way, despite a few obstacles.

Many places were suggested as the birthplace of the Ku Klux Klan, but that dubious honor actually belonged to the state of Tennessee. Six confederate veterans of the Civil War created the original KKK in Pulaski, the day before Christmas 1865. Formed ostensibly as a means of pushing back Reconstruction and its embrace of African Americans, the dreaded Klan used violence to intimidate and influence elections. Henry witnessed some Klan activities in central Connecticut in the early 1900s. The violence sometimes got so out of hand that the KKK's first Grand Wizard, former Confederate General Nathan Bedford Forrest, tried unsuccessfully in 1869 to disband the organization due to its excessive violence.

The KKK spread into other southern states by 1870, bolstered by earlier attempts to resist political and economic equality for

Negroes. As the White and Black populations became somewhat equal, Blacks won elections for southern state governments. At least ten percent of them were victims of violence during those early years of Reconstruction in 1867 and 1868, including seven who were killed. Almost every southern state had some kind of KKK branch by 1870. Not well-organized and most operating on their own, they wore the signature white robes and masks and usually struck at night. Attempts to outlaw them and their pernicious activities failed.

The Klan struck in most areas where Negroes were a minority or where they constituted very small numbers. One of the worst examples of violence in a dark period known for such acts, members of the Klan burst into a county jail in South Carolina in January 1871 and lynched eight Negro prisoners. During that year, Republican state governments in the South looked to Congress for help. The result was the passage of three enforcement acts, the most notable being the Ku Klux Klan act of 1871.

Elected president in 1868, Union General and Civil War hero Hiram Ulysses S. Grant believed in equality for all and committed the use of military and police power of the U.S. government to enforce it. He ordered his generals in the South not only to execute the terms of the Reconstruction Act but also got Congress to pass the Enforcement Act, which made racial terrorism a federal offense. He created the U.S. Department of Justice by signing a bill into law on June 22, 1870, and charged the department with dealing with crimes against federal law.

He also pushed Congress to sign the Ku Klux Klan Act and didn't hesitate to send federal troops and agents to enforce it.

Thousands were arrested, many convicted, and Klan operations either went underground or were disbanded.

The 1952 elections were over in the United States. With a promise extracted from the newly installed congressman from the Sixth District to write a letter nominating Philip to the U.S. Military Academy, Jack sat on a porch chair of the sprawling farmhouse. It was an early Sunday morning in late March of 1953, and the last remnants of winter's snow were receding.

He thought mostly of David, the son he'd never met and probably never would. The letters and birthday cards were still being returned. David would be eleven, and he was probably in sixth grade. Jack's eyes moistened, as he thought of his son, something that always happened when he thought of the boy. How could his ex-wife have taken the boy without ever letting him hold his son? It was cruel and inhumane, and Jack sometimes wished harm toward Cathy and her evil father.

Each time, he collected himself and realized that such thoughts were destructive. He remembered a cogent quote from former First Lady Eleanor Roosevelt, something he always invoked at times like those: "Resentment is like taking poison and waiting for the other person to die." Also attributed to the First Lady was another relevant thought under such circumstances: "Remember that anger is only one letter short of danger."

Thinking of such sayings helped him through the always difficult times when he thought of little David.

Henry, walking onto the porch, sat beside Jack.

"Ever do something you were really ashamed of?" Jack asked.

"Yes, I did, more than a few times, my good friend. I did probably more than my share. A few happened when I played football at the Connecticut Agricultural College, which is now the University of Connecticut. In my freshman year, we played Springfield College, and we got the shit kicked out of us. They were an all-White team and didn't take kindly to Connecticut having a Negro player. I played halfback. On several occasions, I was the victim of some extracurricular stuff in the pile after I was tackled."

Jack leaned forward and smiled. "What kind of extracurricular stuff?"

"You know—the usual things. Some of those bastards tried to stick their fingers in my eyes or twist my nose or ears."

"What did you do in response that was so bad?"

"One of their dirtier players was playing with a bum knee that was wrapped up. We were in a scrum near the goal line, and he was on the ground after a tackle. One of the Springfield players brushed by me, and I pretended to lose my balance. I sat my fat ass down hard on his bad knee. He yelped like a coyote."

The old man gave a hearty laugh. "The sound of a few broken bones and tendons filled the air. I could have easily avoided it, but I enjoyed it for a while. Later, I heard he never played again, and that, too, pleased me for a short time. I came to realize my revenge was too excessive."

"He asked for it. You shouldn't feel sorry about it. An eye for an eye, my good friend."

"Thanks, but I did a few other things in the pile, like grabbing a few guys by the nuts and driving my knee into a tackler's nose."

"You did what you had to do."

"Jack, what was your come-to-Jesus moment?"

"Like you, I had more than a few. I remember playing Pitt in late October of 1939, and they had a mean linebacker. After a tackle, he always tried to drive his flat hand against your jaw and shove it up. It would snap a guy's neck, and it hurt like hell."

Henry leaned forward, eager for more. "What did you do about it?"

"On the halfback option pass play, I told our tackles to let the big goon charge in unobstructed. Remember, we had no face masks back then. I dropped back to pass," Jack said, a twinkle in his eye, "and threw the hardest, tightest spiral I ever tossed right on his ugly, fat nose. He spat out some teeth, and his nose looked like a cracked cherry. I was kicked out of the game, and Coach Crowley was really pissed. We were winning, though, and it was late in the game. It was kind of cool to see it raining Chiclets."

"You cruel bastard." Henry chuckled. "It must've felt good."

"It did, believe me, but I probably took it too far. In the locker room, after we beat Pittsburgh, Coach Crowley called us all together and asked how the team felt about my action. Almost all the guys voiced their approval. Several players said, 'He got what he deserved. He was a dirty bastard.' Coach Crowley was visibly upset and snapped, 'You're all wrong!'"

Henry smiled.

"Then he ripped me a new one," Jack said with a wry smile. "In front of the whole team, he told me I was selfish and put myself ahead of the team. You know something? He was right. I did. I was selfish and deserved that dressing down. It was my first real coaching lesson, and I never forgot it. My mantra from then on was never to put myself before the team."

"Who was the first Negro to sign a contract with the National Football League," Jack asked.

"That's easy. It was Kenny Washington of UCLA. Let me give you one. What great athlete did he play football with?"

Jack pondered that for a moment, then blurted, "Jackie Robinson."

"Right, smart ass. What a backfield that must've been. What was Kenny's number?"

"No idea."

"Thirteen, and it should have been retired, like Jackie's number forty-two."

"No argument there."

"Kenny really got screwed. He led the nation in total yards his senior year and wasn't even drafted. Finally, seven years later, he signed with the Cleveland Rams, but he only played a couple of years."

Henry continued the story of Kenny Washington. "Many people thought he was a better baseball player than Jackie, and he actually out-hit him when they played together for UCLA. In many ways, he had it even tougher than Jackie in breaking the color barrier in baseball. Football, as we both know well, is a full-contact sport, and he took a lot of punishment. I read one time when the Rams were playing Washington, some Redskins players held him down, piled on top, and rubbed chalk in his eyes. The sons of bitches in the NFL never even put him in the Hall of Fame. There were a few Negroes who played in the league when it was first formed in the twenties. Kenny was the first modern-era Negro to play."

"It just wasn't fair, Henry. A friend of mine in Buffalo once told me that the only fair thing in life is a ground ball between first and third."

"A tad cynical, but pretty darn true."

Nellie interrupted the two by storming onto the front porch and shouting, "Paula has a boyfriend! I just got off the phone with her!"

"That's nice," the two men said in unison.

"I hope it doesn't interfere with her studies," Jack added.

"Oh, come on, Mr. Negative. It'll be good for her."

"I guess so."

"He's at Amherst College, and he also wants to be a doctor. She wants us to meet him."

"Uh-oh. Sounds like it's serious."

Henry chuckled.

Paula finished her sophomore year at Smith and continued getting good grades. Meanwhile, Philip did good work at Bentley High and had a good chance to become class valedictorian.

"Boy, these kids have good genes," Molly said. "The Kellys must've been pretty smart people."

CHAPTER 32

B efore the end of the school year, Jack asked questions of the students in his history class. They had assignments to read dealing with U.S. presidential facts, and those who answered correctly were eligible for extra credits. The kids loved it because they wouldn't be penalized for giving the wrong answer. It was late May, shortly before finals.

"OK," Jack greeted them on Friday morning, "I have a few dandies for you. Get them right, and you'll get an exam point added to your final next week."

They leaned forward eagerly. Trivia was always fun, especially if it was interesting.

"Is everybody ready?" Jack asked.

"Yes!" they replied.

"The first question is...." He paused as if waiting for a drum roll. "Who is the only person who ran for president of the United States who won a majority of the popular vote and yet lost the election?"

After a brief pause, one hand shot up, then two more.

"Yes, Julie?" Jack asked. "Your hand went up first. Matt and Linda are next if you miss it."

"Samuel Tilden in 1876, when he beat Rutherford B. Hayes."

"Absolutely right. Good work! The next question is an easy one. Who was the only president to capture every single vote in the Electoral College?"

Five or more hands went up immediately. Jack was hard pressed to determine if the first one was Beth or Andy. "Help me out here."

"I think Beth beat me by an eyelash," Andy admitted.

"Thank you for your honesty. What's the answer, Beth?"

"George Washington, Mr. Morgan."

"Correct! Now here's the second-to-last question." He waited until he had their full attention. "What president won forty of the forty-eight states when he first ran for office, but he lost forty-two of them when he ran for reelection?"

A girl's hand shot up in the back row, followed by others.

"OK, Gretchen. Who was it?"

"Herbert Hoover!"

"Herbert Hoover is right. Good for you. OK, everyone. Here is the final question. What presidents of the United States died in office of natural causes. This is a tough one, and you have to get all four."

One hand went up, then was immediately withdrawn. Many of the students groaned. Thirty seconds passed without any takers.

Finally, Tommy Moran hesitantly raised his hand.

"OK, Tommy. The floor is yours."

He was a quiet boy with bright-blue eyes sitting in the second row. He had lots of pimples and stood up sheepishly to answer. "Um, William Henry Harrison. Ah, Zachary Taylor, and, um, Franklin Delano Roosevelt. I...I can't remember the fourth one."

"Try to guess."

"Grover Cleveland?"

"No. I'm sorry. Class?"

Barbara, a short girl in the front row with pigtails, raised her hand. "Warren Harding."

"Correct, Barbara. Good catch. Sorry, Tommy. You gave a noble effort."

The first of the four questions involved Tilden v. Hayes in the presidential race in 1876, one of the most, if not *the* most, interesting and controversial presidential elections in U.S. history. Samuel J. Tilden, a Democratic governor of New York, won his home state and the swing states of Connecticut, New Jersey, and Indiana on that November 7 election day. He expected to win the solid South and most of the West. His opponent was the Republican governor of Ohio, Rutherford B. Hayes. Both men went to bed that night believing Tilden had won. Most of the country's newspapers reported his victory, just as the *The Chicago Tribune* seventy-two years later mistakenly called Thomas Dewey over Harry Truman in 1948.

CHAPTER 33

It was the end of the school year, and Philip gave his best effort to be class valedictorian. He fell short of the coveted goal by several percentage points, however, and finished second in his class. His considerable disappointment was compounded by the knowledge that his sister had accomplished that difficult objective. His admission tests and forms complete, he had to endure a torturous wait to hear from West Point.

Congressman Robert Byrd did his part, as promised, and sent a copy of the endorsement letter to Jack. It was late June, and Philip would hear soon. Meanwhile, Paula finished at the top of her class again, helping make her case for admission to medical school in two years.

The mailman arrived in midafternoon on June 26, the last Friday of the month. Seeing Philip spring out of the farmhouse to greet him, Pete Henderson pulled the official-looking letter from his mailbag and waved it in his right hand.

"Here it is, Philip." He wore a broad smile. "This must be what you're waiting for."

"Thanks, Pete. He tore open the envelope, scanned it, and shouted, "I'm in! I made it!"

Pete offered him a big handshake and pat on the back. Philip raced back up the drive, whooping in excitement. He made it through the front door in what seemed like three seconds. Nellie, the first to greet him, gave him a congratulatory hug and kiss.

Hearing the racket, Henry, Molly, and Jack ran over to join the celebration. Tina was the only one not at home, counseling a battered woman at the center.

"I did it! I did it!" Philip shouted, shaking with excitement. "Thank you all so much for your encouragement. I can't believe this is happening. I have to write Mr. Byrd a letter to thank him. There's so much I need to learn and know. This is amazing. I have to call Paula."

"You did it, Kiddo," Jack said. "It was all you." He gave the young man a bear hug for a full minute.

The soon-to-be Army plebe asked to borrow Nellie's car and drove to the Bentley Library to do more research on West Point.

Over dinner that Saturday night, Philip couldn't wait to share his findings with the others. Jack barely finished saying grace before the excited young man began reciting what he learned.

"Do you realize that George Washington considered West Point to be the most-strategic point in America? He moved his Revolutionary War headquarters there in 1779. He built a great fortress on the west bank of the Hudson River that was impenetrable to the British, that...."

"Easy, Philip." Jack chuckled softly. "You need to take a breath and come up for air."

The others laughed. Philip's exuberance was infectious, and no one could remember ever seeing him so excited about anything with the possible exception of the arrival of his dog.

"It was really interesting," Philip continued. "Washington allowed Benedict Arnold to have command of West Point on June 29, 1780, and sixteen days later, the traitor offered to surrender it to the British for twenty thousand pounds of sterling and a command in the British Army. It might have worked if Arnold's contact wasn't captured, and the papers he carried revealed the surrender plans."

"That's a great history lesson, Philip," Henry said. "Why was West Point such a strategic prize?"

"The book I read said that West Point is positioned at a sharp curve on the Hudson. From there, it's easy to prevent any ships from navigating the river. Apparently, if West Point was taken by the British, our colonies would have been divided, and Washington would have been forced to retreat from New York."

"Good job, Philip," Nellie said. "By the way, Molly, Tina, and I prepared your favorite meal to celebrate. You'd better eat up."

The young man wholeheartedly devoured every morsel.

"That was delicious," Philip said. "Pot roast with all the fixings is definitely my favorite meal. Thanks for the special treatment."

"Let's break for dessert and tea," Molly said. "Then you can tell us more."

The dishes were carried into the kitchen, and the women prepared the next course.

Thirty minutes later, all were assembled in the living room. Tina made shortcake, while Molly prepared strawberries and blueberries for the biscuit topping. Vanilla ice cream completed the special red, white, and blue dessert.

After they finished their portions and settled back into their favorite chairs and sofas, Nellie said, "OK, Philip. The floor is now yours."

"Well, I don't want to bore anyone," he demurred.

"Are you kidding?" Jack asked. "We're eager to hear all about where you'll spend the next four years."

"All right. Here's some more interesting stuff I learned at the library. The first West Point graduating class was in 1802. Can anyone guess how many graduates there were?"

"Twelve?" Molly asked.

"I'd say at least forty," Henry said.

"Wrong. There were only two in that graduating class. I've got only one more thing to share with you tonight, but this is really, really interesting, especially for Jack and Henry. The West Point football field was built in 1924 and is called Michie Stadium, after Dennis Michie, who helped start football there in 1890. He was also captain and first coach of the football team. He was the first one to challenge the Naval Academy to a game, and that turned into the yearly Army-Navy game that's a pretty big rivalry."

"Neat," Jack said. "So that's how that game began."

"One more thing," Philip said. "He died in the Spanish-American war in 1898, ironically along with the Navy quarterback who he played against. The Navy player, a guy named Bagley, was the only Naval officer killed in the war."

"Son, if you can retain all of that information," Henry said, "you'll be an honors student just like you were at Bentley."

Over the following weeks, Philip received more material and information directly from the U.S. Military Academy at West Point regarding his upcoming introduction to plebe and academic life. He would depart on his journey in only two months.

Paula took the Greyhound bus home from Northampton on a drive that lasted almost eighteen hours, the delay due to a blowout of a rear tire. "It was a very scary experience," she told her family when she arrived home.

It happened on a two-lane road, and the bus swerved from side to side, scaring the passengers. They cheered and praised the driver when he successfully brought the huge vehicle to a safe stop. The wait for a new tire cost them four hours.

She was ebullient when she first saw Nellie and Jack and everyone, despite her unpleasant trip. Nellie knew what that meant, while Jack had no clue. Daisy and Quincy couldn't stop wagging their tails and showing Paula how much they missed her.

While Paula was unpacking upstairs, Nellie took Jack and Molly aside. "She's getting serious about her boyfriend."

"How do you know?" Jack asked.

"Because I'm a woman, and we have an innate sense about things like that. Right, Molly?"

"Absolutely. I saw it, too."

"Wow," Jack said meekly. "I just thought she was happy to be home."

The women laughed.

At dinner that night, Nellie winked at Molly and turned toward Paula to ask, "What's his name?"

"Blake Smithers." Her face blushed crimson. "I really like him."

"Is he the one you told us about, who also wants to be a doctor?" Nellie asked.

"Yes, he's the same one. You'd all love him, even you, Philip." She poked her brother's ribs.

"Where's he from?" Jack asked.

"Hershey, Pennsylvania."

"That's good," Molly added with a smile. "Tell him to send us some Hershey bars. Tell us a little about him."

The others leaned closer to listen.

"He's kind of short, although he's taller than me, but he's dreamy-looking with wavy dark-brown hair and the coolest, most-beautiful eyes you ever saw."

Philip sat back and moaned.

"I'd rather hear more about the chocolate bars," Jack said.

Everyone laughed, even Paula.

The news seemed to be good for the Morgan clan, including Henry and Tina. Philip kidded his sister good-naturedly about Blake Smithers for a few days, but she accepted the teasing with good grace. She knew he was happy for her, just as she was proud of him for being accepted into West Point.

The two siblings spent many hours walking and romping with their beloved Quincy and Daisy, talking about their respective plans for the future. They couldn't believe how wonderful their lives had been after the Morgans took them in, and they were extremely grateful.

Molly and Jack talked many times about having children, but their efforts weren't successful. No one knew whether her bout with the benign cyst made conception more difficult. They were in their mid-thirties in 1953, and they increasingly felt their time had come.

Molly decided to see her gynecologist and seek his counsel.

"Everything seems in order," he assured her after an exam and some tests. "I think you just have to keep trying. You never know when things might change."

In late August, Philip took a bus to West Point to begin his four years at the Military Academy. His sendoff was bittersweet. Jack and Nellie, having raised him since his parents died so tragically, felt the tug of parents letting their last child fly from the nest. The dogs moped around the property without their owners. First, they lost Paula, then Philip.

The adults were happy for the young man's success at achieving his dream. It was quite an experience for him, especially since he never spent any appreciable amount of time away from home.

At first, Philip stayed in touch with phone calls and letters.

"Look, everyone," Nellie said at dinner one night. "Here's a letter from Philip. I'll read it to you."

Hi, everybody,

You won't believe how busy I am. I've got six classes a day, some time for special instruction, and then a three-hour study hall. I also have inspections, formations, and drills. Man, by the time I go to bed, I sleep like crazy!

We start at 6 AM with training exercises, then a 7 AM formation. I have breakfast right after that at 7:30 AM before classes that run from 7:45 to 11:45.

Then there's a noon formation. Lunch and an afternoon break go from 12:05 until 1:30. My afternoon classes are from 1:30 to 3:20, and then I have soccer practice from 4 to 6, with dinner at 7 PM. After dinner, I have study hall from 9:30 to 11. We hear Taps at 11. Don't worry. I'm doing OK and hanging in there. I'm still glad to be here.

By the way, did I tell you that West Point began the tradition of class rings back in 1835 before any other school? Well, that's all for now. My love to everybody.

Philip

"Wow," Jack said when she finished. "I'm exhausted. I'm glad I never went to West Point. I don't think I could handle such a demanding regimen. Thank God it's Philip, not me."

The others nodded.

The next night at dinner, Tina suddenly announced that she and her boyfriend were getting married.

"What?" Jack asked. "I didn't even know you had a boyfriend! That's great, Tina."

"We've been seeing each other for several months. He's kind and respectful and caring—everything I could hope for. His name is Paul Gagliani, and he's the love of my life." Tears came to her eyes. "He's an attorney who did some *pro bono* legal work for the Women's Shelter. That's how we met. He's an amazing, wonderful person, and he makes me very happy."

Suddenly, she brought her left hand up from her lap and let them see her shiny new engagement ring. The women oohed and aahed and told her how beautiful it was.

"That's so wonderful, Tina," Henry and Jack exclaimed.

Nellie and Molly had already guessed about her declaration, although they hadn't met Paul yet."

"We're thrilled for you, Tina," Nellie said. "You certainly deserve it. Are you sure?"

"Absolutely. I couldn't be happier. You've been so good to me, all of you," she added, her eyes filling with tears again, "and I'm so grateful. Paul has a home, so now you'll be able to rescue someone else like you did me."

"We can't wait to meet him," Nellie said.

CHAPTER 34

The football season opener for the Bentley Bears would take place in two weeks. Jack and Henry had a lot to do to prepare the boys. As usual, the team was a work in progress, considering the lack of experience of the players.

On the way home from practice one day, Henry asked, "Why has no Army football player ever worn number twelve?"

"I don't have a clue," Jack replied.

"Because the number represents all the other Army students not on the field. It represents the spirit of the Corps. Philip told me before he left."

"OK, smart guy. What two teams played the first college football game?"

"Rutgers beat Princeton 6-4 in 1869."

"You son of a gun. How'd you know that?" Jack asked in astonishment.

"It was just sixteen years before I was born," Henry said proudly.

The 1953 season began as a disaster, with the young Bears team losing its first four games. Three victories followed in a row, and they had a faint hope for a .500 season if only they could beat their archrival Central. The Chargers lost two games and weren't playing at the same level as past Central teams.

In the last game of the year, everything seemed to go wrong for Bentley. The Bears lost again, 30-7. Jack and Henry, dumbfounded by the result, were at a loss to explain it. That was the first year in their tenure that they really believed they could beat their rival.

There was no parity in the talent levels of the two schools. Central had the best pick, and the really good players always went to the Chargers. New Coach Christy Connor came from Western Pennsylvania, where he established a winning program, and it was considered to be a privilege to play for the man. Bentley got the rejects and kids without experience, although occasionally a blue chipper slipped through Central's hands and ended up playing for the Bears. Fortunately for the Bears' coaching staff of Jack, Henry, and Cliff Hogan, the parents and school administrators recognized the inequities and challenges involved and didn't blame them for the occasional one-sided losses.

Under their collective tutelage, Bentley became a very respected adversary throughout the Mountain League, and no one, not even Central, could afford to take them for granted. The boys always played sound defense, featuring a few skilled players. The kids played hard for Jack and Henry, and all observers knew it. It was manifestly clear that both coaches set a great example for their players, who enjoyed the experience. If only they could have a breakthrough season and topple Central.

Henry, at sixty-eight and less robust, got a horrible cold in the fall that took him seven weeks to shake. Jack and Nellie feared the worst at first, but eventually, Henry rallied and regained his health and strength. Fall turned into the winter of 1954.

Early one morning at the hospital, Nellie met a new nurse who just moved to Bentley from Charleston. Gladys Peters was friendly, vivacious, and full of energy. Tall at almost five feet eleven inches, she had attractive features. Her piercing dark-brown eyes immediately caught Nellie's attention, as did her almost-perfect skin.

At sixty-two but looking more like fifty, Gladys was near retirement but loved nursing and the deep satisfaction and pride she felt in helping her patients. The two immediately became friends.

Over coffee in her first week, Gladys confided in her friend that she left a somewhat complicated situation in Charleston. It was to escape a rather officious, controlling boyfriend hell-bent on marrying her. When she refused on several occasions, he became overly aggressive until he frightened her. He had a good, steady job that prevented him from following her to Bentley, and for which she was very thankful.

Over the next few months, Nellie and Gladys became fast friends. One night, Nellie invited her to the farmhouse for dinner. While preparing the meal, she told Henry, Jack, and Molly about the new guest and asked Henry if he would watch for her car and welcome her into the house. She gave her brother and sister-in-law a knowing glance, which they didn't understand.

Soon, the sound of tires on dirt and gravel signaled Gladys' arrival. Henry jumped up from his seat on the couch, went through the door, and, ever the good host, raced down the steps to greet her.

"Jack and Molly," Nellie said, "watch this." She beckoned them to the window.

Henry was surprised when he opened the car door for her. She was as beautiful a woman as he ever saw. Dumbfounded and at a loss for words, he stammered his welcome and could barely introduce himself. She was a statuesque Negro woman, and he had not expected that.

Gladys graciously introduced herself, and the two walked up the steps to the porch and into the farmhouse to meet the rest of the family.

After the introductions and pre-dinner chatter, the five sat down to enjoy Nellie's pot roast. They had animated, easy conversation throughout the meal. Once done, they retired to the family room for dessert and more conversation.

Jack saw that Henry was quite taken by their guest. "You know, Gladys, Henry played football in college."

"Whereabouts?" she asked.

"Connecticut," Henry said, "though baseball is my first love."

"Mine, too," she said passionately. "My younger brother played in the Negro leagues and even played briefly with Jackie Robinson on the Kansas City Monarchs."

Henry's interest in her went up another notch. "That's really neat. He must've been really good."

"Actually, he'd be the first to tell you he was a scrub. He was a great fielder, but he couldn't hit. He was joining the Monarchs just as Jackie was recruited by the Brooklyn Dodgers. He got to play three games with him, and he's very proud of that."

"He should be. Jack took me on my birthday to see Robinson during his rookie year in 1947. I won't tell you how many birthdays." He chuckled.

His interest in Gladys was clear, and she seemed to feel the same about him.

The two excused themselves to take a walk after the baseball chatter. She told him how she graduated from Bennett College in North Carolina, which became an all-women's college in 1926. She entertained thoughts about becoming a physician but wasn't able to gain admission to medical school. She became a nurse instead and really enjoyed helping people.

They walked for several miles and finally realized it was pitch black outside. Henry held her hand all the way from the driveway to the house.

After thanking her hosts for a wonderful dinner and evening, Gladys said good night, and Henry walked her to her car.

"I would enjoy seeing you again, Gladys."

"I'd like that very much, Mr. Parker," she replied with a smile.

As she drove down the driveway, Henry walked back into the house with a spring to his step. When he walked in with a grin and a twinkle in his eyes, his housemates welcomed him with smiles and laughter. It was a good night.

Henry and Gladys saw each other frequently and soon attended movies and dinners and enjoyed more long walks. The old man felt younger than he had in years, and his friends were happy for him. Nellie bragged to Jack how she could just tell if a couple were suited for each other. Jack had to admit that her track record was pretty good.

CHAPTER 35

It was a cold, windy day in Bentley on a late January morning, two weeks after Henry and Gladys met, when Molly stepped into the shower before work. The hot beads of water on her back felt good, as she applied soap to her neck and shoulders.

As she moved the bar under her arms and onto her chest, she felt a small lump under her right breast. It was hard but not very big, and it didn't hurt. Initially concerned, she thought about it as water pelted her body. If it didn't hurt, it probably didn't amount to anything.

As soon as she got to the hospital for her morning shift, she would ask Nellie or another friend about it. As a nurse, she knew that most of the lumps appearing on women between the ages of twenty to fifty were benign. Since Molly Rivers Morgan was only thirty-five, she fell into the safe zone and wasn't very worried. She would check it at the soonest opportunity.

Although the two women drove to work together that day, Molly didn't mention anything to Nellie about her discovery in the shower that morning.

At her lunch break, Molly met Nellie making hot tea to go with her turkey sandwich.

"Hi, Molly," Nellie said, as her sister-in-law walked into the lunchroom. "How's it going?"

"Nellie," she began hesitantly, her hands fidgeting with her cup, "while I was showering this morning, I found a small lump under my right breast. I'm sure it's nothing."

"Was it painful?"

"No."

"Any discharge around the nipple?"

"No, I don't think so."

"Have you noticed any itching on the breast."

"Yes, now that you mention it."

"How about the underarm lymph nodes—any swelling?"

"A little but not much."

Both knew as nurses that only ten to fifteen percent of breast cancers occurred in women at their age. After age forty-five, the percentage went up exponentially.

"Is there any breast cancer in your family?"

"Not that I know of."

"That's a good sign. Just be careful. You should see Dr. Bittman. He knows breast cancer better than anyone else at the hospital."

Sensing the fear in Molly's eyes, Nellie said quickly, "You're young and healthy. I doubt it's anything, but if it is, as remote as that possibility might be, we should find out as soon as we can."

Nellie squeezed Molly's hand, as she began crying softly. Nellie held her to comfort her.

Dr. Bittman was able to fit Molly in by the end of the day. He had a great bedside manner and welcomed both nurses warmly. He had clearly gone through the situation before and recognized the fear in Molly's eyes. While he knew her from a few mutual patient encounters, he was more familiar with Nellie, having worked many cases with her.

During his examination, it was difficult to find the lump. He proceeded to her underarm and gently touched the area below her right breast. It showed signs of abrasion. Molly explained it itched for weeks.

His countenance showed concern, but he wasn't grim. "I don't want to sugarcoat this, but there are no overt signs of cancer."

Somewhat relieved, she sighed and sat back in her chair.

"We need to take an X-ray, but those aren't always conclusive. X-rays are better at detecting bone problems than finding cancer in the tissue or organs. Let's do it first thing in the morning, if you can."

"OK, Dr. Bittman," Molly replied. "I'll see you first thing. I have to work tomorrow, so is seven o'clock all right?"

"Absolutely. Let's get this done."

Molly thanked Nellie profusely for accompanying her to the doctor's office. "I don't think I heard some of what he said, so it was good that you were there, too."

The big question they discussed in the car on the way home was whether to tell Jack. They were divided. Nellie favored telling him, while Molly didn't.

After talking over the pros and cons, they agreed to tell Jack immediately if Dr. Bittman found something on the X-ray and diagnosed it as breast cancer. They felt that was a fair compromise.

Molly was quiet and fidgety throughout dinner. Jack didn't notice, but Nellie did. Even the dogs sensed something was amiss in the farmhouse that night.

They were at the hospital at seven the following morning for the X-ray. Neither slept well that night. The technician told them Dr. Bittman would look at the results and get back to Molly later in the day.

Molly went through the day in a fog, then Dr. Bittman's secretary called in the early afternoon and asked Molly to come to his office when she was off work. She agreed and immediately sought out Nellie.

She's shaking like a leaf, Nellie thought. "Of course, I'll come with you. We'll get through this, Molly. Good news or not so good, we'll get through."

Dr. Bittman greeted them warmly. "Molly, based upon my review of the X-ray and my manual examination, I'm fairly certain that the mass under your right breast is breast cancer. It may have spread to the lymph nodes under your arm."

Molly, although she tried to be brave, came close to collapsing in Nellie's arms.

"What do we do now, doctor?" Nellie asked.

"I'd recommend that I perform a Halsted radical mastectomy," he replied. "You probably know that's a surgical procedure to remove the lymph nodes, breast tissue, and breast muscle."

The declaration hit the women hard. Molly dissolved into tears and was immediately sick to her stomach. Nellie did her best to calm her down, but it didn't work. Nellie's eyes filled with tears, too.

Recognizing the despair and the women's sense of desperation, Dr. Bittman placed his hands on Molly's shoulders and tried to assuage her. "Remember that you're young, and the numbers are in your favor. You're young and strong, Molly. You must stay positive."

Those words weren't as comforting to Nellie as they were to Molly. Nellie put on a brave face and resolved to see her beloved sister-in-law through the trauma.

The operation was scheduled for Thursday, February 4, just one week off. At first, Molly resisted telling Jack, but she recognized his need to know. It would be impossible to go through the coming week as if nothing were wrong.

Jack and Henry welcomed them home that evening. Despite the women's efforts to disguise their feelings, both men sensed something was dreadfully wrong. Nellie got out the bottle of Jack Daniels and poured everyone a drink—a sign that something was up. A warm fire crackled in the fireplace, although they weren't aware of it.

Jack broke the silence. "Well, what is it? What's the matter?"

Leaning forward from her seat on the couch, Molly said, "Oh, Jack.... I have breast cancer." She immediately leaped to his side, and he opened his arms to envelop her.

"Don't worry, Molly," he said. "We'll get through this and beat it."

She managed to smile through her tears, while the dogs instinctively came up to Molly and placed their heads in her lap to offer comfort. Henry offered the same sentiment as Jack and kept a stoic expression, although his eyes glistened in the soft firelight.

During dinner, Molly could barely swallow any of her food. Nellie was almost as bad. Gloom permeated the room despite all attempts to stifle it.

Molly and Nellie spent a good part of that week learning as much as they could about the Halsted procedure. William S. Halsted, a prominent young surgeon at Johns Hopkins, first performed a radical mastectomy in the United States in 1882. In 1954, it was the standard of care, but it was very difficult for the patient. Unless the surgeon was absolutely positive that the lump was malignant, she would go under anesthesia without knowing if she would wake up with or without her breast.

Dr. Bittman was quite sure it was malignant, although he wasn't absolutely certain. If it was malignant, she would undergo a radical mastectomy and wake up without a breast. If she were fortunate, and the lump was benign, she would not. Undergoing anesthesia without knowing was enormously stressful and a traumatic injustice to women patients, but it was the norm in those days.

The wait until February 4 was excruciating. Neither Molly nor Nellie could sleep those few days. Fear of the unknown was the principal offender, but Molly was anxious about other issues. Would Jack still find her attractive? Would he feel sorry for her? Would her condition affect their intimate moments?

She explained her concerns to Nellie, who quickly pooh-poohed them. Finally, when Molly's anxieties persisted, Nellie urged her to have a frank discussion with her husband, but she alerted Jack about it, too.

Three nights before the surgery, Molly said, "Jack, I'm very worried you won't find me attractive anymore if I come home without my breast."

He promptly held her in his arms and reassured her everything would be fine. "Moll, I didn't marry you for your breasts. I don't love you because of your breasts. Nothing will change no matter what Dr. Bittman does or doesn't do. As long as you're well and healthy, nothing else matters."

His answer reassured her enough that she didn't bother asking other questions. As she lay in his arms, it was the first restful night she had since she heard Dr. Bittman's sobering words.

Molly wasn't the only resident of the sprawling farmhouse on Mountain View Road who had a health problem. Although Gladys definitely made Henry feel years younger, getting him out and about for long walks and day trips five months short of his sixty-ninth birthday, he was finally showing signs of slowing down. His creeping arthritis manifested itself in his knees and shoulders. He started having nose bleeds and chronic headaches without any warning.

The previous week, while moving a few school desks as part of his regular custodial duties, blood dripped from his nostril. That night, in addition to a few before it, he had headaches so severe that he thought his head would explode.

Molly and Nellie thought it might be high blood pressure. Between the two of them and Gladys, they convinced him to see a doctor and arranged an appointment for the following day.

"You were right," he said, thanking them after his appointment. "It was high blood pressure. The doc said we can get it under control. He gave me a prescription, and I have to cut back on salt and caffeine. No more three cups a day for me."

It was very good news that his condition could be controlled, but there was still an elephant in the house regarding Molly's upcoming surgery.

Thursday, February 4, was a dank, miserable day in Bentley, West Virginia. It was cold, and faint mist fell over the town. The farmhouse was a busy place at six o'clock in the morning, when everyone got out of bed. Molly couldn't have anything to eat or drink, and the rest had muffins and juice while Molly got ready.

At the hospital, Henry and Jack waited faithfully in the waiting room with Nellie. All were at the hospital at seven o'clock when Dr. Bittman's nurse asked for Molly to come and prepare for surgery. Despite having the day off, Gladys came to the hospital that day to offer her support. All of them hugged Molly. Jack whispered in her ear, "I love you so much. Everything will be all right."

Fighting back tears, Molly followed the nurse through the double doors.

Although Nellie accompanied Molly for her initial visits with various medical personnel concerning her case, she wasn't allowed in the operating room. Molly was anxious but brave, worried but resolute. The worst thing was not knowing. Would she still have two breasts when she woke up? Her four cheerleaders were also filled with apprehension, although they didn't dare speak about it.

When Nellie returned to the waiting room, she suggested they go to the cafeteria and have a cup of coffee and a doughnut. The men welcomed the distraction. With Gladys' help, Henry tried to be a good patient and had orange juice instead of coffee. Nellie smiled and commended him for it.

When they finished their refreshments, they returned to the waiting room and sat down.

After nearly ninety minutes, Nellie said, "I guess Dr. Bittman decided a radical mastectomy was needed. Otherwise, Molly would have been out by now."

An hour later, Dr. Bittman appeared. All four shot up from their seats when he emerged through the swinging green doors.

"She's doing fine, but I had to perform a full radical mastectomy. I'm confident I got everything. The lump was malignant. I removed her right breast, the underlying chest muscle, and the lymph nodes. We believe it was best that way. Otherwise, the cancer could spread."

"Is there anything else, doctor?" asked Jack, clearly shaken.

"Yes." He placed a hand on Jack's shoulder. "She'll need a full month of radiation and a lot of prayers. She's young and strong, but these things aren't foolproof. I can't sugarcoat this for you," he said solemnly. "Sometimes, the cancer returns. Pray often that it won't. We'll talk more in several days when things are settled."

"When can we see her?"

"Jack, she'll want to see you, but she's still very, very groggy. You should go in for only one or two minutes just to let her know you're here and will see her again in a little while. All of you should give her an hour or so to recuperate. Nellie, I see no reason why you can't be at her bedside right now. When she discovers her breast is gone, she'll be very upset and will need your helping hand. You must tell her again that the cancer is gone, and that's good news. Gladys and the men can join you in about an hour. I'll come in at that time, too."

"Thanks, Dr. Bittman," Jack said. "When does radiation start?"

"Probably in a little over a month. Her tissue needs time to heal." He walked back through the swinging doors.

All four held hands and thanked the Lord for giving Molly a second chance.

"Remember, guys," Nellie cautioned. "She'll feel incomplete, as if she lost part of her femininity. We must be very compassionate, understanding, and patient. Jack, be aware of mood swings and perhaps erratic thinking. Molly has to come to grips with the fact that she no longer has a breast."

Jack followed Nellie through the swinging doors and kissed his wife's forehead, telling her he loved her and would see her in an hour when she was up for it. She smiled weakly at him and drifted off to sleep.

Nellie spent the next hour sitting with her sister-in-law and stroking her arm, reassuring her she would be OK.

A little over an hour later, Jack, Henry, and Gladys walked in. Molly and Nellie were holding hands, and both women had been crying.

"Hi, hon," Jack said, bending over to kiss her forehead.

Henry and Gladys patted her hand and told her she would be fine.

"We're here for you, Molly," Henry said. "We care for you a great deal."

Dr. Bittman arrived soon and reviewed with Molly that he had to do a radical mastectomy. She would stay in the hospital for several days. Once her wound healed, she would begin radiation treatments.

"I know this is a lot to take in," he said. "I'll see you every day while you're here, so you can ask me questions. The surgical nurses will explain how to care for your wound when the time comes, but right now, you need a lot of rest. Your family can stay another fifteen minutes, then they have to leave, so you can sleep."

He nodded to Jack and the others, who reciprocated.

After several days in the hospital, Molly was finally released to return home to the warm, welcoming farmhouse. During her hospital stay, many coworkers stopped in to offer their best wishes, bringing flowers and balloons to cheer her up. Although she enjoyed the visits, she wasn't her usual upbeat, happy self.

Jack and Henry came in several times a day. Because Nellie and Gladys were at the hospital, they stopped in often to see her and check on her spirits. Tina visited a few times at the hospital and also stopped by the farmhouse occasionally. Cards and flowers arrived from Paula and Philip and Jack's parents. Her parents appeared often at her bedside. Molly felt loved.

The understandable crying spells lasted two weeks, then the courageous woman seemed to regenerate. There were a few more crying jags after that, but only the callous and insensitive wouldn't understand them. Even Daisy and Quincy sensed her mood and followed Molly around the house. They were appreciatively cuddled and patted on the head for their unwavering support and companionship.

Since Molly wouldn't be working at the hospital for several weeks, various colleagues and friends stopped by to say hello and bring her flowers or treats to raise her spirits. The mood in the farmhouse remained positive and upbeat to help Molly get through her ordeal.

Almost Heaven

After five weeks, Molly was eligible and healed enough to undergo a daily radiation treatment. She was back at work by then, although on a reduced schedule, so it was convenient for her to receive her treatments right at the hospital. She napped most afternoons, as the combination of emotions and radiation treatments tired her.

CHAPTER 36

Tina Tompkins and Paul Gagliani were married in April, in a small, modest, intimate ceremony, and Nellie served as maid of honor. The couple planned to drive down to Key West, Florida, a trip of almost eleven hundred miles, for a ten-day honeymoon. Everyone was happy to see Tina have a second chance at happiness, particularly after her first marriage turned out so badly. She thanked Henry again for saving her life, but the old man, as always, was gracious and modest about that grisly night's events.

Jack, Molly, Nellie, Henry, and Gladys saw the happy couple off and returned to the farmhouse in a good mood. It was a stressful few weeks for everyone, but Molly was regaining her strength and had completed her daily radiation treatments.

They were in the mood to celebrate, so Jack opened a bottle of sparkling wine to toast the newlyweds and give thanks for a healthy future for all of them.

"Here, here!" the others said, basking in the warmth of genuine love and companionship.

On the first Friday in early May, Jack greeted his history class with the question, "Who was the first U.S. president not born in either Virginia or Massachusetts?"

At first, no hands went up, then Jimmy Rogers, a slight, pimply lad with red hair, raised his hand for a moment before withdrawing it. His classmates laughed.

"Give it a try, Jimmy," Jack said.

"Um, ah, Martin Van Buren?"

"Is he right, class?"

"No, sir," Doug Evans in the front row said.

"Well, then Doug, who was it?"

"Andrew Jackson."

"You're correct, Mr. Evans. Well done. Jimmy, you were off only by one. Jackson was the seventh president, while Van Buren was the eighth. OK, one more. Three U.S. presidents died on July fourth. Name them."

Carol in the third row immediately raised her hand. "John Adams, Jefferson, and Monroe."

"Right. You guys are getting pretty good at this. OK, one last thing. Does anyone know of a special achievement recorded just yesterday?"

"I do, sir," Bob Lombardi, a young man who excelled at soccer and track, said.

"OK, Bob. Tell us what happened."

"Roger Bannister from Great Britain became the first man to run the mile in less than four minutes."

"Right again, Bob. It's getting really hard to stump you guys."

Grades were in by the end of June. Paula finished at the top of her junior year class at Smith. Philip did almost as well as a plebe at West Point, finishing in the top quarter of his class.

At Mountain View, all eyes were on Molly. She returned to work. Though she was doing well, and her spirits were good, if she got as much as a simple head cold, everyone worried that meant her cancer was back. If she coughed, Jack grew agitated and uneasy. If she could make it through five years, the survival rate increased considerably. Before five years, her chances were fifty-fifty. No one was more aware of that than Jack and Nellie. All of the household remained positive and vigilant.

It seemed as if time flew, and another year passed. All were glad no untoward events struck anyone in the household. That June in 1955, Paula graduated third in her class and *summa cum laude*. Her chances of getting into Yale Medical School, the second major step on her way to becoming a neurosurgeon, were greatly enhanced. Philip also concluded a banner sophomore year by finishing in the top ten of his class—not an easy feat in a military academy.

On more than one occasion, Jack mentioned to Nellie and Molly, "Those Kelly parents must've been very bright people to pass along such exceptional genes to those two kids."

With everyone home from school in July, at dinner one night Molly asked about Paula's scholastic achievement. "I never understood the different between *magna cum laude* and *summa cum laude*."

"I was never that concerned about them," Jack said, "because I was never in contention for either one."

The others laughed, especially Henry, who really enjoyed self-deprecation.

After the merriment subsided, Paula said, "*Cum laude* means with honor. *Magna cum laude* means with great honor, while *summa cum laude* means with greatest honor."

"Wow!" Molly said. "You got the best possible!"

"Again, everyone," Jack said, "I want you to know that *cum laude* was never in my stars."

"Paula," Nellie said, "we're all so proud of you, and you, too, Philip. You both had amazing years."

A few weeks later, Paula heard she'd been accepted at medical school. Her academic career at Smith was so distinguished that her professors assured her she didn't need to apply anywhere but Yale Medical School.

Philip, now a junior at West Point, was having a wonderful time despite the rigorous curriculum and physical activity. He declared he wanted to spend the rest of his life in military service.

The rest of the 1950s were momentous for all the residents of 7 Mountain View Road. Molly was cancer free, much to everyone's relief. Paula finished her four years of medical school and began a long, difficult five-year residency in neurosurgery. It was quite impressive to realize she was the only woman in the program. Her romance with Blake Smithers, which had seemed promising, petered out. She found it was almost impossible to maintain a serious relationship through medical school due to the enormous amount of work and study required. It was the same for Smithers, and the couple parted amicably.

Philip finished his four years at West Point and was sent to South Korea as an Army attaché, having graduated as a commissioned second lieutenant.

Nellie took a month off her job at the hospital to be with her aging parents in Buffalo. They all spoke on the phone at least once a week, but, while they weren't frail, neither was in good enough health to travel to West Virginia on their own. Nellie tried to convince them to move to the farmhouse with Jack and her, but they were set in their ways and had a good support system, including their hometown doctors.

They functioned relatively well in their own home, but Nellie told Jack and Molly that soon at least one of them would need additional hands-on care. She had a good visit, and she met with their doctors to find out the truth about their health conditions and to give them her contact information if there was anything she and Jack needed to know. Then they went shopping for new clothes that would be easier to put on and take off. Nellie made sure there was minimal risk of falling from scatter rugs or anything else in the house. The Morgans agreed to move into the downstairs bedroom so they wouldn't have to climb the stairs anymore. Nellie helped them move their belongings into that comfortable room that looked out over the backyard garden.

Nellie prepared meals for them and filled their freezer with precooked dinners they could just heat up. They enjoyed each other's company, reminiscing over old times and catching up on the Buffalo gossip and the goings-on in Bentley.

When it was time for her to leave, Nellie pleaded with them to consider one more time the idea of moving in with her and Jack. "Please think about it, Mom. We'd love to have you both with us. We certainly would feel better. There's plenty of room in the farmhouse, and you could bring your own furniture if you wanted to."

Mary winked at her husband and hugged Nellie tightly. "We'll think about it, honey. We really will. I promise."

John nodded, and they walked her to her car. After more hugs and tears, Nellie left them standing in the driveway, waving vigorously and blowing kisses to her. When she looked at them in the rearview mirror, she knew they would stay in Buffalo forever.

Jack and Henry continued with the vicissitudes of coaching, trying to build a football program that would rival Central's. Victory over the Chargers proved an elusive prize, but both coaches were confident it would happen eventually, although they couldn't guess when.

Henry was fond of saying, "Come hell or high water," whenever he was asked about it.

Henry and Gladys were very fond of each other and managed to spend a lot of time together out and about, at Gladys' house, or at the farmhouse, where Gladys always felt at home. She was wonderful company for Molly, and they often cooked meals or did crafts together.

Nellie became the head of nursing at Bentley Hospital, and, while she dated occasionally, finding a Prince Charming in a small town like Bentley was a formidable task. She wasn't actively looking for him, but a relationship would provide a nice balance in her life. She was deeply committed to her parents and her job. That was fine for now.

The mid-1950s could not be mentioned in West Virginia without a discussion of basketball. It became apparent to college basketball observers from around the country that the Mountain State's own Jerry West was a very special player. He was born into a poor family in Cheylan, West Virginia, on May 28, 1938, to a housewife and coal mine electrician and was dealt a devastating blow at the age of twelve when his older brother died in the Korean War.

He was small and frail as a young boy. There was little to suggest he would become a player, much less a basketball icon and one of the best who ever played the game. Jerry Alan West soon established himself as not only one of the best high school players ever in West Virginia but also one of the finest in the country. He was an All-American during his senior year at East Bank High School and could have attended college anywhere he pleased. Rejecting over sixty offers from interested universities, he chose to stay at home and entered West Virginia University.

In those days, freshmen weren't allowed to play on the varsity team. West had three great years at WVU and averaged 29.3 points a game in his final season. Almost everyone in the state over the age of eight watched West and the WVU basketball team play its final game against the University of California for the NCAA Championship on March 21, 1959. West scored twenty-eight points and snared eleven rebounds, but Cal won in a heart-breaking final score of 71-70. It didn't matter to the great Jerry West that he was the high scorer and the MVP in the tournament. The always modest, unassuming West also led his U.S. Olympic team to a gold medal in 1960.

Jerry West spent fourteen years in the NBA, garnering All-Star honors each year. Considered one of the greatest college and professional players of all time, the West Virginian brought another honor to his state. The eventual choice for the NBA's iconic logo was based on a photo of Jerry West dribbling a ball up the court.

CHAPTER 37

J anuary 1960 brought heavy snows and bitter cold weather to Bentley.

"Holy cow!" Jack exclaimed, as he and Henry sat before a warm fire in the farmhouse.

It was Sunday afternoon, January 17, and they were both reading the newspaper.

"What's up, Jack?" Henry asked.

"It says here that Martin Luther King, Jr., is coming to West Virginia next week to preach in Charleston. Do you want to go?"

"Of course I do. Mind if I bring Gladys?"

"Of course not."

The service featuring Dr. King would be held at eleven o'clock in the morning at the First Baptist Church. If they left at nine o'clock, they could drive the sixty miles in an hour and a half, unless the snow continued mounting up as it had for the past two weeks.

The famous Baptist minister just turned thirty-one nine days before his scheduled appearance in Charleston, and the Negro community eagerly awaited his arrival. He first gained notoriety during a seminal event involving a fifty-year-old woman four years earlier.

She was a Negro named Rosa Parks, who boarded a Cleveland Avenue bus in Montgomery, Alabama, on the evening of December 1, 1955. She took a seat in the first row of the colored section in the middle of the bus. As the bus went to make its scheduled stops, all the seats in the White section filled up, leaving several patrons standing.

The bus driver noticed and signaled to Ms. Parks and several other Negro passengers that they had to give up their seats. Three of them did so reluctantly, but Rosa Parks refused to budge.

When she refused the driver's second entreaty, she was arrested and booked for violating the Montgomery City Code. A trial one week later found her guilty and subject to a ten-dollar fine and a four-dollar court fee.

On the night of her arrest, the head of the NAACP Chapter met with Martin Luther King, Jr., and several other civil rights leaders to plan a citywide boycott in protest of the egregious action. King was elected the group's leader, because he was young, articulate, and a family man with professional standing.

"We have no alternative but to protest," he said in his first speech as the group's president, "for we have shown an amazing patience. But we come here tonight to be saved from that patience that makes us patient with anything less than freedom and justice."

The bus boycott lasted three hundred and eighty-two days and forced boycotting Negroes to walk to work and endure shameful acts of harassment and intimidation. King's home was attacked.

After several court cases and large financial losses, the city of Montgomery finally lifted the law mandating segregated public transportation. One year later, the group helped found the Southern Christian Leadership Conference (SCLC,) which helped organize nonviolent protests to promote civil rights reform.

The following year, the SCLC sponsored numerous meetings in key cities across the South to register Black voters. Dr. King spoke at almost all of these rallies and lectured across the country on race-related issues. The year before he came to Charleston, he traveled to India to visit the birthplace of Mahatma Gandhi in the coastal city of Porbandar. The nonviolent nature of the Great Soul's protests appealed to King and increased his commitment to America's civil-rights struggles.

With Martin Luther King, Jr. being such an icon to African Americans throughout the country, Henry was as excited as he'd been thirteen years earlier when he first saw his hero, Jackie Robinson, in Pittsburgh.

"Let's leave at eight thirty instead of nine," he urged Jack, "in case we run into delays. I don't want to miss this."

On Saturday night, January 23, Henry, approaching seventy-five, could barely sleep. Gladys stayed at the farmhouse and wasn't able to get him to settle down. The two men and Gladys left for Charleston the following morning at eight fifteen. It was a cold, clear day with nary a snowflake predicted.

"Do you think I'll be the only White guy there?" Jack asked.

"I doubt it. Would it trouble you if you were?"

"Not really. Just asking."

They pulled onto Shrewsbury Street and saw the First Baptist Church ahead. It was ten thirty, and the parking lot filled quickly. Jack was fortunate to find a space. As they entered the church, there was no sign of Dr. King or anyone from his entourage, although there were plenty of other people, almost all African American. Jack felt a little strange about that, but walking in with Henry and Gladys comforted him.

The three nodded and said hello to everyone they met. All were polite and friendly, despite a look of, "What are you doing here?" Jack perceived from several in the audience.

They squeezed into the fourteenth row of the beautiful, ornate old structure. As Jack looked around, he was amazed at the number of people in attendance. The entire hall was full, as was the balcony behind him. People stood in the aisles and lined up along both sides of the church. A few Whites were scattered throughout the mostly African American multitude, but that didn't matter.

There was a hush of anticipation, as Dr. King entered the church and approached the podium to begin his talk. The words that particularly stood out for Henry came halfway through Dr. King's remarks.

"If you compete on the basis of being a Negro, you have failed to matriculate in the university of integration. Do the best you can in whatever you do. If you become a street sweeper, sweep the streets like Raphael painted his pictures. Sweep the streets like Michelangelo carved in stone."

Henry swelled with pride, as he listened to Dr. King, because he knew that was what he was trying to accomplish as a school janitor and football coach. He gave everything he had every day, always doing his best, and Martin Luther King applauded him for it.

Gladys, sensing the strong emotion coming from Henry, held his hand.

King's final words were equally powerful. "Progress is not inevitable, and we must work unceasingly for first-class citizenship, but we mustn't use second-class means to get it."

Instead of leaving right after his powerful sermon, the three visitors from Bentley tried to navigate the crowd to shake hands with Dr. King. Unfortunately, everyone else had the same idea, and it took forty minutes just to get close to the man.

Jack encouraged Gladys to go first, then Henry.

"Congratulations and thank you, Dr. King," they said, while pumping his hand. "Your words were so inspirational."

"What's your name, young man?" Dr. King asked Henry with a smile and a wink.

"Henry, sir, Henry Parker. This is my lady friend, Gladys."

"Well, Henry and Gladys, it's a pleasure to meet you both."

How they wished they could spend more time with the famous preacher, but they felt the restlessness of the impatient crowd behind them, all wishing the same thing.

After Jack met the civil rights leader, the three went out the door on their way to their car.

Henry gushed over what it meant for him to meet Dr. King. "Jack, he even asked my name! I'll never forget this day. First, Jackie Robinson, now Dr. King. How can I ever thank you for giving me these unbelievable experiences? Thank you, my friend."

"It was my pleasure and my privilege." Jack intertwined his arms with Henry and Gladys and walked proudly toward the car.

One week later, four Negro college students staged a sit-in protest at a Whites-only lunch counter at Woolworth's in Greensboro, North Carolina, two hundred and forty-five miles southeast of Charleston. That incident touched off a chain of events that culminated in the integration of lunch counters, including the one in Greensboro, in July of that year. The nation's spotlight was on civil rights.

The trip home to Bentley was filled with conversation, ranging from excitement to reflection. Jack felt a sense of gratification that he'd been able to provide Henry with two of the most-memorable days of his life.

When they arrived at the farmhouse, they bolted from the car and rushed up the steps to tell Molly and Nellie about their exciting day.

"You won't believe what happened!" Jack shouted, as he raced through the door.

Both women sat on the couch, while Jack's wife sobbed uncontrollably, as Nellie tried unsuccessfully to console her.

"My God," he said. "What happened? What's the matter?"

"Molly found a lump in her other breast," Nellie choked out.

"Shit!" he shouted. "Shit, shit, shit! It's been six years since the operation. Five was supposed to be the magic number!"

He quickly joined them on the couch and held Molly in his arms. "It's OK, sweetheart. We'll get through this. Besides, it could be benign."

Something told him deep inside that it wasn't, but it was important he maintain a brave face. He greatly admired his sister's *sangfroid* through any crisis, particularly the latest threat. They would see Dr. Bittman in the morning. In the meantime, they would do some serious praying and hope for the best.

Jack feared the worst.

When the commotion subsided, Molly insisted on hearing about their trip to see Dr. King. She and Nellie had to work that day and couldn't go. Henry, Gladys, and Jack described their day and shaking hands with the famous preacher.

"He even asked me my name," Henry said excitedly.

Even with those words of enthusiasm, any observer could see how difficult it was to penetrate the somber mood. Molly was terrified almost out of her wits, and there was little anyone could do to dispel it.

On Monday morning, Dr. Bittman rearranged his schedule to accommodate seeing Nellie and Molly. His examination was inconclusive.

"An X-ray needs to be taken," he said. "Try not to worry about it." Sensing her fear, he tried to assuage her, but he didn't have much luck.

The X-ray that afternoon confirmed it was a mass that could be cancerous. Dr. Bittman saw the seriousness of the situation and scheduled a procedure for Thursday that week.

Everyone knew the potential for a frightening scenario because a recurrence of cancer would significantly lessen Molly's chances of survival.

The following few days were difficult beyond imagination. Molly's mind raced. Would she wake up after the procedure to find she lost her other breast? Was that the last vestige of her femininity? Would Jack still love her and find her attractive? Would she survive?

She struggled with such thoughts despite Jack's assurances that even the worse result wouldn't have any bearing on his love for her. Nellie, Jack, Gladys, and Henry continued their attempts to buoy Molly's confidence and convince her the lump could be benign, although it was a losing battle.

Molly was certain it was malignant, and her life was in jeopardy. All their cajoling did little to lift her spirits. She was a strong, selfless woman, but the emotional burden was too great. She appreciated their efforts and tried her best to think otherwise, but she believed the handwriting was on the wall.

When Molly came out of the anesthesia that Wednesday morning, she didn't need to look at her breast. The combined looks of Dr. Mark Bittman and Nellie told her everything.

The lump was cancerous.

Nellie held Molly's hand, and they both dissolved into tears. Fighting through her tears and the emotional and physical trauma of the procedure, Molly heard the doctor speaking, but she couldn't comprehend the words.

I'm going to die, she thought.

What troubled her was the cruelty of it all, especially after she passed the five-year litmus test for cancer patients.

Jack wished it had happened to him instead. The chances of another recurrence of cancer were greater than ever, and, as Dr. Bittman said, "There's no sugarcoating this."

Molly remained at the hospital for three more nights, and the Morgan clan spent much of that time with her.

"We all know what this means," Nellie reminded them late on the third night at the farmhouse. "We're going to have to work full-time to lift her spirits. Her psyche is very fragile, and she'll be waiting for the other shoe to drop. We must be calm and optimistic. The odds are against her, but we can't allow her to give up or think we have. People survive a recurrence of breast cancer, but the numbers aren't good."

Nellie felt the need to speak frankly. Although she wanted to be positive, she didn't want to lead Jack into thinking the situation would be easy or, in the long run, a simple transition.

Jack brought Molly home from the hospital on Sunday morning, and everyone tried to placate her without sounding too patronizing. It was a difficult balance, but Molly was an extraordinary patient. She tried to be upbeat and positive, although Jack heard her crying softly upstairs in their room almost every other night.

The radiation treatments would begin in early April and would last thirty days.

After the first week, Molly said in the car, "I'm going to die, anyway. Why bother with radiation?"

He held her hand tightly and replied, "That won't happen."

"What do I do if the cancer returns?"

He didn't have an answer. No one did.

Nellie knew several breast-cancer survivor patients, and she was assiduous in contacting all of them. Three lost both their breasts in separate procedures, as Molly had, and they were the first she called. All were local, although two were in their sixties.

The other, an attractive, raven-haired woman in her mid-forties, would be the perfect match for the distraught Molly Morgan. Nellie arranged a meeting for the three of them over lunch.

Carol Hopper wore her hair long and straight and had a captivating, inviting smile. Of medium height, she was slender and possessed a pixie nose and high cheekbones. She went through two reconstructive surgeries well after each radical mastectomy, and she admitted they made her feel better about herself.

She assured Molly, "There is life after mastectomies. I refused to consider the possibility of a recurrence. If it happens, it happens," she said matter-of-factly.

"However, there's one important thing you need, and that's a supportive husband and family. If you have both," she said, taking Molly's hand across the table, "then you're home free. I won't allow myself to consider a possible recurrence of cancer as a Sword of Damocles."

Molly understood the intent but not the metaphor. People didn't use that term often, but it was apropos for the discussion.

In modern times, it meant a sense of impending doom hanging over a person. It came from the writings of the Roman politician, Cicero, who was a superb orator and philosopher. His point was that death looms over all of us, and we need to try to be happy despite that eventual ending.

As the luncheon ended, Molly looked into Carol's eyes and thanked her for her inspirational words. "You've put a new face on our affliction. I can't tell you how much your words and example mean to me. I hope we can be friends."

"Absolutely."

"I'm lucky to have such a supportive husband. You can see that my sister-in-law is here for me, too."

"I can see that. Let's do this again soon."

Nellie knew that Molly's peace of mind wouldn't last, and she would be subject to future crying jags and periods of depression. Meeting someone else who experienced all that her sister-in-law endured was an important tonic. She would make sure those monthly meetings continued.

It was early April before Molly healed enough to undergo one month of radiation treatments. The last time she endured that ordeal, she was surprised that the treatments didn't sap all her energy. She felt pretty good after each one, although she often napped for an hour.

This time was different. Each session enervated her to the extent that she required a nap or some rest just to function properly. Dr. Bittman didn't know whether to attribute that to the aging process or some other unknown factor, but that month of treatments took a far greater toll on Molly than the first time. She became drawn in the face, and her cheeks sagged.

To make it worse, she knew it. Tough and resilient as she was, life went on, and she soldiered through her discomfort like the brave patient she was. She and Carol met frequently, sometimes without Nellie, and they developed a strong bond. Her new friend's optimism was infectious, and she always felt better after a visit with her. There was no doubt of Jack's devotion to her, and their marriage remained strong.

Gradually, Molly's strength returned, or most of it. She looked less haggard and wan.

CHAPTER 38

T he year 1960 brought a new election. There were a host of Democratic candidates for president, but a young, vibrant senator from Massachusetts named John F. Kennedy quickly became the front runner.

On Monday, April 11, Kennedy ended a full day of campaigning with a rally in the Bentley Town Hall. The 1960 Democratic presidential primary provided West Virginia with the rare opportunity to play a salient role in the direction of a national political party. Prior to that, the state hadn't influenced the policies of the federal government. Economically and politically isolated from voters in sister states, West Virginians weren't able to avail themselves of the same technological advancements many other Americans enjoyed.

Those were the issues when Minnesota Senator Hubert Humphrey and John Kennedy tangled in the West Virginia primary. At least one out of six were unemployed, and almost as many depended on surplus government food. Only one out of three residents had finished high school. Less than one percent of the country worked in the mining industry, but fully ten percent of West Virginians made their entire living from coal mining.

Things grew worse for the Mountain State after World War II, when coal production decreased over twenty percent, and almost forty-five thousand miners lost their jobs. Advanced technology and modern techniques decreased the need for coal miners, and, in some cases, one machine was capable of replacing fifty employees. The lifeblood of the state's economy, the coal industry, began a downward spiral.

At thirty percent, Bentley suffered the highest unemployment of any area in the country. In the past ten years, at seven percent, West Virginia had the highest population decrease of any state in the union. In stark contrast to those numbers, it enjoyed a robust four percent increase from 1940 to 1950, when Jack and Nellie moved to the Mountain State. To compound the economic woes, there were less than one hundred miles of interstate highway, which ranked thirty-seventh compared to the other states.

When John F. Kennedy and Hubert Humphrey came to West Virginia in April 1960, seeking votes, many homes lacked running water and electricity. Many people didn't have radios and only a few had television sets. More than a few political pundits felt that a Kennedy defeat in West Virginia would be catastrophic to his overall hopes of capturing the Democratic nomination. To make matters worse for him, Senator Robert Byrd, the fiddler politician, backed Humphrey. Early polls suggested a decisive win for the Minnesota senator.

Jack, Henry, Molly, Gladys, and Nellie eagerly set out for the Bentley Town Hall that April afternoon to hear what Kennedy might do to ease the burdens for them and their neighbors. Several hundred townsfolk filled the building.

Kennedy's closing comments resonated with the attendees. "Why should one state prosper, while another suffers? The Eisenhower administration is talking about prosperity, but they haven't been to West Virginia. The state has been forgotten by the White House."

Later that month, he elaborated on his Bentley remarks by presenting a rather detailed outline of his program to revitalize the state. He would increase unemployment benefits and amplify food distribution. He would create a youth conservation corps to provide jobs for the young and would try to emulate many of the FDR policies that so endeared West Virginia voters to him.

Another frequently spoken comment separated Kennedy from Humphrey. His supporters reminded voters, thirty-five percent of whom were veterans, that Humphrey had not served in the military.

One of Kennedy's more acerbic comments was, "He's a good Democrat, but I don't know where he was in World War II."

That contrasted with Kennedy's valorous service, helping doom the Minnesota senator. Humphrey supporters tried to counter with charges that the Kennedy machine bought the election, but it was too late. The Massachusetts candidate won the May 10 primary resoundingly by a 61-39 margin. Such a decisive victory by a Catholic candidate in a heavily protestant state put to rest religious concerns that were raised about whether a Catholic could be elected president. Humphrey withdrew as a candidate, and Kennedy narrowly defeated Republican Richard Nixon for the presidency.

Something amusing came out of the Hubert Humphrey campaign. Anyone who knew the Minnesota senator or watched him on what proved to be an unsuccessful journey to the presidency was well aware of his penchant for talking and affinity for verbosity.

One day he was speaking on the radio and talked endlessly about a certain issue, as was his custom, when the host felt impelled to interrupt him due to the station's time constraints.

The host told Humphrey and his radio audience, "We have time for one more question, but we don't have time for one more of your answers."

That was how it was for the avuncular man from Minnesota who could more than hold his own with anyone when it came to just plain talking.

CHAPTER 39

As for Jack and Henry's Bentley football team, they had yet another two forgettable seasons. Winners of only two games in 1960 and 1961, they ended the last season being stomped by Central, 50-0. It proved a bitter end to an already disappointing campaign and was the worst record compiled by the two coaches in their tenure.

Paula, in the third year of her neurosurgical residency program at Yale, was still the sole female.

Philip continued moving up the ranks in his Army career and had attained the rank of sergeant major and clearly enjoyed it.

Molly remained upbeat with the help of her friend, Carol Hopper, and the rest of the family continued in good health.

Daisy and Quincy, both almost twelve years old, were displaying signs of arthritis. It was increasingly difficult for them to navigate the porch stairs, especially Quincy, and Nellie and Jack prepared their foster children for the inevitable. Soon, renal failure claimed Quincy, and his sister missed him so much, they considered getting another dog as her companion. She sniffed around all the places where Quincy slept, and she often whimpered into the late afternoon.

On a late March day in 1962, Nellie came home and found Daisy sleeping on the porch, or so she appeared. She was dead, perhaps of a broken heart. It was a very sad day for the residents of 7 Mountain View Road, who fought to contain their tears. The pups had lived for almost twelve years and brought much happiness and joy to those who lived in the sprawling farmhouse. Paula and Philip had been away for several years, between schools and budding careers, but they remembered well how the puppies filled the emotional void when their parents were taken so suddenly.

In September 1962, still smarting from the previous season's 2-6 debacle, the coaches worked the boys particularly hard with conditioning drills. Both agreed that the team seemed to fade late in the games, and the only thing they could attribute that to was lack of training. The boys weren't thrilled about working that hard, but the coaches drummed it into them that it would pay off in the end, when winning the game was on the line.

All the additional labor made a difference in turning a losing season into a resounding success. The Bears finished with a strong 5-3 record and only a two-point loss to their nemesis, Central. Coaches Morgan and Parker also found a very reliable quarterback in Tony Kraft, a sophomore.

"Sometimes kids can come out of nowhere and become stars," Jack told Molly, "if only you give them a chance."

The boy developed quickly into a very able field general, with passing and running skills to complement his talent. There was much to look forward to for the boosters of Bentley High School football.

CHAPTER 40

On a cold, dank, mid-March day in 1963, Molly sat down to lunch in the nurses' lounge and began what had become a regular coughing jag. It was so bad she covered her mouth with a napkin—and then saw blood on it.

She'd had a persistent cough for the past week, but she attributed that to recovering from a cold. She also was more fatigued than usual and had lost her appetite, but that hadn't seemed worthy of attention or concern. The nurse in her, however, told her otherwise.

On raw days, and West Virginia in March always had more than a few of those, her bones ached. Jack and Nellie urged her to see an oncologist, but Molly feared what she might learn. The blood on the napkin gave her little choice. She had to see Dr. Hayward because the oncologist who supervised her past radiation treatments was away on vacation.

After telling Jack what happened, she didn't sleep well that night and nestled into his arms. She was frightened, and Jack did all he could to comfort and reassure her.

The following day, accompanied by Nellie and Carol Hopper, a reluctant, frightened patient appeared in Dr. Hayward's office.

A tall, slender, gray-haired man with thick glasses and an unseemly wart on his right cheek offered his hand and welcomed them. "I'm Dr. Hayward. Which of you is my patient?"

"I am." Molly stepped forward to take his hand. "I'm Molly Morgan. This is my sister-in-law, Nellie Kent, and my friend, Carol Hopper."

He saw Molly trembling with fear, but none of his patients were ever eager to see an oncologist.

He looked over the medical records she brought, then engaged her in a long discussion. She needed blood tests and X-rays. Dr. Hayward desperately wanted to give her good news or say something positive, but he needed to see the results first. He knew from previous consults and other patients that the prognosis wouldn't be encouraging. X-rays would determine if Molly's cancer had spread or whether she had bone cancer. A positive diagnosis would reveal bones with ragged or uneven edges, maybe holes. It occurred mostly in the long bones of the body, like the humerus in the arms or the fibula in the legs. The radiologist would interpret them and tell Dr. Hayward his findings. Molly also needed a chest X-ray to determine if cancer cells had spread into her lungs.

It took two weeks for all the X-rays and blood tests to be performed and interpreted. During that time, Molly's health deteriorated further, and she felt fatigued and weary most of the day. Her face lost color and looked drawn.

Jack wondered out loud one afternoon with Henry how anyone could be an oncologist. "I couldn't do it, seeing all those patients who are really sick and maybe dying. It must be gratifying to help people through their illnesses, but many will end up dying. I really take my hat off to those doctors."

With Henry's help, Jack tried to be positive and believe Molly had beaten the terrifying, insidious disease. All he had to do was look at his beloved wife to know deep down that she probably hadn't.

Discounting his Marine buddies, many of whom died in front of him, Jack wasn't emotionally prepared to handle the death of someone who was so close. He always put on a brave face when he was with Molly, but it was increasingly difficult to process the information and still say something positive. The oncologist hadn't even received all the results of her blood work or X-rays yet. Jack gave Molly's shoulder a gentle caress when they passed, or he kissed her cheek to show his support and concern.

Molly remained as upbeat as possible, exhibiting great courage and fortitude. Her body and bones ached, and there wasn't enough medication in the whole pharmacy to keep her pain-free.

Finally, Dr. Hayward's office called to arrange an appointment for Molly the following morning. He wouldn't comment over the phone, and his office assistant merely said he was free to see her at ten o'clock.

The two weeks of waiting hadn't gone fast enough, but once they were over, a great sense of foreboding overcame all in the farmhouse.

Nellie, Jack, Henry, Gladys, and Molly were in the doctor's waiting room by nine thirty. Just after ten, the assistant ushered them into Dr. Hayward's rather small office.

"Is it all right to have all these people with you?" Dr. Hayward asked Molly.

She nodded, clearly needing all the support she could muster. He tried very hard to be cheerful and not let on prematurely his discouraging news. Jack and Nellie sat on either side of Molly each holding a hand. Henry, an integral part of the family, sat with Gladys on the far side of his best friend.

"Molly," Dr. Hayward said, taking a deep breath, "the news is not good."

As her eyes welled with tears, Jack and Nellie squeezed her hands hard.

"The chest X-rays show that the cancer has spread into your lungs." He gave them a moment to digest that. "Other X-rays detected several masses that could be cancer cells near two organs and into the fibula and humerus bones. X-rays aren't, by any means, a perfect diagnostic tool, but both bones on the left side show ragged edges and a few holes, which are consistent with bone cancer."

The dazed friends tuned out his words. Molly froze and didn't show any emotion, although tears kept running down her cheeks. All were in shock, but Nellie, inured to such unpleasant happenings after more than twenty years in nursing, was terribly sad but calm upon hearing what amounted to a death sentence.

No one spoke. None of them wanted to volunteer any thought, nor could anyone seem to get words out.

Finally, Molly asked, "How much time do I have?"

"I'm so sorry, Mrs. Morgan. Possibly a few more months. There really isn't anything we can do for you except make you comfortable."

Jack sighed and slumped in his chair before catching himself and saying, "We'll fight this, Molly. We'll win this battle."

"Others have done it," Nellie said.

The experienced realist in the room, Dr. Hayward simply said, "You may come to see me any time. We must keep your pain to a minimum and keep you as comfortable as possible."

They drove home together without a word. Finally, Henry, who was approaching his seventy-eighth birthday and was acutely aware of his advancing age, broke the silence as they pulled into the driveway. "Why couldn't it be me? Why not me instead?"

"Thanks, dear friend," Jack said, reaching to grasp the older man's hand, "but I don't want it to be you or anyone else."

As they walked into the front door and collapsed on the living room couch and chairs from mental exhaustion, there wasn't much anyone could say. Their dejected expressions told the story. Gladys attempted to lighten the mood by playing a few tunes on the piano. The others appreciated her effort, but it didn't help.

They had a somber dinner that evening. Molly insisted on opening some windows because it was a beautiful, cool spring evening. She valiantly tried to change the subject that was on all their minds, when she recalled years earlier when Henry saved them from the near carnage that Ray Tompkins attempted to inflict on them.

"Gladys, we all thought we were done for," Molly said, "then Henry saved us."

She toasted the janitor, football coach, and dear family friend.

The modest old man tried to make light of it and inject some humor. "I was trembling so much, I almost shot myself instead of that bastard."

That admission elicited a hearty laugh from all of them, including Molly.

After dinner, they agreed they were spent. They hugged each other and retreated to their respective bedrooms for the night. Jack held Molly closer than usual as she drifted off to sleep, and it was only a short time before he closed his eyes, too.

Molly Morgan accepted her fate better than her husband. After all those years and the bitter disappointment of losing the son he never saw, he finally found the sweet, lovely woman of his dreams. He would have switched roles with her in a second, and everyone knew it. She would waste away in the time she had left, and he was powerless to do anything about it.

He tried in little, everyday ways to lighten the mood and brighten her spirits, bringing her a bouquet of flowers or her favorite chocolate bar. She slept for most of the day, and pain medications were barely strong enough to sustain her. He was eternally grateful to have his sister, a nurse, able to guide them through some of the rougher times.

Occasionally, Molly had a good day. She loved to stroll the grounds of the farmhouse, poking around the garden and breathing the fresh air. Most of the time, though, she steadily languished away.

As Jack observed to Henry once, "It's like a guillotine coming down an inch at a time."

Soon, she didn't have the strength to leave the house. While Molly enjoyed the fresh air while sitting on the porch, even that effort became too laborious and was sheer drudgery.

Throughout the ordeal, brave and resolute Molly never complained. It was difficult for Jack and the extended family to see her struggle just to rise from her chair, and he sometimes had to excuse himself to step outside and cry alone. Above all else, he didn't want to see his courageous wife in that state where he visibly lost all hope.

Try as he might, he couldn't keep his deep sorrow hidden from his students. They knew what the couple was going through, because that was what it was like to live in a small, friendly town. He couldn't contain the emotion of feeling sorry for himself as well as Molly. He knew it was selfish, but he couldn't help himself. It wasn't just her world being rocked. It was his, too. The worst times were when the pain meds didn't work well enough, and he saw her suffering and wincing in pain.

Although chemotherapy was developed in the 1940s, its use in 1963 wasn't very sophisticated. Dr. Hayward tried a few treatments, but they ravaged her so much, he gave up. They did nothing more than stabilize for a very short period of time what had clearly become a limited, poor quality of life for his patient. There was nothing anyone could do for that once vibrant, energetic woman. Death would be a blessing for her, and although no one mentioned it, that was what all of them prayed for—including Molly.

Death took Molly at nine thirty-three on a sunny morning in mid-May. It was Wednesday, May 15, and Jack would always remember it. At Molly's bedside were Jack, Nellie, Carol Hopper, Gladys, and Henry.

Molly's last words were sadly, "I'm so sorry. I love you all. I don't want to leave you."

Then she was gone.

While gloom and sadness pervaded the farmhouse, relief was evident, too. She was at peace with the world, up in heaven and no longer in pain. When the others left her bedside, Jack remained with his beloved, lifeless wife, her cold hand in his, and wept unashamedly and uncontrollably.

The coroner eventually arrived and officially pronounced her dead, and Molly made her final journey to the funeral home.

That Saturday, there was a memorial service and burial. It was a bright, sunny, spring morning with daffodils and tulips blooming. After a beautiful service, with many of Molly's hospital colleagues and friends and Jack's co-workers in attendance, Molly was laid to rest.

Jack was surprised and touched that the football team came to pay their respects. Philip and Paula came home and spent several days trying to boost their adoptive father's spirits, reminiscing about the good times and happiness the Morgan family enjoyed. There were frequent tears and lots of hugs, and Jack spent difficult nights alone in the bed he had shared with his wife, the love of his life.

Several important things kept him functioning—his loving family, including Henry and Gladys, and the thought that his beloved Molly was finally free of pain. Those were enough to sustain him.

When Jack finally returned to school and his history class, he found a gift-wrapped box with attached card on his desk. Johnny Evans, sitting in the front row and apparently designated as the class spokesman said, "This is a small token of our collective esteem for you and to help you through your grief."

He didn't open it then for fear of shedding tears in front of the class. It was clear Johnny spent time rehearsing his brief talk and must have received help with a few of the words. The mood in the room was somber and respectful.

Jack had missed the past few weeks of school due to Molly's decline and death. Upon his return to class, they resumed a discussion about U.S. presidents. Most of the kids considered the thirty-fifth president, elected just three years earlier, their favorite, if not the greatest.

After a long discussion that included comments about George Washington, Thomas Jefferson, and Abraham Lincoln, the class asked Jack to identify his favorite president.

"It's James Garfield, our twentieth president," Jack replied. "Tomorrow, I'll explain why."

When Jack got home that night, he opened the students' present to find a cuddly stuffed golden retriever. He hugged it tightly as he cried. The gift gave him an idea.

Then he read the card.

> Dear Mr. Morgan,
> We're so sorry and sad to hear of Mrs. Morgan's
> passing. We know how much you loved her. Please

know that she's in our hearts and prayers, just as you are. All of us wish there was something we could do to ease your grief.

Your History Class

Below that were the signatures of all the students in small print. He was deeply touched, and his tears returned, rolling unashamedly down his cheeks.

The next morning in class, he thanked the students profusely and sincerely for their thoughtfulness and kind message. Clearing his throat, he explained why James Garfield was his favorite president.

"As you should know, he was the second president to be assassinated. He was a man of many abilities, yet he was always modest and unassuming. Did you know that if you asked him a question in English, he could simultaneously write one answer in Greek with one hand and Latin the other?

"Here's the answer to another presidential trivia question. He was the last of seven presidents to be born in a log cabin.

"He was the only one of our thirty-five presidents to be a sitting member of the House of Representatives while elected president of the United States. What I especially liked about him was the statement he made before the November election. He made a very eloquent, politically compromising statement that somehow has been lost or overlooked in the annals of history.

"'We will stand by the Black man until the equal sunlight of liberty shall shine upon every man, Black or White, in the union.'

"One week before the November 2, 1880, election, Frederick Douglas declared at Cooper Union in New York City that his good friend Garfield must be elected. He won by only ten thousand votes, and he served for only two hundred days before he was assassinated in 1881 by a disturbed, disappointed office seeker named Charles Guiteau."

The students leaned forward, paying close attention.

"The doctors, attempting to locate the two bullets, especially the one in his back, probed with unclean fingers. Joseph Lister, the British surgeon known as the Father of Antiseptic Surgery, discovered as early as 1865 that germs caused pus and infection. Still, Garfield's treating physician, along with some who found him bleeding on the floor of the Baltimore and Potomac Train Station in Washington, D.C., thrust their fingers into his wound in a vain attempt to find the elusive bullet."

Some of the girls in the class groaned in shock.

"As you would expect, poor Garfield soon suffered from fever, chills, abscesses, and infection, all caused by germs. Many people suggested he would have survived if left alone. I admire him, because he raised himself out of poverty and worked his way through school as a janitor and carpenter. His father died before he was two-years old. Garfield persevered to become a kind, brilliant leader who would have been, in my opinion, a great president, but it was his destiny to be shot on July 2 and die on September 19."

He looked at the class. "Have any of you heard the expression, 'Ignorance is bliss?'"

Kenny Daniels, class clown, raised his hand. "I have, sir. My mother says that to me all the time."

The class erupted in laughter with a few catcalls. Jack waited for the cacophony to subside.

"Seriously, who has heard your parents say that?" Jack asked.

Almost all raised their hands.

"Tonight, you can impress them. When your dad comes home from work, ask your parents for the derivation or genesis of that expression."

Seeing perplexed looks on some faces, he added, "What I mean is, where do you think 'Ignorance is bliss' came from? Where did it start?"

As expected, not one hand went up.

"Remember Garfield's attending physician? He was considered a quack by some people, and he ignored good, sound medical advice like Joseph Lister's urging that cleanliness was vital to avoid germs, which can lead to infections, abscesses, and pus.

"What was the doctor's name? It was Dr. Willard Bliss. Some people have suggested that's where we get the expression, 'Ignorance is bliss.'"

Garfield would most likely have survived had he been shot fourteen years later, when X-rays were invented. That new machine would have located the bullet without the need to probe with dirty fingers.

"Ask your parents about that expression," Jack concluded.

He had a knack for making his classes interesting, so his students listened intently and learned.

Approximately three hundred and five miles north of Bentley, in Washington, D.C., the fiddler politician who won a seat in the U.S. Senate a few years earlier prepared for real power within that august body. While he hadn't gone to college before his political career began, he ended up graduating *cum laude* with his juris doctor from American University. His parents would have beamed to know that Robert Byrd received his diploma from U.S. President John F. Kennedy, who was the commencement speaker that day, June 10, 1963.

Byrd was on his way to do more for his beloved West Virginia, the beautiful state of rolling emerald hills, than any living person. Self-educated before he secured his law degree, he was always well read. A master of the Senate's arcane rules, he established a reputation early on for his near-encyclopedic knowledge of parliamentary procedure. No senator in either party wanted to be pitted against Robert Byrd when a rule was in question.

For the kids in Jack's class who thought John F. Kennedy was their favorite or greatest president, they were in for a real treat ten days after Byrd received his diploma in June. On June 20, 1963, the one hundredth birthday of the great state of West Virginia, President Kennedy came to Charleston, sixty miles north of Bentley, to give a speech.

When Jack heard of the president's impending visit, he did something unprecedented at Bentley High School. He asked Principal Mahon for permission to take his class on an extended field trip on that special day.

At first, the principal balked, explaining no field trip had ever gone over ten miles from the Bentley town limits. "I need a day or two to think this over," he told Jack.

By the time their conversation ended, though, Principal Mahon was almost convinced.

"Think about it, Pat," Jack urged. "Some Bentley students should be there on this historic occasion. What a great thing for the school. We could probably get the newspaper to devote a couple columns to it, and they might interview a few of the kids."

"OK, Jack. Back off," Principal Mahon said with a smile. "Let me think about it. See me before class tomorrow morning. I give you my word to consider your request carefully."

Confident that the decision would be in the affirmative, Jack had to admit he hadn't thought about the logistics. He felt the excursion would provide a welcome distraction from the loss of his wife.

The next morning, Jack appeared in Principal Mahon's office and was thrilled to hear his answer.

"It's a go, Jack," Mahon said, "but there are a few things to be done. We'll need parental approval for each student who wants to go. Then there's transportation, chaperones, and other things that only a principal would consider. Can you pull it all together?"

"You bet I can, and I will! The kids will be so excited, and it'll be a great experience for them. Frankly, it'll be one for me, too. Thanks for the opportunity, Pat."

Jack shook his hand and patted his back, then felt as if he were floating on the way back to his classroom. He couldn't wait to inform the students. It would be a special occasion before school broke for the summer vacation, something they all would remember.

Thursday morning, June 20, a school bus pulled out of the lot promptly at nine in the morning for the long-awaited field trip to begin the sixty-mile drive to Charleston. The occupants couldn't wait to hear the thirty-fifth president of the United States commemorate the day one hundred years earlier when West Virginia became the thirty-fifth state of the union. Jack told his students to study the events that led to West Virginia's becoming a state, because some of them would be asked to come before the class and discuss them. It helped that pamphlets were handed out before Kennedy's arrival, explaining how West Virginia became a state one hundred years before.

The speech was scheduled to be given in the West Virginia State Capitol. Given the outing's short time frame, it took considerable effort on the part of the students and their parents to get the required approvals, as well as from the Bentley officials. Henry and Gladys agreed to chaperone, and Nellie changed her schedule, so she came, too. Also very helpful was the Morgan clan's relationship with Senator Byrd, who had become one of the most-important members of the Senate and would also be in attendance that day. It seemed whatever Senator Byrd wanted, he got.

Jack, his students, and their chaperones were excited to be there and hear the president speak.

Early in his speech, President Kennedy said, "I would not be where I am now, I would not have some of the responsibilities I now bear, if it had not been for the people of West Virginia."

Throughout the large chamber, chests swelled with pride at those words, and they gave him a huge ovation. It was three years and ten days since Kennedy captured the West Virginia primary over Hubert Humphrey and later, a forty-six-thousand-vote victory over Richard Nixon in the Mountain State presidential election. During that arduous primary fight, Kennedy seemed to understand the state's plight and promised relief.

In his first act as president, he doubled the surplus food allotment for the state's many poor and extended the welfare benefits for the needy. He began a national food stamp program in West Virginia, and the federal aid channeled to the state increased considerably. During those three years of his presidency, West Virginia's rank in receiving defense contracts catapulted from fiftieth and last in the country up to the twenty-fifth. New buildings were built, and the parks system visibly improved. The building of a major north-south highway system also boosted the state's commerce and gave the people a sense of pride that they elected such a president. All of those accomplishments were achieved with important help from Senator Byrd.

President Kennedy's words to the audience were inspirational. "The sun does not always shine in West Virginia, but the people do."

When he finished, the acclaim he received was long and ardent. Jack's students participated whole-heartedly in the applause.

The excitement and chatter of the students lasted all the way home. The kids thanked Jack many times for the opportunity, and he knew the experience was forever imbedded in their young minds.

President Kennedy would never visit or speak in West Virginia again—but not because he didn't want to. Just one thousand days into his presidency, five months and two days after his rousing speech in Charleston, he was gunned down by an assassin in Dallas.

Still exhilarated from seeing a live president and attending the events of the previous day, members of Jack's history class filed in, buzzing with excitement.

"I'm so glad you had so much fun hearing President Kennedy on the one hundredth anniversary of West Virginia becoming a state," Jack said. "Who wants to be the first to come up here to tell us about it?"

The room became totally silent. All eyes wandered away from Jack's gaze, as if that would prevent him from calling on someone.

"I see we don't have any takers."

Still, no one made eye contact.

Instead of gently chiding them, he stepped forward and said, "Jimmy Howard."

Jimmy sat in the last row. His face sagged, as he realized he was expected to speak before the class. Hoots and catcalls came, as Jimmy, one of the seniors in the class, slipped slowly out of his chair.

Jack raised his hands palms out to calm the crowd. "You might be called upon next." He made a mental note of the biggest offenders. Tommy Peters and Bill Fellers would soon hear their names called, too.

Jimmy reached the front of the class, his face ashen, and turned toward his classmates, as Jack sat on the edge of his desk. Jimmy was a good student, quiet and a bit diffident.

"Our state," he began, "used to be part of Virginia, which was the tenth state admitted to the Union in 1788, but the people were very different from each other. The pioneering mountaineers lived in the western section, while the slave holders lived in the eastern parts. Those in the west wanted to live separately and tried to in 1769, but those efforts failed.

"Finally," Jimmy said with growing confidence, "when Virginia seceded from the union in 1861 during the Civil War, the westerners decided to stay with the union."

"Good job, Jimmy," Jack said.

His classmates applauded as he nearly ran back to his seat.

"Now, who should I call on next?" His eyes scanned the room and noted Tommy Peters and Bill Fellers. Everyone looked away.

A moment later, he looked at directly at Tommy and took a bit of pleasure from the fact that the young man began squirming in his seat. "Tommy, why don't you come up here and enlighten us?"

It was Jimmy's turn to enjoy his classmate's discomfort, as color drained from Tommy's face. There were fewer catcalls, as the other students understood the consequences of their actions.

"Well," he stammered in front of the class, "Virginia had problems, because they had two governments, one confederate, the other with the union. I believe it was fifty counties that decided to join the federal government, and it looked like Virginia would soon become two states."

"Nice work, Tommy," Jack said, as he scurried back to his chair. "Who's ready to tell us the next chapter in the story? How about you, Bill?"

The young man climbed out of his seat and awkwardly sauntered to the front of the room. Again, Jimmy enjoyed the moment.

"Well, um...Virginia was caught in a war just like the North and South in the Civil War. The more independent, western region wanted no part of secession from the Union. Its citizens hoped to create a new Virginia."

"Bill, you've done a good job getting us almost to the point of statehood for West Virginia." He looked over the classroom, as Bill returned to his seat. "Who wants to get us the rest of the way?"

Sally Simpson, a pretty, petite, dark-haired girl in the second row, raised her hand.

"Yes, Sally? Come up and tell us."

She walked to the front of the room. "Well, delegates met at Wheeling and proclaimed what they called the Newly Restored Government of West Virginia. Statehood was later approved in a referendum of the people, and a state constitution was prepared. In April 1863, President Abraham Lincoln proclaimed the admittance of our wonderful state into the union to be effective on June 20. We were there to hear President Kennedy on the hundredth anniversary of that date."

"Wonderful job, all of you. Knowing the history of the founding of our state makes the trip yesterday more meaningful, right?"

"Yes!" they responded enthusiastically.

Almost Heaven

That night, Jack, Nellie, and Henry gathered around Gladys, who was playing piano. She just finished her rendition of "It's My Party" by Leslie Gore, the top pop song. Henry tapped his wine glass with a spoon to get people's attention.

Jack and Nellie looked surprised.

"Gladys and I are getting married," the old man said. "We've been together for nine years, and I think we're young enough to take the plunge."

Jack and Nellie laughed and hugged their friends.

"When's the big day?" Nellie asked.

"We plan to elope on July 6, a Saturday," Gladys said, giggling. "Nothing fancy, just a justice of the peace."

"I hope you want us there, don't you?" Jack asked.

"Of course," they replied in unison.

Later that evening, Jack asked his friend, "Why now, Henry? You'll be seventy-eight soon."

"Jack, I'm going to be seventy-eight anyway."

They were married on a gloriously sunny Saturday in Bentley, with Jack and Nellie in attendance, then the couple drove one hundred and forty miles north to Clarksburg for a short honeymoon. They made the trip in a 1957 Chevrolet their friends gave them as a wedding gift.

"Isn't that wonderful?" Nellie asked, nudging her brother, "that they found happiness together?"

Both of them couldn't help thinking that they, too, once found the holy grail of happiness, but it slipped away.

CHAPTER 41

F or several years, the Morgan clan, particularly Nellie, had wanted to visit the Greenbrier, the beautiful, world-famous resort located sixty miles east at White Sulphur Springs. In the 1800s, it was considered the most glamorous social resort in the entire South.

The resort had a rich history. President Kennedy's parents, Joe and Rose, who had the means to go anywhere for their honeymoon in October 1914, chose the Greenbrier. Their first child, Joe, Jr., was born on July 25 the following year, and it was rumored he was conceived there.

Nestled in a beautiful, lush, green valley near the Allegheny Mountains, it opened for business around 1787. Visitors made the pilgrimage to White Sulphur Springs almost a decade before to enjoy the restorative waters. It was rumored that those soothing, sulfur waters could cure everything from rheumatism to an upset stomach.

Nellie heard from her friend Sally Gardner that the rooms were gorgeous, with beautiful drapes and exquisite wall coverings.

"Just viewing the lobby was worth the trip," Sally added.

More than a dozen times over the years, Nellie had exclaimed, "We just can't live that close to such a fantastic place without visiting it!"

Finally, the time came at the end of July, two months after Molly's passing. Jack was still in mourning and distraught about losing his beloved wife. While it wouldn't relieve his grief, Nellie thought the trip to the Greenbrier would at least be a pleasant distraction, and Henry and Gladys agreed.

The four of them piled into Jack's car on a sunny, beautiful Friday morning, July 26, and drove to the Greenbrier. It was Henry's seventy-eighth birthday, only the trip wasn't a surprise—like the one sixteen years earlier when Jack took him to see Jackie Robinson play in Pittsburgh. Brother and sister would share a two-bedroom suite, while Henry and Gladys shared their own room.

The bountiful flowers and plantings on the grounds were the first to greet them before they walked into the magnificent lobby to check in. They marveled at the lush green grass and perfectly manicured lawns as the bellman opened the front door of the resort. Inside, there were beautiful tapestries, draperies, and ornate wall coverings.

"Nellie," Gladys exclaimed, "oh, my goodness! Look at the vases full of fresh flowers all over the lobby!"

The Greenbrier was breathtaking. The bellmen were eager to share some of its rich history with incoming patrons. On the way to their rooms, they learned that the original building on the site was constructed in 1858 and was called the Grand Central Hotel. The property fell into confederate hands during the Civil War, then was recaptured by the North and almost destroyed.

Ned, the bellman, told them the impact the famous designer, Dorothy Draper, had on the Greenbrier following World War II, which served as a surgical and rehabilitation center for soldiers during the war. Her handiwork gave the resort a special reputation for grace and elegance that few, if any, resorts enjoyed.

Allegedly, Mrs. Draper's favorite movie was "Gone with the Wind," and she attributed some of her Greenbrier designs to what she saw in the film. Ironically, Margaret Mitchell, the book's author, wrote to the Greenbrier in 1936, just before the book's publication, telling the general manager of her listening as a child to many adults tell of their experiences at the resort.

From Atlanta, Georgia, Margaret Mitchell attended Smith College in Northampton, Massachusetts, for a year before becoming a newspaperwoman. Her book brought her such fame and attention, she vowed never to write another one. She was constantly beleaguered by fans either in person or over the phone. Fame brought her over one million dollars from movie and book royalties. Her death at age forty-nine, just ten years after the movie première, was shocking.

On Thursday, August 11, 1949, as she and her husband, John R. Marsh, were crossing Atlanta's Peachtree Avenue at Thirteenth Street on their way to a movie, she was mortally injured by a speeding, off-duty taxi driver. He was drunk and driving on the wrong side of the street. He had twenty-three traffic violations and should never been allowed on the road.

She lived for five days after the accident before succumbing to her injuries.

Nellie and Gladys both loved "Gone with the Wind" and were eager to see it at a special showing at the Greenbrier during their stay. Neither Jack nor Henry had seen the movie and weren't that anxious to see it, but the women prevailed.

At the beginning of the film, Gladys pointed out the dedication that Mitchell wrote: "To J. R. M." "That's her husband," she proudly exclaimed.

For years, the Greenbrier played host to many American and foreign dignitaries, socialites, famous golfers, actors, and actresses. Jack, Nellie, Henry, and Gladys strolled the resort's vast grounds. They visited the Presidents' Cottage, which housed visiting U.S. presidents and their families and had been turned into a museum. They ate lunch at the golf clubhouse.

The foursome enjoyed the beauty surrounding them. Occasionally, Jack went off alone for an hour or so, probably thinking about Molly.

When it was time to leave for Bentley, they thanked their attentive, accommodating Greenbrier staff for making their stay so enjoyable.

"We won't forget this beautiful place quickly," Henry said.

The others nodded.

On the way home, all but Jack kept up a lot of chatter and conversation.

"Jack, are you OK?" Nellie asked.

"I was just thinking how Molly would have loved that place and all the flowers," he said sadly.

The rest of the ride back was pretty quiet. It is interesting to note that Jim Justice, governor of West Virginia, later rescued the beautiful Greenbrier resort from bankruptcy.

It was August 1963, over three months since Jack lost his wife to cancer. Although there was a small respite with their visit to the Greenbrier, every day after her death was a struggle for him. It just didn't seem fair. While serving his country, his former wife divorced him and deprived him of any chance to see his son. Having spent a blissful, joyous decade with the woman of his dreams, that, too, was taken from him.

He wasn't an overly religious man, but he prayed every day and looked to Jesus Christ as his personal savior. He tried to be the kindest man he could, but where had that gotten him? Never before had he taken the Lord's name in vain, but he found himself shouting an occasional epithet intended for the Lord.

Feeling sorry for himself, he closed down on his family and friends, even Henry, and they worried about him. The only place he didn't exhibit his wounds and deep scars was in the classroom, and he wasn't sure why. Perhaps he couldn't afford to appear weak in front of those impressionable young adults. He was becoming an emotional wreck.

One night after dinner, Nellie, Gladys, and Henry asked to speak with him. That was unusual. Ordinarily, conversation among them flowed like vintage wine, without pretense. Suddenly, they felt they needed to make a reservation, so Jack felt guarded about the situation.

"Jack," Nellie said earnestly, "all three of us are worried about you. You haven't been yourself since we lost Molly. A nice young pastor just moved here from Parkersburg to replace Reverend Miller, who retired. His name is Niles Butler, and my friends have many good things to say about him. You haven't gone to church with us in three months, and you've missed some good sermons."

"But, Nell...."

"Hear me out first, damn it! I haven't finished."

Somewhat taken aback by her aggressive demeanor, he sat back, uncharacteristically submissive, and listened.

"Do you want to know why Pastor Butler left Parkersburg to move here?"

"No, but I have a feeling you're about to tell me," he said with a smirk.

"He lost his thirty-two-year-old wife in childbirth," she said sadly. "They couldn't even save the baby. He told us about it in his sermon last Sunday. He even mentioned some people suggested that the doctor made mistakes and should be sued."

She explained that Pastor Butler didn't want to do that, because it wouldn't bring back Sara or Jacob. He also knew the doctor felt bad about it and did his best. He then asked the parishioners how suing the doctor would work for anyone.

"He concluded by saying we need to forgive, and, by doing so, he felt better inside. Jack, please see him for me."

She gave a look to Henry, who took his cue.

"Jack, what do you have to lose?" Henry asked. "Please do this for all of us, including Molly. We miss you at Sunday services."

Jack sat back on the couch and thought long and hard. After several minutes, he finally said, "I'll do it, but only because you three begged me."

Two days later, on Sunday morning, September 1, the Morgan clan walked into the Presbyterian Church.

Pastor Butler spoke eloquently about Martin Luther King, Jr.'s "I Have a Dream" speech delivered in Washington, D.C., the previous Wednesday, August 28.

"Speaking before an unprecedented crowd estimated at two hundred and fifty thousand people, his speech was part of a March on Washington for jobs and freedom. Of that large number, over six thousand were White. The march originated at the Washington Monument and ended at the Lincoln Memorial, where the Baptist minister spoke from the steps. I want to quote to you from his speech what I consider the most important words, though I invite you to read the entire text.

"King was up until four in the morning the night before the speech, and a close advisor told him not to use all of that 'dream' stuff, because it would sound trite. It was a good thing he didn't follow that advice.

"Many of the attendees had already left on that long, hot, humid day and didn't stay to hear the featured speaker, who was the last of many to address the crowd. As for the seventeen-minute speech, I was especially moved by his words toward the end."

He paused, then quoted from the speech. "I have a dream today that one day, this nation will rise up and live out the true meaning of its creed: that we hold these truths to be self-evident, that all men are created equal. I have a dream that one day on the red hills of Georgia, the sons of former slaves and the sons of former slave owners will be able to sit down together at the table of brotherhood. I have a dream that my four little children will one day live in a nation where they will not be judged by the color of their skin but by the content of their character."

He concluded the day's sermon by urging peace and goodwill among all of God's children. There was scattered applause from the congregation.

Henry, Gladys, Nellie, and Jack enjoyed the sermon, although some didn't.

"The preacher shouldn't mix religion with politics," Jack heard someone say.

The foursome stayed until almost all the parishioners left the church, then went up to introduce themselves.

"We enjoyed your sermon, Pastor Butler," Nellie said.

Jack stepped forward. "Could I see you this coming week to discuss a matter?"

"Certainly."

They set a time for Tuesday afternoon, after Jack's last class. Monday was the Labor Day holiday.

Jack arrived promptly at four o'clock in search of Pastor Butler. He found the man in his small office at the rear of the building.

Pastor Butler was a very friendly man with short reddish hair, pale-blue eyes, and protruding ears. His nose and mouth seemed a tad small for his face. Of medium build, he stood very erect and greeted Jack warmly.

"I understand you lost your wife to breast cancer fairly recently, and you're having difficulty coping with your loss," he said.

"Yes, Pastor Butler. I can't seem to get over my anger."

"Jack, please call me Niles."

"Thank you, Niles. I keep thinking how unfair it is."

"Who are you angry with?"

"I guess I'm angry with God for letting it happen. Molly was such a loving, giving person who never harmed anyone. It makes no sense."

"Do you think God was responsible for it?"

"If He wasn't, He could have at least prevented it from happening. He's God, after all."

"Jack, I checked with others about you, and I find you're known as a very kind man."

"A lot of good it did me."

"I understand how you feel, but let's look at the situation. I'm not sure anyone in Bentley is more liked and respected than you are. That's quite a reputation, so I think your kindness to others has had a positive return. God doesn't make bad things happen. People do. Many bad things happen, even to good people, Jack, because of the nature of this world. I really believe that God is deeply saddened by the pain and cruelty that exists in our world, and that includes what happened to your wife and mine."

"Niles, it just hurts so much. My anger is tearing me apart."

"It tore me apart, too, my friend, then I found a place where I came to understand that bad things will eventually happen to all of us. It's how we receive and process those bad occurrences that determines how we'll receive God and experience life. We can't pray for God to make our lives problem-free, but we *can* pray for Him to give us the strength and courage to deal with them and appreciate what we still have.

"If we don't forgive Him or whomever we blame for our troubles, we'll continue to wither on the vine. Jack, bad things happen to good people, but also to bad and indifferent people. No one is spared. It eventually happens to all. It isn't God who's orchestrating or perpetuating these things. It's life and nature at work every day. God didn't cause them, but He can help us through them.

"For Molly's sake and yours, I beseech you to look to God for help, strength, and courage to get through this tragedy. If not, it will continue to gnaw at you, and you'll have nothing but regret to show for it.

"Honor Molly by forgiving God and accepting Him and the help He can give you. Your family misses you and wants you to be at peace, as do all your friends and colleagues to whom you've given so much."

As they walked toward the door for Jack to leave, Niles hugged him and told him to call if he wanted to talk again. Jack thought about their discussion all the way home. Pastor Butler made sense, yet he couldn't turn his emotions off and on like a faucet.

At least it was a start, setting Jack on the path of acceptance. As much as the other three wanted to interrogate him at dinner, they left him alone. The most he acknowledged was that he was glad he met with the pastor, and his words helped.

That same night, Jack began resuming his prayers. That was a positive sign that the healing process began, but it would take lots of time.

CHAPTER 42

T here were plenty of reasons for optimism at the Bentley High School football camp that fall. Tony Kraft, after showing great promise as a sophomore, was back, along with a host of other Bear starters. Relegated to bystander status due to his age, the newly married seventy-eight-year-old Henry appeared at every practice to help any way he could.

Jack's assistant was Hank Bennett, who played at the University of West Virginia. A hulking man who stood six feet four inches tall and weighed two hundred and forty-five pounds, he played linebacker on a good Mountaineer team that finished 8-2 in 1962.

With Hank's help, Jack decided to install a new offense based around the need to get as many plays in as possible. To accomplish that, members of the entire offense would have to be in superior condition and be ready to take positions quickly after the whistle blew to end the previous play. Eventually, the opponent's defense would wear down and wilt as the game's pace increased. Usually after the whistle blew, the defense had thirty seconds to collect itself and prepare for the next play. With a hurry-up offense, as the head coach called it, he wanted the next play to commence within twenty seconds, hopefully fifteen.

The kids would not only need to be in the best shape of their young lives, they had to embrace the new system. Jack would explain why the hurry-up offense was an effective weapon, but he entrusted the scut work of accomplishing it to his new assistant.

Hank was up to the task. He drove the boys almost mercilessly. Several of them complained at first, but eventually, all of them accepted the new concept.

"Wait till you see your opponents dragging their sorry asses at the end of the game," Hank said. "Then you'll be glad we worked so hard."

As they completed laps around the track after each practice, several boys stopped with a stitch in their sides. A few vomited. Some did both. The promise of future success was alluring enough to make them try. Two boys who didn't think the new physical regimen was worth it quit the team.

It didn't take long to find out if their efforts were warranted.

In the first game of the season against Derby, the Bears were barely holding off a bigger opponent. It was 20-13 for Derby as they entered the fourth quarter.

The Derby defense seemed to fold like a tent, and the Bentley offense exploded with twenty unanswered points to win decisively 33-20. It was a great win over a good team, and the locker room after the game was bubbling with enthusiasm.

"What have I been telling you?" yelled Hank during the bedlam.

Team Captain Joe Brady nodded. "Right on!"

The same thing happened in their next game against the Hanford Warriors. They were tied 19-19 late in the third quarter when quarterback Tony Kraft noticed some players on the Hanford defensive line with their tongues hanging out, panting.

"It's working," he told his teammates in the next huddle. "Let's see if we can up the tempo."

Increase the tempo they did, winning 33-19. Clearly, the new strategy was a rousing success, and the emphasis on physical conditioning worked.

They mowed down their opposition, especially in the second half, and found themselves unbeaten and untied in seven games, as they approached their final game of the year against arch-rival Central.

It rained all that morning, leaving the grass wet and muddy. Even with the Bears' new offense, Central was the favorite.

Late in a 20-20 tied game, Tony Kraft got the team moving. They came back from a 20-7 halftime deficit, and it was second and six at the Charger seventeen-yard line with less than two minutes to play.

Then disaster struck. Brian Fallon was the target for Kraft on a pattern that took the receiver straight down the field to the end zone, where he quickly cut left by the sideline, but he never got there. As Tony released the ball, it looked like a guaranteed touchdown, but as Brian reached the goal line and began his quick cut, he slipped on the wet grass and fell.

Pat Hardy, the Central defensive back covering him, made an easy interception on the one-yard line and scampered an unimpeded ninety-nine yards for the winning touchdown, much to the delight of the hometown crowd.

It was the toughest loss the Bears ever suffered, for players and coaches, a grim Jack Morgan admitted after the game. Only that last-minute fluke prevented them from being undefeated that season.

Jack, with Nellie's urging, decided to get a dog. He missed the affections of Daisy and Quincy. When he told Paula and Philip of his decision, they were both enthusiastic and reminded him how the dogs got them through their own grief and transition.

On a sunny Sunday morning, Jack took Henry with him to a local breeder who had placed an ad in the newspaper. After winding down a long, well-manicured driveway lined by a canopy of beautiful shade trees, they arrived at Shady Brook Farms. A beautiful yellow clapboard house with a wide, wrap-around porch greeted them at the end of the drive. Several dogs of different breeds and ages lounged on the porch, as they arrived. All their heads turned, as Henry and Jack got out of the car. The dogs got up and began wagging their tails.

A bark from a large, brown Lab prompted the front door to open, and an older, smiling couple emerged. Leo and Millie Gilmore greeted them warmly.

"Are you the gentleman who called earlier this morning?" Leo asked.

"Yes," Jack replied. "That was me."

They were led to a side yard, to a large, fenced enclosure.

"We have a few puppies from the last litter still available, and they're beautiful," Leo said.

Of the four remaining pups, a chocolate Lab puppy caught Jack's eye, and he went closer for a better look. He bent, and the puppy attempted to scale the fence to greet him. He picked up the dog and held it, while they exchanged hugs, and the dog licked him.

That was all he needed. "I'll take this one," Jack said enthusiastically. "Does he have a name yet?"

"Well," Millie said, "we call him Oscar, but he's young enough to be called whatever you like."

On the way home, Jack and Henry decided to rename the puppy Buddy.

Nellie and Gladys went to a pet store and brought back some toys, chew bones, training treats, dog dishes, a new collar, and a leash. They were excited when they greeted the new four-legged visitor and resident who joined the Morgan clan.

While a new puppy would be an adjustment for all of them, Buddy was a welcome addition to their lives.

CHAPTER 43

Presiden John F. Kennedy's aid to West Virginia was of even greater help than originally anticipated due to the newfound prominence of Japan and China in overall steel production and quality. Their reputation for quality had an adverse impact on the demand for American steel and soon elicited philippic tirades and outbursts from the steel-producing states in America, including West Virginia. Reduced demand meant lesser production and lower profits in the Mountain State.

Fortunately, Kennedy's aid in the form of greatly increased defense contracts, plus the added demand for more steel in the new buildings he promised, helped somewhat to offset the repercussions caused by the new world competitors. Moving from the fiftieth and dead last in defense contracts up to the twenty-fifth spot was largely due to Kennedy's and Robert Byrd's assistance. Byrd was in his sixth year as a U.S. senator, and he delivered for his state like no one before him. He became a member of the Senate Appropriations Committee in 1960 when JFK was elected president.

Byrd delivered millions in federal aid to his constituents in the form of roads, schools, and hospitals. His out-of-state detractors called him the "King of Pork," but appreciative voters named him the West Virginian of the twentieth century. He would be heard from again many times, although not always in a positive light.

On Friday afternoon in late November 1963, Jack was taking a late lunch hour at one thirty to have a much-needed haircut. Suddenly, the sad and horrific news reverberated throughout the barber shop.

A customer bolted in through the door. "JFK's been shot in Dallas! No one knows how badly he's hurt!"

That news was disturbing enough throughout the country, but Kennedy was especially loved in the Mountain State. Its citizens took pride in thinking they helped elect him.

In thirty minutes, almost everyone in the world knew how bad it was. Kennedy was pronounced dead at Parkland Hospital in Dallas.

After processing his initial thoughts of the slain president, Jack's mind turned to how the assassination would affect his history class. They went to Charleston only five months earlier to see him speak.

Principal Mahon recognized the traumatic impact the news would have on his students and teachers, too, so he let them all go home. Most had mothers waiting for them. Those who didn't went to a friend's house.

Jack immediately called Pastor Butler and asked him to address his class Monday morning. He contacted Pat Mahon afterward to ask his permission. The principal quickly embraced the idea and decided to have the pastor address all the students at a school assembly.

Future events complicated an already difficult, tragic event. Lee Harvey Oswald, the assassin, was killed Sunday in the first-ever nationally televised murder. Since Kennedy's funeral and procession would be held Monday, November 26, Principal Mahon canceled school that day, so the students could watch the procession on TV at home.

The following day, a Tuesday, Pastor Butler addressed the students and faculty at an assembly. Those who saw the president only a few months earlier were most affected by the tragedy.

"Students, it's very hard to explain the events that took place on Friday and Sunday," he began. "Talking with your parents and grandparents, if you can, will help you better understand what's so difficult to comprehend. It was a senseless act to kill President Kennedy, but there is evil in this world, and there are bad people living in it. Try to think of the good surrounding us every day. There's far more good than bad, but we don't always hear about those numerous positive acts.

"Not so with bad behavior. It seems we hear about those more often, and it's easy to think they're more prevalent than they really are. John F. Kennedy is the fourth out of thirty-five presidents to be assassinated, and that's a terrible tragedy, but we've had presidents since 1789—one hundred and seventy-four years.

"One of the great things about the United States of America is that, in the few times we've faced such a tragedy, the country goes on, the government goes on, and life goes on. It doesn't lessen the current tragedy in our minds, but history tells us our lives will go on, and the healing process begins right away.

"The nation mourns. We all mourn, but you must understand that things will return to normal soon. Please don't misunderstand what I've said about the assassinations. One is one too many. The nation will come together and heal as one, as we've always done. Grieve and feel shocked, as I do, but take comfort in knowing the healing process will start sooner rather than later."

Principal Mahon thanked the pastor and discharged the students to their teachers' care. Jack knew his history class would want to talk about nothing but the assassination, especially those who saw the vibrant young president only months before his life was so tragically ended. A few of the girls continually wiped away tears during the class discussion, which was a very difficult forty minutes. The students couldn't believe what just happened. Talking about it openly among themselves helped, but not much.

Jack urged them to discuss it with their parents that night. Over time, he emphasized, their sense of shock and grief would dissipate.

"I know you don't think that will happen, but trust me, it will." He wondered if it was a mistake to take the class to Charleston that day, then he decided to address the topic.

"I was just thinking I made a mistake urging you to go with me that day to see the president. Some of you might agree, and I wouldn't be surprised if some of your parents are mad at me for planning that trip."

Several mouthed the word "no" and more vigorously shook their heads.

"Thank you for that. However, some may feel upset with me, but I would do it again. You'll get over your grief and shock, but no one can ever take away from you that you saw firsthand a vibrant, young, sitting president of the United States. It was a special event, and you were there."

Whether or not he was trying to convince himself, the argument resonated with the students, and they applauded. Becoming misty-eyed, Jack smiled.

When Jack came home that afternoon of November 26, he felt exhausted by the day's events. The moment he walked through the door, any negative thoughts immediately vanished. Ten pounds of puppy love can help anyone's soul. Buddy almost knocked him over, barking, jumping, and wagging his little tail. As he picked up the frisky chocolate Lab, the little critter slobbered kisses all over his face.

"Come on, boy. Let's go outside for some business."

When they came back inside, they sat on the couch and played until Buddy fell asleep nestled against his master's side.

Yes, indeed, Jack thought. *The timing couldn't have been better to get a dog.*

Gladys' soothing music in the background also helped.

The following months were somewhat chaotic for the country what with the transition of Vice President Lyndon Johnson to the presidency. Some Americans suspected him of having had something to do with the assassination. Conspiracy theories always abound when a famous person is killed, and Kennedy's death was no exception.

On the afternoon of the assassination, Lyndon Johnson took the oath of office of the presidency aboard Air Force One on the tarmac of Dallas' Love Field. Of special note was Judge Sarah

T. Hughes swearing in the new president, becoming the only woman ever to administer the U.S. presidential oath of office.

The thirty-sixth president had been an old arm-twister as Senate Majority Leader, and he knew how to get things done. He immediately went to work to enact the programs Kennedy espoused before his untimely death. One of the most-notable, interesting measures was the passage of the Civil Rights Act of 1964.

The legislation intended to end segregation in public places and ban employment discrimination on the basis of race, color, religion, sex, or national origin. It was a struggle to find all the necessary Senate votes to pass the legislation. Robert Byrd, the influential fiddler politician who'd been in the Senate since 1958, was opposed to it. The U.S. House of Representatives passed the bill on February 10.

It was Monday, March 30, 1964, and Nellie just finished work with a patient and wandered to the nurses' lounge for a cup of coffee. The TV network NBC brought viewers up to date on the Senate's consideration of the Civil Rights Act.

It was eleven thirty in the morning when a new show called "Jeopardy" appeared on the screen. She had time to hear only the first question before she needed to report to the OR.

Art Fleming, the host of the show, asked the first questions to ever appear on the show. "These rodents first got to America by stowing away on ships," he asked the three contestants.

The correct answer was, "What are rats?"

As she left for the OR, Nellie said to Gladys, who was also watching, "I don't see this show lasting very long."

"Me, neither. I bet they don't even finish the season."

In 1964, Senate rules required a two-thirds vote, or a total of sixty-seven senators to invoke closure and cut off debate. At nine fifty-one in the morning, Wednesday, June 10, Senator Byrd finished a filibuster effort he began fourteen hours and thirteen minutes earlier on the previous evening.

As he relinquished his speaking role and took a seat in the chamber, Georgia Democrat Richard Russell, offered the final resistance, followed by Minority Leader Everett Dirksen, who spoke for proponents of the bill. In typical fashion, Dirksen was particularly eloquent and invoked a Victor Hugo quote the great author wrote in 1852. Dirksen noted that June 10 marked the one hundredth anniversary of Abraham Lincoln's nomination to a second term.

"Stronger than all of the armies is an idea whose time has come," the senator said, "The time has come for equality of opportunity in sharing government and in employment. It will not be stayed or denied, for it is here."

Never before in the history of the Senate had there been a successful effort to ward off a filibuster on a civil-rights bill. The large chamber became quiet, as the clerk began the roll call.

When he reached Clair Engle, the fifty-two-year-old Democratic senator from California, there was no response. The mortally ill Engle, who just arrived by wheelchair, was unable to speak due to a brain tumor. The Senate was quiet, as the man slowly lifted his frail arm and pointed to his eye, signifying an "aye" vote the only way he could.

John Williams from Delaware cast the decisive sixty-seventh vote, and four more were added to the tally.

Nine days later, the Senate passed the act. On July 2, 1964, President Lyndon Johnson signed the bill into law. Just twenty-eight days later, the brave California Senator Engle died from his brain tumor.

In the November election, President Johnson was elected by a record fifteen million more votes than his Republican challenger, Barry Goldwater.

CHAPTER 44

Paula finished her five-year neurosurgical residency at Yale and was ready to go out on her own. It was a long struggle to make it in a male-dominated world. The only female in her Yale residency, she would be one of only ten women in the entire country practicing neurosurgery. She came to visit the farmhouse after completing her program, and the Morgan clan, including Buddy, greeted her warmly.

Perhaps even more than Jack and Henry, Nellie and Gladys totally appreciated what Paula achieved. As nurses and women, they marveled at her dedication, discipline, and perseverance in such a monumental accomplishment.

"Your parents would be so proud of you," Nellie gushed one night over a glass of red wine. "It's hard to believe you were able to stick to such a lofty goal all the way to the end. We're proud of you, too."

Buddy, refusing to leave Paula's side, nuzzled his nose into her lap. He knew she was family.

Her commitment to medicine and achieving her objective took a toll. She had no time to pursue any love interest, save the brief interlude with Blake Smithers, and she was thirty-one and hadn't yet earned a dime.

"Most people don't realize," Nellie told Jack and Henry, "that physician training is so arduous that they don't begin making a living until they reach their thirties. Most people are in the workforce in their early or mid-twenties, while physicians are still preparing for their future."

Paula received a tempting offer from two male colleagues in her residency program to join them in a three-person practice. The only hitch was it in New Haven, Connecticut, a world apart from her beloved state of West Virginia.

"I could start on my own here in Bentley," she said, "or join my colleagues."

"Do you like and respect them?" Jack asked.

"I do, Uncle Jack. I really do."

"Perhaps you should start a practice up there with them," Nellie said, "then after you have a few years' experience, you can return here."

"That's been my thought, too, Aunt Nellie. It could be my ticket back to Bentley. I really want to come back here someday."

That night, they celebrated Paula's amazing accomplishment and the beginning of a new adventure over family dinner. Nellie and Gladys made a pot roast with roasted potatoes and carrots, a wonderful green salad, and a blueberry cobbler for dessert.

Henry raised his champagne flute and said, "Paula, not only have you done your family proud, but your adoptive family, too. I'll be happy to say I knew you when. I know you'll stay the sweet, determined, caring woman you've always been. Good luck in your new practice and new life. Cheers!"

"Hear, hear!" the others said.

There wasn't a dry eye around the table.

They slept peacefully that night.

The following morning after breakfast, Paula was on her way. They were sad to see her go, but they were happy for her, as she began a new, exciting chapter in her life. Buddy, following her to the car, waited patiently for a goodbye snuggle.

CHAPTER 45

O n an early September morning in 1964, Jack wanted to float an idea he had by Principal Mahon. They had become fast friends since their initial meeting nineteen years earlier. Pat received several offers to go to larger high schools in West Virginia, but he rejected them all, because he and his family were so happy in Bentley.

"Hi, Jack," his friend greeted him. "What's up?"

"I've been thinking about something for a long time, Pat. I think the time has come."

"Time for what?"

"Time to honor Henry for all he's given Bentley High School. He was a janitor for more than forty years, and he's been my valued assistant football coach for seventeen years before he stepped down last year. Even though he wasn't assistant coach last year, he was still here for every practice and game, and he helped Hank and me immensely."

"OK, coach." Pat raised his eyebrows. "What do you suggest?"

"I think that beginning this year and from now on, the MVP trophy that goes to the Most Valuable Player of the football team should be named the Henry Parker MVP Award. "That's very generous of you, Jack."

"Not really, Pat. He deserves it. If it's OK with you, I'd like to announce it at our football banquet in November."

"Tell you what. I'll make the executive decision right now and grant it. Henry worked hard for this school and the students. It's a fitting honor for him."

Jack was elated, as he left the office. It would be a surprise until he made the presentation after the season.

Fresh off a 7-1 record the previous year that ended so devastatingly in a last-minute loss to Central, the Bentley Bears had every reason to feel optimistic for the coming season. Their outstanding senior quarterback, Tony Kraft, looked better than ever, and the kids all relished the second year of their hurry-up offense. Hank Bennett drove the kids hard again, but, after the previous year's unqualified success, there were few complaints.

The season began wonderfully with a rousing 34-6 win over Derby. Again, the new offense ran like a machine, and the second half belonged totally to the Bears. Tony Kraft was already commanding the attention of college scouts. He had a superior game in which he ran for one touchdown and threw for two more.

The chances for a great year ended abruptly in the second game with a little more than three minutes left in the third quarter against Hartnett. Running to his right, Tony was blindsided by a defensive end who took him to the ground hard. The humerus bone in Tony's throwing arm was broken in two places, ending his high-school career. Along with it went Bentley's chances for a special season.

Sophomore Jim Clark tried his best to fill in for the absent Kraft, but he lacked seasoning, and the Bears fell to a losing 2-6 year.

At the dinner banquet after the frustrating season, Jack left the head table and headed for the podium to present the MVP award. After talking about the team and its heartbreaking season, he finally moved to the awaited, coveted award presentation for the player who was most valuable to the Bears that year. Henry still didn't know what was coming.

"This year," Jack said, "and from now on, the MVP award will be named for a very special man who has contributed so much to this school and the football program. I don't know anyone who's more worthy of having this honor named after him.

"The first winner of the Henry Parker Most Valuable Player Award is Josh Hunter. As Josh comes up to receive this award, I'd like to ask Henry Parker to come up and present the trophy."

Henry was totally floored by the honor. His eyes flushed with tears.

Hank Bennett sat beside Henry and almost had to shove the older man out of his seat. As he ambled up to the podium from the head table, Henry wiped away tears and stood beside Josh in disbelief.

All Henry managed to say was, "Thank you so much for this great honor. I've been blessed to be here at Bentley High School and to meet so many wonderful people. Josh, congratulations for winning this fine award."

People stood and cheered for the recipient and the presenter. As Henry returned to his seat, he noticed that at the back of the room of the all-male banquet stood Gladys and Nellie, holding hands and grinning while wiping away their tears.

It was a wonderful ending to a very disappointing football season. The honor accorded to Henry seemed to give him a spring in his step. Nellie, Gladys, and Jack sensed that the much-appreciated gesture added ten years to his life. That bright, distinguished gentleman was finally getting the public recognition he deserved.

Gladys and Nellie knew in advance. They, along with Buddy, gave the two men an affectionate welcome when they strode through the front door after a long evening.

CHAPTER 46

It was spring of 1968 and not much had changed with the Morgan clan except that everyone was three and a half years older. Buddy's pranks and energy helped keep the others young and on their toes. Often in the afternoon, Henry and Gladys took him for a long walk, while he retrieved sticks and looked for squirrels to chase.

Paula enjoyed her neurological career in New Haven with her two partners, and she wrote home about some of her more-difficult procedures. The others in her family thought, *of course, for a neurosurgeon, what wouldn't constitute a difficult procedure? Neurosurgery is anything but simple.*

Philip, making a career in the U.S. Army, rose to the rank of colonel. He showed no sign of slowing down. Vietnam loomed rather large on the horizon, and the American commitment was growing each day.

At eighty-two, Henry was noticeably slowing. His knees creaked. Arthritis took a toll on his hands and joints, and he recently had what he thought was a heart scare. Fortunately, it turned out to be a bout of indigestion. Such a scenario was a regular one for those a few months shy of their eighty-third birthday. Gladys, Nellie, and Jack worried about Henry's health but never in front of him.

Nellie and Gladys still worked at the hospital, loving their jobs and feeling happy they could help so many patients. Gladys, at seventy-five, worked only two half days a week, so she could watch Henry. Over the years, the women became very close friends, and it was nice to share stories at the end of the day over a glass of wine.

During those three years, Bentley fielded competitive teams, but the Central Chargers continued to beat them.

The four of them, joined by Buddy, who stretched on the floor near the top step to catch the breeze, sat on the porch on Saturday evening to listen to the radio.

The number-one song in America was Otis Redding's "Sittin' on the Dock of the Bay," and it played in the background.

At six fifteen on the morning of April 4, a voice suddenly broke in. "We interrupt this broadcast for a special news bulletin. Martin Luther King, Jr. was shot several moments ago in Memphis, Tennessee."

The occupants of the porch, except for the snoozing Lab, sat up abruptly with horrified expressions and leaned intently toward the radio.

"We don't know his condition and will bring you further information as it is received."

The music resumed.

They kept the radio on, as they retreated into the farmhouse, followed by a dog that sensed something was wrong.

An hour later, the terrible news came that the Baptist minister and civil-rights leader, whom Jack, Henry, and Gladys met eight years earlier, was dead of a lone assassin's bullet.

King's death sent shockwaves that reverberated throughout the country. Riots sprang up from coast to coast. It was also a presidential election year, and there was extra turmoil caused by an increased American presence in Vietnam. Resistance to that presence helped sitting President Lyndon Johnson decide not to stand for reelection. Several Democrats, including New York Senator Bobby Kennedy, brother of former President John F. Kennedy, slain in 1963, vied in the primaries for the nomination.

On June 6, 1968, Bobby Kennedy won the California primary and seemed in a favored position to capture the nomination. As he walked through the kitchen of the Los Angeles Ambassador Hotel, just after addressing his cheering supporters, shots rang out, and Kennedy became the second American leader to be assassinated within two months, the third in the past five years.

America was at a crossroads, and its residents started wondering who would be next. Protests were becoming the norm, and they spilled over into the August Democratic Convention held in Chicago.

Outside, tens of thousands of Vietnam protesters battled police in the streets, while inside the International Amphitheater, delegates vehemently disagreed on the party's stance toward the war. Richard Nixon, the Republican candidate, became the thirty-seventh president, partly as a result of the discord within the Democratic Party. The country tried to move on.

Eight months later, NASA gave the country something to cheer about. On the evening of July 20, 1969, like many other

Americans, Nellie, Gladys, Jack, and Henry stared at their TV set. It was a sultry, stifling Sunday night. Even Buddy, who preferred being outside on the porch in the hope of catching a breeze, gave up and ambled indoors to join the four adults.

The Apollo 11 mission to the moon was on everyone's mind. Its sole purpose was to photograph the moon walk and broadcast it back to Earth. Although it was later than usual for bedtime, the four had the TV on at 10:51:27 in the evening West Virginia time, the screen zeroed in on the lunar landing. They leaned forward intently while munching popcorn and pretzels and washing them down with Nellie's special lemonade.

Astronaut Neil Armstrong, born in Wapakoneta, Ohio, took the first step ever onto the moon's surface precisely four minutes later, and hundreds of millions of people witnessed the historic occurrence.

Unknown to those viewers who gaped in disbelief, Astronauts Armstrong, Michael Collins, and Buzz Aldrin weren't able to afford the exorbitant life insurance premiums that bordered on stratospheric for astronauts. It wasn't as if their safe return was reliably guaranteed like that of the insurance agent who returned home after writing a policy. The three men devised an ingenious plan to protect their families financially if something untoward occurred during the mission.

Before the lunar launch in July 1969, when the trio were still in prelaunch quarantine, they signed hundreds of autographs and gave them to a trusted friend. If the men didn't return safely, the friend would send all the signed autographs to each astronaut's family. That was their insurance policy—the ability to sell those autographs.

Also unknown to the TV audience that night, something NASA kept quiet, was something Buzz Aldrin did on the visit to the moon. NASA asked the astronauts not to engage in any religious activities to avoid offending the world, but Buzz couldn't pass up the opportunity. He took out a small plastic container of wine and some bread, items he took with him from Webster Presbyterian Church near Houston, Texas, where he was an elder.

He read from the Gospel of John, drank from the plastic chalice, and ate the bread in what was the first and possibly the last Holy Communion performed on the moon. Armstrong and Collins observed the one-man ceremony but didn't participate.

When Apollo 11 returned safely to Earth, the crew was summoned to Hawaii where they were asked, despite their worldwide fame, to fill out the customary forms and declarations at the security desk.

Where the form asked, "Departure from," their collective answer was, "the moon." The flight number was Apollo 11.

During that same weekend of American pride and glee, two hundred and thirty-eight thousand miles away from the moon, an equally striking event happened when Massachusetts Senator Ted Kennedy drove his Oldsmobile off the Dike Bridge, a narrow wooden structure on tiny Chappaquiddick Island, part of Martha's Vineyard, Massachusetts. The car careened into the fairly shallow Poucha Pond, but the senator escaped. Unfortunately, his passenger, Mary Jo Kopechne, wasn't as lucky. Although the car was barely submerged, Mary Jo drowned.

The accident and death hounded Kennedy for the rest of his political life and forever scarred him as a presidential candidate in the eyes of the American electorate.

CHAPTER 47

The 1969 football season was memorable for the Bentley Bears. They didn't go undefeated, and they didn't win the Mountain League, but they accomplished something more important and of far-greater significance. Although finishing the season 5-2-1, they finally defeated their archrival, the Central Chargers, for the first time.

It was a close game from start to finish, but the Bears made a big play near the end of the game. Tied 20-20 with less than one minute left in play, Bentley had the ball on the Chargers' twenty-one-yard line. Quarterback Sam Phelps dropped back to pass but didn't see an open receiver. He tucked the ball under his arm and threaded his way the entire distance to the goal line. But not before a huge block by running back, Hal Paxton, on the safety, the only opponent who had a chance to bring Phelps down short of the end zone.

The local Bentley crowd went wild. The game ended twenty seconds later. The winning Bears celebrated on the home field for over half an hour. The team carried both coaches off the field on their shoulders, and they would have carried Henry, too, if they could find him. When the old man didn't appear in the locker room afterward, Jack worried.

Unfortunately, that wasn't the first time. One week earlier, Jack dropped his friend off at Zack's Hardware to buy screws to repair a screen door on the porch. They agreed Jack would stop at the drugstore and return for Henry in ten minutes.

When he drove back to Zack's, he saw no sign of Henry. He looked inside the store but didn't see him. Puzzled, he went down the street and found his friend in the portico of Peggy Sue's Restaurant.

Jack parked the car and approached Henry hurriedly. Henry appeared lost. He recognized Jack, but he couldn't explain his whereabouts or why he'd left Zack's. While Jack didn't admonish him, he saw that his dear friend of almost a quarter century seemed disoriented.

Later that night, while alone with Gladys and Nellie, Jack told them about the incident.

"You know, Jack," Nellie said, "he just had his eighty-fourth birthday a few months ago. It's easy to be forgetful. I'm fifty-two, and I sometimes forget where I left my keys."

"I know," Jack responded, "but this was different. He looked dazed. His eyes were vacant, and he didn't know where he was."

"I've noticed his forgetfulness on several occasions recently," Gladys said. "It's happening more frequently."

The trio agreed to keep a close eye on Henry.

The incident a week later at the football field forced their hand. Instead of celebrating with the team, Henry was wandering the parking lot. Even Gladys agreed that warranted a doctor's visit.

That night, Nellie called Paula and asked her professional opinion about which doctor Henry should see for consultation.

"I'll look into it, Aunt Nellie, and get back to you tomorrow morning. Tell Gladys not to worry. From what you described, though, it's definitely time for an examination."

Paula called and said, "I scheduled an appointment for Henry next week with Dr. Peter Stevens, a neurologist."

Gladys and Nellie, who worked in the medical field, were concerned about the possibility of dementia. Although Alzheimer's disease was discovered in 1906 by the German physician Alois Alzheimer, it wasn't named until 1910. The sentinel case involved a fifty-year-old woman he identified as Auguste D. He followed her case until her death five years later in 1906, when he first reported on it.

The year before Henry's disquieting episodes, researchers developed the first cognitive measurement scales, although they were still relatively unknown.

Dr. Stevens' findings, after a thorough examination, were inconclusive.

"He showed signs of memory loss," he explained to Gladys, Nellie, and Jack, who accompanied Henry on the visit, "but it's difficult to draw any real conclusions because of his age. At eighty-four, our memories often fade. It's usually short-term memory, that of recent events, that's the first to go.

"He remembers some things very well. He knows his birthday, the president of the United States, and his address."

Once Henry was out of earshot, Dr. Stevens told Henry's loved ones, "Watch him closely and check for any unusual behavior or worsening of his memory."

Almost nine months passed without any ominous signs, and Henry's family began to think his previous spells were an aberration.

On a late August summer day, the foursome was enjoying Nellie's lemonade while reading the Sunday newspaper. Suddenly, Henry had a coughing fit he couldn't control. He was short of breath, and Gladys quickly checked his pulse, which was too high.

Suspecting possible congestive heart failure, she calmly told Nellie and Jack to prepare the car for a trip to the hospital. A few sips of water helped calm Henry's cough, but he told Gladys he was very tired. As a good nurse, she recognized his confusion or state of impaired thinking as another symptom of congestive heart disease.

They hustled him to Bentley Hospital and saw the on-call physician, Myron Rounding. After a close examination and tests, he asked Henry to stay overnight in the hospital. The old man became agitated, but Gladys and Nellie soothed him and calmed him by holding his hands and talking softly to him.

Henry expressed concern about being alone, so Jack offered to sit with him throughout the night. That, plus the sweet bedside manner of the two women, put Henry at ease.

He was checked in with a preliminary diagnosis of congestive heart failure, and further tests would be done the following day.

Once Henry was settled in his room, Dr. Rounding returned to speak with Gladys in the hallway. Jack was with Henry, and Nellie remained with Gladys.

As the nurses knew, and the doctor explained, the prognosis wasn't good. With congestive heart failure, the patient's blood backed up in the pulmonary veins because the heart couldn't keep up with the supply. Fluid built up in the lungs, causing coughing fits. Since the heart couldn't pump sufficient blood required by the body's tissues, it diverted flow away from less-vital organs, like muscles and limbs, creating a feeling of fatigue.

"It's like a domino effect," Dr. Rounding said. "One thing affects another. Further down the line, the heart beats faster to make up for the loss in pumping capacity. As for memory loss or disorientation, changing levels of certain substances in the blood, which are often a byproduct of these other phenomena, could account for confusion and impaired thinking."

The only question left was exactly how serious the illness was and what Henry's prognosis might be.

Henry's hospital stay lasted a full week before he could return to his beloved farmhouse, his home for the past twenty-five years. Buddy often rested beside Henry's chair or bed. Henry had trouble regaining any semblance of his old, robust self, and arthritis wreaked havoc with his joints. He needed numerous medications.

Even a walk to the mailbox exhausted him, and he took several naps throughout the day. Gladys tried to lift his spirits, but he was losing interest in everything.

Unfortunately, he didn't even have the energy to sit on the sidelines for Bentley football games to cheer on the boys. Without Henry there, it was a sad season for Jack. He found himself often looking over his shoulder to the sidelines to see his friend, but it was futile.

Jack admitted to his close confidants he didn't do a good coaching job that year. His heart wasn't in it. He always considered himself a consummate professional in whatever he undertook, but he felt he let the boys down. They counted on him, but he wasn't up to the task.

Any way you slice it, he told himself, *I didn't do my job and didn't really earn my paycheck.*

For a perfectionist who was accustomed to putting out whatever was necessary to achieve a goal, the thought made him feel like an abject failure. Yes, he had an excuse; he was worried about his friend, but it was unprofessional to disengage.

He considered resigning his position as head coach, but he couldn't muster the courage to do it. If it weren't for Buddy and the women, and his chance to see Henry after work, Jack would've lost all interest in coaching.

His history class interactions with the students were always positive and a pleasure, but self-doubt crept in, threatening to overwhelm him. Nellie, sensing the problem, felt powerless to help.

The football season ended on a sour note with a 55-7 drubbing from Central. Although the assistant coach did his best to take on more duties to help Jack through his difficult time, the Bears won only one game in 1970, and that debacle was clearly the fault of Jack Morgan, head coach. Henry was so weak, he wasn't able to make it to the football banquet to present the MVP award named in his honor.

The end came on February 22, 1971. Regularly in and out of the hospital by then, Henry was admitted for the second time that month on Friday night, February 19. He felt excessively weak and coughed more than usual, but Nellie, Jack, and Gladys were confident there was no immediate crisis threatening the old man's life.

The attending physician wasn't unduly concerned, either. Nellie and Jack went home that night, while Gladys stayed over. They spent most of the weekend's daylight hours at Henry's side. It rained hard on Monday, and Jack went to the hospital to visit after his classes.

Nellie looked in on Henry whenever she could during her normal duties. Gladys never left his side.

Henry must have sensed the end was near and drew his wife closer, reaching for her hand. Speaking and thinking very lucidly, which surprised her, he told her how much he enjoyed their seventeen years together.

"I'm so glad we got married," he whispered. "The past seven-and-a-half years have been the best of my life. I don't know why it took me so long to ask you."

She squeezed his hand tightly.

"I've been blessed to have you, Jack, and Nellie in my life," he said. "I remember it like it was yesterday, the first time I met you in the driveway at the farmhouse. You were the most beautiful woman I ever laid eyes on, and you still are."

His eyes grew moist, while her eyes were bathed in tears. He stopped talking and slept.

Late that afternoon, after consulting with the attending physician, they agreed Henry was deteriorating rapidly. Jack decided to join Gladys at the bedside.

By eight o'clock that night, with Henry just shy of his eighty-sixth birthday, he lapsed in and out of consciousness.

A little after nine, he summoned one final burst of energy and grasped both their hands.

"I know I'm going soon," he said. "I can feel it. Jack, you're the brother I never had. Most of the favorite moments of my life were spent with you. Gladys, thank you for loving me."

They tried to silence him, fearing the effort of talking would weaken him further, but he would have none of it.

"You took me to see Jackie Robinson, President Truman, President Kennedy, and Martin Luther King. You know, Jack, that Dr. King asked for my name?"

"I know, Henry. It was very special."

"You're the best friend I ever had." Tears trickled down his cheeks. "I was a Black man, and no one seemed to care about me, but you and Nellie took me in. Then Nellie introduced me to the most wonderful woman in the world."

Nellie had been alerted, and she stood beside a grief-stricken Gladys and her brother.

"Me, too," Jack said, as tears filled his eyes.

Henry's grip on their hands relaxed, and he was gone.

Burying his face in his hands, tears streaming down his cheeks, Jack reached for his sister and Gladys, taking their hands. He glanced at his watch and saw it was just after nine at night. Henry was dead, and their almost twenty-six-year bond of friendship was gone with him.

Jack and Nellie quietly left the room, so Gladys could have some private time with her husband. They would be waiting when she was ready to return home.

It was a quiet ride to 7 Mountain View Road, each passenger deep in thought about the man who left their lives forever. No one felt like eating anything, but Nellie convinced the others to have tea and a small sandwich. They stayed up for an hour, talking about the arrangements for the services.

With tears and a heavy heart, Gladys said, "I want a celebration of the wonderful life Henry enjoyed."

"Absolutely," Jack and Nellie said.

They hugged warmly before going to bed that night, then Nellie walked Gladys to her room.

Henry was raised a Baptist, although he hadn't attended church for at least ten years before he met Jack and Nellie. He wanted to attend the same church that they did, so he was there every Sunday at the Presbyterian church.

Gladys was happy to accompany all of them, so they sat together, along with Molly.

As Henry said more than once, "As long as I thank God, I don't think it matters to Him where the place of worship is." Then, he would break into a big smile.

The funeral home was packed, as was the church. Members of the Bentley High School family included many football players past and present, teachers, and coaches, all paying their respects to a man they admired and loved.

The service was simple. Beautiful flowers were everywhere, and the choir sang uplifting hymns. Niles Butler gave the eulogy, pointing out Henry's faith and the love he had for his adoptive family. He'd known Henry a long time and was able to provide amusing anecdotes that made the congregation nod, smile, and chuckle. Philip and Paula returned home when they heard the news. Henry was a big part of their young lives.

Philip provided a touching remembrance of his younger days, sitting on the big front porch and learning about life and gaining wisdom from his friend, Henry. Jack wanted to say a few words, but he knew he wouldn't be capable, without breaking down, so he wrote a beautiful tribute to his dear friend and had it printed on the remembrance program. Gladys bravely held Nellie's hand during the entire service.

Once the service and private, personal burial ceremony were over, a few close friends joined the family at the farmhouse for a toast and the telling of life stories. Soon, it was over. Gladys,

Jack, and Nellie were left in a daze. Their lives would continue, but there would be a vast empty space.

Gladys handled the situation with grace and courage, although, as expected, she was periodically overcome with bouts of sadness and tears. She and Henry enjoyed a beautiful friendship and a loving marriage. She was grateful for the time they'd had. Nellie was a great comfort to her, and the strong bond between the two women grew even stronger.

Jack took Henry's death very hard, which everyone expected. He spent more time than usual with Buddy, who, at the age of eight, was getting a bit old, too. There was something nurturing and comforting about having a dog, especially Buddy. Those noble creatures seemed to have an uncanny ability to sense emotions in their masters. Jack spent a lot of time walking with Buddy, napping with him, and sitting on the porch together to experience the love and affection that seemed inbred in most canines. His loyal dog kept Jack going. Slowly, time began to heal Jack's wounds.

Jack decided to dedicate the next football season to Henry. Determined not to let the boys down, he vowed he would come back with a vengeance. There was nothing he could do for the graduating seniors, a fact he lamented frequently, but he would again be the coach he was before Henry's illness and demise. He had allowed the distraction to interfere with his job and his debt to his players and assistant coach, Hank Bennett. Jack vowed that the 1971 season would be different.

CHAPTER 48

T he West Virginia economy showed progress in the late 1960s and early seventies. Due to the increased need for sand and gravel to make concrete, a major component of interstate highway and lock-and-dam projects under construction, the state's commercial construction of both underwent a huge increase. As for "king coal," that was a time when mining was politicized, and the state's miners participated in several wildcat strikes. They helped create the downward trend of coal production in the Mountain State, and it was difficult to reverse. The United States encountered strong competition in steel production from China and Japan, which didn't bode well for West Virginia. U.S. Steel in West Virginia felt the same pressure as other steel-producing facilities in the country.

In football, it was a trying, disappointing game for the Thundering Herd of Marshall University. Based in Huntington, West Virginia, the team lost a close one, 17-14, to the East Carolina Pirates at Fickler Stadium in Greenville, North Carolina. Most of the Marshall team, including the coaching staff, traveled to away games by bus, since most were within driving distance. The return trip home on November 14, 1970, by chartered aircraft, was almost canceled. Those plans changed, and Southern Airways Flight 932, a Douglas DC-9, pulled away from the gate on time at Stallings Field in Kinston, North Carolina, with seventy-five people aboard.

As the plane taxied for takeoff, everything seemed in order. The flight was uneventful until six thirty-eight p.m., as the plane was cleared for an approach on Runway 11 at Huntington, West Virginia, airport. The weather was bad, with mist, light rain, and broken clouds at five hundred feet. Visibility was poor.

Descending below the minimum descent altitude, the Douglas DC-9 struck some trees on a hillside one mile from the runway, crashed, and burned. There were no survivors.

Among the seventy-five dead were thirty-seven Marshall players, nine members of the coaching staff, including the head coach, and twenty-five team boosters from the community. The pilot and crew also perished.

The tragedy was compounded when observers learned it was the only flight the Thundering Herd took during the entire football season. It was the deadliest tragedy involving any sports team in U.S. history.

The plane dipped to the right until it was almost inverted before crashing nose-first into a hollow. There was no chance for survival. It burst into flames and left a swath of charred ground ninety-five feet wide and two hundred and seventy-nine feet long. The fuselage was so badly damaged that the National Transportation Safety Board described it as being reduced to a powder-like substance. Sadly, the remains of six passengers were never identified.

The effects of the crash echoed far beyond the Marshall campus. Among the dead were a city councilor, a state legislator, and four physicians. Seventy children lost at least one parent in the tragedy, while another eighteen were orphaned.

News of the terrible accident reverberated throughout the state. Residents spoke of it for many months. Jack and Hank spoke to the Bentley High School team about it in detail, because, as a football disaster, it seemed extra painful. Coming off their own disappointing one-win season, the Bears were already crestfallen. What happened one week after the season's ending loss to Central increased their sadness.

Two years later, a Memorial Foundation was dedicated at the entrance of the Memorial Student Center. The plaque on the base read, "They shall live in the hearts of their families and friends forever, and this memorial records their loss to the university and the community."

While nothing could truly ease the grief of West Virginians, something positive happened in the spring of 1971 to lessen the pain. The connection between John Denver and musicians Bill and Taffy Danoff served as a tonic and brought a smile to all residents of the Mountain State.

The three collaborated on a song titled "Take Me Home, Country Roads" derived from a poem written in a letter from a friend of Bill's who lived in West Virginia. It was first recorded in New York City in January 1971 and was released in April.

There were many interesting things about the song. The Danoffs originally wanted Johnny Cash to perform it and almost didn't bother to play it for Denver, thinking it didn't fit his style.

When he heard the Danoffs play the song, Denver reportedly exclaimed, "Wow. That's great! It's a hit for sure. Did you record it yet?"

"We don't have a record deal," Bill said.

Soon thereafter, the New York recording event took place. The song became John Denver's signature song, although there wasn't much in it about country roads. Danoff had considered using Massachusetts instead of West Virginia, since both were four-syllable names.

The Mountain State won out, and the song was considered an iconic symbol of the state. Far from an instant hit, the song moved very slowly up the charts until it finally took off. By August, it was number two on the Billboard singles chart.

The first words, "Almost heaven, West Virginia," struck a responsive chord for the proud residents of the Mountain State. Henry never had a chance to hear it, although he would have loved it. It was released two months after his death.

Gladys played it almost every night on the piano, and Jack and Nellie sang along.

CHAPTER 49

It was football season in September 1971, and Jack was determined to make it up to the Bentley players, the high school, and its boosters. He would never let his personal problems interfere again.

Jack always admired the successful Oklahoma Sooners football coach, Bud Wilkinson, and managed to employ one of his inspirational gambits.

In the late 1940s, the college football team posted a sign above the home locker room that stated, "Play like a Champion today!" The players and coaches touched the sign for good luck, as they went down the tunnel that led to the stadium. Wilkinson even took the sign with him to away games, posting it above the locker room door for everyone to touch on the way to the opposing field.

Jack liked the idea of a sign but thought of a better one. "How about 'Make a Difference' as a sign, Hank?" he asked one day after practice. "I like it better than the Oklahoma one."

"I like it, Jack. It makes the point that each player has to contribute."

"Make a Difference" it was. The coaches asked the high school art department to make two signs, one for home games and another for away. The boys embraced the idea immediately and took pride touching it before practice.

Assistant Coach Hank Bennett worked them in practice at a frenetic pace until they panted from exhaustion. There was little complaining because the previous year's failure was a constant reminder to all. Hank had a sign made that he kept on the sidelines during each practice. That "1-7" poster showed them their ugly record for the previous year—a statistic they all wanted to reverse.

Tom Martin, a tough junior, won out over Doug Baldwin in the contest for starting quarterback. The coaches molded the team into a squad that was on a mission and that held a team-first attitude. Sticking with their hurry-up offense, they all looked forward to their first encounter with Derby. The Bears went through the Derby Dogs like a hot knife through butter, 37-13. One game was over, and seven were yet to come.

They won their first six games, and only Hanover and Central stood in the way of an undefeated season. It was great to see the Bentley fans out in force to cheer their team. With each win, the crowd grew. The players were confident, yet their coaches reminded them that it was one game at a time. They couldn't take success for granted.

Hanover went meekly at 36-6, setting up the Bears for a big home game with Central, who lost only one game in their 6-1 season. Everything pointed to a victory late in the game.

With the Bears leading 12-7 and having the ball on the Charger thirty-five-yard line, victory was two minutes away, then the impossible happened.

Sam Darnell, the Bentley fullback who played a magnificent game, scoring both touchdowns, went into the line on a third and two. He held onto the ball with both hands, as he was instructed to do, but the Central safety ran up and yanked it free. It popped into the air. The Central defensive cornerback sprinted in and plucked the ball out of the air at full speed, scampering sixty-five yards down the sideline for the winning touchdown.

The home crowd watched in stunned silence, as he crossed the goal line. That bid goodbye to their undefeated season, but the 7-1 record was the opposite of the 1970 debacle that preceded it.

CHAPTER 50

In June 1972, Jack dated a woman named Becky Renert for six months. Although no one would ever take Molly's place, he knew in his heart Becky was the woman for him. He met her one weekend while at the pet store buying dog food and treats for Buddy. She had a little Yorkie with her and started chatting with him in the checkout line. Because they seemed to have a lot in common, including a love of dogs, Jack impulsively asked her out.

One thing led to another. She was an energetic lawyer, involved in the community and had West Virginia values. She was very attractive in many ways—looks, personality, and demeanor. Jack found himself very attracted to her in every way. They spent a lot of time together, going out to dinner and the movies, hiking in the West Virginia hills, and listening to their favorite music. Buddy and Peanut, Becky's dog, became close friends.

It was nine years since Jack lost Molly on that sad May 15, and it was finally time to marry again. He wasn't certain what Becky would say, but she hadn't given him any indication she would refuse.

They were dining in a nice, upscale restaurant in nearby Hanover, and Jack decided that was the night he would propose. Nellie met Becky several times and liked her. Gladys gave Jack a "thumbs-up," too.

While they never directly discussed marriage, Jack hinted about it a few times. Becky was married previously, but her husband died of cancer seven years into their marriage, around the time Molly suffered the same fate. They both endured personal tragedies, and those discussions helped bring them together. Jack was married twice, but the first marriage almost didn't count. Becky was infused with great empathy for those who experienced substantial pain in their lives. It seemed to be in her DNA, and she was genuinely touched by Jack's story of a son he never met.

As he pulled on a jacket over his long-sleeved shirt, Jack was filled with great expectations for the dinner. He picked Becky up at her apartment promptly at seven. After a short, chatty drive, they were seated at their table in La Monico's by seven twenty. Jack hadn't been nervous all day, but now that his proposal was forthcoming, he felt tension creeping into his pores.

La Monico's specialized in roast beef, so they ordered theirs medium rare.

It's possible that this marriage could be made in heaven, Jack thought.

They even ate the same food. Both had salads, baked potato, and broccoli. They engaged in comfortable banter as they waited for their food, each having a slice of crusty Italian bread with butter. Neither wanted the seasoned dipping olive oil. He looked across the table and was taken by Becky's beauty. She was in her early fifties but looked ten years younger. Becky's raven hair was thick and short. Her pale-blue eyes seemed capable of seeing right through him. He loved her full red lips and rather pert nose. Her prominent cheekbones gave her a regal look, and Jack knew the other men in the restaurant were aware of her.

As dessert and coffee drew to a close, he contemplated his next move. Should he get the waiter involved? Should he distract Becky for a moment and drop the ring into her water glass?

He rejected both ideas, because they required some degree of flair and were out of character for him. He took another look at her beautiful eyes, sipped some water, and thought, *here goes.*

He reached across the table and took her right hand in his. She didn't resist, although she looked surprised and stopped her story about a recent court case in mid-sentence.

"Becky Renert," he said, trying not to sound officious, "we've known each other for six months or so, and I think you're very special." He wanted to add more, but he was nervous and forgot his train of thought. "Becky, I love you and would like to ask you to be my wife. Will you marry me?"

He fumbled in his jacket pocket with his free hand and took out a tiny velvet box, presenting it to her.

"I don't know what to say, Jack."

There are many favorable responses to a marriage proposal, but that isn't one of them, he thought.

"How about 'yes?'" he asked, feeling surprised. *Don't grovel,* he reminded himself. *Whatever you do, don't grovel!*

She sensed his embarrassment. "Jack, you're a wonderful man, and any woman would be proud to be married to you."

If that isn't the kiss of death, what is? he wondered.

"I don't know if you can understand this, Jack. I love you, too, but I'm not in love with you."

Son of a bitch. I know exactly what her next words will be. She'll say it's her, not me.

"It's me, Jack, not you." She was trying to let him down as gently as possible.

He'd never been so embarrassed in his life except when he passed gas loudly in church during a moment of complete silence. The nearby parishioners knew he was the culprit.

This situation was different. He'd put his emotions on the line, and all he had to show for it was a big rejection. His mouth went dry, and he didn't know what to say.

I love you, but I'm not in love with you? What the hell does that mean? What does that little word "in" mean? It must be gibberish and bullshit. It must mean something like, "You're an OK guy, but I don't want you in my life other than for an occasional meal."

The short ride home was inexorably long and quiet. There wasn't anything left to say. When he saw her to the door, she apologized again and repeated that he was a wonderful man. For some reason, he apologized, too, then tried to smooth over the whole thing.

"I'm sorry it didn't work out, Becky. You're a special woman." He left without even kissing her cheek.

On the way home, he berated himself repeatedly. It was hard enough to accept the wrong answer, but to be thoroughly embarrassed over the whole shabby incident was hard to take.

Their paths never crossed again.

Nellie and Gladys were watching TV when Jack returned.

"When does Gladys get to meet the future Mrs. Morgan?" Nellie asked, clearly not thinking there was any possibility he would have been rejected.

"She won't. Apparently, she loves me but isn't in love with me. What is it with you women?"

He stalked from the room and went to bed with a bruised ego and heavy heart.

Nellie waved to Jack, as he stepped through the door one afternoon. She whispered, "Mom's on the phone. Get on the extension. It's not good news."

John Morgan had been ill for six months, having been diagnosed with hypertension and chronic respiratory problems. Although they spoke to their parents every week, John's condition hadn't been shared with either of them, and it came as a surprise. John lived a good life and would be ninety on his next birthday—if he lived to see it. He'd been in the hospital several times in the past few months, but the situation was serious.

"I think both of you should fly up," Mary said. "The doctor isn't sure he'll last another week."

"Mom, why didn't you and Dad tell us sooner?" Nellie pleaded.

"We would have been there for you," Jack added.

"He didn't want to say anything." She stifled a sob. "You know your father—the old Don't Tell Anyone."

"Oh, God, Mom. You've been dealing with this all by yourself," Jack said. "We're so sorry. We'll be there tomorrow."

After giving Gladys the news, she assured them she'd watch over the house and take care of Buddy, then hugged them both.

"It's hard losing someone you love," Gladys said. "Goodness knows we can relate to that. Yet, as we all know, there's a time for all of us. While I don't know your mother, please give her my love."

Nellie and Jack were on a plane to Buffalo the following morning. Once aboard and settled in, they became lost in thought for the duration of the trip.

Jack enjoyed a special bond with his father. Many sons acknowledge such bonds, but theirs was special. He held more respect for his father than for any other man. He considered him the most intelligent man he ever met. It didn't matter that John never attended college. Few Americans went to college in the early 1900s. John was a carpenter like his father, and his family needed him home. College wasn't a good fit for him.

He was a voracious reader who eagerly consumed all the classics. A master wordsmith, he loved pithy quotations and often penned letters to magazines and newspapers.

As the plane leveled off on the way to New York City, then Buffalo, Jack sat back in his seat, silently reminiscing about the times he spent with the old man. His father loved fishing and enjoyed baseball. Jack loved hearing the stories John told about the past.

They walked to Offermann Stadium to see the Buffalo Bisons play, often taking in a double-header. Strangely, the stadium was built without any adjacent public parking. It was only a fifteen-minute walk from their house to the corner of Michigan Avenue and Ferry Street.

Jack's first visit was in 1929, when he was only eleven. The Bisons had played there since 1889. The ballpark was built with second-hand lumber hauled from Olympic Park in another part of the city. Before the first game held in the stadium, there was a huge problem. The contractor, who hauled all that lumber for eight hundred dollars, wasn't paid. He didn't take kindly to the oversight.

On opening day, he stood at the stadium gate with a shotgun cradled under his left arm. No one would go anywhere, nor would there be a game, unless he was paid.

The unhappy man was finally paid, and the Buffalo fans saw their first game in the stadium. If one were a Presbyterian, as the Morgans were, it was possible to go to Sunday church and then see a Bison game without crossing the street. The church stood behind the home plate portion of the stands, and it had the scars of many foul balls to prove it.

John Morgan had a friend who was part-owner of a fishing camp in the Adirondacks. At least once a year, John and Jack got in the family Oldsmobile and drove up to spend the weekend catching trout. Sometimes, they cooked over an open fire, and a mug of piping-hot chocolate was the perfect complement.

Over those same lingering flames, John told stories about when he was a kid and other family tales involving Jack's grandfather. Jack, listening intently, learned about the many books his dad loved. His favorite was *The Count of Monte Cristo* by Alexandre Dumas, and that soon was Jack's favorite, too.

John Morgan was all about truth and honesty, fairness and character. Revenge, which played a prominent part in the book, was okay too. He discouraged Jack from becoming a carpenter, not because it wasn't a noble calling, but he wanted Jack to be the first in the family to attend college and get a degree. Both his parents admired teachers and hoped their children would gravitate toward the field.

"A good teacher," they said in unison often, "can have a tremendous impact on the world. Kids always remember the great ones in their lives, and you can have a really positive influence on children."

Those words resonated with Jack, and they influenced his choice of career. Nellie listened but chose the nursing profession, because she, too, wanted to have an impact on people—but on their health. Both parents were pleased by their children's choices and were proud of them.

As a boy, Jack initially played baseball to please his father, but soon he grew to love the sport. There was no Little League at that time, but neighborhoods fielded teams, and Jack later played for his high school team. He played shortstop, the same position his father had, and John never missed a game.

Sometimes, the Offermann Stadium outings included one or more of Jack's friends. One Saturday afternoon, Buffalo was playing Montreal, and the game went extra innings. They stayed until the end, when the Buffalo first baseman hit a game-winning home run just before the game would have been called due to darkness.

The game lasted fifteen innings, and the mothers of the two friends who attended with Jack were frantic with worry.

Mary Morgan's only words of admonishment to her husband were, "John, what were you thinking?"

Another fond memory for Jack was the neighborhood Saturday night oyster party that John hosted once a year, usually in October. He arranged to buy a barrel of oysters, and the men all went to the basement to open them for consumption at the party upstairs.

Once on an early Sunday morning, Jack appeared outside his parents' bedroom. Although he was only five years old, he cursed like a longshoreman.

"Son of a bitch!" he shouted. "You dirty bastard! Shit! Come on, you lousy jerk off!"

That last expression brought a very angry, agitated father through the closed door. "What in God's name are you doing, Jack?"

His son, totally unmoved, stood in his pajamas, manipulating his fingers as if opening something and swearing like a trooper.

John laughed so hard, he almost cried, then he called for Mary to join him in the hall. She didn't think it was as funny as her husband—until he explained everything. Obviously, Jack sneaked into the basement and must have camped under the stairs out of sight. While he watched the men attempt to open oysters with rather sharp instruments, the inevitable antics and related cursing were on display for the small boy to observe and hear.

As the men labored to open the little devils and secure the oysters, many attempts failed, resulting in cut fingers and raucous language. Jack was repeating what he saw and heard the previous night. His parents understood the humor of his actions, but Jack wouldn't be invited again in the basement for an oyster party until he was old enough to open them himself.

Memories continued churning in Jack's mind as the second leg of the flight neared its end. Jack was sure Nellie was remembering the special moments she shared with her father, too.

"How is he, Mom?" Nellie asked, hugging her mother at the Buffalo airport, where Mary insisted on meeting them.

"Stable. That's all they'll tell me." Her expression was worried. "They'll know more tomorrow. Nellie, I'm glad you're here to interpret the medical jargon."

"Can we see him now?" Jack asked.

It was almost seven in the evening, but they drove to Buffalo General Hospital. During the twenty-minute drive, memories of their father stirred in Jack. Although he heard Nellie and Mary conversing in the background, Jack's thoughts drifted off.

He could almost hear his father's words: "Never say in life that you 'should have.' You'll have far fewer regrets."

Jack didn't realize how cogent that advice was until he reached his thirties.

He recalled more of John's favorite quotes:

"Your regrets aren't what you did, but what you didn't do."

"You're what you do, not what you say you'll do."

He especially liked that last one from Carl Jung. He thought of other sayings his father passed on—messages of which to be mindful in life.

Perhaps the old man's absolute favorite quote was from Publilius Syrus, the Latin writer who died in 43 BC. "Trust, like the soul, never returns once it's gone."

John's quotes told a great deal about the man and how he valued honesty. Telling the truth was of paramount importance to him, and he didn't just say that—he lived it.

A light rain fell as they arrived in the hospital parking lot. They had an opportunity, despite the hour, to visit with the attending physician, Dr. Brendan Morrison, a tall, thin man in his late fifties with a slight limp. Piercing blue eyes and a ruddy complexion were the first things Nellie and Jack noticed about him. He greeted them warmly, and Jack was comforted by his firm handshake.

The doctor placed a hand on Mary's shoulder. "How are you doing, Mrs. Morgan? I know this isn't easy on you."

Shrugging, she reached for Nellie's hand. Dr. Morrison began discussing John's condition, and he acknowledged Nellie's background, noting she might be able to explain the situation to her mother and brother.

"John has chronic obstructive pulmonary disease, or COPD for short. It's most likely due, at least in part, to his smoking of cigarettes and a pipe."

It was late, and they needed to get Mary home. She was clearly tired, and the distress of the situation was wearing her down. They didn't want it to affect her health, too.

On the way home, Mary told them it wouldn't be long, then she became quiet. The emphysema and chronic bronchitis were also taking a toll on John's health. He'd given up smoking twenty years earlier. Sometimes, that erased the past effects, but not for him.

They got Mary to bed after making her a cup of chamomile tea. Although they were tired from their trip, the siblings sat at the old family kitchen table to reminisce and discuss their mother's future before they retired an hour later.

Early the next morning, they ate a light breakfast and returned to the hospital to continue their vigil at John's bedside. He came out of his stupor several times for as long as twenty minutes. Mary held one hand, while Jack and Nellie alternated holding the other one.

When he was conscious, John told them repeatedly how proud he was of all of them. "Mary, you've been a rock," he whispered coarsely, "a real rock. I've always loved you dearly. You two, my wonderful children, have made me proud since the day you were born. I have no regrets. I've been blessed by the Lord with a good life and wonderful family. I always tried to do the best I could in everything I did. A man can do no more. The three of you are everything to me."

He looked at his children through cloudy eyes. "Take good care of your wonderful mother. I love you all."

With those final words, he was gone.

They remained silent, while warm, plentiful tears fell from all their eyes. Nellie and Jack were grateful for sharing John's last moments.

They spent the next few days making the arrangements for John Morgan's funeral service and burial. Mary continued to be a rock, but they knew after the frenetic activity died down, and friends and families returned to their own lives, the situation would be more difficult and lonelier for Mary. Fortunately, she knew about the household accounts and was more than capable of taking care of such things. For Jack and Nellie, though, there was more than that. Their worries shifted to their mother.

"I'm so afraid," Nellie told Jack when they were alone, "that she won't last long without him."

"But she's in good health."

"It doesn't matter. I've seen it happen many times. When a couple is happily married for so long and each is dependent on the other, as Mom and Dad were, when one goes, the other isn't far behind."

"Let's not think that way. Let's think how to keep an eye on her. Do you think the Smiths next door can help? Would she consider joining us at the farmhouse in West Virginia?"

"I doubt it, but it's a good idea. Let's discuss it with her."

After the funeral and burial services, they stayed with Mary for a couple more days to make sure she was all right.

Nellie was buying groceries with her mother one day when she ran into an old friend. "Sue! I haven't seen you in almost thirty years! How have you been? You remember my mother, Mary?"

"Of course."

Mary wandered off to the dairy section, leaving the two women to themselves. Sue Weaver and Nellie exchanged hugs.

"Don and I will be married twenty-five years tomorrow, and we're having a party to celebrate. We'd love it if you could come, and bring Jack, if you can. I know Don and his other friends would love to see him."

"Thanks, Sue. I'll get back to you later today. Dad just died, and all our emotions are pretty tenuous right now."

"I'm so sorry." She touched Nellie's shoulder. "We heard about it. He was such a wonderful man. You probably could use a little diversion and some cheer. I hope you can come."

When Nellie told Jack about the Weaver party, he wasn't thrilled. "What about Mom?" he asked.

"What about me?" Mary asked, walking into the room without their knowing, just like the old days.

"Jack and I have been invited to a get-together at the Weavers tomorrow evening," Nellie explained. "Will you be OK for a little while if we go?"

"Of course I will. In fact, I could use some time alone. You two go and give my best to all your old friends. Tell them I remember them and all their antics when you were young and adventurous."

"Thanks, Mom. We won't be gone long. I promise to fill you in on all the gossip."

"You always did, sweetheart. Don't worry. I'll be fine."

Jack, not convinced, finally acquiesced. It would be nice to meet some of his old buddies.

Sam Parks was the first to greet them. He played football with Jack in high school. "You old man," he said with a smile. "You're looking pretty good."

"Back at you, Sam."

"Don't forget your old offensive tackle who opened up all those holes for you and allowed your sorry ass to be here."

Laughing, they shared a beer. Other old friends came up to share funny stories from the past.

"Remember when we took all the towels from the shower room," Phil Miner asked, "and you got caught buck naked by that old battle-ax, Mrs. Crawford?" Jack blushed crimson.

Finally, Lance Kurtz took Jack aside and asked how he was doing in West Virginia.

"Nellie and I love it there," Jack said. "The people remind me of the good people of Buffalo. I love coaching football, and we lost an undefeated season on the last play of the game."

Lance coached football at the University of Buffalo and also taught economics. "We could use you up here, Jackson," he said using his favorite nickname for his good friend. "You could coach with me and teach history. We could have a ball together."

"Thanks, Lance. I know, but I don't want to let my kids down. West Virginians are wonderfully hospitable people. Nellie and I love it down there. Don't misunderstand me. We always loved Buffalo, but we're very happy doing what we do in the Mountain State."

"OK, partner. I understand." Lance lightly punched his arm.

They didn't stay long at the gathering. On their way back to the house, Jack said how glad he was they went to the party. Nellie concurred.

Mary greeted them in the foyer. She'd obviously been crying but asked how the party was. They explained they met old friends and how great it was to catch up with them.

Jack and Nellie toyed with the idea of bringing Mary to West Virginia to live with them. With cups of tea in hand, they sat in the living room to explore the possibility with her.

"Mom," Nellie began tentatively, "we'd love to have you come stay with us. There's plenty of room in the farmhouse, and it's quite comfortable."

"I know you both mean well, and that you worry about me," Mary replied, her voice shaking a little, "but I'm very comfortable here. I have a lot of friends here, too. Right now, I can't even think about leaving the Queen City and our home."

"It's OK, Mom," Jack chimed in. "We understand, but you have to promise to inform us about everything going on, especially your health. Don't do what Dad did and keep us in the dark."

"I promise. And now, I'm very tired, so I'll bid you both good night. I love you both very much, and so did your father." She ascended the stairway.

Jack and Nellie talked for a little while before finally agreeing that Mary knew what was best for her. They also agreed to keep close tabs on her, setting the intention to call several times a week and also ask neighbors to keep their eyes and ears open.

Two days later, Jack and Nellie were on a plane to New York City, the first leg of their journey back to Bentley. Jack mentioned his conversation with Lance.

"He wanted me to come back and work with him," Jack said.

"It's funny. I had almost the same conversation with Sara Reynolds. You remember her? She was the one who had a crush on you when she was ten."

"Yeah, yeah. They all did when they were ten. Then they grew up. The story of my life," he lamented. "Little girls liked me but not the big girls."

"Come on. It wasn't that bad." She snickered. "Sara's a nurse, and she said the hospital is short-staffed and asked me to consider moving back to Buffalo."

"Would you?"

"I honestly thought about it for a moment or two but decided no. I love Buffalo and always will, but I love where we live now and my nursing colleagues at Bentley Hospital. West Virginians are such real people, humble to the core and ready to help anyone in trouble or need. I was tempted, but I told her I loved my life in West Virginia. What did you tell Lance?"

"Pretty much the same thing. It sounded inviting, but I don't want to leave the kids."

The rest of the trip was uneventful. When they were finally back at the farmhouse, they looked at each other and smiled. It was indeed home for them.

Gladys and Buddy were happy to see them. After many hugs and a nice, home-cooked meal, they retired to the porch, where Jack and Nellie told Gladys the events of their days in Buffalo.

"Although I wouldn't mind the company here," Gladys said, "I think your mother is doing the right thing by staying near her friends for support. She loves you two and recognizes that you have your own lives, too. Don't worry. She'll know when the time is right. It might never come. You just have to stay in touch."

"Bless you, Gladys," Nellie said. "Coming from you, it gives me a sense that we did the right thing by not forcing her to move."

"I'll second that," Jack said with tears welling in his eyes. "Thanks, Gladys."

CHAPTER 51

C oming off a 7-1-0 season the previous year, the Bentley
Bears had high hopes for at least duplicating their success
in the coming season. As the players worked and mingled, there
was still conversation about the Munich tragedy, in which
armed terrorists broke into the Olympic village during the 1972
Olympic games and killed eleven Israeli athletes and coaches. It
was almost incomprehensible that such an inhumane act could
occur, especially during such a famous sports event.

Bentley opened its season against Hanover, a good but not
great team. It was a close, hard-fought contest, but the Bears
succumbed 20-14. Things improved quickly for the Bears with
a decisive 37-6 walloping of Derby and another five wins going
into the game with their archrival, Central.

Still smarting from their heartbreaking, last-minute loss to
the Chargers a year before, Jack's team seemed more than ready.
Maybe they were too ready. Sometimes, a team can be too fired
up and end up losing because of it.

Whatever the reason, it wasn't Bentley's day once again. They
went down 27-12. It was a discouraging way to end a season,
but the Bears were a solid team with a distinguished program
and a school that no one took for granted anymore. That was
of little consolation to the graduating seniors, most of whom
would never play another football game. Fortunately for the
coaches and the returning team, there were only two seniors,
so the Bentley Bears would continue to have a strong presence

the following year. Jack and Hank agreed the team earned a B+ for the season.

After several romantic disappointments in her life, Nellie, fifty-two, was going out with a physician friend named Keith Crowley. The pediatrician was eight years her senior, with wide, expansive green eyes, and always seemed to wear a broad smile. At only five-feet-seven-inches tall, he was well-built and worked out regularly at the gym. He played football in high school and had his nose broken enough times that it resembled a splattered carrot from the bridge down. His plastic surgery hadn't gone well.

While the nose wasn't very attractive, he more than made up for that with his infectious personality. They began dating earnestly in early summer, and Nellie really liked him. He was a popular member of the Bentley community, albeit not considered a catch by most women's standards. Nellie had been down that road before—with the nice man who moved to the West Coast.

Nellie sometimes felt like she was waiting for the other shoe to drop. The sixty-year-old physician went for a run one night on the high school track, right after talking with Nellie about their upcoming plans for the weekend. He often followed his running ritual three evenings a week after finishing up his medical practice, and he seemed in superb condition.

A history of heart conditions ran in his family, and one of them manifested itself when he was on the last turn of the quarter-mile track. Had he been running with someone, as Nellie had a few times, he probably would have survived.

The school janitor found him the next morning just off the track surface. It appeared he attempted to crawl after he was stricken.

Although the relationship hadn't reached the point of actual love, at least for her, Nellie felt the loss keenly. The day after Keith's body was found, she mentioned to Jack that the Morgans seemed to be cursed, or at least it felt like it.

Jack quickly dispelled that notion. "If we were cursed, Nell, we all would have died that night with Ray Tomkins."

Although Jack was right, it didn't make her situation any easier. She developed a wonderful friendship that was probably moving toward something even stronger, and suddenly, it was over.

If only I was with him that night, she thought. *I might have been able to save him.*

Six months later, tragedy struck them again. It was a hot, sultry July day, and Nellie and Jack returned home late in the afternoon after grocery shopping. Gladys was out, playing cards with friends.

They opened the farmhouse door and knew immediately something was wrong. Buddy wasn't there to greet them, tail wagging like crazy. Jack felt something untoward happened and was sick to his stomach.

They called for Buddy in cheerful voices, but he didn't show up. When they walked inside, they found their beloved canine stretched out in front of the couch, his body cold. He must have died soon after they left on their shopping trip.

It wasn't a total shock, since the dog was ten years old, but it came unexpectedly, since he hadn't shown any signs of illness or slowing down. They were hurt to the core.

Totally devastated, Nellie collapsed in tears and found refuge in Jack's arms. He tried to fight off his own tears but failed. He loved that dog so much. They sat on the couch, Buddy prostrate by Jack's feet like always, but now his beloved dog was dead. Jack cried bitterly.

"Do you still think we aren't cursed?" Nellie asked.

Jack contemplated the question for a moment, then his optimistic nature returned. "Yeah, I still think so. This wonderful dog gave us ten incredible years. Besides, I really needed him—something good—after Molly died."

"Think we should get another dog?"

The idea brought more tears for Jack. He wasn't able to respond right away, because the thought of replacing Buddy was unbearable and felt a bit disloyal.

Finally, he choked out, "Yes. I think . . .Buddy would understand."

"I think so, too."

When Gladys came home, they met her at the front door and broke the news. She had to reach for the banister when she saw the dog lying in the living room.

"That beautiful dog was a godsend to us," she said in a quivering voice. "I believe we'll see Buddy again."

They held each other for a minute. With tears in their eyes, they buried Buddy in the backyard under his favorite tree.

Standing over the grave, Jack read Psalm 34:18 from the bible: "The Lord is close to the brokenhearted and saves those who are crushed in spirit." He also read from Matthew 5:4, "Blessed are those who mourn, for they will be comforted."

As he shoveled the last bit of dirt on top of Buddy's grave, Jack was reminded of the wonderful, felicitous quote from Will Rogers, which he shared with Nellie and Gladys. "If there are no dogs in heaven, then, when I die, I want to go where they went."

They cried together, hearing that.

The next day, Jack and Nellie went to the pet store to look for another dog. They felt guilty, as if they were being disloyal to Buddy, but they knew it was a compliment to their special pet. No animal could replace Buddy.

The situation reminded Jack of an anecdote he often shared with his history class. When Thomas Jefferson went to France as the new U.S. ambassador, several Parisians came up to the future president and asked, "So you're the man replacing Ben Franklin?"

"No one replaces Franklin," he replied. "I merely succeed him."

That was how Jack felt about finding a new dog.

It took a few weeks before Jack and Nellie finally learned from one of the teachers at Bentley High that another teacher had a litter of chocolate Labs that were almost ready for adoption.

When she heard the news that evening, Nellie said, "Oh, my goodness, Jack. We have to see them right now!"

Jack called his fellow teacher, and off they went. There were six little pups, all beautiful and full of energy. One came right up to Jack and Nellie and sat his little butt down in front of them, staring adoringly up at them with big brown eyes.

It was love at first sight. Enthralled with the little guy, they decided that as soon as he was checked by the vet, he would become the new resident of 7 Mountain View Road.

"Jack, you should name him," Nellie said.

"How about Rudy?" Jack blurted.

Rudy it was.

Rudy and Jack soon became inseparable; Jack even took Rudy to some football practices. The sight of the little dog roaming the sidelines, watched by a student manager, warmed Jack's heart, reminding him of their recently lost, beloved canine.

CHAPTER 52

When Jack first arrived in Bentley twenty-six years earlier, the football program didn't generate any fear from its opponents, but that had changed. The Bears were respected enough by their adversaries that they no longer would be able to sneak up on any of them. Their superb conditioning, hurry-up offense, and trick plays made them worthy foes and not a team to be taken lightly.

Wanting desperately to repay Hanover for the loss they received in their opening game the previous year, Bentley again fell short in a hotly contested battle. The final score was 13-7, and the difference was Hanover's senior all-state quarterback, who almost personally engineered the drive for the winning touchdown. On the plus side was the fact that Riley Brown would graduate and take his considerable talents to the next level at the University of Pittsburgh. That wasn't much consolation, but at least the Bears didn't have to face him again.

A debilitating shoulder injury felled their own quarterback midway through the season, and that loss helped sink their original high expectations for that year. Bentley finished 4-4, and they couldn't muster much offense in a 27-7 loss to Central.

There was little the coaches could do to prevent the slippage from the previous year. The boys still loved the motivating Make a Difference sign in the locker room and even more so when other teams adopted the same concept and created their own slogans. Jack was proud that his idea resulted in copycat imitators and firmly believed that Make a Difference was the best motto of them all.

Life in West Virginia wasn't just about football.

Who would have believed that the man who took sixty-one percent of the popular vote and ninety-seven percent of the Electoral College in 1972, losing only the state of Massachusetts, would resign from the presidency less than two years later? That was what happened to Richard Nixon after the Watergate scandal broke.

Only fifty-five percent of the electorate had voted to reelect him, the lowest turnout in twenty-four years, but the Californian appeared to be in for a smooth second term that never came. Gerald Ford became the nation's thirty-eighth president on August 9, 1974, one day after Nixon's resignation—the first U.S. president to resign from office.

Ford served the rest of Nixon's second term and ran in 1976 for his own election only to lose to Jimmy Carter, a Georgia peanut farmer. Many observers attributed Ford's loss to his full, complete pardon of Nixon. Ford claimed he took the action to stop divisiveness and get the country back on track.

Five days after the pardon on September 13, the Kanawha County schools in east central West Virginia were closed due to violence resulting from a textbook controversy. That issue overshadowed for some in the Mountain State what happened three hundred and sixty miles north in Washington, D.C.

The genesis of the controversy arose out of a decision over the selection of textbooks for the forty-six thousand students matriculating at the county's one hundred and twenty-four public schools. It began harmlessly enough five months previously when all five members of the Kanawha County Board of Education voted unanimously to approve the three hundred and twenty-five recommended books in language arts that were previously available for public viewing.

One month later, one board member challenged the content in some of the books, including *Animal Farm* by George Orwell, *The Crucible* by Arthur Miller, and *The Autobiography of Malcolm X.* Despite a petition from over twelve thousand residents and public condemnation of the books by twenty-seven ministers and other citizens on the grounds of immorality and indecency, the board voted 3-2 in June to accept most of the books.

Anti-textbook attitudes mounted during the next two months. Opponents urged a boycott, and school attendance plunged twenty percent on the opening day of school, September 3. And some thirty-five hundred coal miners staged a wildcat strike to support the dissenters, and other factions of the business community, including industrial plants, became involved. When the Board of Education acquiesced and agreed to remove the offensive books, pending review by an eighteen-member, board-appointed citizens' committee, it escalated the conflict. Shots were fired, cars and homes were firebombed, and schools were dynamited and vandalized.

No one was killed, but eleven protesters were arrested. Schools in the county closed on September 12 for four days. Finally, in December, the board reached an agreement on a set of policies in which several committees were established involving parents who had a say in both textbook selection and adoption. The issue refused to die and simmered for years afterward. It became something other school districts around the country also faced.

The 1974 football season was a rather nondescript, ordinary one for the Bentley Bears. They couldn't seem to put any streak together, winning and then losing for the entire season. Their 4-4 record, culminating in a final loss to Central, didn't accomplish anything. As Hank Bennett quipped, "It's a little like kissing your sister."

A win over the Chargers would have ensured a winning season, but Central upended them by a score of 27-13. The up-tempo offense proved successful, but the defense had holes in it that couldn't be repaired. A few key injuries contributed to the mediocrity, but the Central and Hanover offenses in particular resembled juggernauts and would have prevailed even if Bentley were at full strength.

Jack and Hank continued to work well together, and the school budget allowed for a third coach, Ben Stephens. Jack was fifty-seven and beginning to feel his age. His knee ached, particularly on cold November days, and he actually felt old. Mandatory retirement at sixty-five loomed eight years away, and he actually began considering it, but his teams always had a way of bouncing back after an off year. No doubt in 1975 their fortunes would change for the better, as usual, and the fans would see a more successful Bentley team.

CHAPTER 53

Just before Thanksgiving, Jack was out looking for new tires for his car, and Nellie was the one home to receive an important call. It had been longer than usual since they'd heard from Paula or Philip.

When Jack barged in through the farmhouse door, Nellie said, "Hi, Jack. Good news from New Haven." Without waiting for his reply, she declared, "Paula's getting married."

"It's about time," he shot back.

"What do you mean by that, brother dear?"

"Nell, she's got to be forty-one. It's about time."

"You mean a woman needs to be married to fulfill herself?"

"Come on, Nell. You know what I mean." He smiled. "Don't give me the women's lib routine."

"I know that the poor girl has done nothing but work for the past twenty-five years. She worked her tail off to get where she is."

"I agree. I was just trying to get a rise out of you—successfully, I might add."

Gladys walked into the room. "What's all the excitement about?"

"Our Paula is getting married!" Nellie said.

"Oh, sweet Lord! What a wonderful, blessed surprise. I can't wait to see that sweet girl walk down the aisle. Nellie, we have to start planning right away."

Jack was suddenly left alone in the kitchen, while the women began making up lists of tasks for the upcoming event.

He heard them talking excitedly about cakes, flowers, and food as they went into the living room.

Oh, boy, here we go, he thought.

Paula was to marry Ben Andrews, a family physician who also practiced in New Haven. Paula mentioned to Nellie she hoped she'd have her wedding in Bentley sometime in June, but she wanted to schedule it around Philip's availability; by then, he had become a full colonel stationed in Washington, D.C. He didn't see a problem with a June date.

Clearly exuberant over the news, Nellie and Gladys joyously went to work planning the details. There were many phone calls back and forth with Paula. Nellie was pleasantly surprised by one of Paula's requests.

"Aunt Nellie, would it be possible to do everything at the farmhouse?" Paula asked.

Nellie beamed. "Of course, honey—even the ceremony?"

"Especially the ceremony. The farmhouse, you, Uncle Jack, and Philip are the most special things in my life, along with Gladys, of course."

"We can do it all here without any problem. We're tickled pink you want it that way. You can bet I'll put Uncle Jack to work making it the most beautiful wedding site ever, just for you. Gladys will be happy to be part of it, too. We can't wait."

The date was set for Saturday, June 21, 1975. With little less than six months to prepare, Jack was given a to-do list by Nellie to spruce up the property in time for the wedding festivities. To his credit, Jack took his new responsibilities very seriously and recruited several Bentley football players to help clean the landscape, put a fresh coat of paint on the house, and paint the shutters, doors, and porch floor. They even painted the fence around the property. Nellie hired two men from the church to paint all the rooms on the first floor, too.

Nellie and Gladys made sure the hydrangea bushes, azaleas, and all the flowering bushes were fertilized to be in splendid bloom. The daylily beds along the fence were mulched. In early June, multicolored annual flowering plants would be placed in the beds at the front of the farmhouse.

Gladys ordered a beautiful, white, wooden gazebo for the side yard. The distant mountains would provide a stunning backdrop for the ceremony. It became her special project. She planted flowering bulbs and seeds that would bloom in time for the special day. She wanted to express her thanks to the people and place that was so welcoming to her and her late husband.

Finally, June 21 arrived, and Paula and Ben Andrews were married by Pastor Butler on a balmy, sunny afternoon before a small wedding party of two dozen. The bride's brother, Army Colonel Philip Kelly, walked her down the aisle, looking handsome in his U.S. Army dress uniform. There were just enough clouds in the West Virginia sky to keep the temperature down to the high seventies. The flowering bushes and bulbs were in full bloom as Nellie and Gladys hoped.

When Paula saw the beautiful gazebo Gladys had purchased, she smiled and blew her a kiss. Everything was perfect. They all liked the new groom, who originally hailed from Boston.

"How about you, Philip?" Jack asked. "Any wedding bells in your future?"

"Not for now, Uncle Jack, though I met someone recently who could be pretty special."

"OK," Nellie said. "What's her name?"

"Abby. I met her on leave a few months ago. You'd really like her Aunt Nellie. She's a nurse."

"What am I, chopped liver?" Jack asked.

"Sorry." Philip sounded sheepish, but there was a twinkle in his eye. "You'd like her, too."

"Are you serious about her?" Nellie asked.

"Not yet, Aunt Nell. We'll see." He grinned.

The wedding festivities and reunion were wonderful and fun. Much to the delight of Nellie and Gladys, everyone commented on how beautiful the gazebo, flowers, and landscaping were.

Everyone, including the bride and groom, had left by late Sunday afternoon. Paula and Ben would honeymoon for two days in Washington, D.C, before heading back to their medical practices in New Haven. Paula kept her maiden name of Kelly, because she'd been professionally known by that name since she first opened her practice.

After a few days of rest, they had barely cleaned up the debris from the wedding when Jack and Nellie received, not unexpectedly, news from Buffalo. Their mother was very ill. According to her physician, she wouldn't last more than a week. They had to move fast.

As they disembarked from their plane in New York City and hustled toward their connection to Buffalo, Nellie invoked memories of their previous trip, when they buried their father.

"It's been almost three years," she said. "I'm surprised she lasted this long without Dad. Dr. Ray said she seems to have lost her will to live. I've seen that pretty often, when the survivor in a couple who were married for many years loses interest in living and wants to be with the deceased partner. I'm sure that's what Mom is thinking."

They sat with Mary for two days, each taking time to return to their childhood home to freshen up.

Mary had serious difficulty breathing, and her respiratory problems grew. There was no question of recognition. While there were times when she drifted in and out of consciousness, Mary recognized her children and squeezed their hands with what little strength she could summon. She had lost twenty pounds from her frame, which had never been large.

Both children thought their mother was still beautiful, despite her age, thinning hair, and frail condition. The end was clearly near. It finally came when they were both with her, holding her hands.

Just past seven on Friday, June 27, Mary passed away. Her children were grateful they'd been with her as she ended her odyssey on earth and began her journey to join their father.

They felt comforted to know she was in a better place, but it was an odd feeling to realize they were now orphans—perhaps old orphans, but nonetheless orphans.

It was difficult losing their father, but the emptiness seemed more acute after their mother and remaining parent passed on. Jack and Nellie no longer had a living parent. It was a psychological blow. Fortunately, they still had each other. Time would heal both of them, especially when the relationships were strong and lasting—something that characterized the relationships the siblings had with their parents.

The following days were busy. Nellie took care of planning a visitation and service through the same funeral home Mary chose for their father's arrangements. She would be buried alongside her husband, John.

Jack contacted the family attorney and asked him to handle all the details of their parents' estate.

"It's hard to believe, Jack," Bob Kelleher stated. "Your parents were like an aunt and uncle to me. I've been working for them for so long. Don't worry. I'll take care of everything and will keep you apprised if we need to discuss anything. They didn't have a lot, but your father invested well, and there's the house, too.

"I know you'll need time to sort out the belongings in the house, but when you and Nellie are ready, we can put it up for sale if that's what you want."

"Thanks so much, Bob. Let me talk with Nellie and see what she wants to do. I'll get back to you. By the way, thanks for looking out for my parents' best interests, especially Mom's for the last few years. Nellie and I greatly appreciate it."

A simple, beautiful service was held that Monday for Mary Morgan. Nellie arranged for her mother's favorite flowers, a multitude of colorful summertime blooms—to be placed on her casket and in the funeral home. Mary always spent an hour or two tending her garden of summer flowers, and Nellie thought the bouquet was a wonderful tribute.

While in Buffalo, Jack and Nellie retired each night to their childhood home and reminisced about their days growing up there and their wonderful, supportive, loving parents. They spent time going through important papers left behind, which Jack would take to Attorney Kelleher, and they spent hours browsing the photo albums their mom put together, cataloging their happy family life.

They decided to donate all the house's contents, including clothing, to the local shelter for abused women and children. They each took a few mementos, along with the photo albums, and Jack called Bob Kelleher to have the house put up for sale once all the paperwork was completed.

"You know, Jack," Nellie said, sighing, "this is so difficult, but we know it's the best thing to do. I know the shelter and those women can use everything here. Mom and Dad would be happy with our decision."

"We're definitely doing the right thing. We can take some pretty wonderful, happy memories with us and know we're doing good, something Mom and Dad instilled in us."

The siblings came to terms and were at peace with the passing of Mary and John Morgan.

CHAPTER 54

The 1975 Bentley Bears football team was bound to be interesting. Under Jack's tutelage, an average season was always followed by a good one. Injuries hurt them the previous year, but holes in the defense needed patching. The Mountain League had too many teams with powerful offensive units for any team to neglect defense.

The coaches' number-one mission in September was to shore up the personnel on the defensive side of the ball. They moved sophomore Joe Mack, a six-foot-two-inch, two-hundred-fifteen-pound beast, as they called him, from offensive tackle to defensive linebacker. He was probably the best athlete on the team, certainly the strongest; he occasionally filled in offensively. His main job was to wreak havoc on the opponent's offense. That move probably should have been done the previous year. The defense needed a stopper, a *bona fide* tough guy who could punish the ball carrier.

Joe relished the responsibility and seemed to take it personally if he was beaten on any play. That was the mentality the coaches wanted, and Joe didn't disappoint.

Having Ben Stephens as third coach again was also a big plus. He was no longer a stranger to the team, and he blended in well, contributing new ideas. Having played defensive safety in both high school and college didn't hurt, either. Jack, Hank, and the kids liked and respected him.

A sign proclaiming their previous year's season of 4-4 hung prominently beside the Make a Difference poster in the locker room. The team seemed confident in opening the season against Derby, having won at home the previous year 20-7.

The offense moved the ball well, and Joe Mack was a terror on defense, resulting in an easy 34-6 victory. Everything went well for the Bears as they stormed through their next five opponents, leaving them with a 6-0 record going into a home game with the Tilden Titans.

Tilden beat Bentley in 1974, 21-20, on their way to a 7-1 record, so it was clear the Bears faced a tough game. For fifty-nine minutes, Bentley appeared more than equal to the task and never trailed in the game. With the ball in the Titans' possession on the Bears' thirty-six-yard line and only thirty seconds left to play, a pass play looked incomplete when the ball was tipped twice.

The Titan receiver, Jimmy Warren, was the most-surprised player on the field when the ball fluttered into his arms like a wounded duck. He scored a touchdown and a 23-20 victory for the Titans. Again, a fully undefeated and untied season eluded the green-and-white Bentley Bears.

Central was upset by Derby that same Friday night, which took a lot of luster off their final game with their biggest rival. The anticlimactic 13-13 tie left both teams unsatisfied. The following year for the Bears looked very promising with their one-man wrecking crew of Joe Mack coming back, along with a host of other defensive starters. An unbeaten, untied season was still a dream.

Almost Heaven

The 1975-1976 winter wasn't as cold as it was snowy. Sudden thaws in the temperature led to flooding problems, but things were OK through February. In mid-March, they had a seventeen-inch snowfall in the Bentley area that was beautiful to look at but posed a serious threat. A lot of snow remained on the ground due to three snowfalls in the previous ten days. Freezing weather further complicated the situation.

It rained for two full days, and the temperature rose to the low forties. The snow melted rapidly, and, together with the steady rain, cascaded down the hills and mountainsides, causing serious flood damage. The river became swollen, exacerbating the problems. Five homes on the water were destroyed as the rapid currents ravaged them.

One of those homes belonged to Tom and Rachel Hopkins, good friends of Jack and Nellie's. They had no family in the Bentley area and were suddenly rendered homeless. Once again, the good-hearted Morgans stepped up and offered refuge.

"Don't be bashful, Rachel," Nellie implored. "You and Tom need a place to stay. Besides, you'd do the same for us."

"But Nellie, it would be such an imposition."

"Rachel, the farmhouse is practically empty. We used to have six people here, and now it's just Jack, Gladys, and me. Come on. We'll make the most of it, and besides, it'll be fun!"

"Are you sure they won't mind?"

"Of course not. Jack and Tom are good friends, and Jack will love some male company. Gladys, bless her heart, loves everybody. She's very easygoing."

They became friendly when Tom and Rachel moved to Bentley from their hometown of Pittsburgh twenty years before. They first met through church. Over time, the friendship blossomed, and they had occasional dinners, movies, and evenings playing cards. Their allegiance was natural.

Rachel was a nice woman, although a bit high-strung, and she worked as an X-ray technician at the hospital. She was a good friend to Molly during her illness and helped the grieving family with meals and companionship after her death.

Quiet, calm, and skinny as a beanpole, Tom was a labor lawyer. Their two adult children both had busy lives in New York City. Both hated imposing on a friendship, but they had nowhere else to go. When everything was back to normal, they planned to rebuild, although not as close to the river.

"This is a done deal," Nellie said. "No ifs, ands, or buts."

Tom and Rachel moved into the farmhouse, and no one knew or cared for how long. They shared the upstairs with Gladys and even had their own bathroom.

Everyone was pleased that the other four couples who'd lost their homes in the flood—two with children—found ample accommodations with nearby relatives. Fortunately, the March floodwaters didn't claim any lives. The rest of that spring, thankfully, was uneventful, although there was a lot of debris to clean up.

After over thirty years of looking after her brother and extending a helping hand to so many others, including Henry and Gladys, Philip, Paula, Tina, Rachel, and Tom, Nellie's fortunes were changing for the better. After losing one husband and an almost-husband to unimaginable tragedies, and watching a serious boyfriend move to San Francisco, Nellie was in a happy, satisfying relationship with Greg Carson, a successful lawyer in town for twenty years. A native of Parkersburg, he took several legal jobs in Charleston before completing law school at the age of forty.

Greg was a kind man, a former college athlete, and very protective of Nellie. Tall with green eyes and gray hair, he was considered handsome by all her friends. He actually proposed to her three times, but each time, she said she needed more time.

The third proposal occurred days before she went to Buffalo. Again, her response was, "I need more time."

Somewhat exasperated by then, he bluntly asked, "Exactly how much time do you think you have?"

That caught her by surprise, and she pondered it all the way home from Buffalo. She'd never been asked such a question before, and she found she had no answer.

CHAPTER 55

The middle of May was Jack's favorite part of the school year because he spent a full week with his history class discussing and learning about the signers of the Declaration of Independence. He was reverential about the fifty-six, solemnly believing they were as brave and courageous as any American heroes from any time.

"The kids should understand how patriotic they were," he explained to Nellie and Gladys, sharing his rationale for instituting the weeklong study more than a decade earlier.

His homework assignments were for the class to get to know something about each signer and have the kids understand and appreciate the sacrifices they made when they put their pen to the nation's birth certificate. It didn't surprise him that before his special class, the students had little or no conception about how special those men were or how they compromised their own futures and that of their families.

The syllabus Jack prepared called for the students to read assignments for three nights, then spend Thursday discussing some of the more salient facts about the historic event. Friday was reserved for Jack's special questions about the men. The students who answered correctly were eligible for extra credit on their final exams.

The special week began on Monday, May 17. By Thursday's class, everyone had ostensibly finished the reading assignments and was prepared for the ensuing discussion. As he always did,

Jack set the stage with important background information. He pointed out that the debate in the Second Continental Congress of the thirteen colonies of British America began on June 7, 1776, in Philadelphia, when Virginia's Richard Henry Lee introduced a proposition that would seemingly get wide support.

> *Resolved, that these United Colonies are absolved from all allegiance to the British Crown, and that all political connection between them and the State of Great Britain is, and ought to be, totally dissolved.*

"A simple, declarative sentence," Jack said, "that wasn't outlandish for those times and should have easily passed, right?"

Several heads nodded.

"Wrong! Many delegates thought it too aggressive and far-reaching. Many hoped to return to the status quo before British officers began to regulate the colonies' commerce and didn't think it was necessary to break all bonds with the motherland.

"It took four days of vigorous debate before the proposition was adopted, and then by only a single vote. Edward Rutledge of South Carolina, to the relief of many, deferred the entire question until July 1. Some of the delegates would have been happy to see it deferred forever.

"Meanwhile," Jack said, "the citizens in the rest of the country were way ahead of their representatives in Congress. They wanted full independence from Great Britain. John Adams characterized the movement as a 'wave of independence rolling like a current over the land.'"

The students were very engaged. Many leaned forward in their seats to listen.

"Over the next twenty days, representatives in Philadelphia were instructed to cast their vote in favor of full independence. Some still held out, not because they weren't real patriots, but because they thought the measure was too extreme. Many people to this day don't understand what happened next.

"After four more days in the extreme heat of early July in Philadelphia, John Hancock signed the Declaration of Independence on July 4. He was the first and only one to do so that day, although that was the actual day the document was approved. It was a Thursday, and tempers were flaring. What happened next, class?" Betsy Harris in the front row raised her hand.

"Yes, Betsy?"

"Well, four days later, on July 8, freedom was proclaimed throughout the colonies."

"What did that mean for the delegates?"

"It meant all the delegates who voted for independence were guilty of treason."

"And what was the penalty for treason, Betsy?"

"Death by hanging, sir."

"Ah ha! You've done your homework. I sure hope your classmates were as diligent."

Jack explained how the delegates agreed over those hot, tumultuous days in Philadelphia that the actual signing date for the Declaration of Independence would be August 2. It was a brutally hot day when the signers walked up to the table where the document lay, attended to by Charles Thomson, secretary to Congress.

The temperature was so sweltering, the delegates were glad to forego the usual lengthy and somewhat pompous preliminary comments. They were there for a single purpose—to lend their signatures to a unique, important document. It was actually Friday, August 2, 1776, not Thursday, July 4, when the already-approved parchment was signed—a little known fact many years later.

"OK, class," Jack said, "let's begin our discussion. Who do you think was the biggest hero or patriot of the fifty-six signers?"

Anne Hale's hand went up.

"Yes, Anne? Who has your vote?"

"I think it was South Carolina's Edward Rutledge, because he was the youngest signer and had the most to lose."

"Good reasoning. Do you remember what happened to him?"

"Yes, sir. He was so upset that George Washington died in December 1799 that he had a stroke and died a month later."

"Excellent work, Anne. Before I go around the room, can anyone tell us two very prominent, leading patriots who didn't sign the Declaration of Independence?"

"Yes, Sir," Terry McKay in the second row said. "George Washington and Patrick Henry."

"Very good, Terry. Can you tell us why they didn't sign?"

"Because Washington was away fighting the war, and Patrick Henry was governor of Virginia and attending to state business."

"Right. It appears all of you did your homework. OK, let's move on. I'm interested in hearing who you think was the bravest and most courageous signer. Anne said Edward Rutledge. Do you agree?"

"I don't," Ed Henry called from the back of the room.

"OK, Ed. Who's your choice?"

"I think it was Charles Carroll of Carrollton."

"Why?"

"Because he was the wealthiest signer. Some said he was the wealthiest man in America, and his signature included where he came from. The British would know exactly where to find him."

"Very compelling reasons, Ed." Jack looked around the room to assess the impact of Ed's reasoning and wasn't surprised to see several students nodding.

"Anyone else?" Jack asked.

"It had to be John Hancock," Harry Clark said.

"Why's that?"

"He was the first to sign, and his signature was so large, there was hardly any room left for anyone else."

A few students laughed.

"Besides," Harry said, "not only was he first, he was the only one to sign on July 4."

"That's true, Harry. Does anyone else have a different opinion?"

One of the many things the kids loved about Jack's teaching, something that set him apart from the other teachers, was that he taught them *how* to think and not *what* to think. Many of the parents were aware of that positive practice and thought it helped bring out the best in the kids. They could tell when the kids came home from school and talked about their assignments and what they learned.

Holly Daniels, a pert blonde in the front row, raised her hand.

"Yes, Holly? Who do you think was the bravest?"

"Caesar Rodney from Delaware."

More than a few students gave a blank stare. A few laughed.

"Wait a minute, class. Let Holly explain. She might be on to something. Caesar Rodney was one of the most obscure of the signers, and his name would rarely be involved during any discussion of the subject and hardly ever appeared in print."

"Well," Holly said, feeling nervous about the class's reaction, "he was doing very well in Delaware long before the debate began over whether to break ties with Great Britain." She slowly gained confidence. "He was appointed to the Delaware Supreme Court, even though he wasn't a lawyer. He had a cancerous tumor removed from his face and desperately needed additional treatment because the cancer remained. The only way to save his life was to return to England for treatment."

Suddenly, her classmates became very interested in Caesar Rodney.

"Tell us more, Holly," Jack said.

"On the night before the July 4 vote, it was raining in Delaware, and Rodney was very sick. Upon hearing that his vote was needed in Philadelphia the next day, he got on his horse and rode eighty miles to the city. The trip took fourteen hours, and his vote was decisive in a 2-1 Delaware vote for independence. That's why I think he was the bravest signer."

Much to Holly's surprise and delight, several of the students, as well as Jack, applauded.

"Anyone else?" Jack asked.

The room fell silent.

"OK. Let's take a vote. How many think Edward Rutledge was the bravest?"

Only Anne Hale's hand went up.

"How many for Charles Carroll of Carrollton?"

Ed Henry and one other student raised their hands.

"John Hancock?"

Harry Clark's hand went up.

"All right. How many think Caesar Rodney was the bravest?"

Many hands rose, showing the class was nearly unanimous in agreement.

"That was really good work, Holly," Jack said. "You had doubters, but you persevered, and your knowledge prevailed. Let's hear it for Holly!"

The students applauded.

"That just goes to show you that if you know your subject and have command of the facts, you can change a skeptical body and turn their opinions around. That's an important lesson for all of us, and we have Holly to thank for it."

The pert blonde girl blushed.

"That's all the time we have," Jack said, dismissing the students. "Let's pick up tomorrow where we left off today."

Jack always enjoyed the week spent on the signers of the Declaration of Independence. That night at dinner with Nellie, Gladys, and the Hopkins couple, he described how the students responded to their homework. He took special delight in talking about Holly and how she turned the class, initially hostile to her point of view, into almost total agreement. Making the story even more fascinating was the fact that none of his four dinner partners ever heard of Caesar Rodney.

"It just shows you how captivating some obscure historical fact can be," Jack said, "especially if one isn't aware of it. You should have seen the faces of all those doubting Thomases when Holly blew them away with the tale of Mr. Rodney. Our history is replete with such stories, and that's another reason why I love teaching. I may never be financially rich, but I can't tell you how proud I get of my students and how they enrich my life."

"You have to excuse my brother," Nellie interrupted, "but he really feels it."

"I love his passion," Gladys blurted. "It's so refreshing."

"I apologize for the lecture." Jack said sheepishly.

"Don't you apologize for a second for loving what you do," Rachel said earnestly. "Wouldn't it be great if all of us had the same passion for our work? Right, Tom?"

"She's right, Jack. It's great to feel that excitement and have such a positive impact on the kids. Sometimes, I wonder what the hell good I'm doing for mankind."

"This is dangerously degenerating into a séance without the candles." Nellie chuckled. "Let's go to the other room with our coffee."

The following morning, Jack looked forward to a continuation of the discussion that captivated his class the previous day. He hoped they had enough time to complete their lessons, because the following day was Saturday.

Sitting on the edge of the desk, he again set the stage for them. "I think you're beginning to understand why I think the signers were very special patriots and that their collective bravery and courage should be admired forever. Each and every signer was declared a traitor. The British hunted for all of them. No family was immune.

"Most of them, at least for a while, were unable to visit their families or homes. Almost all were offered forgiveness, freedom, and property rewards to renounce what they did and pledge their support of the king, but none of them did, despite losing their fortunes, their homes, and, in some cases, their families. Their honor and that of their country remained intact. Pretty amazing, don't you agree?"

All the students nodded.

"Let's talk about what happened to those splendid fifty-six patriots. Who wants to start?"

Lenny Travers' hand shot up.

"Educate us, Lenny," Jack said, leaning forward with arms akimbo.

"The houses of twelve signers were all burned down. Seventeen of them lost everything they owned."

"Good, Lenny. Anyone else?"

From the back of the room, one of Jack's football players raised his hand.

"Larry?"

"Nine signers died during the Revolutionary War. Five others were captured and imprisoned."

"Nice job, Larry."

Dennis Roy raised his hand. "The wives, sons, and daughters of some of the signers were killed or jailed."

"Does anyone specifically come to mind, Dennis?"

"Yes, Sir—Francis Lewis of New York."

"What's his story?"

"A few months after the signing, the British took over New York City and destroyed Lewis' house on Long Island. They captured his wife and put her in a cold, dank prison in the city to get back at him. It ruined her health, and she died within two years."

"I want to commend all of you for taking this assignment seriously. Now I'll ask you some tough questions."

The students stirred in their seats, leaning forward to listen. Jack began with a trick question he asked all his classes in May.

"At the time the Declaration of Independence was written, how many of the signers were born in America?"

A wave of hands went up. Almost in unison, the class shouted, "Forty-eight!"

"Wrong!" He tried to hide his grin.

They shouted their protests, but he reminded them, "There was no America until July 4, 1976."

"Unfair! Trick question," some said.

"I'm just kidding. Now for the real questions. Number one: Who was the oldest signer?"

Everyone knew it was Ben Franklin.

"How many bachelors out of the fifty-six?"

Only three knew that the correct answer was two.

"Number three, who was the niece of signer George Ross."

"Betsy Ross!" the class said.

"What two signers became presidents of the United States?"

"Adams and Jefferson!"

"Very good. Now for some toughies: Who was the only Catholic among the fifty-six signers?"

Most of them didn't know. Holly Daniels, the assiduous reader who told them about Caesar Rodney, raised her hand.

"Charles Carroll of Carrollton," she said proudly.

"Correct. Well done."

"He was also the last signer to die," she added.

"You don't miss a trick, do you? OK, class, what was Roger Sherman's important contribution to America?"

"You mean his fifteen children?" Sarah Grimes suggested.

The class burst into jeers and laughter.

"No, Sarah, I don't." Jack laughed, too. "Try again."

"Well, he introduced the Connecticut Compromise that solved a gigantic problem. No one could figure out how to satisfy the bigger population states who wanted more representation than the states with fewer people. Sherman proposed to have representation in a House of Representatives based on population, while each state would have two in the U.S. Senate."

"Great job, Sarah. You nailed that one. We have time for only a few more."

The students groaned in disappointment because they were fully engaged in the exercise.

"Before I ask you the next question," Jack said, "let me tell you a little more about Connecticut's Roger Sherman. He's the only man in history to have signed the Declaration of Independence, the U.S. Constitution, the Articles of Confederation, and the Articles of Association—the only one.

"Now here's the second-to-last question. Who was the first signer to die?"

Again, Holly Daniels raised her hand. Jack looked around, hoping to see another, but she was the only one.

"Yes, Holly, who was it?"

"John Morton of Pennsylvania."

"Right, Holly. You've again demonstrated the advantage of being a voracious reader. All right, everybody. Let's hear a drum roll for the last and final question. This is a tough one. This Virginian was the father of one president and the great-grandfather of another. What was his name?"

The students looked at each other. Several threw up their arms in frustration. George Thornton gingerly raised his hand as if he weren't sure of the answer.

"Good for you, George. We're sitting on the edge of our seats. Who was it?"

George stood from his third-row seat and hemmed and hawed for a moment, then blurted, "Benjamin Harrison. He was part of the only grandfather-grandson duo to ever hold the office." He sat down abruptly.

"That's correct, George. Good work. Let me ask all of you if you found this week's assignment interesting and if I should continue it next year."

They gave him loud, enthusiastic applause and an explosion of positive comments.

As 1976 provided the gateway to the late seventies and early eighties, the fiddler politician Robert Byrd rode high in the U.S. Senate as the Democratic whip. At fifty-seven, he was known as a workaholic. Rarely did he attend any sporting event or other social outing. Even watching TV was kept to a minimum, although he took to the Senate floor once to protest the cancellation of his favorite show, "Gunsmoke."

He was a most unusual elected official in another way, too. Robert Byrd never forgot his roots. He was so poor as a young boy that he was reluctant to go to Sunday school, because he had no socks to wear. Byrd never forgot the plight of his people in West Virginia, and they loved him for it. He was reelected in 1976 with a whopping eighty-nine percent of the vote. His gift to them in return came in the form of "government pork"—highways, grants, and other forms of largesse.

His first refrigerator wasn't even an icebox. It was more primitive than that, just an old orange crate he nailed outside the kitchen window. He knew what it was like to be without, and he easily identified with his less affluent and less fortunate constituents.

The senator never learned how to relax, but on those few occasions when he did, he smoked a cigar and played a tune on his fiddle before retiring.

Unlike most politicians, he never had to worry about reelection. Some people turned out at the polls just to vote for him, such was the hold he had on the people of West Virginia.

He was also capable of considerable kindness. When Democrat Joe Biden was first elected to the Senate in November 1972, tragedy struck before the end of the year, on December 18. Biden's wife, Neilia, and their one-year-old daughter, Naomi, were killed in an automobile accident. Fortunately, Biden's two sons, although injured, survived.

Almost Heaven

At the memorial service held soon after, during the peak of the Christmas season, one lonely figure remained seated at the back of the church, the only member of Congress present. Robert Byrd drove two and a half hours each way in a cold, hard rain to be there. That was the kind of man he was, which endeared him to many, even outside the Mountain State.

CHAPTER 56

The 1976 edition of the Bears started with great promise with the team winning its first five games, but the loss of their quarterback to a knee injury in the third quarter of the Tilden game put a damper on the rest of the season. They finished 5-3, which was a huge disappointment to all.

The ferocious play of Joe Mack caught people's attention, including some college scouts. He made fifteen to twenty tackles every game, despite opponents running the ball away from him. Joe, a junior who stood six feet three inches tall and weighed two hundred and twenty-five pounds, was a dynamite player who could run the forty in 4.5 seconds.

A few months later, on a nondescript February afternoon, Jack sat at his desk in the football office when his secretary indicated he had a call from Mr. Bryant.

"It was hard to understand him, Jack," she said. "He has a strong Southern drawl, but I thought he identified himself as Mr. Bryant."

"Thanks, Barbara. Go ahead and put him through."

When the call connected, Jack heard a man say, "Hello. Is this Coach Morgan?"

"Yes, it is. What can I do for you?"

"This is Bear calling, Bear Bryant from Alabama."

Jack was stunned that the famous college football coach was contacting him and was almost unable to reply. "Hello, sir," he stammered. "Nice to talk with you."

"Well, son, please call me Bear."

"Bear it is."

"Ah understand that y'all have a boy up there who plays a mean defense. When ah say 'mean,' I mean 'mean.'"

"You must be talking about Joe Mack," the excited coach replied.

"Ah sure am, Coach Morgan. Ah understand that under your coaching, this boy is a tremendous linebacker, and ah would like to see him wearing crimson and white when he goes to college. Tell me more about him, Coach Morgan. He's a senior next year, right?"

"That's right, sir. Please call me Jack."

"Will do, son."

"Well, he's a very special athlete, sir, and he makes everyone around him perform better. Joe's very popular with the team. They have great respect for him. One thing for sure is he'll give you his very best for the whole sixty minutes. You wouldn't have to worry about him in the classroom or off the field, either. He's a solid honors student."

"Well, Coach Morgan, ah mean, Jack, ah sure thank you for talkin' with me. Please say hello to Joe for me and put in a good word for Alabama. By the way, is there anything else you can tell me?"

"Sir...Bear, one other thing. His mother is famous for her strawberry shortcake. If one of your assistant coaches comes up to recruit him, they might mention that."

"Ah sure do appreciate that, Jack. Ah'll make certain he does."

The line went dead.

"I just spoke with Bear Bryant! I can't believe it!" Jack shouted.

His reaction was no surprise. After coaching at Maryland, Kentucky, and Texas A&M, Paul "Bear" Bryant became a college football coaching legend during his twenty-five years at Alabama, having won six national titles.

It was a full year since Tom and Rachel Hopkins moved into the farmhouse with Nellie, Gladys, and Jack. It didn't present any problems for the Morgans or for Gladys; they all enjoyed the company. The Hopkins were growing restless, and the construction of their new house was delayed several times due to West Virginia's inclement weather. Rachel worried that she and Tom had used up their hospitality, but Nellie assured her everything would be fine until their house was built.

By June, the house was finally complete, and the latest round of Morgan boarders moved into their new abode.

One month later, an Alabama assistant football coach named Lance Dodge called Jack.

"I'm just checking in with you, as I plan to visit with the Macks tomorrow evening. Mrs. Mack asked me over for dinner, and Bear told me about her strawberry shortcake. By the way, Bear wanted me to be sure to convey his best to you and say thanks, too."

Jack couldn't help thinking that the great coach's ability and ease with people had something to do with his success. He hoped Joe would select Alabama, but Jack's ethics wouldn't allow him to push the subject. If Joe asked him about it, that was another thing. Then Jack would be free to put in a word for the great Paul "Bear" Bryant.

Joe Mack's last season with the Bears was eventful. There were fifty or more people than usual in the stands to watch the games. Some locals were eager to see Joe in action, but many college football scouts were also in attendance. In Jack's years at the helm of Bentley High football, it was common enough to see a scout, but the current situation escalated into a *bona fide* phenomenon.

Joe told his teammates that Notre Dame, Michigan, Alabama, and even UCLA expressed an interest in him. He didn't say it in a pedantic or offensive way, more like a matter-of-fact casual response to a question. Clearly, the attention hadn't changed his behavior. He wasn't getting egotistical over the accolades, and he remained the same steadfast, shy, young man he was before his enormous football talents manifested themselves. Jack knew his parents, Helene and Vincent, and they were regular people with strong West Virginian family values.

Jack hoped the other players on the team would step up their own games, knowing there were scouts watching, and it seemed that was the case. The first five games for the Bears were almost too easy. With Joe Mack fortifying a proud, aggressive defense, Bentley gave up only fourteen points in winning those games by a collective 103-14.

Tilden offered more opposition than the previous five opponents, but they also fell 20-12.

Derby was a very physical, big team, and they were undefeated as they came to Bentley. The contest was a barnburner in every sense of the word, as the old-timers called it. The Demons kicked a twenty-yard field goal just as time ran out to seal a 13-12 victory. It was another late season crushing defeat for the Bears.

The highlights of the game were the play of Captain Joe Mack and his fellow defensive marauders, as they pridefully referred to themselves. Somewhat out of character for the modest, unassuming young man, he practically guaranteed a victory the following week at the Bears' away game against Central. It would be his last high school game, and the Charger stands were packed with fans. Joe wasn't the only player they came to see.

Central junior running back Billy Lee was also considered a blue-chipper. For the first time in Bentley football history, they pummeled their worthy opponent and nemesis by more than a few points. The final score was a shocking 30-0, and Billy Lee was limited to only seven yards. He averaged over one hundred yards a game, but the Mack Marauders never gave him room to breathe. To make the moment even sweeter for Mack, he scored the game's final touchdown on a thirty-five-yard pass interception.

Jack was right. The entire Bear team stepped up to the plate to support their star player.

Amid all the hugs and bedlam in the Bear locker room after the game, Joe asked Coach Morgan to step outside for a moment.

"I've decided to go to Alabama, coach, and play for Bear Bryant, if that's OK with you."

"I think it's a great choice, Joe. I'd be surprised if you didn't help bring them a national championship. I'm proud of you, not only as an athlete I've had the privilege to coach but as a great student who'll go far. Your parents are very proud of you, too, and so are the people of Bentley. Stay the course, Joe. You're a wonderful young man with great character and integrity. You have a bright future ahead. Someday, you can be a role model for many youngsters."

"Thanks, coach. You had a lot to do with it, too."

Hugging, they rejoined the celebration inside.

Joe Mack played at Alabama. The Crimson Tide rolled to an 11-1 season in his freshman year in 1978 and was co-champion of college football along with the Southern California Trojans. They did even better the following year, winning all twelve games in an undefeated season. In his freshman and sophomore years, Joe started in every game, and his team won two national championships.

Without him, the Bentley Bears didn't fare as well and dropped 3-4-1 and 4-3-1 in those two years.

As a junior at Alabama, in 1980, Joe had great expectations, as did his teammates, but it wasn't to be. He went down with a leg injury in the eighth game against Mississippi State, and it was a long, painful trip back to Tuscaloosa. The Bulldogs won by a 6-3 score and ended the Crimson Tide's twenty-eight-game winning streak. In Joe's last season, they finished 9-2-1 and achieved the same number-six national ranking as the year before.

Bear Bryant retired the next year after winning six national championships over his twenty-five years with the Crimson Tide. Joe Mack's only regret was that his wasn't the final team the Bear coached.

The Bentley Bears improved to 4-4 and 6-2 over Joe's final years at Alabama, but the fans still spoke in awe of the way he impacted a football game.

CHAPTER 57

The year 1982 was a seminal one in the life of teacher and coach Jack Morgan. He was sixty-five in December, and the school required him to retire from both his positions at the end of the calendar year. His classroom teaching and football team leadership were about to end, and it was difficult for him to wrap his mind around that fact. What would he do with himself? Hang around the farmhouse, cut grass, and pick flowers? He was still healthy, and his mind remained keen. He and arthritis weren't strangers, but he could still outwrestle anyone ten to fifteen years younger.

Nellie felt his angst but didn't know what she could do about it or how to help. Jack always seemed to be planning for his classes or practicing and preparing for a football game. As he faced retirement, something mandatory and unfairly imposed on him, as she saw it, how would he deal with it? He never showed any sign of depression, except extreme sadness when his beloved Molly and then Henry passed away.

Nellie spoke with many wives whose husbands faced retirement, and some of the stories weren't good.

While Jack could still watch the team, he couldn't coach it. Nellie hoped they would honor Jack in some way and hoped she'd be included in whatever plans they chose. Jack was an icon at the school, had positively impacted so many lives, and lived a selfless life.

In recognition of Jack's impending retirement, honors came swiftly and often. The Rotary Club honored him for his community service, and the Home for Battered Women recognized Jack and Nellie for their supportive efforts. Jack greatly appreciated those awards.

They paled, however, in comparison to what his students did for him. On the last day of school in June 1982, the students in his history classes presented him with beautiful matching silver frames engraved with the following words: "To Jack Morgan, the best teacher ever." Underneath the inscription on each frame appeared the words: History Class June 1982. The frames showed photos of Jack's two classes with the students grinning at him. The gestures moved him to tears. He hugged each student as class was recessed for the last time that year. He was sensitive enough not to show his gifts to the other teachers for fear they would feel left out.

Nellie knew those associated with the football team planned something after the fall season to recognize Jack's thirty-seven years of coaching the Bentley Bears, with thirty-five as head coach. She didn't know exactly what the plans entailed, but she knew it would mean a lot to Jack. Whatever those plans were, she resolved to do whatever she could to make the event unforgettable.

That night at dinner, Nellie mentioned she was flying back to Buffalo for a visit. "You remember Harriet Donald, don't you? We stayed in touch."

"No, not really."

"She's having a really rough time with breast cancer and may not make it."

"What a shame," he said, sympathy and pain in his voice.

"I just need to see her."

"Of course. You should go." He recalled the tough, heart-breaking battle Molly fought. "Somehow, I think Gladys and I will make it without you."

"Gladys will, I'm sure, but you? That's debatable."

All three chuckled.

Nellie returned four days later to report Harriet was doing better than expected.

The principal thought it would be an easier transition for the students if they welcomed a new teacher in September, rather than January. It helped with continuity, and Jack agreed. Without any classroom responsibilities, he could concentrate entirely on the football team. He was glad he could coach the 1982 seniors.

Jack poured all his energy into his last football campaign. He, Hank Bennett, and Ben Stephens drilled the kids hard each practice. The players knew it was Jack's last team and season as coach, and they wanted to make it a winner. While no one talked openly about it, they knew that Bentley had never gone undefeated and untied, so they dedicated themselves to that scenario and worked harder than many thought possible.

After seven games, the Bears were perfect. Their dream was within reach. If they could defeat Central, the players would send Jack into retirement with a perfect season, something the school never attained.

As usual, the Chargers had lots of talent and were also undefeated. Some observers claimed Central also had its best team ever, but Bentley was loaded, too.

It promised to be the game of the year. Jimmy Rodrigues, arguably the most explosive running back in the entire conference, should have been playing for Central, but instead, he was the most valuable player on the Bentley roster.

James, Jimmy's father, moved to the Bentley area one year before Jack's last season and sought to place his son in the football program. It was early September, right before the football season began. He went directly to the Central High School administrative offices with Jimmy to inquire about his son playing for the Chargers. They were referred to the office of Christy Connor, the head coach, where they met Ed Oliver, the assistant coach. He took one dismissive look at the five-foot-six-inch scrawny sophomore who barely weighed 128 pounds and immediately discouraged him from coming to Central.

"Our first game is this coming Friday," Ed told them, "and we've already been practicing for the greater part of three weeks. Let me check with Coach Connor. I'll get back to you in a few minutes. Why don't you wait for me here? Feel free to have a cup of coffee or some water while you wait."

He quickly excused himself and went to the next office to talk to his boss. "Christy," he whispered, "I've got this kid and his father who just moved here. The kid wants to play football for us."

"Is he a big kid?"

"No. He's real skinny. His legs are like sticks, and he can't be over five foot-five."

"Shit, Ed. We don't have room for him at Central. Maybe if he were a big, strapping boy around six feet and two hundred pounds, we could find a place for him. Tell his father to go to Bentley High and ask for Jack Morgan." Wearing a sardonic smile, he winked at his assistant. "We don't have time for a kid who won't contribute to our program."

That was the biggest mistake of his coaching career.

Jimmy and his father went to Bentley High and talked to Jack Morgan and his assistant, Hank Bennett, for over 30 minutes.

During the discussion they learned that Jimmy, although small in stature, had exceptional speed and played football and ran track at a small Ohio school in the eastern part of the state. He finished third in the state one-hundred-yard dash with an outstanding time of ten seconds. Also, he was still growing. Jack would have accepted the boy on the team anyway because that was his nature. Knowing his athletic background and abilities clinched the deal.

"We'd be glad to have you join us, Jimmy," Jack said. "You can pick up your equipment when you register later today."

"Thanks, Coach!" Jimmy said. "I can't wait! Thank you for the opportunity. I won't disappoint you. I promise."

While passing on Jimmy Rodrigues constituted the greatest blunder in Coach Connor's football career, it was also the best decision Coach Morgan ever made. The scrappy little kid from Ohio immediately paid dividends for the Bentley Bears. Initially, he was used on the kickoff and punt return teams, but his blazing speed forced Jack to use him as a running back, too.

CHAPTER 58

Both Central and Bentley High were undefeated going into the final game of Jack Morgan's coaching career. Without Jimmy Rodrigues, Jack's final game would have been an event, but suddenly it became one of the most anticipated high school football games in West Virginia history. It was little undefeated Bentley High versus the undefeated perennial powerhouse, Central, and promised to be a memorable game.

It was six o'clock in the visiting locker room, one hour before kick-off. Jack assembled the boys for their pre-game prayer and then addressed the team.

"Boys, even if we lose this game, it's been a remarkable season. I want you to have fun out there and enjoy every minute of it, especially you seniors playing your last game for the Bears. Bentley has never gone undefeated and untied before. For the first time since I've been here, we match up well against our opponents.

"In previous years, we didn't have the all-around talent to compete with them and had to work extra hard just to keep it close, but not this year! We're as good as, if not better than, Central in all areas. They might be a slight favorite, but there's no reason why we can't go out there and kick their asses. Play hard. Play from the heart, but don't get any stupid penalties. They like to talk a lot and get into your heads, but don't fall for that. If we play our game for sixty minutes, we'll win."

The boys nodded, formed a huddle, and gave a high-five cheer. There was no mention of its being their coach's last game.

Co-captains Matt Doyle, Mike Conrad, and Jimmy Rodrigues broke the temporary silence by asking the coaches to leave the room, then the boys huddled together again.

"This is coach's last game," Matt said. "Let's send him off a winner."

"Bentley's never been undefeated," Mike said, "until today."

"Work harder than we ever have before," Jimmy implored his teammates. "We must win tonight."

They all knelt on one knee in the middle of the room and clasped hands. "For Coach Morgan!" they shouted before charging out of the locker room door.

The three coaches stood just outside the door. They hadn't heard what the boys said, but they caught the cheer and saw the players were fired up.

At five minutes after seven, Central kicked off to the visiting Bears. It was a bright, clear Friday night with little wind. The temperature was fifty-five degrees, perfect for football.

The Central kicker did his job just as Coach Connor told him, sending the ball away from Jimmy Rodrigues and right at Lance Davis, who was only twenty yards away. Jack, however, had anticipated that strategy and told his team how to counter it.

Lance took the ball on one hop at the ten, then ran directly to the left toward Jimmy. Rodrigues hesitated for a moment, then sprinted right to intercept his teammate and accept a short lateral pass. Davis flattened the first Central tackler, as Jimmy raced straight ahead toward the sideline. No one even came close to touching the speedy ball carrier, who raced untouched into the end zone.

Pandemonium reigned on the Bentley side of the field, while the Central side stared in stunned silence. The only noise came from Coach Connor, who threw his hat to the ground in outrage.

The teams almost matched each other point for point into the beginning of the fourth quarter.

Bentley had a slight lead, 27-23, with six minutes left to play, but Central had first down on the Bear's seven-yard line. It took the Chargers three downs to score, and their fullback, Chuck Clancy, finally bulled his way into the end zone from the two.

The score stood at 29-27 in Central's favor, and the extra point was very important. The kicked ball veered right, struck the upright, and careened forward just inside it, giving Central the extra point through luck. A Bentley field goal would give them only a 30-30 tie. To win, the Bears needed a touchdown, and they had less than three minutes to accomplish it.

Coach Connor wouldn't take any chances to let Jimmy Rodrigues get his hands on the ball. The Central kicker deliberately squib-kicked the ball short to the Bentley forty-yard line, where defensive player Tom Gallo fell on it. Jack knew Central would try something like that and made sure his players with the best hands were on the field.

It was first and ten from the Bentley forty-one-yard line with two minutes and thirty-seven seconds left to play. On first down, quarterback Pat Ryan threw a safe screen pass to fullback Sam Reynolds, who took it to the forty-nine.

It was second and two with two minutes and nine seconds left to play after a Bear timeout, then, despite having two opponents on him, Jimmy made an end run to the left and wriggled his way to the Central thirty-two-yard line and a first down.

Time was crucial, with only a minute and forty-seven seconds to play after another timeout.

Jack Morgan took a chance. Faking a hand-off to Jimmy, quarterback Ryan raced to the right sideline and took the ball down to the sixteen, but it cost them another fifty seconds on the clock.

With less than one minute left to play, and the Central defense concentrating on the speedy Rodrigues, fullback Sam Reynolds took it over the top to the twelve.

On third down with only ten seconds to go, Pat Ryan took the ball from the center and tried to complete a pass on the left to end Phil Peters, but it fell incomplete. Bentley called its last timeout, and the players quickly retreated to their bench with Coaches Morgan, Bennett, and Stephens.

They were down to one last play, and it was time for something especially dramatic.

It was fourth and six to go for the first down, twelve for the touchdown. Only six seconds remained on the clock, so the next play would be the last one of the game. A field goal would give them a tie, and the Bentley Bears would finish with an undefeated season and a tie, not a bad way to end a good coaching career.

During the timeout, Jack had a grandiose idea. "Why not fake a field goal?" he asked Hank Bennett. "Let's go for the win!"

"Do you want to risk it, Jack? A tie against these guys would be spectacular and preserve our undefeated season."

Jack wouldn't consider it. His mind was made up. They would fake a field goal with the snap going to the kicker, Tom Kenney. Tom would move slightly to the left and loft a soft pass to Jimmy in the right end zone. They practiced that move several times during the season and used it once in the past week, but they never sprang it on an unsuspecting opponent in an actual game.

That's the joy of it, Jack mused. *Christy Connor won't expect it at all.*

The referees signaled the end of the timeout and resumption of play. Everyone would soon know if Jack Morgan was a brilliant strategist or a foolish gambler. It was one or the other; no in between.

The Central Chargers filled the line of scrimmage, intent on blocking the kick. Tom Kenney made all three of his field goal attempts that season, and Connor would go all out to avoid a dreaded tie that would tarnish his own undefeated season.

Bill Allen made a good snap to Kenney. The impact of the two lines clashing emitted a savage, ferocious sound, but the Bears held. Two Central linebackers and a safety joined the rush, leaving only one teammate back to cover any pass. Christy Connor was sure that Jack Morgan wouldn't have the balls to go for the win.

Tom took a step to the left to freeze the charging linebackers and then threw the ball toward the end zone. Jimmy took a blocking position just to the right of the holder when the ball was snapped, then he suddenly and unobtrusively jogged toward the sideline and cut directly for the end zone.

Everyone heard the defense shout, "Pass!" but it was too late. Their lone defender in the backfield raced in vain to cover Jimmy, but he was open by at least six feet, and the perfectly placed ball fluttered into his open arms for a touchdown.

The Bears won and were undefeated and untied in Jack Morgan's final year as coach. The roar of the Bentley fans thundered throughout the playing field. Nellie and Gladys, along with the Hopkins, jumped up and down and shouted their approval of the victory, especially since it was Jack's last game. Half the Bentley team cried with joy, as they raised Jack to their shoulders and marched him to the middle of the field.

Christy Connor held out his hand and begrudgingly shouted over the din, "Nice call, Jack."

That was all Jack would get from the irascible old coach, but it didn't matter. He almost couldn't believe what happened, as he basked in the adulation of his team and the Bentley supporters in the stands.

Back in the locker room, amid slaps on the back, hugs, and near chaos, Jack told the players, "If I asked you whether or not to go for the win versus a field goal to tie, how many of you would have gone for the win?"

Every hand went up.

Jack laughed and said, "Way to go, bullshitters!" He bent over double in laughter.

It didn't matter. They went for the win, and they got it.

It was pitch black by the time the Bentley bus pulled out of Central's parking lot. It was a twenty-minute ride to their own football field, where the boys, many for the last time, would take off their uniforms and deposit them in their grimy lockers.

As the bus neared downtown Bentley, the boys and coaches were treated to a spectacle. Townspeople gathered along both sides of the road, each one holding a candle and a sign or poster that read, "Thank you, coach!"

Jack was stunned at the reception.

Approaching the gate to Bentley Field, Jack saw more candles and lights. He recognized Fred Giganda, the team's captain from the previous year. He stood beside Jeff Lewis, the captain from the year before that.

Others crowded the bus when it stopped, and Jack recognized many other kids and their fathers from prior teams. They cheered, as he stepped down from the bus, moving him to tears. He saw Nellie with an unfamiliar man beside her, and Gladys, too. After the game, the two women had left quickly to be at Bentley Field for Jack's homecoming.

"Jack!" Nellie shouted. "This is your son, David!"

Jack was speechless. He walked toward the younger man, tears streaming from his eyes. "David? Is that really you?"

"Yes, Dad. I've been waiting to say that word for a long time."

The two men nearly collapsed with emotion. Jack clutched his son desperately. "David," he choked out, "I...I would never have left you. Never! I tried so hard to find you all these years...."

"I know, Dad. Aunt Nellie explained it to me when she finally located me last week in Buffalo. We'll be able to catch up later tonight. I'll be staying with you at the farmhouse for the whole weekend."

Bentley's athletic director, a huge man named Buster Crane, slithered through the people swarming around Coach Morgan. "Jack," he bellowed, "we want you to come up onto the podium we set up on the field."

He pulled and helped direct the bewildered coach to follow him. Hundreds quickly gathered around the pair at the lectern, all clearly visible in the four theater lights illuminating the area.

Crane bellowed, "Now!"

The lights in the middle of the field went on. Jack stood open-mouthed, gaping in amazement. A few yards away stood all but two members of his first team as head coach, and they all wore their original team numbers, standing behind a sign that read, "Your First Team—1947." In front of them was Joe Mack.

The players raced up to embrace Jack, and he could barely stand the excitement. With tears streaming down his cheeks, he hugged each one.

Buster Crane stepped forward and announced, "We aren't done with the surprises yet, Jack!"

Suddenly, at his direction, all the lights went out, leaving them in total darkness. "Now!" he shouted.

Big, bright lights appeared over the scoreboard at the end of the field and formed the words, "Welcome to Jack Morgan Field" in big, block letters.

The crowd went wild with cheering and applause, whooping and hollering.

"Well, coach," Buster asked with a chuckle, "what do you think?"

"I...I...I'm stunned. I can't believe it. This was my last game, and my boys gave me an undefeated season. I'm so proud of them and their efforts, but I'm also immensely proud of the many boys, players, who came before them and labored through some tough years to help Bentley get where it is tonight. Everyone, thank you for this great honor. I accept it in the name of all my players over the past thirty-seven years and in the name of my fabulous assistant coaches."

Taking a small step back from the microphone, he looked upward. "Henry, this is for you, too, my friend. I hope you're watching."

He saw Gladys several yards in front, wiping tears from her eyes with a big smile.

"This is the happiest day of my life for many reasons," Jack continued. "I just want to share with you all what just happened before I received this incredible honor. It's a long story and has a happy ending. I just met my son, David, for the first time."

People gasped. Jack seemed to stumble a bit and backed away from the microphone. The emotion of the game, seeing David for the first time, and the tributes got the better of him. Someone offered him a glass of water, which he eagerly accepted.

"I apologize. All this is taking my breath away. I want to thank all of you—yes, all of you. I'm so...I'm so...."

He collapsed to the ground, dropping the water glass. Crane, the first to reach him, tried to help Jack to his feet.

Blair Horton, a family doctor, whose son played tackle on the Bentley team, ran up to the stricken coach and the dazed athletic director and immediately called for an ambulance.

One of the good things about small towns was that the ambulances weren't usually very busy and were readily accessible. An ambulance arrived in six minutes. Jack lay on a blanket on the ground, which, by that time of evening, was cold and moist.

Nellie accompanied Dr. Horton, as the ambulance threaded its way through the crowd and drove toward Bentley Hospital. Gladys and David followed in the car.

Dr. Horton told Jack, who was still awake and lucid, as well as Nellie, "Please be silent while the paramedics administer oxygen and monitor Jack's vital signs." He leaned over and whispered to Nellie, "It may be a heart attack, possibly a stroke, though a heart attack is most likely."

It was ten after ten when Jack was settled into a hospital room. Nellie, Gladys, and David remained at his bedside until eleven thirty, until it appeared Jack was out of danger. All the monitors attached to him revealed stable vital signs. He was able to sit up and take food, so Nellie felt comfortable leaving. She wanted father and son to have time together after so many years, so she took Gladys home with her.

Something went wrong. After appearing to have made a strong recovery, Jack relapsed at five in the morning, while David snoozed in a chair beside the bed. A monitor suddenly burst into alarm, and the nurse saw Jack's rapidly deteriorating vital signs.

She called Code Blue and ushered the alarmed young man from the room. Medical personnel rushed in with more equipment.

David, waiting in the visitor's lounge, immediately called Nellie. She and Gladys rushed back to the hospital even though they knew it was probably too late. She wanted to say goodbye to her brother, and hug him one last time. Gladys, although quite distraught, stayed strong for her dear friend, although she couldn't stop the tears streaming down her face.

No one saw Jack alive again. He succumbed to a severe heart attack that worsened quickly. Beloved football coach and history teacher, a stalwart of his community, Jack Morgan was pronounced dead at eight thirty-five on Saturday morning.

The shock of the tragedy devastated the Bentley community. Jack's impact far transcended the positive influence he had on the football program, which molded the character of all the boys who played for him. He was a hale, hearty man, robust and vital in everything and everyone he touched. It seemed impossible that such a vibrant man could die at sixty-five. Most affected other than his family were his history class students and the football players. His sudden death cast a pall over the entire community.

CHAPTER 59

Nellie, Gladys, and David drove solemnly back to the farmhouse, each lost in thought. They knew arrangements had to be made, but Nellie wanted to speak further about her brother.

As they walked to the porch of the house she shared with Jack for over thirty years, she took David's arm. "I want to show you something."

While Gladys went into the kitchen to prepare a light meal, Nellie led David upstairs to Jack's study. Once inside, she directed him to a desk with large drawers.

"This is what I told you about. Sit down and look at these." She opened the large top drawer.

Crammed into the drawer were clumps of letters, cards, and small packages, each bearing "Return to Sender" stamps. Tears fell down David's face, as he pored over the contents.

"You see what I've been telling you?" Nellie asked the distraught man. "He never forgot you, and he tried constantly to reach you. Your father assumed you didn't want anything to do with him. When I finally caught up with you last week, entirely by chance, you told me you took the name of your mother's second husband. That name change made it virtually impossible to locate you."

He wiped away tears. "I'm so grateful you found me," he said, still sniffling.

"A dear high-school friend named Julie Crawford went to college in Massachusetts with your mother, Cathy Mumford.

They were roommates for their junior and senior years. Julie always had a crush on Jack, but nothing ever developed. I saw Julie periodically through the years and confided in her about the situation between Jack and Cathy. They married young, right out of college. Her wealthy family, prominent Philadelphians, never thought much of Jack and didn't think he was good enough for their daughter. They tried unsuccessfully to prevent the marriage.

"When Jack enlisted in the Marines the day after Pearl Harbor, Lewis Mumford saw his son-in-law's absence as an opportunity. Cathy gave birth to a baby boy—you—on March 20, 1942, just a few months after America entered the war. By the time Jack received furlough from training, he returned home to find an empty apartment. His wife and child had vanished. He spent that entire week looking for you to no avail. Thanks to Mr. Mumford's connections, Jack found himself divorced against his will."

David, riveted by the story, wiped his eyes periodically and shook his head in disbelief. "Please continue, Aunt Nellie."

"Jack's first military action was at the terrible place called Tarawa, a frightful battle in the Gilbert Islands in November 1943. He also participated in the Battle of Peleliu, again in the Pacific Theater, and he landed at Iwo Jima in February 1945. The National Museum of the Marine Corps called Peleliu the bitterest battle of the war for the Marines, although Jack said Iwo Jima was just as bad. He was lucky to survive and come back to Buffalo when the war ended.

"His reward for distinguished service to his country was to come home and find no trace of his former wife and his almost four-year-old son. Mr. Mumford arranged that, too.

"Your mother remarried in 1944. Her father managed a quick adoption of you to his new son-in-law. Your name ceased being Morgan and became Webb.

"Without my friendship with Julie, you would never have known the truth. She saw your mother a month earlier at a Smith College reunion. After Julie prompted her a few times, she told Julie that you were practicing law in Buffalo. Feigning a need for an attorney, Julie asked for your last name in case she needed to contact someone. Your mother said it was David Webb and added, 'He's a star!'

"That's how I was finally able to reach you one week ago." Nellie sniffled. "I'm glad I did."

David hugged her. "Aunt Nellie, I'm so happy you found me and that I had the chance to meet my real dad. Can I keep these things? I want to read them all, and I'll cherish them always. My only regret is that I didn't get more time with him, to get to know him...." He stopped, overcome with grief and regret.

The two held each other and cried for a long time, thinking about the man they both lost.

Nellie recalled that she shared with her brother Greg Carson's question about getting married just before her trip to Buffalo.

"Nell, he has a point," Jack had said. "None of us is getting any younger. You, above all the people I know, deserve some happiness in your life. Since we moved to Bentley thirty-seven years ago, you've taken care of everyone but yourself. If you love him, you should marry him. Mom and Dad both had long lives, but that's no guarantee for either of us. Greg's a good man."

Jack had chuckled. "He asked you a very important question. How much time do you think you have? How much do I have? We don't know. Please think about it."

Coming from the person she most respected in the world, those words resonated.

By the time Nellie fulfilled her mission to contact David in Buffalo, her mind was pretty much made up. Thinking about it on the way home, she would give Greg a resounding, "Yes!"

Unfortunately, she had other compelling things on her mind—the death of her beloved brother.

The town of Bentley, West Virginia, never saw anything like it before. Practically everyone was there. Even though Jack died early Saturday morning, the funeral home was able to prepare his body for a service and burial the following Monday. Even Christy Connor, the crusty old Central High coach, came.

All of Jack's old players who made the journey to dedicate the stadium stayed to attend. The church, unusually large for such a small town, seated about four hundred. Back in its heyday fifty years earlier, almost all of those pews were occupied each Sunday, but that was before several major employers and industries shut down or failed. Those failures rocked the town, and Bentley began a struggle for survival.

None of that mattered now. There were so many people who came to pay tribute to Jack Morgan that every available pew was filled, with a lot of overflow in the back of the church.

As the townspeople, friends, colleagues, and family entered the church that Monday morning, they saw that the casket was positioned in front of the altar. Many gasped when they saw Jack's loyal but very sad chocolate Lab, Rudy, stretched out beside it. Women immediately clutched their handkerchiefs, as soft sobbing and sniffling reverberated throughout the building. School was closed that day, so everyone could honor the man who touched so many lives.

Nellie sat in the front row with Philip, dressed in his officer's uniform, Paula and her husband on one side, and David on the other. Gladys, Tina, and her husband, Paul Gagliani, sat with the Hopkins in the row directly behind them. Soft organ music played in the background.

As Reverend Niles Butler collected himself at the pulpit, he looked at the ever-expanding crowd. Every seat was taken, and the back of the church had standing room only, with more people still coming in. He'd never seen anything like it in all his years as a pastor. The church was absolutely full, and the side aisles under the stained-glass windows were filling, too, yet even more people kept streaming in. Soon, even the wide central aisle was full of grieving people wanting to show their respect.

Fire Marshall Tom Stanley was nearly apoplectic at seeing such a fire hazard, but he said nothing.

The attendees came in all forms of attire. Some wore dresses and suits, while others were simply adorned in slacks, sweaters, and T-shirts. It didn't matter. That was one of the great things about Bentley. Ostentation and grandiloquence weren't part of the culture. It was a mill town comprised of hardworking, sturdy people of modest means. They were a natural, hard-scrabble group who would never impress anyone with false pretenses, nor would that thought occur to them.

It was America at its best, showing once again why the United States was the greatest country on Earth. They came to the church to honor and pay respect to one of their own, a man who gave so much to his community and his fellow man, someone who served his country, worked hard for his extended family, and who showed others how to be their best while still being kind.

The gathered crowd hushed as Reverend Butler signaled the choir to sing "Rock of Ages." The popular Christian hymn was written by the Reverend Augustus Montagne Toplady in 1763, who survived a terrible storm in England by seeking refuge in a narrow pass between rock formations. The Rock of Ages also referred to the smitten rock found in the Old Testament. Paul wrote about it: "And all drank of that spirited Rock that followed them, and that Rock was Christ. The hymn was a favorite of the church members and began a moving tribute to their deceased brother."

The entire congregation rose, joining those already standing, and people sang out the words that most knew by heart. It was probably the loudest refrain ever heard in that church. Whether it was the cacophony of different sounds or the organ music, no one knew, but the chocolate Lab left his post by the casket and stood, too. Handkerchiefs came out again at what appeared to be Rudy's sign of reverence. If anyone missed that signal of piety, the children made sure they pointed it out to the adults.

Following the hymn, those who could sit down did so. Reverend Butler commenced the service.

"Before I deliver the eulogy, I want to introduce Jack's son, David, who some of you met Friday night at the dedication of Jack Morgan Field. David, please come up."

He walked forward. "Thank you, Reverend Butler. I feel honored to appear before you like this. My Aunt Nellie and Gladys both told me how so many of you loved my father. I'm sure you know how much he loved you."

More tissues came out, and the assembled listened while seeing Rudy lie down again beside his beloved master's casket.

David glanced at Nellie, who gave a small smile and nod. "Today is the happiest day of my life and also the saddest. You see, I never knew my father, not even for one day, until I first met him on Friday night at your wonderful dedication. I can't tell you how happy and honored he was by that incredible sign of affection and esteem. Seeing his former players again was incredibly special to him, too."

David took a deep breath. "When he was first stricken at the ceremony, I went with him to the hospital and sat at his bedside all night. After he was treated and stabilized, his doctors allowed him to talk with me. Dad and I talked from eleven that night until two in the morning, when he finally fell asleep again. He woke up briefly, and we talked a little more, then he went into a coma and died around eight-thirty that morning." Everyone was riveted, mesmerized by David's words.

"As many of you probably know, Dad enlisted in the Marines the day after Pearl Harbor. I was born on March 20. He came back from duty in May 1942, but I was long gone. My mother and her father pirated me away where Dad couldn't find me. My mother divorced him later that year, back when it was easy to arrange such things if you had the right connections. Unfortunately for me, my grandfather did. I grew up being told," he said with great difficulty, "that my father left us and didn't have any interest in seeing me."

Tears welled in his eyes, as he looked at Nellie, who constantly wiped her own eyes.

"My Aunt Nellie finally found me just a few days before you honored my father, and she explained how he sent me cards, letters, and gifts at Christmas and on my birthday, but they were all returned unopened. I learned how he opened his heart and his home, along with Aunt Nellie, to those in need."

Reverend Butler, looking out at the congregation, saw there wasn't a dry eye to be found, including his.

"I don't want to take any more of your time," David concluded, "but I thank you for knowing him, loving him, and honoring him the way you did. He's looking down at us from heaven right now, and I know he's got a big smile. My dad loved you all. I can certainly see why."

The congregation erupted into applause. Those who were fortunate to have seats jumped to their feet to acknowledge father and son.

Reverend Butler embraced David, who left the pulpit and took his place beside Nellie, burying his head against her shoulder.

"When Jack Morgan and his sister, Nellie, first came to our community," Reverend Butler began, "we felt blessed, but we didn't know how long he, or they, would stay. Jack had many opportunities to better himself and leave us, but he didn't. He taught our children and coached them, teaching them values, the importance of self-respect, and doing your best. Coach Morgan was a father to some, an uncle to others, but he was always a friend to all of us. He and Nellie opened their home to people who had no place to stay. They helped feed the indigent among us. Sometimes, their home resembled a hotel."

A chuckle went through the crowd.

Nellie held tightly to Philip and Paula, while in the pew behind them, Gladys, Tina, and the Hopkins held each other's hands and wept unashamedly. They relived their memories of the kindness Jack and Nellie bestowed on them.

"During his years as a teacher of U.S. history, it was his idea to bring cereal, milk, apples, and bananas for students who had little or no food at home for breakfast." He paused and gave a sigh. "I guess our Lord considered Jack's work was done here and was eager to have this great and wonderful man and war hero join His flock to help still many others. We won't see the likes of him again."

Once the service concluded, the reverend sat down, and the choir and organist began a litany of beautiful hymns and songs Nellie requested to honor Jack.

After several minutes of silence, the pallbearers, all former students of Jack's, carried the casket down the main aisle toward the church doors. Rudy walked dutifully beside it.

The burial was attended by all the surviving veterans in the Bentley area, as well as many of the churchgoers. It was fortunate that the cemetery was directly behind the church, so people could get there on foot.

Nellie and David spoke briefly, followed by Paula and Philip. Reverend Butler said the burial prayers, then the casket was lowered into the ground. Rudy whimpered and ran uneasily around the grave. Suddenly he bolted away from Nellie and jumped onto the casket as it was being lowered. The pneumatic lift was quickly stopped, and the casket was raised again to avoid crushing the dog. Nellie held him closely as he whimpered.

There was more than enough sadness for everyone that day. No reception was planned at the church or the Morgan home afterward. The newly reunited family felt the need to spend time with each other.

Philip would soon return to his latest military assignment, while Paula and her husband would return to their medical practices in Connecticut.

David returned to his native Buffalo, where he maintained a law practice. He would always remember that four-day experience in Bentley. He visited West Virginia as an obligation and favor to Aunt Nellie, returning with a full heart and lasting remembrance of a loving father whom he never had the chance to know.

Life was good for David. His only regret was he hadn't brought his own son to meet his grandfather. How was David to know what those ninety-six hours would come to mean to him? He wasn't sure how to approach his mother about the situation and all he missed out on, but he was very angry and deeply disappointed.

Nellie and Greg walked hand-in-hand to the car, while Gladys and Rudy followed closely behind.

Almost Heaven

"Don't you think it's time that we finally got married?" he asked softly. "I love you and want to make you happy. You deserve that. I love the farmhouse. We can make a new family life there, Gladys included. I know this is a difficult time, but please, let's share the rest of our lives together."

Her eyes, still moist from the services, looked up at him, then she smiled broadly through her tears. "Yes, Greg. It's time."

Acknowledgements

We live in a marvelously connected time when there are so many unprecedented and valuable resources available through the internet to any writer.

I am indebted to many of them, especially the Biography and History Channels, Wikipedia, American Experience, The New York Times, Harold S. Kushner, author of *When Bad Things Happen to Good People*, and Dennis B. Fradin, author of *The Signers*.

My gratitude is further extended to a number of individuals who read the manuscript and offered constructive advice and encouragement. They include Clark Bell, Jim Bernene, Don Gilmore, Tony Romanovich and Ed Smoragiewicz.

Special thanks to Kiki Keating and Jaime Morton of the KikiNetwork team and to Janice Beetle of Janice Beetle Books, for their editing and other ideas to improve the manuscript, and to Amy Herzog and Tessa Avila at Why Not Books, for their help in bringing this project to fruition, especially including Tessa's guidance and perseverance in choosing the best cover and interior layouts.

I am especially indebted to my wife, Michele, for her work in typing the manuscript and its many edits and versions, and for her excellent editing skills and valuable suggestions. And to Trouper, who sat by me in her bed and let me pet her when I needed a little levity.

This has truly been a team effort.

About the Author

Tim Norbeck worked in the healthcare arena for 53 years and was, most recently, the CEO of a national health-care-related foundation. During his career, Tim enjoyed the opportunity to speak on behalf of physicians in all 50 states. His numerous writings, Op-Eds, articles, and speeches have appeared in a variety of industry related and other publications including Vital Speeches and periodic blogs for Forbes.com.

Tim began writing novels near his retirement and his first, *Two Minutes*, was published in 2018, while his second novel, *No Time for Mercy*, was published in mid-2022. Tim is also participating as a volunteer course instructor with the OSHER Lifelong Learning Institute at various colleges throughout the country. His topic centers around transitioning from a health-care CEO and changemaker to a novelist.

A Buffalo, New York native who also spent 30 years in Connecticut as the state medical society's CEO, Tim is an avid tennis player, dedicated gym goer, and a major history aficio-nado. He lives with his wife, Michele, and their rescue dog, Trouper, in Estero, Florida.